I0698831

only mostly dead

afterlife incorporated
book one

Alli Temple

Copyright © 2024 by Alli Temple
Only Mostly Dead
All rights reserved.

ISBN 978-1-990719-13-4 (ebook)
ISBN 978-1-990719-17-2 (paperback)

No part of this book may be reproduced in any form or by any electronic or mechanical means, including information storage and retrieval systems, without written permission from the author, except for the use of brief quotations in a book review.

This is a work of fiction. Names, characters, places, and incidents are a product of the author's imagination or are used fictitiously. Any resemblance to actual events, places, or persons, living or dead, is entirely coincidental.

Cover design is for illustrative purposes only, and any person(s) featured is a model.

Cover Design: We Got You Covered Book Design
Developmental Editing: Jen Graybeal, Jen Graybeal Author Services
Copy Editing: Adam Mongaya, Tessera Editorial
Proofreading: Lori Parks

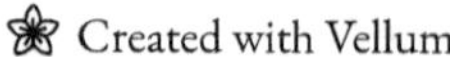 Created with Vellum

For Ed
It's been 25 years. I assume I can call you Ed now.
This is book #16. You probably saw it coming long before I did.
Thanks for reading the words of a goofy earnest kid out of her depth
and telling her they were something to look forward to.

join the a-list

For news on future releases, join the A-List, my monthly newsletter at AlliTemple.com/newsletter.

content warnings

This is a book about death. I tried to make it funny, people are still going to die. For more details, visit the Only Mostly Dead content warnings page.

chapter
one

THE UPSIDE to dying is that I will never again hear the phrase "all of our agents are currently busy." Let's be honest, if you've been experiencing a higher-than-normal call volume at work for more than six months, that's not actually higher, that's your new normal. Hire more people.

But none of that is my problem anymore.

The nice thing about life (and death) in Canada is you can opt out whenever you want. Or whenever the cancer wins. Officially it's called Medical Assistance in Dying, or MAID. You sign some paperwork, wait the mandatory reflection period for liability reasons, then close your eyes, relax, and boom. It's over. Easy peasy.

Or it was supposed to be easy peasy.

I planned to die on Tuesday. I had everything prepared, even the goodbye message.

"Hey, Sparks," I say, trying not to squint at the ring light while my phone silently records. "If you've been following me the last few weeks, you'll know that this is probably going to be my last message. I know this is uncomfortable. Cancer sucks. No one wants to talk about it, so I'll try to keep this short . . ."

The flickers of reaction emojis pour over the screen as I say farewell to the community I've spent the last six years building.

People think it's silly. That followers aren't the same as friends. But I've made some amazing connections and learned from everyone. In the end, it's important to give relationships closure, even virtual ones.

Okay. Moving on. Dying is easy. My family—parents and siblings; we decided my little nieces and nephews are too young to be here—have gathered. Soft music plays. My eyelids get heavy, and at the last second, I hear the gentle sound of a snore rattling at the back of my throat. Then there's nothing. Or at least, nothing more.

I crack open one eye to find the same overhead bulb that was there a minute ago. Where is my white light? My clouds of angels playing the harps and welcoming me to a better place? I was hoping my grandparents might be waiting for me. Or at least Teddy and Bear, the family cats who died when I was in high school. They should be waiting at the gates of heaven, just like they used to wait at the front door, ready to scream their protests that they hadn't been fed ever. Not once in their entire feline lives. Never mind that Teddy was the size of a corgi and Bear had single-handedly decimated the squirrel population in our Don Mills neighbourhood. Even in life after death, they would believe they were starving.

But I'm still in the hospital room. Still lying in the narrow bed with the crisp sheets. No sign of Nana and Poppa, Mimi or Grandpa. Not even a whisker or paw print to say Teddy or Bear were ever here.

"Dr. Sutherland?" I say, and my voice doesn't feel like scraping razor blades over my throat for the first time in a while, so that's an improvement at least. "I don't think you did it right?"

She did something, though. Maybe the sedation is still taking hold. The world is bleary, like I'm looking through an old pane of glass that ripples in the light. Everything undulates slightly. The doctor says something, but the words are muffled. She turns to go, and I push up from the bed.

"Hey, wait," I say, following after her. "What happens now?"

Panic flickers just beneath my collarbone, but also relief. I'm moving on strong, sturdy legs. And there's no pain. For the first time in what feels like a lifetime, I take five steps, then five more, then another ten, and nothing hurts. There isn't the grinding ache as my cancerous bones try to crumble. The weakness from muscles that haven't had to do anything but keep me breathing since I became bedridden. I feel healthy. Alive.

The novelty of being able to follow after her with ease doesn't do much to offset a growing unnerving sense that I don't know what I should be doing. As I always used to tell the Sparks, unease is a sign of inaction. It's your body trying to put you in motion toward the next goal. But what goal is there after death? Do I wait? Am I still technically dying? I thought things would be more obvious on the other side of this mortal coil.

The doctor rounds a corner. Everyone around me is fuzzy, like the way my eyes go wonky sometimes after a multi-hour Netflix binge, only when I blink it doesn't get better.

"Hello?" I ask. No one replies.

As I pass an open hospital room door, a low voice filters toward me.

"And if you'll just sign here. And here. And initial here. And here. Okay, now next copy—"

A handsome young man is standing by a bed. He's white and looks like he's in his mid-twenties, with curly brown hair and a yellow golf shirt and khakis. He's also crystal clear, but when I glance quickly back out to the hallway, a blurry nurse in scrubs rushes by. Something weird is going on.

"Is that everything?" In the bed, a woman who looks like she has to be at least a hundred is holding a pen. She's got a tube in her throat, and I don't even know how she spoke around it, but the man takes the pen and clipboard from her and flips through the pages before he finally nods and says, "Yup. That's everything. If you'll just follow me," and suddenly her tubes are gone. So is her hospital gown. Her wispy hair has settled into white curls and she's wearing a soft pink sweater and pearl necklace. She swings her legs over the side of the bed and hops up to her feet, smiling brightly.

"Will I see Joel?" she asks.

The man in the yellow shirt is putting his papers into a leather briefcase. "I don't know. We can ask at the Reunification Desk. That's not my department."

"Um, excuse me." I'm still hovering in the door. Both the man and woman look up suddenly, startled to see me. "Hi. Sorry to bother you, but—"

"What are you doing here?" the man asks.

"I don't know. I was down the hall and I heard a voice. I thought—"

"Are you looking for afterlife? I don't have any other pickups today." He pulls a tablet from his bag and scrolls through screens. "What's your name?"

"Me? Ember."

"Amber?"

I flinch on old instinct. Mom called me Ember. She said I was her spark of inspiration. It's where I got the name for my business after my first viral post. Find Your Spark. But the number of times I've been called Amber in my life—and now my death apparently —means sometimes I wish my mother had just called me Anne. Kate. Beth. Something short that couldn't be mistaken for anything else.

"Ember," I say again.

"Last name?"

"Munro."

He's tapping at the screen with a stylus. "Date of birth?"

I tell him and he keeps tapping. "What's your mother's maiden name?"

"My mother?" What are we doing? Resetting the password on my mortality? I just want to know how to get out of here.

He glares at me in annoyance. "Her maiden name?"

"Kleisath."

The man stares at his screen, brows furrowed. He scrolls some more.

"Ember Munro. Age thirty-two years, seven months, twenty-nine days. Terminal bone cancer, metastasized to your lungs and lymph nodes." He says it with all the compassion of a mechanic telling me my cabin filter needs replacing and I wince. Still, the fact he's found me in whatever records he's checking is a relief. Maybe he can drop me at that Reunification Desk too and I can find Nana and Poppa after all.

"Yeah, that's me," I say.

"Scheduled for medically assisted death at—" His frown deepens at the information on his screen. "But you're not dead yet."

"I'm not?" I glance at the old woman—though she still seems to be aging backwards and now doesn't look like she can be more than sixty—who gives me an impatient smile. She's definitely dead and has places to be.

"No." The man taps on his tablet screen. "It says you have a few months to go. See here. November fourth. That's more than six months away. What are you doing here?"

I open and close my mouth a few times. I hate this feeling. The one like I'm expected to know the answer when I'm in over my head. I'm supposed to have all the answers. That's the whole point of being a life coach. Though I guess I'm not that anymore. You can't be a life coach when you're dead.

"November fourth?" I say, craning my neck to see his screen. Even if I'd let the cancer dictate the timing of things, the doctors didn't think I had more than a month or so left. I'd have never made it to the fall.

"Yes, see here." He points at his screen. "Four, eleven. That's the date they filled in when they filed your paperwork."

I stare harder, puzzling it through, and finally chuckle when realization hits.

"No, see? You got it backward. They put in the date month-day-year, not day-month-year. It's April eleventh, not November fourth."

He frowns, first at the tablet, then at me. Finally he sets the tablet down so he can fling both hands up in the air. "Well, that's just great. I thought we standardized these things in the last century. It's not that difficult, but no. No one thinks of the reapers." He paces in a circle. The old woman sighs in irritation. Her gaze says she knows exactly what's going on, and I really wish she could tell me where she got her intel, because no one left me so much as a *So you're dead. Now what?* pamphlet.

The man is still ranting. "Do you know how many correction forms I'm going to have to fill out because of this? What am I supposed to do with you?"

"Uh . . . take me with you?" That much should be obvious. What am I going to do here? Wander the halls of the oncology ward?

"I don't think so. Look at my schedule." He picks up the tablet again and scrolls through a seemingly endless list. "I've got to drop Hazel off. Then there's a flash flood in Germany that's got my entire afternoon booked, then an early flu outbreak at a nursing home in Montana. Then I'm pulling a double on a wildfire in Australia. Fucking Australia. It's always tomorrow there, so regardless of when I show up, I'm always behind. So no, Ms. Munro." His gaze swings back to me, and I've never felt so small in my entire all-too-short afterlife. "I don't have time to be picking up entitled ghosts who think they can jump the queue."

"Entitled? Ghost? What queue?"

But he's done with my questions. "Best I can do is leave a note when I get back to the office so someone can swing by to collect you later."

"So you're just leaving me?" There's a quicksand feeling opening up beneath me and I have to reach out for the wall to steady myself, then nearly fall over when my hand slides right through the drywall like it's not even there. "Wait. It's not my fault. I was—"

Before I can plead my case, he takes the older woman by the hand and says, "Come on, Hazel. Let's go find your husband." Then they both vanish with a tiny popping sound like when the flames of a gas barbecue go out.

"Hello?" I say, but I already know no one will answer.

Dear Sparks, being dead really sucks.

chapter
two

OKAY, girlies. No need to panic. Here's what I learn on my first day of being dead:

1. No one can see or hear me. Despite my best efforts to find someone else who is dying in the hospital and plead my case to whoever arrives to retrieve them, I come up empty. Everyone else, from the exhausted-looking nurse at the charge desk to the man in coveralls I find patching the ceiling in a vacant part of the building, just flat-out ignores me. The first time someone walks through me, the sensation is something like plunging into a frozen lake while having a panic attack. I don't like it and do my best to dodge others in the hallway as I explore.

2. I can leave the hospital. This comes as a relief. For a moment, as I stand at the hospital's main exit, a wave of fear washes over me that maybe there's some invisible boundary and I truly am trapped here. I don't actually need my life after death to be harps and peeled grapes. But it has to be more than wandering the hospital. I hurry through the doors, and I'm three blocks away before my heart stops racing.

Or actually, my heart doesn't race, because I have no heart. It's more like the feeling that my heart *should* be racing. It's hard to wrap my head around. Do I even have a head? A brain? If I have no heartbeat, how can I have any brain activity? Any thoughts?

Plagued with existential questions, I make my way up University Avenue. The towering buildings of Toronto's hospital row line each side of the boulevard. Cars crawl slowly past me. It's late afternoon. Rush hour. Hordes of people wait at the crosswalks, making their way to the subway to head home. No one gives me so much as a sideways glance. I am truly invisible. It's unnerving.

Eventually, I find myself circling around Queen's Park. It's a round green space in the heart of downtown, with the provincial legislature buildings at the south end. I used to jog here, back in my undergrad days. It's a weird mix of serene and overwhelming as other joggers, dog walkers, and pedestrians gather their thoughts while an endless roar of traffic passes nearby. Despite the familiar surroundings, I keep blinking, trying to make them come into focus. I didn't live long enough to need glasses, but I wish I had them now.

Closer to the legislature, a group of protesters argues for better harm reduction for drug users, and another passes out flyers in support of a minority group in China. No one offers me anything. Just a typical day in Toronto, and I am no longer part of it.

"Dear Sparks," I say, though no one can hear me. "I guess I should have been more specific when I said I was going. I thought there would be something else. *Somewhere* else. Instead—"

Before my monologue can dive into melodrama, though, a flash of movement behind a tree catches my eye. The world has that soft-around-the-edges texture, but as I spin, I catch a glimpse of a form disappearing behind a tree, sharp and bright, almost like a comet. I follow after it, but when I circle the tree, no one's there. Just an empty paper cup and some cigarette butts.

Behind me, someone giggles. It's a high sound, like a child's, though it echoes oddly in the outdoor space. It's the sort of sound that would make my nerves stand on end . . . if I had any nerves.

How long until this stops being weird? You know what, better not to find out. The odds are, it will only get weirder until I—

The giggle comes again. I'm spinning in circles, but I stop suddenly at the sight of the girl crouched on the ground. Or maybe not a girl. A young woman. Maybe. She might be twelve or twenty-two. Hard to say. Her hair hangs in long stringy strands over her shoulders, almost like it's been dipped in grease. In fact, all of her is dark, like she's covered in shadows. Except her face, which is several shades too pale to be healthy . . . or alive.

And she's looking right at me.

"Can you see me?" I ask, though I don't know if I want the answer to be yes or no. Something says I'm better off waiting for another guy with a tablet than following this woman wherever she's headed.

"Shh." She presses a finger to her lips, and her smile reveals a set of rotting teeth. I haven't seen myself since I died, but given how healthy I feel and how Hazel went from decrepit and full of tubes to upright and judgy, I assume I look better than I have in a long time. Certainly better than whoever this woman is.

"Are you dead too?" I ask, despite the way my head aches and my knees wobble. I need to run. To get away. Something feels like it's unravelling inside me and I can't move.

She doesn't answer. Instead, she's off again, moving too fast to be anything human. I'm not even sure her feet touch the ground. She zips between people who are oblivious to her erratic movements. As she gets farther away, the unravelling feeling settles, and I take off after her.

"Hey—wait!"

She laughs again. She's glowing with a light that has nothing to do with the sun overhead. When she swerves for the street, I steel myself for the harrowing experience of running through traffic when no one can see me.

At the last second, though, she veers to one side, and crashes with a woman walking her German shepherd. The woman has no reaction, but the dog loses its shit. The giggling woman lifts off the ground, soaring overhead, and the dog lunges for her, jaws snapping. The dog's owner is unprepared and can't react fast enough as the leash is yanked from her hand. She calls out, but the dog doesn't care. It also isn't bothered by the woman on the bicycle currently coming to the curb, who has to stop short to avoid hitting it. Her bicycle bounces, shaking the basket in front of her handlebars, which causes a paperback to eject itself. The bottles of wine inside tumble onto the ground with a crash. The woman curses, while the other is still chasing her dog. Neither of them notices the third woman, who is now trying to redirect her stroller to avoid the shards of glass on the sidewalk and the snarling dog. The only option is to turn directly into the path of a second oncoming bicycle.

The giggle comes again, louder than anything else around us. She's perched in a tree, watching the whole scene unfold with wicked glee.

"Watch out!" I call, though no one can hear me. I close my eyes because while I've spent so much time thinking about and planning for my death, I can't watch someone else's.

"All units, assume position."

Soldiers in tactical gear run by me. Where did they come from? Toronto's a busy place, but you don't see active military very often. There are four of them, and they rush past me without a glance. Unlike everyone else around us, they don't have the fuzzy watercolour edges. Instead they have the same clarity as Hazel and the man at the hospital. Does that mean they're dead too? But whatever's going on, they clearly have a plan. The giggling woman shrieks a protest as they lay out poles on the ground, like they might be setting up a tent.

"Ready!" one of the soldiers calls. Another is holding what looks like a phone, but when he swipes at the screen, the poles on the ground, now arranged in a square, begin to glow. They form a column of light that extends upward toward the shining woman. She wails as she starts to struggle.

"More," the first soldier says. "We need more."

The one with the phone swipes over the screen again, and the lights from the rods grow brighter. The woman howls, but slowly she is engulfed. The beam sinks, dragging her down.

"Ready for containment."

She shrieks. The light is so bright I have to shield my face, but I still see when one writhing hand bursts through the column, reaching out for help. A buzzing sound starts up in my head. I clench my teeth and even if there's no blood left to pump in my body, I can still taste metal at the back of my throat.

Her scream nearly drops me to the ground. Whatever is happening here, I don't want to be part of it anymore. I stumble away. It doesn't even matter when I run through the woman as she chases her dog. The sticky frozen feeling is better than the abject terror that pulses through my head as the screaming girl gets sucked into whatever the hell the light is.

That is not what I signed up for. None of this is what I signed up for. I wanted a peaceful death with no fear and no pain. That was the plan. It looked nothing like this.

The soldiers don't try to stop me. I don't even know if they can see me. But it doesn't matter. As I cross the street, the scream cuts off abruptly. The silence is even worse. I should look back. Check on the woman and her dog, the others with the bike and the baby. But they're not for me to help anymore.

Lungs I don't have anymore burn, and I gasp grimy city air that I can't taste. Somehow I can still cry, or at least it feels like I can, so I do. I sob as I run past the legislature building. The long line of hospitals comes into view again and I rush for familiar territory. It's fine. Hospitals aren't that bad. I've spent enough time in them. What's a few more days or weeks? Months, even? Maybe this is all there is. Welcome to death. Please have a seat.

But as I pass the emergency entrance, the shine of a leather jacket in sunlight catches my eye. For a second, I think it's the giggling woman again, but when I blink, my vision clears and it's not. This person is taller. More substantial somehow, even as they hunch into their jacket and stuff their hands in their pockets. They're walking away from me, purple and blue dyed hair shining in the sun, but they're clear. Not blurry like the humans.

"Wait!" I call. Their back is still turned, but they flinch at the sound of my voice, and my absent pulse beats faster. They can hear me. "Wait. I'm dead and I need help!"

Their steps come faster as I rush after them. At first, I try to dodge around the fuzzy-edged people going about their daily lives, but I'm losing ground, so soon enough I just start running through them. The person is headed for the subway. In this dead-but-not form, I feel like I could run forever, but I don't want to chance losing them underground.

"Please. I need help. Please."

At the last second, just before the steps at St. Patrick Station, they stop. Relief pours over me.

"Oh, thank you." I gasp. "Thank you so much. I didn't want to get left behind again."

They turn to look at me, and all the air rushes out of my not-lungs. The guy in the hospital room looked like an everydude customer service employee. Even the soldiers were unremarkable. This person is . . . completely remarkable. Possibly not human. Or human, but with the same vibe as supermodels. Thin, angular, flawless, but when you start to catalogue the features, they don't fit together. Their eyes are too wide, their nose too long. I can't even tell if they're white or some other ethnicity. But now that I'm looking at them, I can't look away. They're magnetic. Powerful. If they're on social media, they must have millions of followers, regardless of what content they make. Everyone would want to hear what they have to say.

"What do you want?" Even their voice is compelling. Gravelly. Serious. Their accent is none of the hundred or so you can hear on any given day in Toronto, yet each word is clear and precise.

For a second, I'm dazzled. They're too beautiful. The leather jacket is paired with distressed jeans and chunky white combat boots. Their black T-shirt fits perfectly over a flat chest, and they wear about six chains in gold and silver around their neck, which would seem douchey on just about anyone but here makes sense with the rest of the look. They're the opposite of a generic polo shirt and khakis.

I pull myself together. I'm not intimidated. I'm the customer, and the service I've received has been less than stellar. If heaven has email and they send me a feedback survey, I will be clicking on the frowny face for sure. There better be some follow-up. A celestial gift card is not going to cut it. Even Teddy and Bear were probably treated better than I have been.

"My name is Ember Munro," I say, squaring my shoulders. "I've been dead since this morning, and so far I'm giving the experience zero stars. Now get me out of here."

The blue-haired person blinks. It's a slow action, like an owl's. They wet their lips while gazing down at me. I suddenly feel very small, even smaller than I did with polo man in the hospital, but I force myself to hold their gaze. No more bullshit. I've done nothing wrong. Not my fault they got the date mixed up. Dead is dead, isn't it? Doesn't matter whether it's April or November.

"No."

It's the shortest sentence in the world, and hearing it now makes my heart stop. Or it would stop if I still had one.

"Excuse me?"

"No," they say again. The word is flat and emotionless. There's no apology. No excuse. A simple statement of fact before they put their hands in their pockets again and turn to go.

"Wait." I reach, grabbing at leather. I gasp when I actually manage to make contact, then yank my hand back at their annoyed glance.

"Someone is coming," they say. "Don't worry. You've still got time even if someone doesn't arrive until later today."

Someone like the soldiers? Will I get sucked into a pillar of light? I don't want that. The screaming and the struggling. I want clouds and angels and harps and Mimi asking me how come I never met the right boy? She always did think being a lesbian was some kind of phase, but even so, it would be a relief to see her right now. Also, what does this person mean I've still got time? Time for what?

"No. No." I shake my head. Somehow the word doesn't have nearly as much impact coming from my lips as it did from theirs. "Take me now. The last guy was too busy. Nursing homes. Forest fires. I don't give a shit. Isn't death the great equalizer? They're no more important than me. So get me out of here."

They watch my little tantrum with an unmoved expression. When I'm done, they put a hand on my shoulder. It's probably meant to be a comforting gesture, but the overwhelming sense of their presence just leaves me feeling rooted to the spot.

"Someone will be here soon. Wait," they say, then turn to the subway stairs.

Oh. Turns out I really am stuck. I try to follow after them, but my feet won't move.

"No. Stop. Where are you going?" I'm back to calling out like a child. Their blue and purple head disappears into the crowd, and by the time I free myself, they're long gone. I finish the sad little performance with a stomp of my foot and a cry of frustration.

Dear Sparks, live as long as you can. There's nothing good waiting for you on the other side.

chapter
three

WHEN MY FEET finally unstick themselves, I go back to the hospital. I hate it. I swore I'd never come back here once it was all over. My throat hurts as I pass through the sliding doors. And I mean *through* them. They don't open. I walk through the glass panes like I'm not even there.

"Oh my goodness, there you are."

At first, I don't realize the observation is directed to me. The ER waiting room is packed with all kinds of people, and the conversations range from kids asking their worried mothers how much longer the wait will be, to an old man with jaundiced skin who's clearly left his hearing aids at home as he tries to understand the triage nurse's questions.

"I take these for my blood pressure," he says, shaking a pill bottle at her.

"I need your health card," she says in reply, enunciating each word carefully and loudly.

"Mommy, my tummy hurts," a little girl says, then promptly throws up all over her shoes.

"Excuse me. Excuse me? Ms. Munro?" This time, it comes from much closer, and I turn to find a man in a suit and tie. He's white, mid-thirties, with brown hair neatly combed back and a thousand-watt smile.

"Yes?" Just the sound of my name means all my attention is on him.

"I've been looking all over for you," he says.

I could cry. "Me? You have?"

"I got lost. These hospitals have so many floors, you know? And then when I found your room, you weren't there." His eyes widen, giving him the appearance of a small-town boy who just arrived in the big city. I wonder how long he's been doing this job and who he was before. "I'm sorry I'm late. There's a window, you know. To get to the other life. If you get lost or wait too long, that's when they send the troops to retrieve you, and you won't like what happens after that."

I shudder at the memory of the woman in the park, then collect myself. No need to worry about that anymore. Things are finally on track. Years from now, when I've been chilling in heaven for a bit, I'll be able to talk about the last hour like it's all a big funny joke.

"I'm ready," I say. I've been ready for days. Weeks. Ever since the doctors said the chemo wasn't working anymore. The plan got diverted for a minute, but that was temporary. Time to get on with the business of dying.

"Excellent. I'm Zach. Follow me." He starts down the hall, then pauses, eyeing me up and down. My hands ball into fists unconsciously. If he says he's changed his mind, we're going to have a fight. But instead, he says, "Actually, why don't I take you somewhere special?"

I jerk back. "Excuse me?"

He holds up his hands in a placating gesture. "Nothing weird, I promise. I don't usually get a say in where new souls go. But since I screwed up, how would you like a choice?"

There are options? Is he saying I can pick between a perpetual lounger on the beach or my own planet full of virgins?

"Just anywhere that isn't a hospital," I say. I have spent enough time in hospitals to last an eternity.

His smile returns. "Perfect. I know just the place. This way to the other life." He holds open a door. I catch my breath. Dear Sparks, this is it. The end. "You'll like it. We just opened up a new district."

"What's a district?"

"Things get crowded." Zach gives me a wink. "People keep dying, and they need somewhere to go. You could go for a more traditional afterlife experience, but the new place is better. More like communal living, less like a holding pen. I can get you in. There's no waiting list."

And now time for Ember's Life Tip #112: *If it sounds too good to be true, it probably is*. Just like all the miracle cures and promising clinical trials. In the end, they failed.

"What's the catch?" I ask.

"You don't tell anyone?" he says quickly. "I'm new. We have to hit certain targets when we're retrieving souls, and if anyone finds out I was late picking you up, I could be in big trouble. So you get a comfy place to chill, and I don't get another lecture from my boss. No foul, no harm, right?"

"That's it?" Am I even ever going to see him again? I don't care what secrets I have to keep. Everyone takes something to the grave, after all.

"Also, the district is really new. More like a pilot project. There might be some areas that aren't quite ready. A few amenities that may not be available immediately."

I laugh. "You're telling me my options are being stuck here or having early access to a shiny new part of heaven but the sauna might not be open to the public yet?"

Zach laughs too. A warm feeling spreads through my chest and all the way down to the tips of my fingers. Relief. That's what it is. More than acceptance, the thing I've been looking for at the end of all the grief was relief.

"Something like that." He hums to himself as he flips through screens on his tablet, tapping here and there. "I could fit you in here. You'd have a view of the meadow. The other units on your floor aren't done but should be ready in another month or so. They're working on the finishings, painting, that sort of thing, so you won't hear any real construction noise or anything. Let's take a walk. I can show you around."

He stuffs the tablet back in his briefcase. We pass through the ER to a bank of elevators. I flinch a few times when people get too close, but no one ever walks into me or through me.

"Stick with me," Zach says. "They can't see us, but they know I'm a presence to be avoided. As long as we stay close, they'll avoid you too."

That's a nifty feature. The first few hours of my afterlife were rocky, but things are finally turning around.

So of course, as the elevator dings and the doors slide open, there's a deafening crash from the direction of the ER.

"Fuck. Shit." Zach ducks, stumbling forward into the elevator.

"What was that?" I ask.

"Not our problem," he says. "Come on, let's go."

Dust billows up the hall. The sound of people crying follows. I put a hand over my mouth and nose like there's anything to protect.

"Ember. This way." Zach holds out a hand.

A dark shape shuffles toward me, bringing its terrifying laughter with it. As it solidifies through the debris cloud, I don't know if it's better or worse. It's not the woman from the park. It's a man. A big one. He looks like he's rotting. Skin hangs from his face and arms in ragged strips. He bares his teeth and they're dripping with dark sticky fluid, like blood from a black and white movie.

"Ember," Zach says again. I should go with him. My heavenly condo awaits. But I can't look away from the man—creature?—coming toward me. He seems to know he has me entranced, and his growl—which is definitely not human—shakes me all the way down to my bones.

"Move in!" A voice calls from farther down the hall, and the sound of several pairs of running boots follows. Shit. More soldiers. I whirl just in time to see the elevator doors slide shut. Maybe Zach looks apologetic, but it happens so fast I can't say.

"You're leaving me?" I ask—but when I bang on the door, my hand slides through the metal, leaving me with no other option but to scream in frustration.

The thing in the hall is closer, and when he laughs this time, it starts high then slowly drops until it gives me Jabba the Hut vibes, only I'm no Jedi. I'm just me, and this is very, *very* bad. The soldiers are getting closer too. Will they ignore me a second time?

The counter above the elevator clicks upward. Two, three.

When it stops at six, I run.

The lights overhead flicker, and a howl chases after me. Second floor. Third, fourth. Fifth floor. The stairwell plunges into darkness. The howling is so loud I put my hands over my ears. When I go to run through the door on the sixth floor, I collide with metal, but when I try to yank on the handle, my hand goes through it like it's not even there. Pretty sure I've had this nightmare before, except now I can't wake up. I claw at the door, but the undead physics are impossible. No matter how I push and pull, it's both too solid and not solid enough. I'm trapped.

A monstrous snarl comes from down below. The crackle of a radio follows close after. The soldiers in pursuit.

"Charging!" someone yells.

I duck just as the blue light shoots up the column of the stairwell contained only by the winding railing that rises upward. Every single hair on my body stands on end. The air is full of static, and the snarl turns to a wail. I'm pressed against the wall, and with every second, the glow creeps closer to me. I don't want this. Wherever this light is sending ghosts, I didn't buy a ticket.

The wailing cuts out abruptly, and the light goes with it. A soldier's radio crackles.

"Report?" a voice asks.

"Contained. It was a big one. We're returning to the office." Then the whole stairwell goes silent. I peek over the railing. Six floors down, a giant scorch mark is the only evidence anything has happened, but as I watch, even that vanishes until nothing is left.

I try the door again, and this time it opens obligingly, leaving me to curse softly. The only sound in the hallway is the squeak of small wheels on the floor as a man in a hospital gown shuffles past me, dragging his IV stand with him.

Where's Zach? What the hell is the point of having someone promise you comfort and ease if they dump you at the first minor inconvenience? Zach was worried he'd get in trouble for being late to pick me up? Wait until his superiors find out he abandoned me in the hospital to save his own neck. I wonder if there are professional development workshops in heaven. Maybe that's my purgatory; delivering Leadership Basics for a few centuries before finally crossing through the pearly gates.

No sign of Zach anywhere. Or anyone else but the watery shapes of the living. How is there not an app for this? A welcome package? They—whatever faith or organization it is that Zach, the soldiers and polo man all work for—clearly suck at the person-to-person stuff. The least they could do is provide some self-directed resources. A brochure discreetly left at your bedside or in the inside pocket of whatever suit jacket your family decides to bury you in.

I trudge back to the stairwell and upward. Maybe there's a stairway to heaven next to the hospital helipad. I'm not opposed to a self-serve option at this point. When I reach the top, I'm not even breathing hard. Or at all. That's a perk, at least. So far death has not been awesome, but from a physical perspective it's at least been better than having bone cancer. So there's that, I guess.

But, speaking of the clothes you get buried in, what am I wearing? With everything else that's happened, I haven't had a chance to consider my appearance. Leggings I threw away after the seams wore out where my thighs rub together. A chunky cable knit sweater I thrifted in Kensington Market a couple years ago and never actually wore because it was never as cute on me once I got it home as it had been in the store. This is what I get to wear for eternity? At least Hazel got some pearls. All I have are a pair of green acrylic hoops that always hurt my ears. When I take them out and fling them into the early evening air, they reappear in my ears like they were never gone in the first place.

No stairway to heaven on the roof. At least the sunset is pretty.

Holy shit, I'm bored. This is why ghosts start haunting people, isn't it? It's not about vengeance or unfinished business. It's about killing time for who knows how long. If eternity is sunsets and running from black ooze monsters, why wouldn't you spend a few decades going bump in the night just to break up the monotony?

I spend a few hours plotting ways I'd haunt the people who wronged me in my life. The boss who stalked my LinkedIn profile for two years after I quit working for him. The TA I dated in university who dumped me after I stayed up for a week straight helping her finish her master's thesis. They'd never see me coming, but they'd sure as hell notice the table spinning and the cupboard doors slamming. May their conference calls disconnect and their PowerPoint presentations freeze at the worst possible moments.

As I imagine increasingly elaborate plans for vengeance, I don't even notice as the few stars that are visible through Toronto's urban glow fade as the sun rises. I can't stay up here forever. And that boss and that old girlfriend aren't worth my dearly departed time. Slowly, I climb down the stairs. Maybe I'll go see my parents. My sister and her kids. We agreed no funeral. Just a celebration of life later this summer. What are they doing today, on the first day without me to look after? It's a bit of a trip to Don Mills where Mom and Dad live, but hopefully the subway is still accessible to the newly dead. At least I won't have to pay a fare?

I'm so caught up in the logistics of my trip, I don't see the young woman with the tattoos and short hair walking out the ER doors until she also walks through me.

"Oh, for god's sake, watch where you're going!" I shout, trying to shake off the gooey transparent feeling of being insubstantial.

She stops. She's got a pair of earbuds in while she talks to someone on her phone, but she pulls one out, glancing around her.

I catch my breath. Did she hear me?

"Hello?" I ask. Her gaze settles in my direction, though she isn't exactly looking at me. "Hello? Can you hear me?" I do some jumping jacks and make a few funny faces, but soon enough she puts the earbud back in.

"Anyway," she says, hefting a backpack on one shoulder. "Like I was saying . . ." And she continues on like I'm not even there.

But she heard me, though. Right? It wasn't just a fluke? She doesn't quite look like everyone else. Not as clear as Zach or the soldiers, but less blurry than most of the other people around her. That means something, right?

She descends to the subway station. It's early morning, and the stairs and escalators are busy with commuters coming into town to start their workday while the tattooed woman seems to be wrapping hers up. I follow her through the turnstiles and down to the platform.

At first, I try talking.

"Did you spend the night at the hospital?" I ask. "Were you visiting someone? Or were you a patient?" I glance at her wrist, but there's no ID bracelet there. She's got her phone out and her sleeve has fallen back, exposing a winding snake tattoo that disappears under a thick leather cuff at her wrist. The cuff is carved with neat geometric designs. It's stylish. Something I might have worn back in the day.

"Maybe you work there?" I ask. "Night shift? Are you a nurse?"

No answer. A breeze picks up, signalling the arrival of a subway, though I can't feel it. She looks up from her phone to watch it pull in and doesn't even give me a flicker of a look.

People get off and she waits quietly. I can follow her on the train, but maybe this is as pointless as everything else. Maybe she didn't hear me. I'm kidding myself and wasting time. I should go see Mom. That's a better way to spend my second dead day.

At the last moment, before she steps on the subway, I dart in front of her, holding my arms out wide. If I were alive, I'd be blocking her way onto the car. Her gaze is down, watching her feet to make sure she doesn't trip on the gap. I brace when she walks through me like I'm not there.

Goddammit.

Her muffled "Ugh" comes just as the doors start to close, and it's the signal I need. Just a hint. A tiny bit of hope. Enough for me to follow her a minute longer.

"Can you hear me?" I ask again as I settle into the seat next to hers. She closes her eyes as the subway pulls out of the station. "Hello?" I poke at her shoulder, but my finger goes right through her shirt, and maybe she shrinks away from the phantom touch or maybe she just settles a little more deeply into her seat. Her chin droops as she dozes off. We're the only people in the car. The subway is headed away from downtown and at this time of day most commuters are going the other direction.

Might as well go all in.

I shift, scooting along the seat until slowly I engulf her. Or am I engulfed by her? Ick. The sensation is even more unpleasant when it goes on for longer than the momentary contact of being walked through. Like wearing too many clothes on a hot day. It feels like I'm being suffocated by something I can't escape.

But if she can hear me, she must be able to feel at least some part of this, right?

When she raises her chin again, I practically crow in victory.

But she only pulls her phone out of her backpack and flips through some screens until she's watching a video.

She's watching porn, to be specific.

Two women naked in bed. One is splayed out and tosses her head while the other has her hand halfway up—

I spring to my feet. Surely this is some kind of violation. I'm not one to shame. Watch what you want. But not on the subway, and not while you have a visitor.

"That's just rude," I say, stumbling back until I slump into the seat across the way.

She crosses one leg and wordlessly watches her phone. From here, with her earbuds keeping the sound private, she might as well be watching cat videos. Her mouth quirks up on one side and her tongue rolls under her bottom lip, popping out for just a second to expose a stud before she grips the phone with both hands and starts typing something.

This is ridiculous. Humiliating, even. But still, when she gets off at St. George—by which I mean she disembarks and not anything else—I follow and wait until she's on the other line going west. Might as well go all the way.

Of course I would choose to follow someone who lives in the outer wilds of Etobicoke. Formally, the City of Toronto is an amalgamation of older communities, the same way New York City is made up of the boroughs that used to have their own administration. New York has places like Manhattan, the Bronx and Queens. We have Scarborough, North York and Etobicoke. But lifelong Torontonians will always debate which ones are truly part of the city and which have their own identity. Officially, the western boundary of the city is the edge of Etobicoke. Realistically, when someone says "the west end" they usually mean the borders of the original city of Toronto. Something like Dufferin Street, or maybe as far as High Park. Etobicoke might as well be another planet.

And yet, as we pass Old Mill and Royal York stations, she makes no move to leave. I can't imagine having to do this commute every day. My condo in Fort York was perfect central: walking distance from everywhere I'd ever want to be. Why would anyone live way out here if they needed to be downtown?

Finally, the subway shudders into Kipling Station. The end of the line. I'm not sure I've ever ridden all the way out here. Not even once in my entire life. Death truly is a new experience. The station looks beyond dated. The pillars that divide the platform are tiled in a rust-brown that was probably the height of interior design around 1970, while the floor is an indistinct colour of greige.

The doors slide open and everyone else exits. The young woman slings on her backpack and heads for the platform. I stay where I am. Will this be worth it? I still don't even know if she can hear me, or if I'm just desperately looking for signs that aren't there. The blue-haired person from yesterday told me to wait at the hospital. I'm so far from the parts of Toronto I know. What if I'm missing my chance right now? Some guy with a clipboard may be standing in the hospital atrium looking for me, and I'm not there.

At the last second, she glances over her shoulder.

"Are you coming?" she asks. "You made it this far."

Euphoric relief shoots through me like a Canada Day fireworks display. I knew I was right. How dare she play coy? I don't have time for games. I'm in over my head and I'm done being patient.

Am I coming? Damn right I am.

chapter
four

THE QUESTIONS TUMBLE out of me almost as fast as I trip up the stairs, following her from the station.

"You can hear me?" I ask. "Can you see me too?"

"You're an excitable one, aren't you?" She puts her earbuds in their case and drops them into a pocket.

"Where are you going? Do you know who I am? Ember Munro. Bone cancer. I died yesterday, but the records say I'm not supposed to die until November. Can you check your files? They know I'm coming, right?"

She doesn't answer. We emerge into daylight, and I squint. She slips on a pair of sunglasses and pulls the hood under her down vest up over her head, hunching into the wind as she walks up the hill away from the station.

Oh, is it cold out? Have I already lost track of things like whether or not I'm supposed to be cold? The people around us are all dressed to protect themselves against the early spring elements, and I'm still here in my leggings and sweater.

I'm getting distracted again. The tattooed woman is waiting at the curb for the light to change, and I'm still only halfway up the hill. This end of Etobicoke is a sea of condo towers, both finished and under construction, along with the usual selection of chain fast food places. Red and orange buses rumble by, dropping off even more people at the subway.

I hurry to catch up, cursing as she starts to cross the street. The upside to being dead is I don't have to worry as a red hatchback takes the corner too close on a right-hand turn. I just keep my gaze locked on the hooded shape as she reaches the far side of the inter-section.

"Wait!" I call, but I'm starting to doubt if she really can hear me. She hasn't answered a single question. I put a shoulder down and run at her. Through her. She's going to stop and listen to what I have to say.

This time, her sound of disgust isn't muffled. She does a full body shudder as she stops on the sidewalk.

"That's really rude, you know," she says, though she's still not looking directly at me.

"Rude?" I say. "I'll tell you what's rude. Ignoring me since the hospital. Watching two lesbians go down on each other in a public place. Picking your nose." Okay, she hasn't done that last one, but I'm on a roll. "Can you hear me or not?"

She's still looking at some middle distance beyond me. "We're almost there. Come on. Kelly's going to be pissed," she says conversationally. "I'm not supposed to bring any more ghosts home. So if the question comes up, you followed me, okay? I didn't have anything to do with it." Her worn leather boots scuff on the pavement. Along with the tattoos, she's got several hoops in both ears and another in her nose. The backs of her knuckles and her throat are tattooed in the same geometric patterns from her cuff. She's younger than I am. Probably early to mid-twenties, with warm brown skin that speaks of some South Asian heritage. Her hair is dyed a coppery brown, and darker black roots peek through at her temples and along the back of her neck.

We turn onto a dead-end residential street, then up the driveway of a small stucco bungalow about halfway down from the corner. It's like nearly every other house on the street and would be completely unremarkable except for the fact that it has flowers in bloom by the front porch, while everywhere else the plants have just sprouted hopeful early spring leaves.

"Come on inside," she says, holding open a side door. "We'll be able to talk properly in private."

When I do as she says, something washes over me. It's an entirely new feeling. Not the sick cloying sensation of walking through someone. Or the tingling feeling beneath my skin whenever one of those monsters is nearby. This is louder. More stable. More grounding.

"Ah." She sighs as she undoes the zipper on her vest and hangs it on a hook, dropping her backpack and undoing the laces of her boots. She kicks them off and they roll to a stop next to a pair of white ones in far better condition. When she lights a candle on the windowsill close to the door, the grounded feeling somehow becomes even stronger. I kick at the white boots. Before I died, the motion would have been enough to knock one over, and that doesn't happen now, but the one closest to me does slide on the fake hardwood an inch or two.

She smiles. "Feels better, doesn't it?"

"What is this place?" I ask.

"It's a rental," she sighs. It's the first time she's directly answered a question, and I do a little happy dance right there in the entryway that makes her grin, even though her gaze is still aimed somewhere over my shoulder. "If they knew how many candles I go through in a week, they'd probably up my security deposit. Come on, I'm going to make some coffee. I'm Jupiter, by the way."

"Ember. You really can hear me?" I ask as I follow her up a small set of stairs to the house's main floor. It's simple. One of those wartime era houses that regularly get torn down in Toronto only to be replaced by something two stories taller that takes up every single inch right to the property line. At the top of the stairs is a hallway. To the left are what looks like a bathroom and a very messy bedroom. The door at the end of the hall is closed. To the right, there's a kitchen and a small table for eating. The table has several stacks of old books and an open but empty pizza box on it. Half-empty glasses and pop bottles dot the landscape too. The kitchen isn't in much better shape, with several days of dirty dishes piled up in the sink and stacks of papers, envelopes, cleaning supplies, and miscellaneous other housewares scattered on every other surface. Two of the piles have avalanched off the counter and onto the linoleum. My fingers itch to pick them up. Another opening at the end of the hall looks like it leads to a living room. That's it. That's the entire house.

"I can hear you now," Jupiter says as she goes about filling the machine with water and starting the grinder. "Outside is harder. I can feel ghosts, but I can't really communicate." She sets the brewer to start and opens the fridge, pulling out a carton of milk and a tub of yogurt that she opens to sniff. With a grimace she sticks it back inside. I've followed her so closely that when she turns she walks right into me, then laughs as we untangle ourselves.

"That's so gross," she says with a shudder. "Even with the candles I can't actually see you. Better to give a wide berth, if you don't mind."

"Why can't you see me?" I ask.

"Beats me," she says as the coffee maker gurgles. "It's not something I've ever been able to do. I have a sense of where you are. It's like static that moves around the room. A mosquito I can almost hear. But I can definitely hear your voice. At least in the house. That's why we have the runes."

"Runes?"

"The candles," she says, and I realize the candles are also decorated with the same markings as her cuff and tattoos. "I carved runes into them. They work best when they're lit. And I carved some into the house too, around the foundation. Don't tell the landlord, okay? She'll be pissed."

I zip my lips shut, then remember she can't see that, so I say, "I won't tell a living soul."

"Not like you could anyway." Jupiter laughs again as she pours coffee into two mugs. To one she adds a splash of milk and a spoonful of sugar. To the other, she adds what has to amount to a quarter cup of vanilla syrup. Then she adds a similar amount of milk, so the dark coffee fades to pale beige. Like a muddy puddle after the rain.

"What are you anyway?" I ask as she puts the milk away. "A psychic? A witch?"

"Something like that. I prefer the term medium, but you can say I'm psychic too." She bangs the fridge shut with a hip, then lifts her voice to call across the house. "Kelly! Wakey wakey. Coffee's ready."

In my mounting excitement at finding a new connection, I've missed some important clues. The most obvious should have been the two mugs, because it's not like one of them is for me. The others are less obvious, but the closed door at the end of the hall indicates the possible presence of another bedroom. It could be something else. Jupiter might use it as an office or a studio or a room to hide the bodies of the people she suckers into believing that she can talk to ghosts. But Toronto rent being what it is, the odds she lives in this whole house by herself are slim.

And there were the boots. The white ones. New and pristine and—now that I think about it—several sizes bigger than the battered ones Jupiter was wearing.

Someone else lives here.

Anxiety thumps in my throat, reviving my poor dead heartbeat. Out of sight, a door opens, and someone groans.

"What did I tell you about bringing stray ghosts home from work?" The voice is deep and smooth, neither distinctly male or female, with an unplaceable accent. The footsteps on the hall floor say the speaker is large, or at least taller than me and with feet to match.

I should have stayed at the hospital. The grounded feeling from the candles is changing. Something big is coming toward me.

Powerful. It sucks all the energy toward itself like a black hole until I drop to my knees.

"She followed me," Jupiter is saying. "All the way from downtown on the subway."

The candle on the table flickers, and the power coming from the hall is like the wind in a fall storm, sudden and fierce. I hold up a hand to keep invisible grit out of my eyes. The flame wheels on its wick, trying to stay lit.

As they round the corner, I know who it's going to be. The accent. The too-perfect features. The ageless disdain as they look down at me cowering on the kitchen floor.

"You again?" they ask.

It's them. The one from yesterday. The person with the leather jacket who told me someone would come and pick me up, and all I got was lousy Zach who bailed at the first sign of trouble. Their blue and purple hair has been replaced with a bleached blonde so pale it's practically colourless, but I'd still recognize them anywhere.

"Ember," Jupiter says, "this is my roommate, Kelly." She looks pleased to have made the introduction. Kelly looks like I'm in the way of their coffee.

Well, tough shit, Sherlock. I know your name, and I know where you live.

The flame rights itself and the falling sensation in my chest subsides. I pull myself up to my feet and walk right up to Kelly. Whoever or whatever they are, they can see me, and they look all the way down their perfectly shaped nose with eyes that still blink too damn slowly to be human.

"You," I say, stabbing a finger into their chest. "You are going to get me out of here. Right now."

chapter
five

DESPITE THE FACT that I just saw them yesterday and they are unmistakably Kelly—whoever or whatever that might be—they are not the same, and I don't only mean their hair colour. For one, the leather jacket is gone, replaced with a grey T-shirt so big the sleeves reach their elbows and the hem almost reaches their knees. Beneath is a pair of similarly baggy white sweatpants. No boots. No socks, even. Just plain, clean, hairless feet.

Also, if I'd had to guess a gender yesterday, I'd have said they were male, but their face is distinctly feminine this morning. Pink lips and eyeliner that would make a beauty influencer weep with envy. Maybe a hint of blush on cheekbones that seem endless as they sweep upward.

"I told you to stay at the hospital," they say, which saves me an argument about whether or not we've met before.

"Yeah, about that. I am deeply unhappy with the service I have received since my death. I've essentially been on hold for twenty-four hours and I'm out of fucks. So who or whatever you are, tell me which way to the complaints department before I ask to speak to your manager."

Their expression changes. Maybe it's a laugh. Maybe a grimace. Some of the feminine softness goes with it. They put a hand on my shoulder and I nearly melt. Even their gentle push to get me out of their way feels like they could knock me into the next room with a finger flick. I stumble and bump against the kitchen island. They pick up the beige coffee and take a sip, closing their eyes as they inhale the steam.

"You know each other?" Jupiter asks, sounding disappointed her big reveal wasn't met with the enthusiasm she'd hoped.

"No," Kelly says.

"Yes," I say. "We met yesterday."

"We didn't meet. You accosted me at the subway."

"Accosted?" I squawk. "Who says accosted?"

"No one says accosted anymore, Kelly." Jupiter sounds tired, like maybe they've had this discussion before.

They purse their lips, considering. "Cornered? Confronted? Propositioned."

Jupiter snorts. "Been up late reading the online thesaurus again?"

"I didn't proposition you," I say. "I asked for help. You knew exactly what I needed because you told me someone would come."

"I knew what you needed because you're a ghost." They're rooting through a kitchen cupboard until they pull out a bag of salt and vinegar chips. Taking both chips and mug, they settle down at the table for the most stomach-rotting breakfast I've seen in a while.

"This can't be my ending," I say. "My name is Ember Munro. Bone cancer. I died and now I need to go to . . ." I pause. Shit. Where? Do I really know where I'm supposed to go? A reunification desk? A condo complex with all the other dead people? Will there at least be shuffleboard?

Jupiter and Kelly are both watching, clearly waiting for me to finish the sentence. I rack my brains. What was it Zach called it yesterday? I don't even care about whether the air conditioning works or the pool is open. I just don't want to wander aimlessly around Toronto forever.

"The other life," I say. "Take me to the other life."

Silence consumes the kitchen. The faucet drips once. Out of nowhere, a fat orange cat strolls into the kitchen. It winds its way around my ankles, meows, then wanders over to the little dish I didn't notice before next to the fridge and helps itself to the kibble there.

Jupiter and Kelly burst into laughter. Or Jupiter does. She tips her head back and screams with hilarity. Kelly chuckles softly once before returning to their coffee, but the effect might as well have them laughing directly in my face. Humiliation scalds my cheeks. Even the cat glances up from his breakfast to give me a look of derision.

"What's so funny?" I ask, trying to stuff down my embarrassment. Ember's Life Tip #12: *You can't control other people's reactions or feelings. You can only control your own.* How many times have I said that when I'm doing live chats with the Sparks? Time to take my own medicine.

Kelly simply shakes their head. Jupiter wipes at her eyes with a gross-looking tea towel.

"The other life? What is that? Some discount brand service offering named for search engine purposes? Like a restaurant called Thai Food Near Me?" She cracks up again at her own joke.

"Does it really matter what it's called?" My efforts to achieve peace of mind are failing. "How am I supposed to know? This is my first time being dead."

Jupiter's laughter subsides and she waves a hand. "Sorry. Sorry. I've just never heard anyone call afterlife that before."

"You've only made it harder by following Jupiter," Kelly says. "The records will show you're at the hospital. They won't know to come looking for you here." They stuff a handful of salt and vinegar chips into their mouth, then chase it with coffee. The vinegar and vanilla mixture has to be revolting.

"Okay, first off," I say, "the records show I'm not supposed to die until November, which is their fuck-up, not mine. Secondly, who are 'they'? And third, I saw two of them—three if we're counting you—yesterday, and none of you were any help. The first took the old woman and left. The second ran as soon as the soldiers showed up."

This gets Kelly's attention. "You saw the quarantine team? Where?"

But at the same time, Jupiter says, "He's a reaper."

"Who is?" I ask.

She jerks a thumb in Kelly's direction. "Him. You asked who they are. They're reapers."

I sift through the statement. First factoid to come to the surface is Kelly is male. Interesting. Second is that he is a . . . My mind skitters over that realization, even as a memory scratches its way forward. *No one thinks of the reapers.* Didn't the man in the hospital room say something about that?

I hadn't really thought about it until now. Not with any of them. The other two, Zach and the first man, looked so human that I assumed they were dead people with new jobs. And even Kelly, while not exactly looking like someone you would pass on the street, still looks person-shaped.

"A grim reaper?" I ask and even to my own ears I sound a little awestruck.

"He's actually hilarious," Jupiter says, which only makes Kelly scowl at her. Her gaze drops and she mutters, "Sorry, I just wanted to clarify you're not always grim."

He looks plenty grim now. But still not like the grim reapers you hear about in books and legends. Where's the hood? The scythe? The bones of his face are sharply angled enough to make it clear there's a skeleton underneath, but he's still very much flesh and blood.

Also, if he's the grim reaper, what does that make the others?

"So you're not the only one?" I ask.

"The only one what?" Here he looks genuinely confused.

"You know." I hunch in like I don't want to be overheard, even though it's just the three of us in the kitchen. Maybe the cat is a spy. "The only reaper?"

"The only—How exactly would that work?" Kelly asks, sounding like it's the most ridiculous thing he's heard all day. "There are hundreds of thousands of souls that need collecting every day. What do you think I am? Santa Claus?"

My annoyance is replaced with something like surprised wonder. Death was supposed to be simple, but I'm starting to question everything. "Wait. Is Santa Claus real too?"

He pushes back from his chair, crumpling up his empty chip bag. "This conversation is over. Jupiter, take her back downtown."

"I know how to get to the hospital," I say, folding my arms over my chest.

"Great." He points to the door. The power is back, along with the sensation that I'm about to be crushed like a bug. Still, I am in charge of my own destiny. No know-it-all grim reaper is going to change that.

"No," I say simply. The shortest sentence in the world. Two can play this game.

His nostrils flare and his eyes go wide. They're pale blue, almost like ice on a pond. Between that and the platinum hair, if either one of us was going to get pegged as a ghost, it would be him.

"Excuse me?" he says.

"But maybe we could—" Jupiter starts to add, but I cut her off.

"I did what you told me to do yesterday, and all I got was chased by monsters and abandoned by your associates. So, no. You know how to get me out of here. I'm not going anywhere until you do." To prove my point, I plop into the chair he's just vacated and wrap my ankles around the legs. Almost immediately, the orange cat jumps up in my lap, rubbing his face against my knuckles until I unfold my arms and pet him. He starts purring and it's only a second later that I realize he's standing on my legs as opposed to in them. I rub him harder and he makes biscuits on my thighs. It's so normal, I can't stop the delighted laugh that bursts out of my throat.

Kelly leans in and blows out the candle on the table. The cat sinks as though I've sprung a leak, paws going through my legs until he hits the wooden seat beneath. He reacts like we've tried to drown him, arching and hissing as he leaps away. His nails skitter on the kitchen floor before he runs up the hall with a yowl.

"Kelly, you're such a jerk." Jupiter sounds horrified. She relights the candle while Kelly smirks, then hurries up the hall in search of the wailing cat. "Carrot Stick! Come here. Good boy. You're okay."

Kelly puts his dirty mug on the counter next to the dozen or so others. The empty chip bag goes next to it, which makes sense I guess, given that the garbage can at the end of the island is over-flowing with takeout wrappers and what looks like the hose from a shower head.

"Are you listening?" I say as he exits the kitchen and heads to the living room where he flops down on the stained oatmeal-coloured sectional.

"I can hear you," he says. "Whether or not I'm listening is a separate question." To prove his point, he loops a pair of pink cat-ear gaming headphones over his head. The TV flicks on, and a gaming console on the leaning stand beneath glows blue as it powers up.

"We're not done," I say, marching toward him, but before I can touch him, he holds out a palm. It's already an infuriating gesture from any dude bro on the street, but from Kelly, it's even worse because I nearly faceplant into the sofa when my feet somehow glue themselves into the floor. I grunt with the effort of trying to pick them up, but I am well and truly stuck. "What did you do?"

He puts a long finger to his lips. "Shh. The mission is starting." On the screen, a group of soldiers in drab olive and grey uniforms walk in formation through a spooky warehouse. A flicker of red light is the only warning before a giant spider-like monster crashes through a wall and roars at them while the soldiers begin blasting in the monster's direction.

"Let me go!" I shout.

"I'm not doing anything." Kelly doesn't look away from the screen as I continue to struggle to free myself. His reply is so infuriating I growl right along with the spider monster.

"Kelly, let her go," Jupiter says from the hall. She's holding the orange cat who appears to have recovered from his trauma and is rubbing his fluffy head against her chin.

Kelly glances at me, then at Jupiter, before he continues his game. It's like watching a toddler test the waters of parental defiance, and the effect is only amplified when Jupiter says, "If you don't let her go, I'm not ordering takeout for dinner. I'll cook what I want, and you'll just have to eat it."

This does the trick, because he lets out a heavy sigh. In the game, one of the soldiers is tossed off his feet by the spider, and the whole screen goes red again, though this time digital blood slowly drips down over the display.

"Now look what happened," he says. He pouts at the screen. But I stumble forward as my feet are released from their invisible hold.

"I know," I say, shaking myself. "Dying really sucks, doesn't it?"

He glares at me. Or, actually, he stares with that same flat expression and slow blink that drips with contempt. He better get me to the other side, or the afterlife, or the other life, or whatever the hell it's called soon, because I am quickly learning to hate that look.

"I can't help you," he says.

"What do you mean? It is literally your job to help me, isn't it?"

Jupiter makes a squeaking noise. Kelly's expression hardens.

Oh, there it is. Now he really is glaring at me. But I hold my ground and glare right back until he finally looks away.

"It's not my job. Find someone else to take you over."

"Who?" I ask, looking around as though someone might pop out of the walls like a spider monster and drag me to hell. Honestly, at this point I'd hardly even be mad about it. I could negotiate my way out of hell. Better than talking to the brick wall that is Kelly. "You're a reaper. Reap me, goddammit."

He glances quickly at me again and works his jaw. He's fighting not to say something, but he's going to lose. I can wait him out. I can literally wait forever.

"Kelly got fired," Jupiter says quietly, then ducks when Kelly shoots her a look that would incinerate even the most fearsome of spider monsters. The cat wriggles free and escapes.

"I didn't get fired. I quit." Kelly goes back to his game, sulking like a teenager.

I can't take anymore. Furious, I spin and stomp up the hall. In my anger, I try to walk through the door to the driveway, but Jupiter's candles are still burning, and instead all I get is a smushed nose against the glass for my trouble.

I don't go far. There's a stained and faded chaise lounge in the backyard, and I flop onto it, throwing an arm over my eyes to shade myself from the bright morning sunlight overhead.

What a disaster. It all seemed so straightforward back at the hospital. Sign some forms, wait ten days. Boom. Done. No one warned me what an administrative nightmare it would be on the other side. They probably don't even know. Someone really needs to send the doctors a memo.

"You okay?" Jupiter has followed me outside. Her gaze is fixed above my head, but I appreciate her checking.

"Peachy," I say. "Best day of my life, except wait. I'm not alive anymore. I'm dead. It sucks."

"I'm sure." She sits down at the end of the chaise, and I make sure to tuck my feet underneath me so we don't touch. "At least you know, though? A lot of the ghosts I talk to still think they're alive. They want me to take them back to their houses or call their bosses to tell them they'll be late for work."

I sniff, trying to force a laugh for her benefit.

"I am my own boss," I say. "And we sold my condo last month." My parents said there was no hurry. That they could take care of cleaning out my stuff after I was gone. But it made sense to do it before. Less stress for them. Less hassle as they settled my estate. I used the money to clear old credit card debts. Even made a video about it. Ember's Life Tips for the month before you die.

"That's cool." Jupiter says. "I'd love to be my own boss. I'd open up a little store. I'd do readings for people. Sell crystals and tea. What kind of business were you in?"

After everything, talking like I'm still a normal living person helps a bit. It doesn't change anything, but it makes me feel less alone.

"I was a life coach," I say.

"Like a counsellor?" She tilts her head. The morning sunshine makes her copper highlights glow.

"More like a content creator. I had a YouTube channel. Find Your Spark." Okay, maybe less normal. Talking about my business in the past tense hurts. One-on-one coaching was part of my five-year plan. Too bad the plan got cut off at year two.

Jupiter's eyes get big. "Find Your Spark? I used to follow you. Oh my god, you're so pretty. Look." She pulls out her phone, scrolling through screens, and before I even realize what she's doing, she's on my channel, opening the most recent video. The one I sent from the hospital.

"No. Wait." I reach out, but she can't see me.

"Oh." Her excitement vanishes, and even I have a hard time watching. My face is skeletal, my head covered in a kerchief. No one tells you when you lose all your hair that you will be cold all the time. The kerchief helped a little. Didn't do much about the cancer, though.

Here in the yard, I run a hand through my hair, long and red, pulled up in a high ponytail the way I liked it best when I was about Jupiter's age.

"I'm better now," I say. "I mean, I look better."

She closes the screen, which I appreciate.

"That really sucks," she says. "I loved your channel. Ember's Life Tip: Having needs does not mean you're needy. That one saved my ass. Broke up with my shitty ex the next day. He was a dick."

"He?" I ask before I can stop myself. "You're straight? I thought after the porn—"

She laughs. "About that. You were in my lap. Shit like that will give me a migraine."

I duck my head in an apology, then realize she can't see that either and say, "Sorry. I didn't know."

"It's okay. But to answer your other question, I'm equal opportunity. After that guy, I dated a woman named Hy. Then another man named Ethan. Then a nonbinary—"

"It's fine," I say, cutting her off. "I don't need the list. I shouldn't have assumed."

She grins. "Not like you can revoke my queer card since you're dead."

"Yeah." I sigh. "Seems like I can't do much of anything. I'm stuck."

Jupiter yawns. "Don't worry about Kelly. He's always grumpy in the mornings. I'm really sorry, but I have to crash. I work nights in the hospital sanitation department. I need sleep. If you're still here later, we can talk to him again."

Jupiter makes her way back to the house. Sleep sounds amazing right now. Maybe I'd wake up and everything would magically be better. But even though I've been awake since I died, I don't feel tired at all. Might never feel again.

But I'm not ready to give up. I stare at the house. Everything I need is inside. A medium and a reaper. Ember's Life Tip #273 says that if you don't get the result you want, change your tactics. My video on negotiation strategies was one of my most popular a couple years ago. I heard from moms, solopreneurs, executives, and creatives. They'd all had success when they changed their approach. The truth is the same for everyone.

Including me. I've tried getting what I want by being organized and clear in my needs. Kelly is going to help me. I know who he is and where he lives. He can't run away from me like the others did.

He said I was a ghost, and I'm going to do what ghosts do best.

I'm going to haunt that asshole until he wishes we were both dead.

chapter
six

DEAR SPARKS, you ever have one of those days where it feels like nothing is going your way? It's time for *Ember Munro's Ten Easy Steps for a Successful Haunting to Get Your Life Back.*

Get your life over with?

Get your afterlife back? Started?

Whatever, the title is a work in progress. And I'm not sure it really will take ten steps, but the only way to know for sure is to get started.

Kelly and I give each other a wide berth all day, which is to say, he spends all day on the couch blowing shit up in virtual space. Jupiter spends most of the time asleep. And I just sort of . . . hang out. As long as the candles are burning, I'm solid enough that I can pick things up, though it takes more focus and strength than it did when I was alive. I think about washing the dishes. Maybe if I can ingratiate myself with Kelly and Jupiter, I can change Kelly's mind. But all it takes is for me to lift the first mug and find mould growing inside the one beneath it before I decide these two don't deserve my kindness.

When Jupiter leaves for her night shift, I sneak into her room, dodging around piles of clothes and a sprawling assortment of succulent plants in various pots, cups and chipped teapots. I spotted a ukulele hung on the far wall earlier and figure—since I've never played one in my life—a few hours of me trying to figure out the tune to "Somewhere Over the Rainbow" by Kelly's bedside, ideally in the darkest hours of the night, should do the trick.

I grab a chair from the kitchen table and wait quietly outside Kelly's bedroom, watching the thin strip of light that spills under the door. I've got my fingers poised on the strings. The second the light goes out, the serenade begins.

But it doesn't go out. Every so often Kelly shifts inside or clears his throat. The light stays on well past three in the morning.

Maybe he fell asleep? More than once I smacked myself in the face falling asleep with a reader in my hand and my lights on. A day full of incinerating spider monsters might really take it out of a reaper.

I wait a little longer. There are no more sounds. Gently, I put my fingers on the doorknob. My concert is imminent. Slowly, I twist the knob and nudge the door open.

Kelly's gaze meets mine immediately. He's very much awake, sprawled out on the bed, still in his T-shirt and sweats. Still has the cat headphones on, but he's traded in the TV and gaming console for a handheld device. He stares at me silently while lights flash against his face. Honestly, if death had happened the way I'd expected and I'd woken up to find him standing at the foot of the bed telling me to go with him, I might not have. Zach and the other guy were so much more approachable. Kelly is intimidating and otherworldly. Case in point: I give the awkward white lady smile that is reserved for when you accidentally make eye contact with a stranger on the street and slide the door shut again.

Okay, so the ukulele is out.

Time for Plan B. The hours tick away as I consider my options while petting Carrot Stick. I could go full poltergeist and resort to property damage. Flood the basement? Rip all the stuffing out of the cushions? But it looks like someone's already done that. The entire house might as well have been hit by a tornado. From the moldy cups to the dirty clothes. The empty pizza box on the kitchen table isn't the only one. There are eight more stacked up by the front door, and—based on the very brief glimpse I had— several more lying around Kelly's room.

The small unfinished basement is no better. Clothes spill out of the dryer, clearly waiting to be folded and put away, and when I open the washing machine, the smell of damp clothes left for too long makes me gag, which is saying something since my sense of smell is seriously muted since I died. Even poor Carrot Stick is pawing in a litter box that is clearly not scooped regularly, and here at least I hold back my disgust long enough to clean out the biggest clumps and take the nearly full garbage bag outside. I make it halfway to the bins before the effect of Jupiter's candles wear off and I almost drop my revolting load. Fortunately, the lids on the garbage cans are open, so I gather everything I have and do my best three-pointer impression to get it the last ten feet. The bag goes in with a pretty satisfying swish.

On my way back in, I collide with Kelly, who is coming down the hall.

"Sleep well?" I ask.

"Still here?" His hair isn't blond anymore. It's shaved super close to his head and dyed a vibrant green. When did he do that? I didn't hear him leave his room up until now.

"If you keep that up, you'll go bald," I say, pointing toward his head.

His lips twist. "You're not my employer, Ember."

"I think you mean 'you're not the boss of me,'" I say, then narrow my eyes as a better retort presents itself. "I thought you didn't have a boss. Why don't you? Oh yeah. You were fired."

He's lined his eyes with dark liner that wings up in the corners, and they make him look extra mean as he sneers at me. I brace for the argument.

"Play nice, you two," Jupiter says from where she is once again making coffee in the kitchen, having recently returned from her night shift. The tension between us breaks and Kelly walks around me, leaving me feeling a bit like a duck trying to steady the course as I bob in his wake.

"Why doesn't Kelly make the coffee?" I ask. "Doesn't seem fair that you work all night then have to do that too."

She arches an eyebrow, making the ring that pierces it sparkle. "Kelly's not allowed to cook. That's how she got stuck with me in the first place."

"She?" I ask.

Jupiter gives me a friendly smile, then gives Kelly a once-over. "Yeah. Feels like a she day, don't you think?"

Kelly's pulling another bag of chips out of the cupboard. The bag from yesterday is still sitting crumpled on the counter.

"Gender is a ridiculous human construct," Kelly says, sounding like the sage on the mount as he (she? They? Maybe it's safer to go back to they?) munch on their chips. "Nothing about my identity requires me to fit myself into your irrelevant classifications. If you feel the need to pick one or another term to make yourself comfortable in your world view, that's on you."

Oh, for god's sake. Man, woman, or neither, Kelly is such a pompous jerk.

"You really don't care?" I ask.

"We aren't going to know each other long enough for it to matter," they say around a crunch.

"Where the hell is the vanilla syrup?" Jupiter asks.

"Oh, I put it away," I say. Sometime overnight, as I'd waited for Kelly to go to bed, I found Carrot Stick on the counter licking the neck of the bottle where Jupiter had left it standing since yesterday morning. One more strike on the public health disaster that is this house. I did the bare minimum by putting the cap back on and stashing it in a kitchen cupboard.

She laughs and taps her forehead. "ADHD. I'm terrible with putting stuff away. Out of sight, out of mind. We ran out of mayo a few weeks ago, and I bought four jars because I kept putting them in the cupboard and forgetting they were there."

"This isn't your house. None of the things here are yours to touch," Kelly says. "And I know where everything is. The piles are part of a system." Without any further discussion, they head over to the living room, no doubt to start up on today's mission of slaying monsters.

"This isn't a system, it's a disaster," I call after him, but he doesn't reply. Or they don't reply. She doesn't reply. Shit. The whole situation is too complicated without me having to play "guess the pronoun" every day.

Not that I'm going to be here every day. Like Kelly said, our acquaintance will hopefully be very few days, in fact. Already a new plan is forming. The ukulele didn't work. I cannot possibly be as annoying as Kelly, so I'm going to do the next best thing.

I'm going to kill them with kindness.

It's surprisingly easy. I wait until Jupiter goes to bed for the day. Kelly's still in the living room. I start with the obvious stuff, collecting the pizza boxes and carrying them outside. Ditto with the overflowing garbage in the kitchen. I work out a system of pushing the bags with a long-handled broom from the boundary line provided by Jupiter's candles to the outdoor bins. I'd rather put the trash inside them, but this will have to do.

Then I go downstairs and restart the laundry machine, adding vinegar from one of the four half-empty bottles I find in a cupboard of dry goods and toilet paper to get the wet, musty smell out of the clothes. I carry the ones from the dryer upstairs in a hamper, then realize I have no space to work, so I get started on collecting the dirty dishes all over the house.

Kelly's in the kitchen pouring another cup of coffee when I return.

"This won't help," he says. They say. Yeah. They. I'm going with they. It feels safest unless they tell me otherwise. "Cleaning my house won't convince me to do you any favours."

I smile sweetly at them. "I'm not expecting any favours. If you're unemployed, you're of no use to me. I'm just keeping busy until one of your buddies comes to find me."

"You'd be better at the hospital," they say.

I take a risk and stand on my toes, rubbing my palm over their bristly green hair. They flinch and duck away, leaving me to smirk. It's a small victory, but I'll take it.

"After I'm done cleaning."

I wash the cups. Many are stained at the bottom, and even after I've done my best to scrub, they still have a brown ring. Table clear, I fold the laundry. It's all too big to be Jupiter's. Must be Kelly's. Perfect.

I don't ask before I let myself into their room. Time for my plan. I open drawers, fold what's inside, add what I've brought up, then help myself to a few things. The handheld game console from last night. Every left shoe I can find. I leave the right ones behind. I unplug Kelly's phone, tucking the charging cable into the laundry basket but leaving the phone on the bedside table. It has just under ten percent of a charge left, which is ideal. Next to it is a leather wallet. I grab that and add it to my spoils. I top the basket up with more clothes.

"I'll put these in the wash when the current load is done," I call cheerfully from the top of the steps. There's no reply. Downstairs the machine is spinning. I pile the dirty clothes on the floor, then take all the things I scooped from Kelly's room and put them in a small closet I noticed behind the litter box. The door is badly warped in the frame, and as it swings open, it carves a crescent shape in the floor where the dust is thick. No one has opened this door in a long time.

Carrot Stick has followed me down from the main floor and watches the whole thing with detached interest, but I think there's an approving gleam in his eye as I carry the basket back upstairs. My mom always did say cats can see ghosts. Turns out she was right. I put my finger to my lips, and Carrot Stick gives me a slow blink in reply. It reminds me of Kelly, but it feels nice to at least have an accomplice.

There's another closet in the hall. I repeat the same steps with the shoes there. Kelly's leather jacket from the first day is hung up on a peg. I take that.

On my way back down the stairs, I grab one white combat boot and also the set of keys hanging on a hook by the door. Everything but the keys go in the little closet before I latch it shut again and push the litter box back into place. The keys go to the kitchen and inside the container where Jupiter keeps the coffee. Even if they find the rest, I might still have some leverage.

Haunting complete.

And look, by traditional gothic standards, it may not meet the definition. More like a passive-aggressive prank. But I'm a ghost. If I say it's a haunting, it's a haunting.

Though now that I'm on a roll, I might as well keep going. Just being in this house makes me itchy. I scrub the sinks and mop the kitchen floor. I pull the dank towels off the racks in the bathroom and throw them down the basement stairs where they can join the rest of the laundry in waiting. I'm filling a plastic watering can I found under the kitchen sink to try to revive some dismal-looking plants in the front window when my grip slips and the can tumbles into the sink. When I reach for it, it slides right through my fingers like I'm not even there.

"Shit." I glance at the candle on the table. Nothing left but a puddle of wax and a thin stream of smoke where it has burnt itself out.

The tap is still running. At least my efforts to clean up mean the water pours down the drain instead of backing up and over-flowing the sink. But I can't turn it off. Despite repeated futile attempts, the faucet also passes through my hand without moving.

It's just after noon. Jupiter's still asleep. But I don't want to run up her water bill. I take a chance and poke my head into the living room.

"I'm really sorry," I say. "Can you help? The candle's burned out, and I can't turn off the water."

Kelly gives me a flat stare that says they really aren't inclined to help—as opposed to their flat stare that says I'm being annoying or the one that asks why I didn't have the decency to float off to the afterlife on my own—but Carrot Stick lets out a yowl from the direction of the kitchen, and somehow that's enough to spur Kelly into motion. They walk through me, which I protest loudly, and a second later the water turns off. Wordlessly, Kelly returns with a fresh bag of chips and settles on the couch again. They haven't lit another candle.

I hope it's enough. I won't be able to touch anything else properly until Jupiter wakes up. In the meantime, and to make sure Kelly feels there are no hard feelings, I flop down on the sofa. Or I go to. At the last second, I worry that it won't hold me. That I'll just sink through it like I dropped the watering can.

Sure enough, I do. It's like the sofa's not even there. One second I'm sitting down, the next my ass is hitting the floor, and there's a mess of springs and upholstery all around me.

"Oh, for god's sake," I say.

"Your god has nothing to do with it," Kelly says, and I almost can't believe they've acknowledged anything has happened.

"It's just an expression," I say as I push myself up again. I stare at the couch like a predator, but when I bend down to put a careful finger on the cushion, it sinks through, and I nearly lose my balance again.

"You're thinking too hard," Kelly says, though they still don't look away from the video game.

"I didn't ask for your input," I say.

"You've sat on things here before, right?"

I did. The chair in the kitchen. In the hall by Kelly's bedroom door.

"The candle," I say.

"The candle helps. But you don't need it for things like that.

You just have to not think about it. If you sit without questioning whether the chair will hold you, it will. If you walk through the wall like it's not there, it isn't."

"You're saying the physics of ghosts is the same as the Road Runner and the coyote?"

On the screen, the spider screams as it bursts into flame. Kelly leans back, and even with the headphones over their ears, I can still hear the cheering coming through from whoever they're playing with.

"I don't know about the behaviour of desert animals. I'm just telling you, if you don't wonder whether you'll fall through the couch, then you won't."

Desert animals? I shake myself. Kelly's probably never seen Looney Tunes.

It takes a couple more tries. I fall through the couch again before I finally get frustrated and come at it with a flying leap and a war cry. I imagine a pillow-soft landing. Those clouds and harp-playing cherubs that continue to elude me. This time I settle with a gentle thump. When I open my eyes, Kelly's playing again, but in between blasts, they say, "Good job."

Watching Kelly play video games is eye-wateringly boring. Endless gunshots and hit points. It's hard to keep track of time without the usual daily landmarks like eating and sleeping. God, I wish I could sleep, if only so I didn't have to listen to the plastic clack as Kelly mashes buttons on their controller. Eventually, Jupiter emerges from her bedroom, only to disappear into the bathroom to shower.

"Hey, where are our towels?" she calls.

"Hall closet," I answer. "I did laundry."

"Did you? That's super cool!" The closet door opens and closes, and the water in the bathroom comes on.

It takes another ten minutes before Kelly finally pulls themself off the couch.

"I'm going out," they say.

"Have fun," I reply, though I don't get up. Instead, I listen for the sound of the front closet door being opened and shut again. Then opened again. There's the sound of Kelly pawing through things before shutting the door again. I lie back and enjoy. They walk up the hall. There's a small shout that says they nearly knock Jupiter over as she comes out of the bathroom, then more sounds of someone searching for something in the back bedroom. Maybe some swearing? Do reapers swear?

Finally, Kelly says, "Jupiter, have you seen my wallet?"

Bullseye. I can't help my smile. Let's do this.

chapter
seven

IS IT CHILDISH? Yes.

Will it get me what I want? Hopefully.

Am I sorry about it? Not even a little.

Kelly pulls open the front hall closet.

"Where's my jacket?"

"I don't know, Kelly. When was the last time you wore it?" Jupiter asks.

"The other day. When I met—" Kelly glances at me, and I give them a bland smile. They already got frustrated looking for their wallet and said not to bother. That they'd pay for things with their phone. Makes me wonder how a grim reaper gets credit cards to load onto a phone. Or how they even have a phone. Or the ID you'd need to open a bank account to pay your phone bill. So many questions. None of them my problem.

Also not my problem is the location of Kelly's leather jacket. I close my eyes and pretend to nap.

They're back in their room, throwing things around.

"Where are all my shoes?" Now they sound genuinely confused, and I have to smother a laugh with my hand.

"Which shoes are you looking for?" Jupiter asks. She's in the kitchen lighting a fresh candle. Carrot Stick hops up on the couch next to me and snuggles against my chest. He purrs as I scratch behind his ears. We watch chaos unfold.

"Why are there only right shoes?"

"All my shoes are here," Jupiter says.

I tighten my hold on Carrot Stick as Kelly comes around the corner and stares down at me on the couch.

"Something wrong?" I ask.

"What did you do?" Their pale eyes are wide with fury and even the green in their hair seems to ripple with barely suppressed rage.

"I tidied up." I have to bite my lip to keep from cackling in their face.

"Where did you put my stuff?"

"I don't know what you're talking about."

We get locked in a staring contest. It goes on for a while. I don't have to blink anymore, and apparently neither does Kelly. As I get twitchy from boredom, I release the cat, wiggle my fingers and make my very best spooky noise. "Oooooooh. Did the ghost move your things? Are you being haunted?"

I expect the curl of power to engulf me. There's a chance I could get smited for this. Smitten? Smoted? Whatever. The point is, Kelly's not human and could probably zap me off this plane of existence with a finger snap. But isn't that what I want anyway? So what do I have to lose?

Also, I'm enjoying myself, which is unexpectedly delightful. They've stomped back up the hall, muttering curses, and pleasure rolls through me in lovely waves. It's been a long time since I really enjoyed myself. Even in the early days of chemo, when I still had the energy to see people, it was hard to have fun. There was always worry in the back of my head. Worry I might exhaust myself. Worry my deteriorating bones would get hurt. Worry I was bringing the vibe down, which I undoubtedly was, between my vanishing hair and the unexpected bouts of weakness and nausea. Now, though, I don't have to worry about any of that, and it's amazing. Like getting reacquainted with an old friend. Hey, Sparks, have you lost your spark? Have you considered dying as a solution?

Yeah, no, that's kind of bleak. Time to dial it back. It's the sort of thing that would get me and all my social media accounts cancelled. *Canadian life coach encourages suicide.* The headlines and talking heads would be merciless. But if only they knew . . . when life is irredeemably sucky and all treatment options have failed, maybe death isn't so bad after all.

"Where's my phone charger?"

I roll to bury my face in the pillow as I giggle. I feel ten years younger. Maybe there's a future for me in this haunting thing.

When I roll back over, Kelly's standing above me.

"Where's my stuff?"

I let my smile free. "Help me cross over and I'll tell you where I put it all."

"You've been here all day. It can't be far."

I spread my hands wide. "So keep looking."

But they don't move. They cross their arms over their chest. Jupiter is standing just outside in the hallway. The corner of her mouth is also twitching like she's trying not to laugh. I wonder if she's done this before. Or thought about doing it? If I were staying longer, I'd want to hear the story of how she wound up living with a grim reaper. But I'm not. Maybe she'll learn to stand up to them a little bit better, though.

"I could just buy more shoes," Kelly says.

Once again, I shrug. "Go ahead."

"Your credit cards are maxed," Jupiter says. "You can't keep applying for new ones, you know."

I hiss in mock sympathy. "That sounds like a problem if you don't have a job anymore. How are you going to pay those off?"

They narrow their gaze, and I hold my breath. The smiting will happen soon. Anticipation tingles along my undead nerve endings. Hopefully it's just a bright ball of light and then I wake up in a white room or wherever it is that I've been supposed to be for the last few days.

"Go on," I say. "Do it."

First thing I'm doing on the other side is writing a book for the newly dead. *How to Train Your Reaper*. Step one: Hide their stuff. Step two: Success!

"Fine," they say. Even as I'm lying there in anticipation, Kelly's sudden capitulation is surprising.

"Fine?"

"I'll take you to afterlife."

But I don't go anywhere. Disappointment flickers behind my confusion. So much for instant smiting. Still, Kelly sounds sincere.

"Really?" I lift my head up, still waiting for the plot twist.

They sigh angrily. "Yes. Just give me back my wallet and my charger. And my keys. If I can't start the car, you're stuck here."

"Where is it?" I ask.

"You're the one who took them." Their voice rises impatiently.

"No, where's the afterlife? Are you saying we have to drive there?"

"Not the afterlife. Just Afterlife. Afterlife Incorporated, officially." It looks like saying the words is physically painful for them, and I'd sympathize, but my sympathy is quickly drowned out by growing excitement. Because their words also sound true. This isn't some ruse to ditch me. I'm going to win, and all it took was to keep them from charging their phone.

"Great." I stand. "Let's go."

"My keys," they say.

I lead them both to the kitchen and retrieve the keys from the coffee tin. When Kelly lunges for them, I ball them up in my fist. The relit candle means Kelly's hand smacks uselessly off my knuckles, though there is a brief zapping sensation like an electric shock on a dry day. I grin and take a step back.

"Afterlife. Now, please," I say.

Jupiter claps her hands. "Road trip! Can I come too?"

"No," Kelly says quickly. "Where's the rest of it?"

"I'll tell Jupiter. You can get it back after you drop me off." I waggle my eyebrows at Kelly. "Let's go." But they stay where they are. I hold the keys out and jingle them. "What's wrong?"

They clearly struggle with answering, but eventually concede. "I need shoes." They wriggle their bare feet against the kitchen floor.

For a moment, I consider telling them to drive without them, but finally I pass the keys over. "Go get in the car and I'll show Jupiter where everything else is."

It's a heady thing to order a reaper around. I could get used to it. They stomp off, and Jupiter and I wait wordlessly in the kitchen until the door to the driveway slams shut.

She laughs. "That was amazing. You really are this incredible girl boss. I'm going to rewatch all your videos. Are you sure you have to leave?"

I really do. I can't spend eternity bickering with Kelly in this kitchen. I'd like to hug her, but even her candles aren't strong enough to make me totally solid and huggable.

"No more porn on the subway," I say.

She nods. "Send a message from the other side if you can. Kelly doesn't talk about it much, and I want to know what it's like."

"As soon as they get my internet hooked up, I'll send you an email," I say. I'm surprisingly sad to be leaving her, even though we've only known each other for a day. She was kind and interested to meet me when no one else was. I wasn't prepared for death to feel so lonely, and she made it better for a little while.

I take her downstairs and show her the closet behind the litter box.

"I would have never found that," she says, shaking her head.

"Try to mop occasionally after I'm gone, okay? You can't live like this. Someone's going to get food poisoning."

Jupiter groans. "Been there, done that. Ever tried to explain vomiting to a reaper? It was not pretty."

These two need so much help. But they're not my responsibility.

As we climb the stairs from the basement, a car horn honks impatiently. Jupiter rolls her eyes and blows the candle out at the door.

"Good luck," she says. Once again, I go to squeeze her, and my hand slides through hers. She shivers. "Rude."

Kelly's already backing the car out of the driveway as I head outside and I hurry to catch up.

"Jupiter will give you the rest after," I say as I slide through the door and take a seat. I hand over their shoes and they park the car properly long enough to put them on, then we're off.

Two minutes later, we pull into a parking spot at the subway station.

"That's it?" I ask. "Why didn't we just walk?"

"I don't like walking," they say. "And it's going to rain."

Overhead, the late afternoon sky is clear. A few wispy clouds float by, but there is zero indication of rain. We head back through the station, retracing the steps Jupiter and I took. Kelly swipes their transit pass. I walk through the turnstiles without a pause. The subway is waiting on the platform as we come up the elevator.

"You're not taking me back to the hospital, right?" I ask. "Remember I know where you live."

They settle on a red upholstered seat, tipping their head back and closing their eyes. The other riders who are boarding all give Kelly a wide berth. I sit next to them, careful not to touch, though they don't feel as overwhelming as they did the day before. A few more days together and I might actually get used to them instead of having to concentrate hard to keep my knees from buckling whenever they walk past me.

The chime warns the doors will be closing. Two teenage boys jump through the opening, laughing to each other. Around us, everyone settles in for their journeys.

"Can I ask you a—" I start to say, but a giggle stops the rest of the sentence in my throat. Beside me, Kelly stiffens. "What is—" But I know what it is. Or who. At the last second, one more boy hops onto the train, though in his case, he doesn't squeeze in the space as they shut. He walks right through the panels while the train pulls out of the station.

"Shit," Kelly mutters. They shift in their seat. It's the first time I've seen them look uncomfortable.

"That's a ghost, right?" I ask. "He's dead too? Should we take him with us?"

"Shh," Kelly hisses.

The first part of the subway ride isn't underground. We rumble along the tracks in daylight. The ghost boy walks along the centre aisle of the car. He's in a hoodie and ball cap that look like they've been dipped in oil. He glances from one passenger to the next, baring his teeth and moaning softly. His skin is palish blue-white, and his eyes aren't eyes at all. They're dark circles that sink into his skull. Still, when he approaches me, our gazes meet, and it gives my whole body a jolt.

"Look down," Kelly says, grabbing my hand. I gasp at the contact, but it's enough to break me out of the connection with the boy, and I look directly down at my feet.

"What is he?" I ask softly. We aren't the same. If I'm a ghost, he's something else entirely. Like the woman in the park and the man-creature in the stairwell.

"Shh." Their hand tightens on mine as the thing stops in front of us. In my line of sight, there are three pairs of shoes. Kelly's white combat boots. My soft pink sneakers. And the boy's leather skateboard shoes. The leather is cracked and split, revealing the black rotten toes inside.

We stay like that as the subway rolls into Islington Station, grimy white tiles glistening under old tube lights as we come to a halt. The recorded voice announces our arrival and the doors open. People get off and more get on. Every instinct tells me to make a run for it, but the thing in front of us doesn't move, and even Kelly seems to be holding their breath, so I stay where I am. And while none of the passengers have any visible reaction to the monster boy's presence, everyone who enters the car turns away from us, walking toward the other end while the doors slide shut.

A puddle is forming where the creature is standing. Something black oozes from the cuffs of his oversized pants. It collects around the soles of his shoes and slowly curls toward me. I make a soft squeaking noise when it touches my toe. Kelly interlaces their fingers with mine, and I can't help myself when I lean into them. They may be a pain in my ass, but they're the safest option in my vicinity.

"It won't hurt you as long as you're with me," Kelly says, voice tight. I nod jerkily while still keeping my gaze down. "But do not look at it or talk to it."

He must get bored, because when the train rolls into Royal York, the doors open and the monster boy gets off. The air around me changes. People sigh in relief, as if they're confused about why they might have done that.

It's only when we're moving again that Kelly relaxes and lets go of my hand. I immediately clear my throat and create a little space between us again. The puddle at my feet has disappeared, but I still rub my toe on the back of my calf like there's something to wipe away.

"What was that?" I ask. "I saw them before. At the hospital and outside near Queen's Park. The one at the hospital chased me up the stairs. The one at Queen's Park attacked a bunch of women."

"Living women?" they ask, sounding surprised.

"Yes." It's not like Toronto has a wealth of dead ones wandering around, at least not in my limited experience.

They stare out the window as we pull into Old Mill. It's the only aboveground station on this stretch of track, and the failing afternoon light feels cleansing after the encounter we just had.

"Wraiths don't attack the living." Kelly says it like there's no room for discussion, but I know what I saw.

"Well, this one did. It started with the German shepherd, then . . ." I pause, replaying the sequence of events. Did it really attack the others? There was a lot of dodging and weaving, and people found themselves in dangerous situations, but did anyone actually get charged? Bitten? I don't even know what these things are supposed to do. So I focus on the little bit Kelly has told me. "Wraiths? Like in *Lord of the Rings*?"

They scowl. "What's that?"

"You know. Tolkien. Frodo. The one true . . ." I trail off. Of course they don't know. I'm not here to educate a stuck-up reaper on human pop culture.

We rumble on. Jane Station. High Park. Keele. The longer we sit there, the less certain I become. There is so much more in existence beyond anything I know, and Kelly hasn't exactly been helpful. Who's to say where we're really going? They said the thing before wouldn't hurt me as long as I was with them, but who knows if that's true? Maybe Kelly's going to take me out to Toronto Island and leave me there for monster chow. Maybe that's all there is in this Afterlife place and I should never have played haunting hardball in the first place. Careful what you wish for, Sparks. You just might get it.

We pull into Bay Station, and Kelly gets up without warning. I hurry after them. I expect us to go up to the street, but instead Kelly leads me to the end of the platform to a door that says *No Admittance*. There's a keypad above the handle, and they punch in the numbers quickly before stepping aside to let me pass through. The steps beyond have a single tube light overhead as it leads down to something dark.

The door swings shut behind us with a bang and Kelly walks past me down the stairs.

"What's with all the commuting?" I ask as I follow. "The guy at the hospital just poofed him and the old lady out of there. Why are we taking the long route?"

Up ahead, there's a rumble, like an approaching subway. It's not possible, though. Lower Bay is closed. It's an old station that got replaced by the one above us. Now it gets used for things like movie shoots, but there's no sign of anyone around. Still, Kelly picks up the pace on the last few steps.

"I'm not supposed to use my powers," they say absently.

I go to ask what powers those are, but I'm stopped short by the crowd of people standing on the platform as the subway pulls in. It's packed, like a Thursday at rush hour. It takes me a second to realize that everyone is crystal clear. I'm already so accustomed to the people around me having the blurred edges of the living that I forget it's possible for them to appear otherwise. But everyone here looks totally normal.

"You're also not supposed to be here."

A man comes alongside Kelly. He's Black, wearing a nice grey suit and wire-framed glasses. His smile is predatory, and he does the same slow blink Kelly's done. Beside him is a woman, also Black, also in a suit, with a modest skirt that reaches her calves and a matching blazer. The two of them could be on their way to a business meeting. She stares blankly ahead, like she isn't listening or maybe can't even hear us.

"Relax," Kelly says. "I'm dropping off a soul to Minerva."

The man's smile grows. "I'd like to be a bug in the office for that. We need you back. Things have really slipped. So many souls being left behind. All I do now is shuttle them up and down the subway line while everyone else is running around. Quarantine team can barely keep up with the wraiths."

We step onto the train. Subways are not the most sociable places in the world, but this one is unnervingly silent. The people around me are all staring straight ahead like the woman in the suit, and there is a seat for each and every one of them. That never happens in

Toronto. The train pulls out of the station, and while it sounded normal enough on its arrival, on the way out, it doesn't roll so much as it lifts up and glides away into the tunnel. Way too fancy for the TTC. The normal concrete grey out the window glows blue.

"Are they all dead?" I ask, looking around.

The suit man looks at me with an arched eyebrow. "You're very lively, aren't you?"

"There was a wraith on the Bloor line, and she said she saw two others yesterday," Kelly says. "Who's in charge of quarantine oversight now?"

He sighs. "Goran. There was another round of restructuring a few years ago."

Kelly doesn't look pleased about this. The idea of restructuring and reaper office politics is fascinating. As are all the motionless people around me. I wave my hand in front of the woman's face. She blinks a few times but otherwise doesn't respond.

"Do you mind not doing that?" suit man asks. "We found her in her apartment. She'd already been dead for a week. Much longer and she'd have been ready for the quarantine team."

I shudder at the thought, first of her body being left there for so long, but then at the realization he means her soul. Is this what would have happened to me? Zach said there was a window for me to be picked up before the soldiers got dispatched. Would I have been blank and empty if I stayed in Toronto too long?

Doesn't matter, though. We're nearly there. Soon I'll be at Afterlife, and the what-ifs won't matter.

"So there are no wraiths at Afterlife?" I ask Kelly as the other man wanders away, checking his passengers.

"Not where you're going."

That feels like only half an answer. There's still a chance this is all a trick. They might be about to dump me at some prison for the dead. I force my voice to stay level, but I'm not letting Kelly hold back.

"But where do they come from? And where do they go if it's

not Afterlife? The soldiers came and took the other two away. Why didn't they come for the one we just saw?"

They pinch their lips in annoyance. "Why do you think Afterlife exists? We aren't some benevolent race that wants to help you find eternal peace. Humans are a menace. Your souls are so bright. Powerful. But after you have no body to contain them, they degrade. You're like plastic bags in the landfill of existence."

"Plastic bags?" I say, confusion winning over fear for the briefest of seconds. "They never break down."

"No." They wave an impatient hand. "That's not right. What's the thing? What did Jupiter say?" But they turn their attention fully to me, which feels like a small victory. "What's the thing I'm not allowed to throw out because it will poison everything?"

"Motor oil? Old paint?" I rack my brain, like finding the answer will somehow protect me. "Batteries?"

"Right. Batteries. Human souls are like batteries in the landfill of existence. You die faster than anyone wants, and if we throw you away with everything else, you eventually start burning holes through things you shouldn't."

"So Afterlife Incorporated is a cosmic recycling plant?" That sounds awful. It's certainly a far cry from what I imagined.

"The reapers don't know how Afterlife started or where we come from," Kelly says. "All we know is we're the guardians of your plane and ours. If we don't get you off yours fast enough, you become wraiths and spread chaos. Disease. War. You consume other newly dead spirits and you never burn out."

I don't like the way they lump me in with these wraiths. I'm obviously not one of them.

"And the soldiers?" I ask, hoping for a small subject change.

"The quarantine team. When reports come in of wraiths, they're deployed to contain them and send them to HELL."

"Hell? Like flames and pitchforks?" I went to Catholic school until I finished grade eight. I've never thought of myself as particularly religious. I did first communion and confirmation with the rest of my classmates, but my family never went to church, but, it turns out that the early messages in elementary school religion class have stuck pretty hard.

Kelly rolls their eyes like they know what I'm thinking and find it particularly silly.

"The human concepts of heaven and hell are silly and punitive. It's more like a containment centre. HELL stands for Hostile Entity Lifespan Limitation. Wraiths are no more stable on the Afterlife side than they are here. We send them somewhere safe before you can cause any real damage. They burn out eventually; it just takes you a millennium or two longer than with normal ghosts."

I still don't like the way they say "you." I don't want to hurt anyone. Or become like those things. Uncontrolled and terrifying. All I've wanted since it was clear I wouldn't survive was to limit the pain and inconvenience around me.

But also, there's something in the way Kelly said "we." Like they're still part of that team.

"What happened to your job?" I ask. Maybe I've been too hard on them. So many people attach their sense of identity to their careers. It can't be all that different for reapers. Fired or quit, they're probably feeling lost.

But they only press their lips tight as the train comes into a new gleaming station.

"We're here," they say, rising. I follow, though my knees tremble as I do. This is it. I finally made it.

Time to see Afterlife.

chapter
eight

THE DOORS open and everyone files off. The suit man waits until we're the last on the car. He puts a hand on Kelly's shoulder.

"Good luck. We miss you."

Kelly doesn't reply. Just walks past the others who are now lining up in rows on the platform. A giant light-up board overhead says "Welcome to Afterlife Incorporated" and beneath are signs that say things like "Arrivals" and "Reunification." In the distance, an office building stretches up toward the sky. It's slate grey with walls of windows. Looks like the skyscrapers on Bay Street. The sky is full of stars, and the lights in several offices inside are on.

"Busy night," Kelly says to themself as we walk past the waiting souls.

"Can't be that bad. What about plagues? Natural disasters?" Relatively speaking, the last year has been a peaceful time for humanity.

They glance over their shoulder. "Those are worse. But there are more of you now."

At the head of the line, people—reapers, I guess—in jumpsuits are doing some kind of scanning thing with wands that look like metal detectors.

"What are they looking for?" I ask.

"Decay. Too far gone and they go to quarantine."

Before I can ask more questions, they're already opening one of the glass doors that lead into the office tower. Inside is a sprawling lobby. More reapers walk back and forth. Their backs are straight and their strides official. No one gives us a second glance, except for a female reaper—is she female? Kelly doesn't care about pronouns, but I have no idea if that's a reaper thing or a Kelly thing—sitting at what would be a security desk back home. She's in cat-eye glasses and a pale blue Chanel-inspired suit complete with cropped jacket and knee-length skirt. When she sees us approaching, she scrabbles backward, looking frightened.

"What are you doing here?" Her glasses have lenses thick enough to be magnifying glasses, and she nudges them back up the bridge of her nose with a nervous push.

"I need to see Minerva," Kelly says. It's not a request.

"You can't go up there," the woman says. But we walk to the elevators, where one is open like it's waiting for us. "She's in a mood. I've already been up there twice today and—"

"Nice to see you too, Bang," Kelly calls back as the elevator doors slide shut. They press the button for the forty-third floor, and we rise with a whoosh.

"I see your manners aren't any better here than they are in the real world."

"This world is real," they say.

I roll my eyes. "As much as I've barely enjoyed our acquaintance, I don't want my last memory of you to be a semantic argument."

For once, they almost crack a smile.

"I've met a lot of souls. They've offered me many things for me to leave them behind. Others have begged me to take them away. They've asked me if I'm an angel, a god, a demon. But I've never met someone who speaks to me quite like you, Ember Munro."

My smile is more than a crack. I pat their sleeve, enjoying the shiver of their power as it runs over me one last time. "I'll miss you too, you jerk."

The doors slide open and we step into an office hallway. Compared to the lobby, this is far shabbier. I don't know what I expected. Something like a spa, with soft-coloured walls and the muted sound of water trickling somewhere. Instead it's cinder block and peeling linoleum. The lights overhead are the same neon tube lights from Lower Bay and they flicker as we walk.

"I'll do the talking," Kelly says as we come to a door at the far end of the hall. "You'll only annoy her."

"She must have a pretty good tolerance if you think she's going to listen to you."

This time they really do laugh. It's a short, sharp sound. "She won't. We didn't part on good terms. But she can't have you running loose either, so I'm hoping that works in our favour."

Without another word, they push the door open and we step inside the office.

If the hallway outside is lifeless and the lobby downstairs is sleek and modern, this office is something else entirely. There are so many colours that I have to shield my eyes as I figure out where it's safe to look. It's like a Lisa Frank poster threw up on itself, painted the walls, and bought furniture to match. Tattered sofas frame a painting of a winged tiger in neon pinks and yellows. Two antique chairs with clashing velvet cushions are settled around a block of glass that I guess must be a coffee table.

The desk is large and made of solid dark wood. There are stacks and stacks of file folders on top of it, enough that I'd worry their landslide would crush me if I wasn't already dead.

From behind them, an annoyed voice says, "Yes, I know that, Ziggy, but you are the keeper of HELL. It is not my job to come down there every time one of the inmates gets a little whiny. Feed them, give them a hot water bottle, and figure it out. It's HELL, not a Hyatt, they don't have to be comfortable." There's a pause. A sharp inhale. I go to say something, but Kelly gently clears their throat and I refrain. A thump like a palm slapping the desk makes me jump and the files teeter ominously. "No! You wanted this job, so do it. I don't have the bandwidth to keep bailing you out." The speaker slams the phone down and the papers all shift again.

Sure. Kelly can do all the talking here. I'm dead; no need to suffer anymore.

They clear their throat again, louder this time. Behind the desk, Minerva snaps, "What?" The tone is a hundred percent "don't fuck with me," and I very much do not want to fuck with whoever it is. All I want—all I've wanted from the very start—is to walk through the gates from which no one returns and never have to worry about anything again. Who knew the path would be so complicated?

"Special delivery," Kelly says.

She rolls from behind the desk barrier, and I can't help my shocked inhale when the occupant is a girl. And I don't mean a young woman that we'll call a girl because gendered language is weird, I mean an actual child. She might be fifteen at the most. Her pink hair is braided in two pigtails, and she's wearing a pink T-shirt with a unicorn on it. When she sees Kelly, she gives them a narrow glare while blowing a pink bubble gum bubble so big her face vanishes behind it. When it pops, she chews it quickly back into her mouth.

"I fired you."

"I think you'll recall I quit. And I'm not here to fight," Kelly says. They jerk a thumb in my direction. "One of your model employees forgot someone."

She puffs up bigger and her gaze flicks to mine. Despite her soft teenage features, there's age in her eyes. A lot of it. I'm looking at someone ancient.

"You know, this is why I don't have time to fix the real problems around here," she says, turning back to Kelly. "People coming to me with every little thing. Why didn't you leave her downstairs with the others?"

"She'd already been left behind by two reapers. Who's to say she doesn't get lost in the shuffle here? You've got a real quack team working these days, Minerva."

"Crack team," I say softly, but neither reaper acknowledges me. They have a standoff. It reminds me of the moment right before the big final battle in movies, where all-powerful wizards face off and begin hurling blue and red fireballs at each other.

Surprisingly, Minerva is the first one to look away.

"Fine." She motions me to come forward as she moves files from one stack to another so I can see her as she wheels back behind her desk. She poises her fingers over her laptop. "What's your name?"

"Ember Munro. Bone cancer. Medically assisted death."

Minerva raises her eyebrows. "Been asked those questions before, huh?" She sighs, but starts typing. "Date and location of birth?"

I tell her and she types some more.

"Profession?"

"Life coach."

This earns a giggle, and when we make eye contact, she laughs even harder.

"The concept of a dead life coach is pretty funny, don't you think?" she asks.

Is this what they mean about facing judgement in the afterlife? Because I'm not here to be made fun of by a teenager.

"I'm also a Gemini and like pina coladas and long walks on the beach," I add, which earns yet another uncomfortable throat clear from Kelly, but Minerva is busy muffling her laughter. She gives us both a second back and forth, and her lips turn up in a smile.

"You two must get along like a burning home," she says. Kelly huffs but doesn't answer. Minerva turns back to her computer, looking at the table that pops up there. "That's weird. Ember Munro's been picked up. Dropped off here three days ago."

I shake my head. "That's not possible. I'm right here. And I wasn't even dead three days ago."

"No, the file is complete. Medically assisted dying." She looks up, lips moving silently like she's counting something. "It says Ember was collected by the SRU three days ago."

"SRU?" I ask.

"Soul Retrieval Unit," Minerva says.

"My old team," Kelly says softly, which earns them a dark scowl.

"You walked away from that team," Minerva says. Her glare is back, and it's possible the floor rumbles ominously beneath my feet.

"Can we get back to me, please?" I say before the clash of reaper titans resumes. "I am dead. I have been for a few days. No one seems to want to help me, and based on what Kelly says, I'll be a chaos zombie if you don't step up soon."

Minerva's eyes narrow and maybe I've gone too far. A good boss never likes it when someone trash talks their employees, no matter how incompetent they might be.

Kelly must see it too, because they say, "I've been with her for two days. The records are wrong."

I should thank them, but their momentary backup doesn't guarantee I'll get what I want here. Minerva stares at the screen a while longer. She blows a new bubble and lets it pop before she pulls the gum from her mouth and flicks it into a trash can beneath the desk. Finally, she leans back in her chair, tilting it as far as the padded leather will reach as she covers her face in her hands to muffle her screams. The whole office around us shudders, and the stack of files closest to the edge of her desk drop to the floor. Even Kelly puts a gentle hand on my arm and pulls me back a few inches.

"I really didn't need this today," she says, dragging her palms away from her cheeks. Instead she points at Kelly. "And you. I definitely didn't need it from you."

Kelly gives her their impassive blink. "Good thing I don't work for you anymore. I can do what I like."

"It's pandemonium up here. You know that, right?" she asks, like Kelly didn't say anything. "The number of wraiths is going up exponentially and no one knows where they're coming from. I've had to send SRU members to WQU with Goran."

"SRU? WQU?" Kelly wrinkles their nose like they smell something unpleasant. "Can't you just call them by their name?"

"Acronyms are efficient," Minerva says. "And Ziggy's losing his mind down in HELL. He's running out of room and Goran's adding more wraiths every day. It's like they're coming from nowhere. Half have been dead for decades. I don't know how they were missed and the data quality team can't tell me either. Everyone's understaffed. You decided it was a good time to walk away. It was inevitable that mistakes were going to happen. What did you expect?" This last part is directed in my direction, and there should be some kind of apology in her tone, but all I hear is accusation.

"I'm not a mistake. And what kind of organization is this? It's not like population growth is a surprise. If you're overworked, can't you hire more staff?" I've seen this so many times. Managers who refuse to hire and just keep piling on more work to their top performers instead. It's why I started my business and my channel. No wonder Kelly left. I don't know how things work here, but the look on the woman's face at the desk downstairs and the man on the subway's smile said Kelly held some sway when they worked at Afterlife, and reporting to someone like Minerva is no picnic. Good for them for looking after themself.

Minerva snorts. "You think there's an endless supply of reapers? We've been overworked for centuries. It's been all hands on deck since the Industrial Revolution and your insistence on procreating like rodents doesn't help. On a good day, we're equipped to handle eighty to ninety thousand new soul entries, and you've been past that for centuries. We're strapped. I'm sorry you fell through the cracks, but here we are."

The office gets quiet. I have a feeling I'm not equipped to problem solve personnel issues on this scale, but I'll try.

I pick up the first folder on her desk.

"Maybe I can help?" I ask. "Do you know the expression 'the mess spreads to fit the desk'? If you feel like you can never get ahead, maybe start with a list of daily tasks and have a look at what can be delegated. On my YouTube channel, we—"

She grabs hold of my wrist. Her grip is like iron, and slowly she drags my arm down until I've replaced the file on the top of the stack. But she doesn't let go. A smell like burning fills my nostrils, sharp when everything else has been so dampened. I glance down at the file, and a small ring of smoke is forming in the shape of my palm and fingers.

"I will not be talked down to by a frumped-up ghost who thinks they know better," she says through gritted teeth. "I've been in charge of Afterlife for four hundred years. You've been dead for a few days. Do you think a little desk organization and some to-do lists are going to solve my problems?"

It would be a start. Better than changing nothing and hoping her issues resolve themselves. But right now I'm more worried about her melting my hand to a stump. I pull away, and she releases me with a smirk, casually blowing smoke away from her fingertips.

It's Kelly who finally says, "Can't you just take her?" Their voice is pained.

I whirl on them, ready to point out I'm not an overtired preschooler who needs supervision, but Minerva speaks again before I get a chance.

"And do what with her exactly? She's already in the system as collected. I can't create a duplicate entry. The DQ review team will have my head." She goes into a drawer and pulls out a fresh piece of gum which she chews furiously. "Take her back where you found her."

"No!" I actually stomp a foot in protest. "That doesn't solve anything. Won't I just turn into a wraith and then you'll have to come get me anyway?" The idea is chilling. I did not hasten my demise just to wind up blowing around Yonge Street like a plastic bag in the wind. And whatever Kelly said about HELL not being the way we think it is, it still doesn't sound fun. Yay! No eternal flames and torture. Boo! Welcome to lockdown.

Minerva looks at Kelly tiredly. "You quit, so you don't get to make demands anymore. But I'll make you a deal. Give me a couple weeks. You know what it's like up here. If Richard ever comes back . . ." She sighs. "Let me figure out the wraith problem, and then I can review your friend's file and how we override the collection record. I'm sorry, Kelly. It's the best I can do."

"She's not my friend," Kelly says, which really seems like the least of our concerns here. But short of staging a protest sit-in in Minerva's office, I'm not sure what the alternative is. Maybe Kelly knows a way to sneak me in. If they're processing that many souls a day and they can't even keep track of who's dead and who's not on Earth, surely they won't notice one more.

But just as I'm planning my great assault on heaven, an alarm sounds. Heavy metal shutters bang down over the windows of Minerva's office, and the whole room is bathed in some kind of red backup lighting.

The desk phone rings. Minerva stabs at the display to bring up the speaker.

"What?" she says without any greeting.

The voice on the other end is crackly and anxious. "We've got a problem at intake. Someone's trying to sneak their husband in. There was a delay with the SRU. The one guy is clear, but his husband's scans show too much decay. They got past reception and no one from IIC is answering my call."

Minerva swears. "Call Infection Control back! Tell them to stop being so mother-lucking useless."

"I did call them back. Three times," the voice turns apologetic. Maybe it's the reaper with the glasses. Dang, I didn't get a chance to ask Minerva about pronouns, though the way she's chewing furiously on her gum says now is not the time.

"I'm on my way down," she says, wheeling back from the desk as she hangs up. "We're done here. Give me two weeks and we'll revisit this."

"What if I've decayed into a wraith by then?" I ask. I have no idea if two weeks is too much or too little time for a full wraithing, but the question itself makes my throat go tight. Talk about the short end of a deadly stick.

Her ancient eyes are filled with regret.

"Try to hold on," she says as she rushes out of the office. She doesn't acknowledge Kelly as she goes by.

Excuse me? Hold on? Hold? On?

"That's bullshit," I say to her retreating back. "Hold on is what they told me while I was puking my guts out from chemo. Hold on is what they told me when they said the new treatment just needed more time to work." I'm supposed to be done all of that. In frustration, I kick at the desk. Another tower of files falls to the floor. It doesn't make me feel any calmer.

Kelly and I are alone in the office. The sirens are still going off in the hall. Now would be the time to get me in while everyone is distracted.

They say, "Let's go."

"Where? Toronto? No."

"I can't force you," they say, sounding almost as tired as Minerva. "But if you stay here, they will find you, realize you're unregistered, and send you to quarantine."

Hell. They're talking about hell. Or HELL, I guess. H-E-double-hockey sticks, as we used to say.

"There has to be a better answer," I insist. "This can't be it.

You've had thousands upon thousands of years to figure out a better system, and this is all you have? Paperwork and . . ." I gesture at the disaster area that is Minerva's desk. No wonder the house in Etobicoke is a mess. Reapers don't clean. "Corded phones?"

They slip their hands in their pockets, shoulders slumping in something like defeat.

"Trust me. I know."

But their acquiescence only pisses me off more. How is this happening? How is this the ending? I guess I really believed there was something out there after we died. A place to welcome us after our lives were over. And instead it's no different than when I was alive. My call is very important to Minerva. Please stay on the line . . . at least until you're a ravenous monster that can't be reasoned with. Then we'll suck you off to HELL where Ziggy will give you cookies and send you back to your cell.

This is the literal worst.

We ride the elevator in silence. I catch Kelly glancing down at me a few times, but they don't say anything. Probably for the best. Their cool detachment makes me want to punch them, and even if I'm already dead, my odds in a fist fight with a reaper are not good.

The doors slide open and the pristine lobby is controlled chaos. The busy office workers have been replaced by guards in tactical gear. The lights are low as well, and the nervous reaper with the glasses at the reception desk is talking to a tall man in a Kevlar vest.

"Come on." Kelly's gaze is fixed directly on the front door, and their tone has hardened. They're walking quickly and I have to hurry to keep up. No one tries to stop us as we pass through the sliding doors. Outside, the neat rows of people waiting to be let in move and churn uneasily while reapers call out to them to stay still and calm so they can be counted. The atmosphere feels like it's about thirty seconds from a riot. Despite my misgivings about Minerva and Kelly, I don't want to be left here. Not right now.

"Train's closed." A guard steps into our path as we walk up to the station, but their eyes widen when they see Kelly. "Oh. It's you." They step aside and let us by. The train is sitting at the platform with all its doors open. We're the only ones on board, but the second we sit down, the doors slide shut and we pull away. I watch out the back window as the tower of the Afterlife office sinks over the horizon.

After everything, I don't know if I want to come back here.

chapter
nine

THE RIDE back somehow feels longer than the ride to Afterlife did. I don't know if that's true. Who can say how time works here? It makes my head hurt, and I'm already having too many thoughts at once. I itch with the need to do something when there's nothing to do.

"Okay, so now what?" I ask, pacing up and down the empty subway car aisle. "What's the next step?"

"We wait to hear from Minerva," Kelly says, rousing from a supposed doze. Not that I believe for a second they were actually sleeping. Just avoiding me.

"Oh yeah. She was such a help. Might as well get it over with and send me to HELL with Ziggy. He sounds like a prince. Seriously." Now I'm pouting. "Why can't you have flames and pitchforks like they do in the books?"

"You wouldn't like either version. Though Ziggy is actually very compassionate. He didn't want that job, but after Richard left . . ."

I pounce on the name. "Richard. He sounded important. Can we talk to him?"

"No."

I reach up, dangling from the bar that runs overhead. My

muscles pull and stretch. The tension is good. I feel more alive than I have in a long time, and giving my hands something to do keeps me from strangling Kelly, which is a very tempting second option right now.

"What do you mean no? Why not?"

Kelly stands, walking toward me. My grip tightens on the bar, bracing for contact. They stop when we're nearly nose to nose, studying me. The closeness is probably meant to be intimidating, but as worked up as I am, it's invigorating. I raise my eyebrows in a silent command that they give me a full answer for once.

"Because nobody knows where Richard is. He took a sabbatical four hundred years ago and never came back." Their voice is flat as always, but there's tension in the corners of their eyes and mouth.

"Sounds like somebody quit. You wouldn't know anything about that, would you?" I release the bar, and warmth flows through my arms. I'm bouncing on my toes, spoiling for a fight. Back at Afterlife, I fully believed Minerva would blast me into oblivion if I pissed her off too much, but if Kelly's capable of that, they haven't taken the opportunity so far. Maybe they want an argument as much as I do.

"Richard left Minerva and me in charge," Kelly says, following after me as I resume a slow exploration up the aisle. The subway looks very similar to the ones in Toronto, right down to the advertisements plastered above the windows. But closer inspection shows they're not real. The text isn't even an alphabet I recognize. Just letter-shaped symbols spelling gibberish. Maybe it's some ancient reaper language. Maybe it's meant to give the dead a sense of familiarity as they take their last ride. It's a sham is what it is.

"Your co-administration appears to have gone well," I say, glancing over my shoulder to make sure they hear my sarcasm.

They grimace. It's a strangely vulnerable expression from them. "Richard was the only one who knew how to make new reapers. He did it once every thousand years, but then he didn't come back. We're overdue by over three hundred years, and Minerva and I had a difference of opinion about the future of Afterlife without Richard or more reapers. Several differences, in fact. For a couple centuries. In the end we agreed it was best for one of us to walk away."

I snort. "And you left the fate of humanity in the hands of a teenager?"

Kelly's discomfort turns to amusement. "Teenager? She's older than I am."

"And how old is that?" If I had to guess, I'd say Kelly is in their twenties. And sure, I've read enough vampire books to know appearances can be deceiving when you're talking about beings who exist outside human mortality, but I'd still only give them a few centuries.

"She's over nine thousand years old."

The train rattles and I nearly fall over. "Nine thousand?"

They grin, clearly pleased to have the upper hand once more. Maybe there's a sense of humour in there after all.

"You think she looks like that every day? She probably had a meeting. The last time I saw her, she was eight feet tall with blue skin and could breathe fire."

"When was that?" I try not to picture what they're describing. The burning hand trick was frightening enough.

They shrug. "The day I quit. Blue and burning is her preferred form. There wasn't much arguing with her at that point."

The train slows. Outside the platform at Lower Bay is empty. Given what's going on at the other station, have the reapers and their souls been diverted somewhere else? There's nothing worse than a transit disruption at rush hour.

"Do you have a preferred form?" I ask because it seems unfair for Minerva to be able to negotiate workplace conditions looking like a dragon while Kelly can only pull off a pop star.

They glance down at me with a gracefully arched eyebrow as

we walk through the shining doors. From this angle, they look the most surreal they ever have. Carved. Airbrushed.

I gasp.

"You've changed before. All the time." That's not hair dye. Neither is the way their features go from hard to soft and their lips seem fuller or thinner from one day to the next.

They don't seem nearly as surprised by my realization as I am. We climb the stairs up from Lower Bay and they say, "Humans alter their appearance frequently. You wear different clothes. Change your hair. Jupiter showed me those videos. What are they called? Contouring?"

The idea of Kelly watching contouring tutorials makes me giggle, but quickly enough I drag myself back to the topic at hand. "Yeah, but even in my awkward femme fatale lip liner phase I was still starting from the same basic structure."

Kelly squints down at me. No wait. It's not squinting. The lighting in the stairwell is poor, but it soon becomes obvious they're shifting. The eyes move closer together. The mouth tilts up at the corners, but there's no accompanying muscle tension. It's either really good Botox or some freaky shit is happening.

Then their cropped green hair changes into a wave of bright pink, cascading from root to tip and falling over one eye.

Yeah, Botox doesn't do that.

We're at the top of the stairs and Kelly walks out into the moving masses of travellers without a backward glance. I practically trip over my feet in my amazement.

"How—Why—You—Why?!"

We stand on the westbound platform. Kelly's bright pink hair flutters as the train pulls into the station and we climb aboard. I can't help but stare as we sit. Suddenly all the confusion makes sense. Masculine, feminine, something in between and something other. I was literally seeing different people.

"It's a necessity of the job," they say. "If I show up looking like this at the bedside of a ninety-year-old Polish woman who never got over the trauma of your Second World War and hasn't left her village in decades, do you think she's going to come peacefully? We change to be something that will be comfortable for you."

Pride swells in my chest. Didn't I have that very thought back at the bungalow? That no one would follow Kelly looking the way they do? Apparently, this is just their Casual Friday look.

"So the reaper who wouldn't take me at the hospital . . . he looked like he worked in tech support at a chain store because that's what the old lady wanted?"

They shrug. Across from us, a man coughs. It's a hacking sound and he spits something gooey on the floor. I wrinkle my nose. Kelly does their slow blink that I'm quickly learning speaks volumes about how they truly feel about most puny humans around them.

"He probably looked like her grandson or something," they say.

We stop at St. George. Spadina. Getting farther away from Afterlife. I should ask Kelly more questions about decay. Minerva said a couple weeks. Does that mean exactly two? How long will I be a ghost before I become a wraith? Does it happen all at once? Or is it gradual? After my diagnosis, I realized I'd probably had cancer for six months or more. I'd assumed the pain in my leg was just wear and tear. I'd joined a high-intensity interval training gym. You can't go to one of those and not ache the next day, so I assumed the pain was a sign of my improving fitness, not impending doom, but looking back I'd ignored so many warning signs. Will that happen to me here too? Or will I go from Ember to monster in the blink of an eye?

"What exactly is a life coach?"

We've just left Christie Station and the question—possibly the first one Kelly's ever asked me other than "Why won't you leave?" —is so unexpected I choke. Old reflexes die hard apparently, because my trachea desperately tries to stop me from breathing my own saliva. Honestly, what's the worst that could happen? A few weird glances from my neighbours, but since they can't hear or see me, all I get is an exasperated glance from Kelly that clearly says *Why do you have to be so fragile?* Two questions in one minute. That's a record!

Finally, I manage a proper inhale.

"I made online content for people looking to make a change."

"What sort of change?" they ask.

"Any change. Career. Personal. It started out as a social media thing, then I added a YouTube channel so I could reach people more directly. Most of my followers were women in transitional periods in their life. They'd just left a marriage, or they'd started careers and were struggling to adjust to working life."

"Did you ever leave a marriage?" they ask, a small frown furrowing between their brows. They genuinely seem to be listening and considering what I've said.

"No." I pick at my cuticles. "I thought I might get married some day. Got close once, but then she—"

Kelly doesn't care about my love life.

"Then how can you coach someone through something you haven't experienced?"

I bite my lip to hold back my initial response, which is a sarcastic "Gee, no one's ever asked me that before." The running joke, of course, is that those who can't do teach instead. But I never saw it that way.

"It's not really about life experience. More about problem solving. Identifying people's strengths. Their values. Half the time when new clients come to me, they just know something isn't working. That they aren't who they used to be or their circumstances have changed so much they can't be that person anymore."

As I speak, I wonder if Kelly can hear themself in my words. I haven't had much time for compassion since we've met, but they have to be in a weird spot. Any career change is a huge upheaval, even if they're the one who quit, and from what Kelly said on the trip to Afterlife, reapers only exist to save humans from themselves. Not like them losing their job means they can suddenly explore alternative career prospects in candle making or advertising.

"Did you like it? Life coaching?" they ask. "Did it align with your strengths and values?"

For some reason, I really want to tell them everything will be okay. I'd probably finally get smoted for my trouble.

"I did," I say. "Coaching doesn't always work. The Sparks have to want to change."

"Sparks?"

"That's what they were called. My clients. They would come with the spark of an idea, but even with coaching, they have to do the work and the self-reflection. The people who did really created something amazing. There was a woman who commented on one of my videos once. She'd just left her husband and her corporate job. Blew up her whole life and then panicked because she didn't know who she was without those things. We talked a lot online. It took about eighteen months, but she found her way. Started working for a senior citizen's non-profit and found a new partner who wanted the same things she did. They were really great together. Last I heard, they were having a baby." We sway in time with the rumble of the subway. Finally, I say, "If you ever wanted to talk . . ."

But we roll into Kipling station, and Kelly stands before I can finish. Probably for the best. I loved my career, but it's not a quick fix, and we only have two weeks together.

The stairs outside the station are slick. It's pouring out. Kelly did say it was going to rain. Their pink hair turns dark purple in the glow of the overhead light towers and I can't help but wonder if it's the water doing that or their mood.

"Well," they say, hunching against the rain. "Good luck."

"For what?"

"Someone will come get you in a few weeks and take you back to Minerva."

I can't feel the rain, but even if I could, I wouldn't be able to anymore. All I can feel is rage. "You're ditching me? Again?"

They shrug. "I did what I could. She knows who you are. Give them the time they need to figure out the wraith problem and a team will be by for collection. You shouldn't be decayed to the point the SRU can't take you."

Shouldn't be? Or won't be? Either way, I'm not taking my chances alone.

"Fine," I say, spinning on one heel. "I'll walk to Jupiter's. No need to drive me."

"What? No." They sound genuinely surprised. "It's not just her place. I live there too."

I don't look back. "You're just a subletter she tolerates."

"I can't help you," they say. "Did you miss the part where I'm unemployed? I have no authority to cross you over."

"So you're going to leave me here to rot until one of those corporate stooges finally remembers I exist? You might as well pack my bags and send me to HELL. Do not pass Go, do not collect two hundred dollars."

Their anger evaporates into something like confusion. They give me a puppy-like tilt of their head.

"We don't get paid to send anyone to HELL," they say. "That would be unethical."

I throw my hands up in the air.

"Look," I say, pointing a finger toward them. Their eyes narrow. It's still raining, but Kelly's hair has turned a bright flaming red. Definitely a mood thing. They square their shoulders, readying for the fight, and if I still had blood, it would be pumping so hard right now.

The parking lot plunges into darkness as the explosion knocks me off my feet.

chapter
ten

IT'S a good thing my bones aren't full of tumors anymore, because the impact of landing on the concrete would have shattered them all to dust. I lie there, gaping at the rainy blue-black glow of the city sky at night.

"What was that?" I ask.

"Death," Kelly says. "A lot of it."

I push up on my elbows. I'm farther away from them than I thought I was. The blast must have pushed me back at least fifteen feet. Kelly's still standing where we were a second ago, staring at something beyond the subway station.

A shiver runs through me. Then another. My teeth are chattering, which is weird considering I haven't actually been able to feel the sensation of temperature changes since I died. Now suddenly it's like I've been lying in the rain for hours.

"Kelly?" I ask, or try to. It's hard to do around the shivering. "What's going on?"

Because it actually looks like nothing's going on. The lights are back on, and now I'm wondering if they were ever off at all, or if it was just that my vision went black. Around us, people are coming and going from the subway like it's any other day.

"Kelly," I say again. Despite all the normal around me, something is very wrong inside. If I get any colder, I'm not going to be able to speak.

They blink, and it's like they remember I'm there. Their movements are jerky as they bend down to help me up, but just the touch of their hand in mine helps settle me, though I'm still colder than I ever remember being before.

"We have to go," they say. To my relief, Kelly seems to have forgotten their earlier plan to dump me at Kipling Station. They help me to the car where I collapse into the front seat. My hands still shake so badly I can't get the seat belt clipped in, and I giggle a delirious little giggle as Kelly gets into the driver's side. It's not like the seat belt will do anything, anyway. What exactly are the Wile E. Coyote physics of a car accident? Will my body stay in place while my neck slingshots forward like an elastic band?

I laugh again at the mental image, and Kelly shoots me a worried look.

"That was wild," I say. The cold is still receding, but I'm left with a giddy feeling that has me wanting to flap my hands and hum a little tune like an excited child. "What was that? A paranormal hiccup or something? Did something change in the Matrix?"

"Keanu Reeves has nothing to do with this," they say flatly.

I huff as I fold my arms over my chest and shake my head. "So you know *The Matrix* but not Tolkien or Monopoly. Got it."

They don't reply. It's only as we're speeding down Kipling that I realize we're headed the wrong way. Jupiter's house is north of Bloor, not south.

"Where are you going?" I ask.

"Bang?" Kelly asks.

"Bang what?" I ask back.

But they don't look at me. Instead, they talk as they hurry along the rain-slick street.

"Where is it?" they ask. There's a pause, like they're listening to someone talking on the phone, but they're not wearing an earpiece or headset, and no sound comes from the car's speaker. Still, they nod, so someone must have answered somehow. "How many? No, Bang, I don't care. Tell me."

I shiver, though this time it isn't the cold that makes me do it. It's Kelly. Their voice. I've heard them angry. Annoyed. Even polite with Minerva. This is something else. Authoritative.

They speed up to blow through an intersection. A car coming the other direction at the green light honks, but Kelly doesn't slow down. I'm clutching the handle on the door, but when I realize I am, my hand slides through it like it's not even there. Damn road-runner. Am I about to sink through the seat onto the pavement too?

But just as I'm about to fall, Kelly's fingers curl in mine. The whiteness of their knuckles says I should feel pain, but all I feel is strong. Their strength. The same power that made candles flicker as they walked down the hall at Jupiter's.

As we approach the on-ramp of the Gardiner Expressway, the highway that runs along Toronto's south end, blue and red emergency lights flicker behind us.

"Pull over," I say, but they don't slow at all. Maybe they don't know what the human expectation is in this situation. "Kelly, pull over and let the police through. There must have been an accident or something."

"Where do you think we're going?" they ask.

The cop cars swerve around us. A sick sense of dread settles in the pit of my stomach. Up ahead, the roadway is a sea of red brake lights. It takes me a second to realize there are no cars coming toward us in the opposite lanes. That's never a good sign. If there are two things you can be sure of in Toronto, it's that the Maple Leafs will blow a perfectly good hockey game whenever they can and that there is always traffic on the Gardiner, regardless of the time of day or night.

The cars up ahead are stopped. The police cars that passed us are trying to navigate a path, and Kelly follows closely behind them. Pretty sure this is illegal, but what does a reaper care about human laws?

Kelly swears and pulls over against the median. In front of us, the outline of people standing lit against bright orange is obvious on the highway.

"Why are they out of their cars?" I ask.

"You stay here," they say as they undo their seat belt.

"Why? Kelly?"

"Just do it." Their gaze is fixed at some point through the windshield. "It's not safe for you."

"But I'm dead. How can it not be safe?"

For a second, they flick a look at me. Grim reaper. They shove the door open and slide out, vaulting over the median.

Stay in the car. That's what they said. Like I'm a liability. But what will it hurt? Something big is going on. I flinch as an ambulance comes up alongside me. It's also on the other side of the median, so it came the wrong way along the Gardiner. A second ambulance arrives an instant later, followed by four fire trucks. I push the car door open and step outside.

The road is chaos. The air is full of shouts and cries. People are running toward the glow. A woman is slumped against her SUV, tears streaming down her cheeks. Her face is smudged with dirt, and her gaze is wild as she looks at the bright orange glow in the inbound lanes where a bus lies on its side, engulfed in flames.

As I get closer, it becomes apparent it's not a transit bus or a Greyhound. It's a school bus, and it's in two pieces. Beyond it, a tractor-trailer is crushed up against the concrete barrier.

"Holy shit," I breathe. The scene is horrific. Apocalyptic. Several other cars have also smashed into each other, no doubt in an effort to avoid the central carnage of the bus and truck. The first responders are rushing toward the scene, barking orders and telling bystanders to get back in their cars. No one seems inclined to listen.

Above the unfolding tragedy, menacing shapes swirl, like vultures searching for carrion. Wraiths. Maybe a dozen. They're like black voids against the inky, stormy sky overhead. They wheel and dive for the bus, screeching. Every so often one passes through the metal shell, and the others wail in something that sounds like wicked triumph.

A fresh blast shatters the atmosphere, throwing me backward, and I bounce off the hood of a minivan before I even have a chance to understand what's going on. It's like the explosion at the subway station, in that it doesn't seem to have any impact on the cars and the living people nearby. But even the wraiths are momentarily blown off course, scattering across the sky.

Something inside me stretches; I feel like pie dough that's been rolled out too thin. Small tears form inside me, and I don't mean torn muscles. More like the very essence of me is about to get passed through a meat grinder. My head bounces off the metal, leaving a ringing sound between my ears.

No, not ringing. Screaming. Crying. Like children. Frightened children, and a lot of them.

Dear Sparks, this is not it. Whatever we think death is, this can't be it. Please, someone. Take me away from here.

I whirl, looking for the source of the sound, only to find myself face to face with a group of reapers, walking in purposeful formation toward the wreck. About ten of them. They're all dressed in the same tactical gear I've seen before, the feeling of their collective power as they walk toward me has me curling protectively against myself as I try to squeeze under the van. If they're here for wraiths, I don't want to be a part of it.

"Get ready," the reaper at the front of the platoon says. Not that it means anything since he could shift to resemble my grandmother at a moment's notice, but he looks male, and also like he's about forty-five, with close-cropped hair. The others around him renew their attention as they climb over the barrier.

Another blast comes, and maybe I'm more prepared this time,

or maybe the van shelter helps, but I feel a little less like I'm being peeled apart from the inside.

The crying is closer.

Tentatively, I squeeze back out from under the van. A girl, maybe nine or ten, is sitting on the ground by the van's sliding door. She's got a purple backpack between her knees and her head is bowed against it.

"Are you okay?" I ask.

"Mommy? I can't open the door." She sounds so frightened.

"I'm not your mommy," I say. "How did you get out here?" I go to pull on the door handle and my hand slips through it. I curse and peer through the window. A woman is sitting in the front seat, frozen as she watches the accident scene. I try to tap on the window to get her attention, but of course she doesn't hear me.

"Mommy?"

"It's okay," I say. The sick feeling is coming back. "I'll help you."

"Mommy?" Her voice is clearer, like she's lifted her head.

When I glance down at her, glowing blue eyes shine up at me. She smiles, and her blackened teeth shine slick with something like rotten blood.

Wraith.

"What are—" I ask, but I'm already stumbling backward, feet scraping on the concrete until I bump into Kelly's abandoned car.

"Mommy?" The wraith follows. She swells, growing bigger than her preteen frame should be.

"No," I shake my head. "I'm not your mother. I can't—Are you—" I'm trying to keep something between us. The car. The median. But she follows, passing through the car like it's not even there. She reaches for me, and her fingers are twisted and swollen like an old woman's. She climbs over the median while smiling a hunter's smile. This side is clear, with all the cars on the other side of the burning bus, so I spin and run. But my healed bones aren't enough to outrun a wraith. I can feel her, even though she's not touching me. My stomach cramps with nausea, and the thin pie dough feeling is so bad I can hardly put my feet one in front of the other. Like bits of me are being torn away one hole at a time. I'm running toward the fire. I don't even know why. Are wraiths fireproof? Am I? But surely it will slow her down, right?

"Mommy!" The voice isn't childlike anymore. It's monstrous. Furious. Whether I'm her mother or not is irrelevant. She's coming for me, and when she catches me, she'll consume.

An arm catches me around the waist, swinging me hard. I yelp and struggle. Too late. I'm too late.

chapter
eleven

"I **TOLD** you to stay in the car." The voice in my ear is a harsh whisper. Kelly. They're running us away from the fire. Away from our car too. Toward the far side of the highway and the ditch near the off-ramp.

"Mommy!" The wraith's cry is behind us, but further away. I squirm to look toward the fire, and she runs straight into it. As she disappears into the flames, another blast comes, knocking Kelly forward. They drag me along with them, and we tumble down the embankment, rolling over each other until we land with a grunt at the bottom.

"Get off me." I push at Kelly's chest, blinking when I realize they've changed appearances again. Their face is softer. Decidedly feminine and younger. Their eyes are icy blue and their blond ponytail has come loose on one side, leaving the hair to clump along their neck, mixed with water and mud. They look like your favourite babysitter or camp counsellor.

"Did it touch you?" They run their hands over me like they're checking for injuries. "Did the wraith touch you?"

Did it? Everything happened so quickly. One moment she was a lost little girl on the side of the highway. The next she was running me down like a hungry wolf.

"I don't think so," I say breathlessly.

"Why didn't you stay in the car?" They sit up, looking over the rise toward the accident. The flames are dying out as the firefighters do their work.

"What's going on?"

"Bus crash," they say with a heavy sigh. "Forty kids coming home from a field trip. Truck driver had a heart attack. There was no avoiding it."

My stomach is in knots at the very thought.

"Are they okay?"

Kelly's raised eyebrow in my direction is the only answer I get. Though I guess their softer, friendlier appearance is an explanation of its own. If I were a scared, newly dead kid, this is the kind of face I might trust to help me figure out what's going on.

"I thought you didn't work at Afterlife anymore," I say.

"Kids are a special case." They slump back on their heels and retie their ponytail. "And a mass casualty like this needs all the help they can get. Wraiths are attracted to the energy of newly dead souls, and children are the brightest of all. We have to get them out of here before the wraiths contaminate them and the only option is to send them to HELL."

My heart sinks. Not because of the idea of wraiths making more wraiths, though that's its own kind of horror. Forty kids. It's the kind of thing that will be in the news for days. There will be memorials and flags flown at half-mast. People asking how this could have happened and what god or force could cut so many little lives short.

"Mommy?" A small hand slides into mine and I scream, ripping myself free. There's a short cry followed by the splat of a body falling into mud, and I turn back in time to see a boy sprawled in the mucky water at the bottom of the ditch. He's got on a blue toque and plaid shirt and stares up at me with frightened eyes that pool with tears. "You're not my mommy."

Not a wraith, though his sharp-edged appearance says not alive either. I step toward him, but Kelly gets there first. They lift him up, hiking him against their hip with gentle ease.

"It's okay," they say. "I've got you." They smooth a hand over the little boy's back, and he relaxes against them almost immediately, turning his face against their neck. Kelly nods and shushes him as he cries. "I know. Let's find someone who knows where you're supposed to go."

This kinder side of them is startling. If someone offered comfort like that, I'd probably follow them anywhere. As they start climbing up the side of the embankment, the little boy has his arms in a stranglehold around Kelly's neck and his ankles locked around their waist.

"Stay behind me," Kelly says in the same tone they told me to stay in the car. This time, I listen. We pass through the firefighters and paramedics. All their attention is on the accident scene. The truck driver has been cut out of his cab and is being loaded onto a stretcher. Also, he—or his ghost, I guess—is standing by the median, arguing with a frustrated-looking man wearing a heavy work jacket and holding a tablet.

"You don't understand," the truck driver says. "I have to get to Windsor tonight. If I'm ten minutes late, they take it off my paycheque."

"And you don't understand," the reaper says, tapping their stylus on the screen, "that you're dead and that this is no longer your responsibility."

The trucker spits on him. The reaper gasps, putting a hand to his cheek, and the truck driver takes off, running down the open stretch of highway.

"Hey! Windsor's the other way." I turn to Kelly. "So you'll freeze me to the spot for asking you for help, but he's going to run away from you and you don't care?"

Kelly's still holding the boy and gives a lopsided shrug. "Not really. I'm here to help the children."

Of course they are. They're such a humanitarian.

The other reaper growls as their features shift, so they're no longer an average guy from the garage and instead look like a teenage girl cosplaying as an elf. Fine features, pointed ears. Their cheeks sparkle with glitter and their pink and lime eyeliner game is on point, even under the garish streetlights above.

"Give me the confidence of a mediocre and newly dead white man," they—she? Dammit, I really have to find someone to explain this to me—says, watching as the man disappears into the night.

"Aren't you going after him?" I ask.

"On a night like tonight?" She sniffs. "He can take what's coming to him. I've got lots to do." Her gaze slides to Kelly, who is still holding the little boy. "Are you back to work?"

"Call it a special temporary assignment," they say.

She grimaces, but nods. Then her gaze shifts to me. "You're one of the teachers?"

"A teacher?" I ask.

"Cerise wants to know how you died," Kelly says, but as I flap my mouth open and closed a few times, they take over. "She's a tough case. Leave her with me."

She glances between us, lingering on Kelly, before she shakes her head, streaks of her hair shimmering in the overhead lights like she's got tinsel in among the shining strands. She really would be better suited for a Ren fair than an accident scene.

Kelly sets the little boy down.

"Take him," they say to me. "But stay close."

I flinch when the boy holds his hand out to me, but Kelly makes an impatient sound, so I take it, and the anticipated devouring sensation doesn't follow. Not a wraith. I repeat it over and over because this little boy doesn't deserve my fear.

The road is a mess of emergency vehicles now. First responders of all stripes move back and forth, carrying out their grim work. The air is full of the sound of crying. Every so often, the wailing scream of wraiths soars over it, only to be cut off as a blue beam of light shoots into the air. The quarantine team, doing their best to catch their prey. Each time they let loose their illuminated trap, I shield my eyes, and the ghostly boy shrinks back with a whimper. Finally, I pick him up like Kelly did.

"What's your name?" I ask.

"Liam," he says, burying his face in my neck.

Instinctively, I kiss the top of his head, the way my mom would when I was small and scared. "You're going to be okay, Liam. We've got Kelly. They're the best reaper out there."

We're close to the smouldering remains of the bus now. The firefighters are investigating the scene. Every so often, the blue-black flicker of a wraith has me dodging out of the way, but they don't seem interested in me now that we're closer. Instead, they swoop in and out of the bus, cackling. Sometimes, as they emerge, it's in pursuit of a phantom child who rushes from the wreckage.

My grip tightens on Liam. Kelly has disappeared into the mayhem. I position myself behind an ambulance, like it might protect us from wraiths, but I can't help myself when I peer over the hood. The scene before me is like watching two pieces of film overlaid on top of each other. In one, slightly out of focus, firefighters desperately try to extinguish the flames that consume the bus. Paramedics wait with stretchers. In the other image, razor-sharp in its clarity, wraiths swarm the bus. There must be twenty of them now. They howl in ecstasy.

The quarantine team that passed me before rounds the bus. The serious leader shouts commands and the beam shoots up. A wraith is sliced in half as part of it is trapped inside the column. It lets out a painful scream that has me ducking back behind the ambulance and smothering Liam against my chest. When I glance up again, the light is out and the soldiers are moving on. The firefighters have put out the flame in the central part of the bus, and Kelly and Cerise walk through the opening. Frightened children grip each of their hands, and Kelly has another on their back.

"We need some help here," Kelly says, and their camp counsellor persona is at odds with the stern authority in their voice.

"We're a bit busy," the quarantine leader says. "And you're not supposed to be here."

"You want Cerise to deal with all of this alone?" they ask.

"Really not time for a genital comparison challenge," Cerise says. The little girl holding her left hand makes a break for freedom, crying out for her mother as she rushes toward the first responders. Cerise swears. I finally realize she meant a dick measuring contest. Not that I need to be thinking about reaper dicks—or anyone else's—right now.

"Where's the rest of your team?" the quarantine leader asks.

The little girl is headed straight for me. I rush forward, shifting Liam against my hip. I catch her in an awkward one-armed motion, but she's small enough that's all I need. We all go down in a tangle of limbs.

"I've got her," I say. Not a single reaper acknowledges me.

"My team is at an earthquake in Sicily. It's just me and Kelly," Cerise says.

"Kelly's not supposed to be here," he says again.

Overhead, a new wraith screams. I have just enough time to see the flash of dark teeth before I roll, covering both kids with my body. The impact doesn't come though. Boots scuff on the ground.

"Dammit, Goran. Do your damn job." Kelly sounds much closer than they were a minute ago. The wraith shrieks in fury, followed by the sound of a body hitting the ground next to me. When I open my eyes, Kelly's on their back, arms and legs raised as they fight off the wraith. Its hands are curled in talons and its mouth snaps at Kelly's throat. The children Kelly had gathered are close by, huddled together as they scream in terror. I scramble toward them, dragging Liam and the girl with me. Cerise is shouting, and another wraith drops out of the sky, dive-bombing us.

"Get those children out of here," Goran shouts, but the

soldiers around him are getting into formation, setting up their machine.

"Watch out!" Kelly shouts, still wrestling with the wraith, but the warning is meant for me. We're in a straight line; me and the kids in line with Kelly and the monster, who are directly in front of the machine. As it starts to glow blue, realization hits. We're staring down a one-way ticket to HELL.

"Liam, take her hand," I say, pushing the first girl we picked up toward him. He does as he's told, and I scoop up the smallest of Cerise's charges. Hopefully the others follow. The light machine is charging fast and we need to get out of the way.

As we sprint to safety behind the ambulance, there's only a second to glance at Kelly before the blue beam shoots forward, swallowing them and the wraith. The second wraith slams into the ground where I was a second before and is immediately consumed by the light too. Both monsters howl in rage, and I want to watch so I can see what happened to Kelly, but the children are crying, so I gather them close and squeeze my eyes shut and wait for it to be over.

The screaming of the wraiths cuts out suddenly, though it echoes in my ears for a few moments longer. I open my eyes. Five kids are basically stacked on top of each other in my lap. I pat some heads, rub some backs. Cerise appears in front of us, breathing hard. Two of the kids dislodge themself from our pile and run to her, wrapping themselves around her legs.

Slowly, I reorganize my little group so we're all holding hands. They move reluctantly as I straighten, but I need to see what happened.

The machine lies on its side, with no remaining glow. Not far away, a blackened, motionless form lies on the pavement.

"Kelly?" I ask. My non-existent heartbeat races. They're the closest thing I've had to an ally in this whole ordeal. If they're dead, I doubt I'll find anyone who will be anywhere near as considerate, which is saying something considering how low Kelly's set the bar.

The figure on the ground coughs. Once. Twice. Finally, a third body-spasming time as they roll onto their side. They cough again, pushing up to their knees and spitting black on the ground.

"Goddammit, Goran. You couldn't have given me a warning?"

They are black from head to toe. Hair, clothes, shoes. Charred like a hot dog forgotten on the grill. But as they stand, the char falls off. They shake, and a giant dust cloud floats up around them. The babysitter persona is gone. They're back to being tall. Mouth too wide, eyes a shade too far apart. They shake the ash out of their hair and what's left isn't even blond. It's just white, to go along with the inhuman flat white of their eyes as they glare at Goran. In return, Goran smirks as the soldiers around him pack up their machine and move on to another target.

"You're off the team," he says. "If you get caught in the cross-fire, who's going to phone me out on that?"

"Are you okay?" Cerise asks me. "You didn't touch the beam, did you?"

I shake my head. Slowly, she untangles the kids around her. They protest and she speaks to them softly, her cheeks glittering with sparkles. She really does look like a fairy princess. Is this what all kids see when they die? It would be a small comfort to me if that were true.

Kelly and Goran are still shouting at each other. Cerise rolls her eyes as she passes me the last child.

"I'll be right back. There were at least three more in the bus. Hopefully the wraiths didn't get them. What's your name, anyway?"

"Ember," I say.

"Ember Munro?" she asks. Even her eyebrows sparkle as they rise up toward her hairline.

I nod. "You know me?"

"You're living with Kelly?

The way she says it sounds cozy. Friendly. Wait 'til she finds out Kelly literally tried to leave me in a subway station parking lot not fifteen minutes ago.

"Temporarily. I—"

But her attention is already turning to the kids. "Everyone, listen to Ember," she says, raising her voice. The frightened children all nod as I hold them close. Cerise gives them all a glowing smile, then strides toward the two arguing reapers. She steps between them and shoves Goran so hard he stumbles back, nearly knocked off his feet.

"That's enough," she says, breathing hard. "Kelly's on special assignment with me. We've already lost ten kids to the wraiths tonight. Minerva is going to have my asshole. If you have a problem with the personnel on this scene, take it up with her. We have a job to do."

Goran's expression is livid, and he squares his shoulders like he might fight back, but as she speaks, Cerise grows. She's now over six feet tall and a set of translucent butterfly wings sprouts from her back, glistening in the light. She's like a child's toy come to life, and one of the kids in my lap even gasps at the sight of her.

"Pretty," the little voice says, though they don't make any effort to get closer to her. Probably safest. Look but don't touch.

And Goran must have the same idea, because he clenches his jaw, shoots a nasty look at Kelly, then turns abruptly as a wraith wails in the distance. He curses and heads off toward his squad of soldiers.

"Good," Cerise says. "Let's get this spit show done."

She disappears back into the bus. My kids are slowly calming. The last few minutes have left me too agitated to sit still, so I make work by getting them organized into two small rows, standing hand in hand like the little duckling lines you see when the daycares take everyone out for a walk. We're ready and waiting by the time Kelly and Cerise return a few minutes later with the last group of kids.

Cerise eyes my little formation appreciatively. "Good job." She kneels down in front of Liam, who stands at the front. "You're in charge, right?"

He gives her a serious nod, and my heart breaks for him. He's all of ten years old, and this is it for him. No more field trips, no summer camp. He'll never fall in love or get a job. And while that last one is overrated, the rest of it is just a fucking tragedy in the highest order.

Unexpectedly, a young man with brown skin and neon yellow hair runs up to us. He's dressed like he was out for a jog and just happened to come across the accident scene, except the way his gaze is locked on us means he's from Afterlife, not from the living world.

"Sorry. Sorry. I just got the call," he says, breathing hard. "I was picking up someone who had a heart attack while doing a marathon. Fifty-six years old. Finished four marathons this year with no problem—then boom!" He claps his hands while he smiles, but a few nervous squeaks from the kids draws his attention and he seems to realize maybe now isn't the time for shop talk. "Sorry. Where do you need me?"

"Take these ones," Cerise says, motioning to the line. "I'll have a look for stragglers."

"You too?" he asks me.

"She stays," Kelly says.

The new reaper frowns, but he inclines his head. As he's been standing there, his appearance has slowly shifted. He's lost the reflective windbreaker and battered sneakers, replacing them with something like a Boy Scout uniform sized for an adult. His bucket hat covers a new mop of dark brown hair, and the green vest he's now sporting is dotted with brightly coloured badges.

"Okay, everyone!" He claps his hands, then lifts a whistle to his lips and gives a sharp tweet. "Let's get rolling. It's time for an adventure."

The kids shift nervously. A few glance back at the bus. One of them asks if he can see his mom when they get where they're going. My chest aches at the question, but it's drowned out quickly by an uneasy tug deeper inside me that says there are wraiths close by. Time to roll out indeed.

I kneel down next to Liam. His little face is tight with anxiety.

"Remember what Cerise said." I hate putting so much responsibility on someone so small who's already been through so much tonight. "You're in charge."

His lower lip trembles for a second, but he nods again and, with a serious expression, holds out his hand. The reaper passes him the whistle, and when Liam blows on it, the kids behind him snap to attention.

"Let's go!" he says. The reaper gives them all a pleased smile and they march off, backs to the bus and first responders. Their little feet beat a steady rhythm on the asphalt for a few seconds, before they fade into silence just like the kids fade away too, disappearing into the ether with their guide.

"We can go," Kelly says suddenly behind me, making me jump. Sometime over the last few minutes, they've returned to something like the form I know them best in. Wide-set eyes, hawk-like nose. Their white hair has turned black and is braided along the top of their head, revealing the shaved sides. One thing I'll give Kelly: they can turn a look, even in the most chaotic of situations.

"We should stay," I say. "What about the other kids? Cerise said there might be more."

"Hey, don't do me any favours," Cerise says, returning just in time to hear my question. The tinkling bell sound of her voice turns hard and sharp. She, too, is back to her original fairy-like appearance and walking directly toward Kelly. Neither they nor I have a second to prepare ourselves before she balls up her fist and slugs them in the face.

Kelly grunts and staggers back. "What was that for?" They look positively astonished.

Cerise sneers. "Special assignment my asshole. You walked

away and now you just show up when you feel like it? It's been forty years. Do you know what it's been like since you left?"

I sigh. "Oh, we do. Minerva already gave us an earful tonight."

She whirls on me, and I duck, anticipating a punch that doesn't come. No one's ever told reapers to solve their personal problems with words, not fists, but at least they seem to draw the line at hitting helpless ghosts.

"She's the worst," Cerise says. "First Richard, then Kelly bailed, so now there's no one to fight with her. Do you know how many seminars she makes me attend? How many SOPs she's written instead of getting her hands dirty and figuring out what to do with the backlog of souls we have to pick up? Every month is a new pilot project and a new acronym no one remembers." Her gaze is furious as she stares Kelly down. "You left us, so you don't get to play the hero now. Not with those kids and not with . . ." She looks me up and down. "Whoever you are. You don't get to keep pets, Kelly. That's just weird."

"I already have a pet," Kelly says, because of course that's the part they'd focus on. "A cat. His name is Carrot Stick."

"I'm not a pet," I say. "I'm a guest." Seriously, just when I think this reaper superiority complex can't piss me off more, it climbs to new heights.

"A guest? How considerate." She purses her lips, and for a second the sparkles in the corners of her eyes almost look like tears, before she blinks and they vanish.

"Walking away wasn't the answer," she says to Kelly, then shakes herself. "Excuse me, I have a job to do."

Awkward. The way Kelly watches her as she walks away says they heard her, even if their face is still impassive. There's history there, just like there was with Minerva. Thousands of years, possibly. The very concept is unfathomable. My closest friend was Lindsey. We worked together at the same law firm for a couple years before I quit when my channel took off. Sometimes we felt like sisters, even after only a few years of dealing with the same asshole partners and associates. What would we have been like if we'd known each other decades? Or even longer?

A pang goes through me at the thought I'll never find out. I've mostly made my peace with leaving everyone behind. Lindsey came to see me last week. I told her she didn't need to be there for the final procedure. She hugged me carefully and said she loved me. She's getting married this summer. When Lindsey asked if it would be morbid to set up a little memorial for me, I said yes. We laughed until we cried.

Shit, I'm going to miss her.

"Did you work together a long time?" I ask as I follow Kelly to the car. They don't reply, and the stiffening of their shoulders says it's not a good idea to push.

Traffic has started moving again, though slowly. Rubber-neckers gonna rubberneck. We merge into the line and make our way to the next off-ramp in silence. For the first time in days, I'm tired. I nod against the headrest, feeling worn out like I used to after the worst rounds of chemo.

Kelly's hand on mine jolts me back to full consciousness. Now that the crisis is over, this touchy-feely version of them makes me uncomfortable and I pull my hand away, which only means their palm drops to my knee instead.

"The wraiths," they say. "They take a lot out of you. Especially when there are that many. Swarms like that are very rare."

I swallow, the childish cry of "Mommy" ringing in my ears. Having kids wasn't ever really on my lifetime bingo card. Maybe fate knew I wouldn't live long enough to see them grow up. And now the word so many moms long to hear is permanently terrifying in my psyche, as is the ravenous howl from the monsters overhead as they tried to consume young souls.

"How long before that happens to me?" I ask, though I don't know what answer will make me feel better.

"It varies," they say. "I've retrieved souls who were too decayed after a few days, and others who hung around for a month or two.

And now with Minerva . . .” They trail off, staring out the window.

“Don’t spare my feelings.” The thing about having cancer is platitudes no longer work for me. If Kelly says not to worry about it, I’m only going to worry more. If they say I’ve got a week at the most, then I’m back to storming the gates of heaven and demanding they let me in.

“We never saw eye to eye after Richard left. The longer he’s been gone, the tighter her grip on Afterlife has become. We’re the two oldest and most powerful reapers at Afterlife, but she has more seniority than I do. It was her way or the driveway.”

“Highway,” I say.

“Highway,” they say softly. “There are so many more of you after the Industrial Revolution. We couldn’t keep up. Her immediate solution was to lower the threshold for allowable decay within the districts.”

“The districts?” I ask.

“You’d think of them like communities. Reunited families. There were reaper supervisors to keep the peace and make sure needs were met. After Minerva’s changes, she reassigned many of them to the quarantine team, as if that’s some sort of long-term solution. The boundaries of HELL are finite, and it takes such a long time for wraiths to burn out. At least two or three times longer than souls. I tried to explain that, but she’s more powerful than I am, so . . .”

I poke at my chest. What is that? Sympathy? Compassion? For Kelly, when I can barely get them to treat me with the slightest amount of consideration? But their words sound genuinely sincere, and the way they won’t finish their sentences says a lot about the emotion they’re carrying.

“And Richard was the only one who could make more reapers, but you don’t know where he went?” This still seems like the best solution. There must be reapers all over the world. Surely one of them has seen him.

"He said something about a vacation. But our sense of time is different than yours. You take a vacation for a week. Among reapers that might be a decade or more. I left Afterlife nearly forty years ago. But by your understanding, that would only be a few weeks or a month."

Which explains why the feelings are still raw. Even Cerise is obviously still carrying some resentment. I can't picture holding a grudge about an old coworker for forty years. The joke is always that no one wants to be on their deathbed wishing they'd spent more time at the office. Imagine being in the business of death and never being able to let anything go.

We pull into the bungalow's driveway, and I follow Kelly silently into the house. We don't say anything before they walk into their bedroom and close the door. The stub of a candle flickers on the small kitchen table. Jupiter must be back at the hospital, and she didn't expect me to come back, so I can't blame her for not leaving the house better prepared. I flop down on the sofa. Carrot Stick appears and hops up, curling himself against me. I let my fingers twist in little circles behind his ears as the nugget of an idea rattles around inside me.

It's pretty clear we can't trust Minerva's promise of "a couple weeks" to cross me over before I decay. Partly because it might not be soon enough, and partly because I have no doubt a couple weeks could easily become a month or two, then more. I can call the Afterlife help desk over and over only to be told they still don't know what happened to my application, but if I fax in a new one, someone will follow up with me shortly. And suddenly it won't matter because I've degraded to the point all I want is to chase and eat and destroy. The only option left for me at that point is HELL or staying here to hurt innocent people.

There has to be a better way. I roll, and Carrot Stick makes an annoyed *mrr* sound before he hops down and wanders away, feet padding softly in the hall.

The answer still must be Kelly.

One of the most common kinds of people I heard from were the overachievers. They'd gotten a good corporate job straight out of school and climbed the ladder. Ten to fifteen years later, they found themselves doing the job of three people because their efforts to make themselves indispensable had been so successful that now the place would fall apart without them, even though they themselves were falling apart under the pressure.

"I love my job, but it's everything I can do to make myself get out of bed in the morning," they would say. They blamed themselves for not working harder and being more committed. The truth was almost always they were working for a boss who was more than happy to take advantage of their work ethic instead of going to the trouble of spending more money on recruiting. They were overworked and often not even doing the job they'd been hired to do.

With the Sparks, I would have told them to take a step back. Which parts of their work did they truly love? What was meaningful? Fulfilling in terms of their personal values, not just in terms of corporate speak about success and accountability? What changes can they make to get back to more of those things? Sometimes the solution is to walk away, but for those who truly love what they do, the answer is usually about boundaries. Prioritize the tasks and responsibilities that drive advancement and achievement, turn down things that aren't part of their job description or don't actually benefit themselves or the company long term.

A plan forms, gelling together quickly in my head. I wish I had a way to film a little announcement about it. The enthusiasm I'm feeling is guaranteed to win everyone over, even a grumpy reaper. It's a win-win for everyone, really. For me. For Minerva. For Kelly too, and that's the critical part. I can't wait around to become a wraith. Kelly is my ticket through the pearly gates, regardless of whether they really are pearly or if there are even physical gates or just a reaper with a metal detector. This isn't something I can do on my own, but if there's something in it for Kelly—something *big* —even they won't say no. Right?

The first time I tap on their door, I do it so quietly even I barely hear it. The second time, the sound is sharp, confident, and professional. The light is on under the door, but even so, the time it takes for Kelly to open it feels endless. When they do, their face is flat and expressionless, but at least they haven't changed their hair colour or added tattoos and piercings to their appearance, so I don't have to take stock again.

"Yes?" they ask, already braced to be annoyed.

But I'm not here to annoy them. Haunting isn't really my skillset. I've got something so much better.

I can barely contain my excited smile. This is it. I can save us both. No more couches and apathy. No more wandering the streets and being told to wait. We can do this, and then everything will be back on track.

"No need to thank me. Just listen. I'm going to help you get your job back," I say. "And it will be better than it ever was before."

chapter
twelve

I DON'T KNOW what I expect. Kelly's obviously not one to drop to their knees and thank me for my magnanimity.

What I definitely don't expect is for them to give me a tired once-over, then say, "No thank you," before they close the bedroom door, leaving me alone in the dark hall.

Sometimes resistance is a natural part of the process. People need to stew or try to find their way around an obstacle before they inevitably come back and admit I was right and it's time to do the hard work. But I might wake up a wraith tomorrow, so there's no time to lose. I don't even bother with trying to open the door. I simply step through it. Kelly's already gone back to bed, where they're lying with an arm flung over their eyes.

"I didn't invite you in," they say.

"I'm not a vampire," I say. "I can come in if I want."

"There's no such thing as a vampire."

"Just because you've never seen one," I say. "That's like saying black swans don't exist."

They drop their arm, looking confused. "There are black swans. I once picked up a prospector in Australia who had been pecked to death by a whole flock of them."

I wave an impatient hand. I don't want to hear about swans or vampires or any of it. We're here to talk about my genius plan. I nearly drop down onto the edge of the bed, but with the way they're sprawled out, taking most of the mattress, the closeness feels too much. Too intimate when what I have to say is basically a mutually beneficial business proposal. So instead, I settle into the large white leather gaming chair by the desk I so meticulously cleaned up earlier. I have a split second to once again wonder how an unemployed reaper can afford a chair like this before I remember the task at hand. Doesn't matter. When Kelly gets their job back, they can buy all the gaming chairs they want.

"I saw you tonight," I say. "You were amazing at the accident scene. It's like you were born to do that."

Their heavy brows furrow. "It *is* what I was born to do. I'm a reaper."

"Exactly," I say, not bothering with Kelly's semantics. "It's what you should be doing. Not hanging out in a bungalow with nothing to do all day." When their frown doesn't resolve itself immediately, I barrel on, in case their next argument is that they can play video games if they want to. Sure they can. Just as soon as I'm off the unclaimed list at Afterlife. "What if there was a way to patch things up with Minerva?"

They snort. "Not possible. She holds a grudge better than anyone. In the Middle Ages, there was a reaper who worked on my team. They accidentally let souls of Crusaders into an area designated for the Muslim families they'd killed. The conflict was so fierce they became wraiths within the confines of the districts. By the time infection control got it contained, six districts were unusable for close to a century. Minerva demoted them to heck."

"Heck?" Why does talking to Kelly always feel like I'm learning a new language? Come to think of it, how many languages do they speak?

They heave a long sigh, but they sit up, leaning against the headboard. "Afterlife isn't about—"

"Punishment," I say, impatience rising. We need to get back to my plan.

"But occasionally souls refuse to believe they don't need to do some sort of penance. We have to put them somewhere."

"Purgatory." Finally, something I already understand.

"Heck." Even though the word is only one syllable, they say it very slowly, like they're explaining astrophysics to a first grader. "We aren't there to adjudicate, only to make sure you don't hurt yourselves or cause decay in others. In heck, souls stand in line for a help desk that never opens or pick at splinters that never come out. Too much trauma and souls degrade, even once they cross over, so we try not to overdo it."

"That's very considerate of you," I say dryly. "But it's not important. I don't care if hell is a waiting room or a place where library books are always on hold and your name never gets to the top of the list."

"It's not hell, it's heck," Kelly says, annoyed. "HELL is completely different. HECK stands for Human Existential Cleansing and—"

"Kelly." I snap my fingers in front of their face. "Do you want your job back, or do you want to spend the rest of your existence stuck among boring, fragile, self-absorbed humans?"

They pause, gaze darting back and forth around the room. The question requires far more consideration than I would have guessed. They can't really want this, can they? A human life? It's so pedestrian. Though how many times while I was in the hospital did I wish to wake up and find myself back at my condo? One more morning to sleep in without nurses poking me? One more afternoon sitting on a patio in the sunshine pretending I like craft beer?

Okay, yeah, life's not so bad. But Kelly's seen all of human history. They're powerful and important. Why would they not want to go back to that?

Suddenly they stand. It's a fast, fluid movement that is a firm reminder there's nothing truly human about Kelly.

"I want pizza. Would you like some pizza?" They push past me and hurry down the hall to the kitchen. By the time I catch up, they're digging through the freezer, which I must have missed in my cleaning spree yesterday and is full to overflowing. They pull out a box of frozen pizza, tear open the packaging, then throw the whole thing into the microwave. Kelly slams the door shut, stabs at some buttons, then paces the kitchen while the microwave turns. They pull at their hair in an agitated motion, and while I'm sure the room is starting to smell like warming pizza, there's probably also the scent of the rubber burning in Kelly's brain while they consider my proposal.

"I haven't even given you the plan yet," I say, trying to hide laughter. I still only have the barest of details about what went down with Kelly and Minerva, but she clearly did a number on them. Kelly's not panicking . . . yet . . . but just the suggestion of going back to Afterlife is making them nervous.

They practically leap out of their skin when the microwave beeps to say the pizza is ready. At the very least, Kelly's hair turns silver and grows about four inches before they clear their throat. They don't make eye contact as they hurry past me to collect their meal, carrying it—glass microwave dish and all—to the living room. I follow after, grabbing a bag of chips as backup, just in case. Kelly's clearly going through something, and I'm not above bribing them with emotional support snacks.

"Well?" I ask, taking a careful seat next to them on the sofa. Carrot Stick hops up into my lap and I pet him while he makes happy purring noises. I always wanted a cat. Kept meaning to stop by the shelter and adopt one. Somehow it never happened. It's fun to have one now, even if only for a little while.

Kelly chews. "I'm thinking about it." A glob of tomato sauce lands on their thigh with a splat.

"Looks like you're making a mess," I say. "I just washed those pants."

"I'm eating pizza," they say, gaze straight ahead. "This is my thinking pizza."

My laughter is so loud and sudden that Carrot Stick yowls as he leaps off my lap. Unfortunately, he lands in a second splatter of tomato sauce that has fallen to the floor. He briefly tries to kick it off in annoyance before giving up and tracking it across the carpet like bloody fluffy footprints as he disappears back up the hall.

Kelly's watching me as I get control of myself again. It feels good to laugh. I haven't done it much since I died, or even before. That it's Kelly who made me laugh is even more surprising, to both me and them, because they ask, "Was that funny?"

"Thinking pizza? Yeah, pretty funny." Another giggle threatens to escape, and I have to compose myself because we're supposed to be having an important conversation right now.

Kelly still looks confused, though it doesn't stop them from starting in on another slice.

"Jupiter can't talk about anything in the morning without coffee. I don't see how this is different."

I could explain, but they're not wrong. Coffee is most people's drug of choice, but salt and fat work nicely in a pinch. In fact, I'm practically salivating as I watch them swallow and pull a third slice free. It was never my preferred comfort food, but it would be nice to taste it, just one more time.

"When you go back to Afterlife, you can tell them all about thinking pizza. You can shake up their whole way of doing things."

They give me a sideways glance. "It won't be easy."

Now is not the time for doubt. "Sounds to me like humanity is a daily disaster. Minerva's in over her head." If I push too hard, they'll retreat. Find a radioactive spider to blow up online and pretend I'm not there.

"It would take a lot to change Minerva's mind," Kelly says

slowly. "They're probably still cleaning up the mess from our last confrontation. She torched a few buildings at Afterlife when I told her I was leaving."

"Everyone deserves a second chance," I rush to say. "And if you find where the wraiths are coming from, isn't that worth more than a few angry words at the office?"

They blink quickly several times like they're reeling at the very suggestion.

"Find the source?"

Gotcha. They're hooked. All I have to do is walk them through the door.

"There are so many. More than usual, I mean. That's what she said, right? That they were popping up in larger groups and more frequently? You said they don't normally swarm like that. Afterlife is stretched too thin. If you can figure out where they're coming from and how to stop them, you'd be a hero. Minerva would be on her knees thanking you for saving her bacon."

Their smile is slow, but their gaze is direct. "And she'd have time to figure out why you didn't get collected and how to put you back in the system before you degrade."

I should have known they'd see through me. But they still haven't said no to the idea.

"I won't pretend there isn't something in it for me too," I say with a shrug. "But think of it as a partnership. A win-win scenario. You get me out of your house, I escape decay and HELL. You finally go back to what gives your existence meaning. Maybe Minerva will even give you a promotion." I'm overselling it, so I bite my tongue to keep from ruining the whole thing.

They extend their hand, holding their palm up.

"What are you doing?" I ask even as excitement lights up my senses.

"This is how humans seal an agreement, right?"

I smile at them as I take their hand, turning it sideways so we can shake.

"Partners. Find the wraiths, kick some ass, and we both go back to Afterlife as heroes," I say.

Their handshake is firm and decisive, and it sends a tremor of excitement through me.

"Ember Munro, you have yourself a deal."

chapter
thirteen

BECOMING A WRAITH HUNTER SEEMS EXCITING. Action-oriented.

I didn't anticipate it would come with a side order of bickering. Maybe that was naïve on my part. It's what reapers do best.

"Where do you usually find wraiths?" I ask.

Of course, Kelly goes for the literal answer.

"I don't actively go looking for wraiths. That's the quarantine team's job."

I strain with impatience and try to think what I'd tell the Sparks.

Ember's Life Tip #634: *Take the leap.*

Sometimes, when you make a big decision, it takes so much energy just to get there, putting your plan in motion feels overwhelming. You decide to start your own business or approach a potential romantic partner. It's exciting but also terrifying. So instead of doing anything, you nurse the perfect idea in your head a little longer because it's safer than risking failure.

Kelly isn't one to show fear, but their departure from Afterlife wasn't amicable. Working with me might win back some favour, or they might discover even solving the wraith problem isn't enough and they're still on the outside looking in. I get it. Embracing my death was just as scary. Maybe it would be something. Maybe it would be nothing. I had no way of knowing, and sometimes the alternative of staying in a morphine haze at the hospital felt safer. And look, it hasn't exactly been smooth sailing since then, but at least I've taken some control back. Kelly needs to do the same. One step at a time.

In contrast, Kelly's gaze is locked on the game du jour. It's not nightmare spiders today. It's a bubble gum–coloured foot race through hallucinogenic mushrooms. Kelly's not very good at it, but they keep trying.

I ball my fists in frustration. This is supposed to be a partnership. If they think they can ride my coattails straight to redemption at Afterlife, they are very wrong.

"So, you figure we'll just hang out here until one pops up in the living room and we can ask it why there are so many all of a sudden?" I ask.

They smirk. "This was your plan, remember? And anyway, they can't get into the house. Not with Jupiter's runes in the foundation."

But like the very mention of her name has summoned her, the side door bangs open and Jupiter's cheery "Honey, I'm home!" sounds up the hallway. The air in the house shifts, in part because of the open door, but also—as something inside me settles and solidifies—because she has no doubt lit a fresh candle at the bottom of the stairs.

"Hey there. How was—" As she rounds the corner, she freezes, her gaze settling on the general direction of where I'm sitting on the far side of the couch. "Oh. Um. Hi?"

"Jupiter? Where'd you go?" This is a man's voice, coming from the direction of the side door.

"I'm in the living room," Jupiter says nervously, still glancing my way. We all wait silently as footsteps walk toward us.

"Sorry, I couldn't get my shoe untied. I did a double knot last night because they keep coming undone. One of these days I'm going to get it caught in a subway door, you know?" the man says as he comes down the hall. He's young. Well, as young as Jupiter. Early twenties, with tanned skin and dirty blond hair. He's in a hoodie and faded jeans. "Health and safety would so get on my ass. Like the time I put a box opener in my pocket and—Oh hey, man. How's it going?"

"X, you remember my roommate, Kelly?" Jupiter says, still looking toward us. Kelly is—woah. Kelly's changed appearance again. They're now much shorter than usual, and their skin has gone a deep brown. Their hair is black, as is the goatee that has sprouted from their chin. They've got their cat-ear headset on and all their attention has returned to the TV screen where their avatar has to duck out of the way of a slavering mushroom that swings pudgy arms toward them.

"Yeah. Nice to see you again, man." He smiles and waves. Kelly ignores him.

Jupiter's still watching me, and I can't understand why she's being so weird. Yesterday was all friendly welcome. Today I'm clearly an intruder. Not like I'm going to fling myself at X shouting "boo!" or anything.

Kelly clears their throat. The sound is an obvious dismissal. X keeps smiling blandly in their direction, not picking up on the hint. Jupiter is looking tenser and tenser by the second. Finally, she says, "X, didn't you say you needed to use the bathroom?"

X's mouth—seriously, his name can't really be X, can it?—drops open, like her suggestion is a revelation. "Oh yeah. I've needed to pee since like Christie Station."

She hurries him down the hall, loudly telling him to take his time. Then she scurries back to the living room and yanks the headset from Kelly's head.

"Hey!" they protest.

"What is she still doing here?" Jupiter asks in an agitated whisper. She's speaking to Kelly but her gaze is directed at me. Or somewhere just past my left ear, anyway. "Weren't you supposed to cross over?"

"There were some complications," I say.

Her eyes get big. "Complications? How can it be more complicated than my boyfriend coming over to find a ghost in my living room?"

"You're the one who brought her here in the first place," Kelly says. On screen, their avatar has been crushed by a mushroom and the screen splatters bright pink goo. They sigh dejectedly and sign out of the game.

She glances over her shoulder toward the sound of the toilet flushing. "Do you know how hard it is to date when you work the night shift?"

"It's not like he can see me," I say. Carrot Stick jumps up in my lap, purring, and Jupiter's eyes get bigger.

"No, but he'll be able to see the cat floating above the sofa cushions. How do I explain that?"

I stand, ignoring Carrot Stick when he protests being dumped to the floor again. "It's fine. We have stuff to do, don't we, Kelly?"

But Kelly doesn't show any indication they're getting off the couch any time soon. They've abandoned their game, but now they're scrolling through YouTube, which is full of recommendations for walkthroughs of other people playing video games.

Also, X is coming back up the hall.

"Hey, I noticed the toilet paper roll was empty, so I changed it for you," he says, though he's still out of sight.

Jupiter puts a frantic finger to her lips. "Just don't be weird, okay?" she says to me.

"You're the one who's being weird." I fold my arms over my chest.

"Whew. I feel better," X says as he comes around the corner. "This is probably too much information, but I had to piss so bad my back hurt, you know?" He laughs. No one else does. His gaze drifts from Jupiter to Kelly, who is still ignoring him, before finally it slides to me. "Hey, I'm X. Jupiter's boyfriend. It's short for Alexander, but that's my dad's name. I should have said hi before, but my bladder had other ideas. Nice to meet you."

I didn't think the tension could get worse, but it does. It's a sign of how shocked we are when Kelly's nostrils flare in surprise. We all stare at X. Even Carrot Stick has paused in his quest to make the perfect carpet biscuit and is glancing up suspiciously.

"You can—" Jupiter says tentatively.

"Ember," I say quickly, cutting her off. "I'm Ember. I, uh . . . work with Kelly."

"You can see her?" This time, it's Kelly who asks, and coming from them, when they've so far done their best to pretend X doesn't exist, I don't have time to cover it with another quick question.

"Sure." X laughs like the question is silly, but very quickly his expression grows serious and his gaze turns to Jupiter. "Sorry. Am I not supposed to? Are we pretending that— I thought—"

"Are you like Jupiter?" I ask.

"I, uh . . ." His face is turning bright red under our scrutiny. "Maybe? We've never talked about it, but it was one of the reasons I said hi to her the first time." He looks at Jupiter again, and his smile turns soft. "I thought there might be something special about you. Looks like I was right." His gaze is tender and adoring, though less like a man in love and more like a golden retriever staring up at a person holding their favourite stuffed animal.

Jupiter isn't one to be distracted by such insignificant things as adoration, though. "But you can see her? Not just hear her?" She points at me accusingly. How is this any of my fault?

"Sure," he says. "Do you mean you *can't* see her?"

Jupiter shakes her head, dropping her gaze in something like shame. She bites her lip and won't look at anyone. It's enough to soften my irritation. In our brief acquaintance, I never got a chance to ask Jupiter more about herself and her history. That anyone with abilities like hers exists was astonishing enough. I didn't think to ask if she knew anyone else who could do the same. If this guy is here to make her feel inferior because he can do something she can't, I really will have to go full wraith on his ass. Maybe that's what true haunting is after all.

"Hey, sorry if I'm making things awkward," X says, redeeming himself with a minimum of emotional intelligence. "My abilities are hit and miss. My grandmother had it too. She used to say they were like a TV antenna in a snowstorm. Sometimes it's all crisp and clear, sometimes it's just a vague sense of something different in the air. Like indigestion."

Nope. No redemption here.

"I am not indigestion," I say.

His easy smile broadens. "No, you're a real firecracker, aren't you?"

If he couldn't see me, I'd step inside him. Sure, it would be uncomfortable for me, but I'd stay long enough he'd feel it too. Make him feel what supernatural indigestion really is.

Since he *can* see me, though, it's best to make myself scarce.

"Let's go," I say, grabbing hold of Kelly's wrist.

"Where?" they ask, but at least they stumble after me.

I glance between Jupiter and X. Her earlier discomfort has passed and instead she's looking at him with interested curiosity. Their date appears to be back on, and we are in the way.

"Not here," I say. I plant my hands squarely on their shoulders and guide them out of the room. They keep glancing toward Jupiter and X. I'll explain the niceties of not being a third wheel once we get outside.

"Keys," I say as we pass the door.

"Are we driving somewhere?" they ask. Kelly's confusion has turned to amusement. Reapers probably don't get manhandled—ghosthandled?—very often.

"We're letting Jupiter have normal human experiences instead of hanging out with ghosts and socially inept reapers."

They frown. "I've been around you for millennia. I'm excellent at reading human social cues."

I can't contain my indignant snort. "Not that I've seen."

"You mistake my lack of response for a lack of understanding. I can read them. I don't choose to do anything about them. It's not part of my job."

Oh, zing. Here at least I have a snappy comeback.

"In case you've forgotten, you don't have a job. Now let's go. Jupiter deserves a few hours without you parked on the couch. And we need to talk somewhere private."

"No one can see you," they say, putting their hands in their pockets. "So let's talk here."

"You don't know that. No one thought to mention Jupiter had a psychic boyfriend. What if there are others?"

A woman walking her shih tzu pauses at the foot of the driveway. Maybe she only sees Kelly talking to themself, but I don't know that for sure. I feel like I need to wait until she's gone again, or at the very least whisper.

Kelly sighs but holds out their arms. "Come here."

Are they asking for a hug? The idea of hugging a reaper feels like hugging a hungry mountain lion.

They wave their arms impatiently. "You wanted somewhere private. Let's go."

I hold the keys out to them, but all they do is roll their eyes as they enfold me in their arms. There's no lion attack, but the sensation of being so close to them and their power is all-consuming. I want to curl into it. Carry a piece of it with me like it will keep me safe. Kelly is infuriating, but there's so much more to them than their superiority and disinterest.

"What are you doing?" I ask, desperately trying to hold on to my sense of self.

"Hold on tight," they say.

"How tight do you—"

But I don't get to finish. There's a sucking sensation, like we're being pulled down a drain, followed by a soft pop.

The world goes black.

chapter
fourteen

I'M NOT SUPPOSED *to use my powers.*

They said that back on the subway platform.

Turns out reapers are very powerful indeed.

I've seen this once. The guy in the khakis took Hazel's hand in her hospital room and told her it was time to go. Then they popped off this plane, leaving me behind.

Of course, witnessing it and experiencing it are two very different things.

Imagine you're on a roller coaster taking place entirely inside a pan-dimensional blender, with a soundtrack of a thousand different animals all trying to cover the same Adele song, even though they can't sing and all are tone-deaf. It's like that. The thrill-seekers might line up for it, but I have zero desire to repeat the experience ever again.

At the same time, though, it all happens so fast I barely even have time to register that we're no longer standing on Jupiter's suburban driveway. And a big part of the swirly, dizzy feeling I'm left with may have nothing to do with the fact that we just cata-pulted through time and space and everything to do with the way we are now standing on top of the CN Tower. All of Toronto and Lake Ontario is spread out beneath me. The world spins and my arms wheel. Only Kelly's firm grip on my waist keeps me from plummeting off the platform a thousand feet off the ground at the top of Toronto's landmark structure.

"Careful," they say, holding tight until I get my footing. They're back to their green buzzcut and whiter skin tones. "It's a long way down."

"But I'm already dead." Even so, a fearful giggle escapes my lips.

"Falling that far would still be unpleasant. There wouldn't be any pain, but the drop would be the slowest, most terrifying ten seconds of your life. There's a theory that extreme fear accelerates decay in ghosts, though it's never been fully proven. Either way, we don't need you degrading any faster than you already are."

And telling me about it will help me stay on an even keel? I smooth my clothes, like I can fight back against the constant threat of this so-called decay.

"Whose theory is that?" I ask, trying to focus on less frightening things.

"Afterlife used to have a department of ghost and wraith studies, but Minerva closed it when the number of dead started surging. She said the researchers were better used working in HELL. Most of their research went to archives and hasn't been touched since." The thin set of their mouth says they disagreed with this decision, but since it sounds like it was made a few hundred years ago, that argument has long been put to bed.

"Will I even be able to tell when it starts?" I ask. "The decay?"

They gaze off into the middle distance, clearly considering the question. If we hadn't rushed out of the house so fast, I would have brought some thinking pizza.

"I don't think that was ever documented. Wraiths aren't usually very forthcoming." Their far-off stare turns into a wry arch of their eyebrow as they focus their gaze on me. "When we find one of these wraiths you think we're going to catch, we'll see if they stop trying to devour you long enough for a conversation."

Sarcasm? From hyper-literal Kelly? It would feel like an accomplishment if it weren't tarnished by the frustration of still not knowing what to watch out for.

Up here at the top of the tower, the wind swirls around us, though my hair lies flat against my back anyway because the dead aren't bothered by something as trivial as wind.

"You thought this would be a good place to talk?" I ask. Even if the wooziness after our little flight here has worn off, it's still unnerving to be so high up.

Kelly, of course, is unfazed.

"You wanted somewhere private. No one can hear us up here."

I'd meant a park, or maybe the back corner of a coffee shop. With a sigh, I settle at the edge of the platform that circles the perimeter of the tower. It's part of a tourist attraction where people can wear a harness and walk around the edge, but it never appealed to me. In life, I always had what could be described as a healthy respect for heights. I may have been a big fan of helping people push their boundaries, but some boundaries exist for a reason.

When I pat the spot next to me, Kelly gives me a skeptical look.

"Oh, Kelly," I say. It sounds nothing like Minerva's stern voice. More like an adoring fangirl, but it's the best I can manage. "Thank you so much for solving our wraith problem. We couldn't have done it without you, Kelly. We missed you, Kelly, please come back. We'll give you a pay raise and a promotion. From now on, you only have to collect souls of the rich and famous. No more slumming it among the rabble like bossy Ember."

Is that a smile? First a joke, then Kelly's lips twist for a second. I'm winning them over, second by second.

"I've worked with your rich and famous," they say, coming to sit next to me. "I wasn't impressed. So many of them seemed to think they carried any pull at Afterlife. I've been offered fortunes, cars, airplanes, houses. Any number of things if I'll help them get back in their bodies and live a few more years."

"Were you never tempted?" I ask.

"Oh, I took what they offered. I have a castle in Scotland and millions of dollars and a pretty impressive collection of jewels in one of your Swiss bank accounts. It just didn't change that they were dead. Nothing changes that."

Guess that answers how they can afford thinking pizza.

"So you have a castle in Scotland, but your credit cards are maxed?"

They shrug. "The reason humans pay off credit cards is so they can continue to participate in capitalism and to protect their worldly possessions for themselves and future generations. I have no desire to contribute to your exploitative economic structures or attachments to any of the things I've been given, so why would I bother protecting it? The castle is mostly crumbling stones now. It was very impressive in the fourteenth century, but I didn't bother maintaining it. I thought . . ." They trail off. Along with the shaved head, they've accessorized with a silver skull stud in one earlobe. It flashes in the growing morning sun as they stare out toward the lake.

"When you thought you'd work at Afterlife forever," I say for them, leaning in to grasp the opening they've presented so neatly for me. "See. This is what I'm talking about. Let's find out where the wraiths are coming from, put a stop to it, and we can both go back where we belong."

Kelly narrows their gaze at me. "You're sure this is what you want to do? It's dangerous. You felt it at the accident site. If you get too close to a wraith, it will consume you. A soul is nothing but energy, and wraiths will leave nothing behind. If we go looking for them, it will be at your peril."

It sounds ominous. But what's the alternative? I don't believe for a second Afterlife is going to clear things up and come get me. Corporations are never that agile, even ones that exist outside human capitalism.

"Are you worried about me?" I ask, bumping their shoulder.

"What?" The way they widen their eyes is adorably flustered. "Not at all. What do I care if you turn into wraith snacks? You don't mean anything more to me than the castle does."

Ouch. Yeah. They're a master at human social interactions. They should give a TED Talk.

"So how do we find them?" I ask. "Minerva said they were popping up everywhere. Are there like wraith hotspots? Wraith dive bars?"

Kelly studies me for a moment longer. Their eyes have turned a brilliant catlike green. Maybe they're not so bad. If I'd died and woken up in the hospital to find them standing at the foot of my bed, I'd have been intimidated, but I might have trusted them to help me. Maybe.

Unexpectedly, Kelly puts a finger to their ear like they're trying to hear something in an invisible earpiece.

"Bang," they say.

"What?" I ask.

"Bang, are you there? Bang! Pick up!"

"What's bang? Do you mean a gun? A bomb? Kelly?"

"I'm really busy right now, Kelly." The reaper who pops into existence on my left has me jerking so hard I nearly fall off the platform. Once again, Kelly keeps me from plummeting into open air. The new reaper laughs. "Whoops. Didn't mean to scare you."

"I didn't think you were going to show up," Kelly says.

"You were shouting. Everyone at reception could hear you," she says with a little pout as she pulls a pair of glasses from the purse she has slung over one shoulder. "You know how much trouble I could get into if anyone at work knew we were still talking?"

Suddenly I recognize her. Or her glasses at least, which have the effect of making her eyes look three sizes too big for her face. She was at the front desk of Afterlife's sleek office tower.

"You work with Kelly," I say.

Her annoyed glance swings from Kelly to me. "Used to. I don't know why they think I'm supposed to answer their calls when they got fired."

"I didn't get fired. I quit," Kelly says stubbornly.

"Calls? They didn't—" I start to say, then pause as more pieces click into place. The finger to the ear was probably for my benefit, but I've seen them do it before. In the car on the way to the bus accident. They'd called for details. I thought they were talking to themself, but instead they were talking to—

"Your name is Bang?" I ask.

She gives me a proud smile. "Edwina Beladorania Bangtilian Mumblebee the Fifth."

"Edwina Bel—"

"Reapers didn't bother with names until sometime around your fifth century," Kelly says. "Richard said we could each pick our own."

"So you chose Kelly, and she chose"—I wave a hand in Bang's direction—"all that?"

Bang laughs. "Oh no. Kelly's short for—"

But I don't get to find out. In a split second, Kelly's disappeared and reappeared on the far side of where Bang is sitting. They shove her so hard she drops off the platform like a rock. The end of her sentence trails after her until she vanishes, then reappears beside us, this time standing next to Kelly. She kicks them, looking hurt. They hop away, rubbing their shin, but don't look particularly apologetic.

"That was uncalled for," she says, wrinkling her nose and making her glasses shift. I wonder if they serve any purpose. Do reapers need glasses? Or is it some human accessory she's adopted because she thinks it looks cute, and her reaper powers mean she can see, even with Coke bottles on her face? "I only get two slides a day, you know. I'm not like you."

Kelly rolls their eyes impatiently. "And you never leave the desk, so what does it matter?"

"Well, now I'm going to have to take the train back to work. Thanks a lot, Kelly. You've always been a pain in my ass."

"You can't poof back to Afterlife?" I ask.

"Poof?" She sneers, but her irritation still seems to be directed at Kelly. "No, I can't just poof. Not all of us have the same powers as Super Kelly here. Administrative reapers, especially ones who are only a few millennia old, get two slides a day, and I've just wasted mine."

Ugh. I need a glossary. A beginner's guide to Afterlife terminology. The best way to alienate potential customers and business partners is to bombard them with unfamiliar jargon and acronyms. Someone draw me an org chart of the different tiers of reapers so I can stop looking completely ignorant when I'm the only one actively trying to solve their problems.

"This is great," I mutter to myself while the reapers bicker. "Not like she's going to do us any favours now."

"What kind of favours?" Bang asks, suddenly interested.

"Tell us about the wraiths," Kelly says. "The unaccounted ones. Minerva mentioned the quarantine team didn't know where they were coming from."

Bang's eager smile vanishes. She takes a step back, and for a second I think she might drop over the edge again.

"I can't."

"It's not a request," Kelly says.

She shakes her head, looking increasingly frightened. "We've known each other a long time, but that's not information I can share. You're not authorized. If Minerva found out—"

"If Minerva finds out about Manila Bay . . ."

Bang blanches even farther, and her glasses drop from her face. She catches them, swallowing hard.

"You wouldn't."

Kelly gives her a cunning smile. Bang's cautious step backward is understandable, because it's the sort of smile now that would bring nearly anyone—reaper or human—to their knees.

"What's she going to do if I tell her? Fire me?"

"She could downsize you," Bang says, eyes narrowing. Kelly's smile dims. Clearly Bang's threat holds almost as much weights as theirs does.

"How can they be downsized if they already quit?" The way reapers throw mangled idioms around is almost endearing, though there are still times where they're just plain wrong.

But Bang and Kelly are watching me with twin expressions of reproach, like I've asked who gets the house in the middle of a funeral. Their expressions make me suddenly feel small.

"What?" I ask.

"Downsizing isn't about employment," Kelly says slowly, like even talking about it is uncomfortable.

"She'd make them human," Bang adds quickly.

I wait for the punchline, but they both stay silent, like the implication should be enough to shock me into understanding.

"What's wrong with being human?" I ask.

"Food poisoning, for one," Kelly says.

"Taxes. Green peppers." Bang ticks the additions off on her fingers, while Kelly nods.

"Fascism. Systemic discrimination. Racism, homophobia. Golf. Global warming. The art form you call—"

"Okay. Okay." I hold up a hand. "You made your point. Let's go back to the other thing. What happened at Manila Bay?"

"Wraiths," Bang says with a scowl. "During the Spanish American War."

"They weren't wraiths," Kelly says, waving a dismissive hand. "They were perfectly fine."

"The paperwork had already been submitted. They were at the gates of HELL awaiting processing." She stomps an exasperated foot.

Kelly pats her head in a patronizing gesture. "And you did the right thing by changing the forms so I could take them back up to main intake."

Kelly? Breaking the rules? The very idea sounds preposterous, but Bang shrinks into herself, wrapping her arms around her torso like she's seeking comfort, so they must be telling the truth.

"Minerva wouldn't see it like that," she says quietly.

"Then it's best if we don't let her find out, isn't it?"

Bang looks absolutely miserable. This is not the way to go about it. We need an inside man—an inside reaper?—but an unwilling one is bound to fail. She'll only be loyal to us until Minerva makes her fear something more. Then she'll spill the whole plan. Kelly's clearly never read *How to Make Friends and Influence People*. They're much more of a *How to Piss Off Allies and Blackmail Coworkers* kind of reaper, and the blunt approach will not work here.

"Excuse me," I say, stepping between them. I have a hand on each reaper's chest, and even with my barely-there understanding of how Afterlife works, the difference between them is tangible. Kelly is a vortex. Something I could dive into and be surrounded. Bang's more like a hot tub jet that hasn't been fully turned on. I know she's there, but she doesn't feel like she can do much on her own. I give her a sympathetic smile before looping my arm through Kelly's and guiding them away from Bang. In a low voice, I ask, "How much do you understand about the concept of consensus?"

They sigh impatiently. "Do you want her help or not?"

I tighten my grip on them, even though they could fling me away without a thought. "Of course I do, but have you ever considered being nice to people instead of intimidating them?"

"Bang's not a person. She's a reaper."

And here I thought they were just prejudiced against people. Turns out it's everyone. To make sure I have their full attention, I tug on the silver stud in their earlobe, hard enough that even Kelly winces.

"Go away," I say, giving them a hard stare.

"What?" They look surprised as they massage their ear.

I point imperiously out into the open air above Toronto, making my request clear. "You heard me. You got Bang here, now let me do the talking. She looks like she could use a little girl's time instead of you threatening to ruin her career."

Kelly purses their lips and flares their nostrils. I should probably be afraid, but honestly at this point if they could have just flicked me like an ant at a picnic off to some dark corner of Afterlife, they would have done it by now. We need someone like Bang to help us find the wraiths.

They vanish without another word, leaving me and Bang alone on the blowing tower platform. I smile, but Bang is now looking at me like I might be planning something even more nefarious than blackmail.

"How did you do that?" she asks, once again pushing her heavy glasses up her nose.

"Do what?"

"Make them leave? No one tells Kelly what to do. Even Minerva could only ever manage to argue with them so long they got frustrated and gave up. But no one ever gives them orders. Not even Richard when he was around." She stares at me, absolutely awestruck.

I can't help myself when I preen. I've had so little control over anything. Not just since I died but since the day the masses showed up on my scans. To impress a reaper—even a minor one like Bang—is incredibly satisfying.

A rattling sound comes from behind us. The doors into the tower swing open, and a half dozen tourists in red jumpsuits and harnesses step outside, gasping and squealing at the view. Six women in their twenties giggle excitedly as a guide gives them the opening speech explaining what they are about to experience walking around the tower's edge. I take the opportunity and lead Bang past them, slipping into the elevator inside as the doors slide shut.

chapter
fifteen

EMBER'S LIFE TIP #98: *If it doesn't cost you anything, give the people what they want.*

"Can we go to a cat café?" Bang asks as we emerge from the CN Tower. It's a nice morning in Toronto. The bright sun does a good job of offsetting the fact it's still too early in the spring for most of the trees to have leaves yet. Bang's watching me with barely concealed excitement, and who am I to say no to a simple request like that? We make our way through Union Station to the subway —the human one, not the Afterlife version—and a few minutes later we're walking up to *Café Meow* on Queen Street, a few blocks from Chinatown.

"Oh my god, hi, babies!" Bang taps on the front window. The café isn't open yet, and most of the cats inside are adults perched on various shelves and cat trees. The majority don't even open their eyes at Bang's knocking, but a trio of orange kittens run up to the window meowing for our attention.

"Can you pass through glass?" I ask. I think about the cool solid barrier of the window, and when I put my hand against it, I slide through until the lower part of my arm is inside while the rest of me is out.

Bang's eyes get big, but she shakes her head. "Reapers can't do that, but I think—" She closes her eyes and squeezes her face together, like she might be in pain, but before I can ask what's wrong, she disappears, then reappears a split second later on the other side of the glass. She smiles at me proudly, waving from inside the café. I close my eyes and think more about the glass until I feel myself drop through it and I'm inside as well.

"I thought you were out of poofs for the day?" I ask.

She smiles. It's a bright, confident expression. In a normal human office, she'd probably be well-liked. "It's called sliding. And technically, admin reapers only get two for emergency purposes, but I've been practicing. If I don't have far to go, I can manage a third."

That information shared, she falls to her knees and is immediately mobbed by the kittens. They look like tiny versions of Carrot Stick, and they scramble over one another in an effort to get into Bang's lap. Her expression is delighted at all the attention.

"I've heard about places like these. I always wanted to visit. When I get promoted from the admin team to the SRU, I'm going to go to cat cafés all over the world."

"I don't suppose you can call in sick and take the day off?" I ask, settling myself beside her. Spending the day with a lapful of kittens wouldn't be awful.

She gives me a rueful glance. "My next day off isn't for a couple more decades."

"Decades?" My voice is sharp with shock.

Bang makes kissing noises at the largest of the kittens, lifting him up toward her face. "Time works differently for reapers. What's a decade or two when you've been alive for thousands of years?"

Kelly said the same thing. Doesn't mean it's right. A day off is a day off regardless of how long you've existed.

"But everyone needs a break," I say.

"We'll take a break when you stop dying," she says, giving me a sympathetic look.

It's an impossible shot, but I take it anyway. "I don't suppose you can get me into Afterlife? It doesn't have to be anything fancy. A tent in the woods. The bottom half of a bunk bed. Anything before the decay is too bad and I don't make the cut anymore."

She laughs ruefully, snuggling a kitten. "I can't help you. I'm sorry. I looked up your file after you left yesterday, and the kind of system override involved would be above my capabilities."

"But you can tell us about the wraiths?" I ask. I had to try, about her sneaking me into Afterlife, but I knew it was a faint hope. "The ones Minerva said you can't keep track of?"

Bang eyes me over the frame of her glasses. "Are you bribing me with kittens so I'll like you and do what you want? Isn't that what humans call kind police officer, mean police officer?"

No point in being coy. "It's good cop, bad cop. But yes, it went something like that. I figured kittens would be more effective than blackmail."

She nods glumly. "You can't blame Kelly. They don't know any other way. When Richard left them in charge with Minerva, it was only a matter of time. He probably figured they would balance each other out, but they've always clashed. Kelly wants things done their way, and Minerva doesn't believe in change. The old ways are the best ways. Just make them better."

A brown tabby with orange splotches has hopped down from its cat tree to come sniff tentatively at me, but when I offer it my fingertips to smell, it puffs up and hisses at me before it scurries back inside a cat bed shaped like a shark, where it glares with bright green eyes. They look like Kelly's and are full of just as much judgement.

"Do you know what happened? What finally made Kelly leave?"

Bang shakes her head. "We were too busy trying to stop the whole building from coming down around us. Most of us aren't powerful enough to cause more than a minor earthquake when we're really angry. But Minerva and Kelly?" She whistles low.

"Whatever it was, it caused a breach in one of the districts. Souls escaped, tried to hop the train back to the living plane. Some got all the way down to HELL where the wraiths down there drained them dry or turned them into wraiths themselves. It was a mess."

Once again, the level of disorganization in an operation the scale of Afterlife is staggering. Usually when there's a row between bosses, the worst damage might be a few paintings knocked off the wall and some frantic messages between coworkers warning to give them a wide berth for the afternoon. Here, there are literal lives on the line, and the reapers at the top of the pyramid meant to keep things running smoothly can't even be in the same dimension together.

"Do you think she'd let them come back?" I ask. "If we figured out where the extra wraiths are coming from, do you think we could hold some kind of peace talks and make things better?"

Bang is silent for a long time. She's got an armful of kittens and looks utterly at peace. I wish I could make things better for her right away. Snap my fingers and everything at work would run smoothly and she'd have time to go on a little vacation to . . . wherever it is reapers go when they have a break.

"I'm going to call this one Noodle." Bang kisses the top of the biggest kitten's head again. "And these ones are Nigel and Narberth, after that town we stayed in when Richard and I had to go pick up a dead king in Wales and we got to hang out among the humans because it turned out he'd been buried alive. They dug him up, only for him to fall down the stairs and really die a few days later." She wrinkles her nose on a soft laugh. "Humans are really accident-prone, aren't you?"

It must have been a different job, way back whenever that was. Relaxed enough that reapers had time to hang out and see the sights while they waited for kings to die, instead of the frantic back and forth I've seen so far. If Minerva thinks that's the goal, to get back to that kind of pace without adding to their staff headcount, they really are doomed, and so unfortunately are we.

Without further prompting, Bang says, "I don't know if Kelly will be able to change anything if they come back. But they're the only one who might. Minerva is too stubborn and too powerful to listen to anyone else. Or else you can find Richard, but I'm starting to think he must have died. Because if he's not dead, he has to know how bad things are, and he doesn't want to come back." She lets out a long sigh. It sounds defeated when I was hoping we could end this conversation with her feeling empowered. "I'll help you. It's better than passing on proposals like the ones other reapers leave at my desk outlining potential operational enhancements, hoping Minerva will read them and realize there are better approaches than ending every meeting with something like 'That's not how we do things here.'" Her impression of Minerva is much better than mine. She puts her face in her hands. "I'm so tired of the meetings."

Why couldn't Bang be my friendly neighbourhood reaper? I know how to help her. Or I would, if there were literally any other kind of job she could do besides work at Afterlife. But she doesn't have enough influence. I need someone with pull who can change the system from outside. For better or worse, Kelly is my guy . . . er . . . person. Reaper.

"Bang," I say carefully. "Can I ask you a question? What do I do about reapers and pronouns?"

She rolls her eyes. "Gender is a ridiculous—"

"Human construct. Yeah, that's what Kelly said." I slump, feeling disappointed to not get more clarity.

But Bang pushes her glasses up her nose, then runs her fingers through her hair. It's a warm dark brown, but as she watches the kittens playing around her knees, slowly it takes on hints of orange, until she's looking tiger-striped.

"I mean, you humans can't even come to an agreement. English has all sorts of pronouns for people and anthropomorphized things like pets and boats, but none for other objects. Some languages have the same pronoun for everything. Others have them for things but not people. Some have three, two. Some languages have nouns to differentiate genders, but in casual conversation just refer to individuals as a person without specifying gender at all. It's like—" She launches into a full explanation about how intricate languages and grammar can be and how confusing it is for reapers who might have to speak a dozen or more languages a day. At least she looks a little happier. Reapers are always at their most relaxed when they're talking down humans, it seems.

Being the butt of the joke is the price I'll have to pay for a successful transition into the waiting arms of what comes next. Maybe in the process I can make things easier for the ghosts who follow after me.

We play with the cats until the café opens so Bang can walk out the front door. Since she's out of slides, I take her to the subway and walk her to Lower Bay. The surprised look on the suited reaper's face when he opens the door to find us standing at the top of the stairs is worth the detour before I head west back out to Kipling Station.

When I walk back up the street to the little house, Jupiter and X are sitting on the porch. They've got matching coffee mugs and they've got a ragged quilt wrapped over their shoulders. When they see me, they break into twin smiles. X waves excitedly, which is unnerving. I'm getting pretty used to being invisible to the citizens of Toronto. To be greeted like an old friend from people I basically just met would be uncomfortable when I was still alive. Now it makes me jumpy. Or maybe that's the decay. It's almost like I can see inside them. They glow. Just a faint aura around each of them, a bright outline that makes them look almost like they've been photoshopped onto the porch. Unless that's just how psychics look when they spend time together. Post-coital glow might mean something else entirely among the spiritually inclined.

There's still so much I don't know.

"We've been waiting for you," Jupiter says, smile getting even wider.

"Did Kelly come back?" I ask.

"For a little bit," X says. "Dropped off a bunch of shopping bags and said something about going to the archives. I didn't even know it was Kelly. He looked completely different. Jupiter explained it to me. Isn't that cool? A real live grim reaper." He frowns like he's just had a realization. "Which archives was he going to?"

Leave it to Kelly to be dismissed from the top of the CN Tower and take that as an excuse for a shopping trip. Probably got a shiny new credit card just for the occasion. I have to admit I have no problem with their commitment to fully ignore things like interest rates and collection agencies. The living should be so lucky.

Jupiter says, "We want to help you. Me and X."

"Help with what?"

She looks excited, which is a big change from earlier. "Whatever you need. You didn't get to Afterlife, so you need help now, right?"

I sag unexpectedly. After arguing with reapers for days, I should have known Jupiter would come through. A million requests get tangled up in my throat. I want her to call my family. Check my channel. Send the Sparks a message from me. A message from beyond the grave would keep my social media presence going for ages after I finally crossed over.

"Are there more like you?" I ask. "Mediums? Psychics? People who can see or hear people like . . . me?"

They glance at each other, one of those silent conversations that I seem to be on the outside of more and more lately. Reapers, psychics, even doctors and nurses who don't want to deliver bad news.

"I'll take that as a no," I say, slumping down to the steps. The world is damp and muddy, but the flowers on either side of Jupiter's porch are bright and vibrant as ever.

"My grandmother," X says. "But she's almost ninety and most

days thinks I'm my dad, so I can't promise anything she'd say is accurate."

"I used to know a girl in high school. We'd do seances and things," Jupiter says. "But I'm not sure how much was real and how much was her pretending while I did all the work. She moved to Alberta after graduation, and we don't talk anymore. All I know is we're the reason you can't take a Ouija board into the Starbucks on the corner of Bloor and Montgomery anymore."

"Woah," X breathes, looking at Jupiter tenderly. "That's badass."

So much for an army of psychics who can help with our monster hunting. And X hasn't done much to shed his puppy dog persona since this morning. He seems like he'd be good for a cuddle, but maybe not so much when the wraiths are going for my throat.

"Do you know anything about how ghosts decay? How long before they become wraiths?" Despite the fact I can't feel the exterior temperature, a chill sweeps over me, and I have to rub my arms to settle myself.

"Uh-uh." X shakes his head. "Wraiths are some heavy shit. You don't want to mess with them."

Thank you, Captain Obvious. "I don't want to mess with one any more than I have to. I want to know if I'm going to become one."

"We can look into it," Jupiter says eagerly. "Research. I'm good at research."

"I have research," a voice says as the front door swings up. Jupiter and X shout and jump up. I had a little bit of warning, since Kelly's power is basically like a beacon whenever they're close. They're standing in the doorway. Blue hair, blue eyes, denim jacket, denim shirt, denim jeans. The Canadian tuxedo. I don't remember seeing the shirt or jacket in the laundry the other day. Must be the result of their shopping trip. They hold up a stack of papers. "Minerva loves a paper path, and Goran with the quarantine team is just as obsessed."

"Do you mean paper trail?" X asks.

"What?" Kelly looks at them blankly.

"What are those?" I ask, motioning at the paper. I don't know X very well, but something tells me if he and Kelly start arguing idioms, we could be here all day.

"Incident reports. They're part of the intake documentation in HELL. Each one documents the wraiths they bring in," Kelly says.

"Where did you get those?" I ask.

"The archives." Their tone implies it should be obvious.

"How'd you get into the archives?"

"The archives are open to everyone?"

"Like the library!" X says, finger pointed upward in an adorably wholesome eureka moment. Jupiter pats his knee to tell him he's a good boy, and I'm surprised he doesn't ask for ear scritches as a reward.

I should probably ask for more information about the ins and outs of archives and how Kelly, who is reaper non grata at Afterlife, can just waltz in and help themselves to stacks of records, but I just don't have it in me. I may not need to sleep, but existential fatigue transcends death.

"If you want to know about the wraiths, this will have everything Afterlife knows about the recent ones." They retreat into the house, and the rest of us follow. Good thing I cleaned off the kitchen table, because they set them down with a flourish and the papers scatter over the surface, covering the whole thing. Pages and pages of neatly typed forms. Names, birth dates, death dates. It's all there, along with details on where the wraiths were found.

"No one's going to notice these are missing?" Jupiter asks with her hands on her hips.

"Minerva loves a paper trail, but no one ever goes back to look at anything that goes into the archives. If we cleared them out, she'd have more space for souls, and she wouldn't—" They shake their head. "No one will notice these are gone. But we might be able to find a pattern in where the wraiths are coming from. If we can figure out which team from the SRU isn't meeting their quotas, we can help."

Their gaze is intent, darting over the papers they collected. Pride swells in my chest. I was right. It's the first proactive thing Kelly has done since we met, and I'm going to claim some responsibility for it. They want to go back to Afterlife as much as I thought.

"Let's get started," I say. "Take a stack and let's see if we notice anything suspicious. Patterns. People who died on the same day or were found in the same place. Jupiter, do you have some highlighters? Maybe sticky notes?"

Minerva scoffed at my offer to help organize her office. Now her carelessness has directly delivered information into our laps. Pride turns to excitement. Everything is better with an action plan. You can nurture future dreams forever because it feels safer, or you can dive in and take what comes.

Our return to Afterlife is getting closer all the time.

sixteen

"THIS IS IMPOSSIBLE." I slump back in my chair. The kitchen is a multi-coloured disaster area. Stacks of papers and neon-coloured notes line the floor and the counter. "We've been through everything over and over and it makes no sense. There's no pattern or anything."

We've looked at hundreds of files. Hundreds of wraiths sent to quarantine in the last two months. There's no common factor. Ethnicity, gender, age. Some died in accidents or of disease. Some died and were found as wraiths a week later; others had been dead for fifty years. Some had no date of death at all, but when I asked Kelly about them, all they could do was shrug.

"There's no quality control on these?" I ask.

"Quality control was reassigned to quarantine in the late 1890s."

Of course they were. If there's any recurring theme to find, it's that one by one, all of Afterlife's various departments have been pulled off the work they did for thousands of years and reassigned to either retrieval or quarantine. Research, quality control. Deemed unnecessary in the face of the onslaught of souls after the industrial revolution.

Kelly gets up to turn on the coffee maker. Jupiter and X disappeared a few hours ago to get some sleep before they have to go to work. They tried to help, but apart from periodic commentary from X about things like "Oh, hey! This lady was born in Souris, Prince Edward Island. That's where my Aunt Cheryl lives," they haven't had any better luck than we have. But at least their involvement has meant Kelly relies on Jupiter less as a personal servant and has learned to make their own coffee.

Still don't do their own dishes, though. The stack by the sink is getting taller and taller, and no one seems to notice but me.

"Do you turn back into a mermaid if you get wet?" I ask, surveying the wreckage. Kelly clearly appreciates the human obsession with caffeine, but they don't understand the concept of reusing the same mug. Every fresh cup is a literal fresh cup, and now there are more than a dozen mugs waiting to be washed.

Kelly frowns as they turn the brewer on. "Mermaids aren't real."

"How would you know?" I ask as I turn on the water. While not needing to sleep has given me more hours to comb through the reports from Afterlife, it's also meant more hours for my frustration to mount, and I'm about to reach a tipping point. "Have you been to the bottom of the ocean? Maybe they're immortal and don't need your services and know what disorganized dicks reapers are so they've never bothered to reach out."

The longer I talk, the faster Kelly's painted fingernails change colours until they're blinking like holiday lights. I'm not the only one who's frustrated.

I turn the sink on and add soap before lifting a mug from the counter. "If you're so insistent on having a clean mug every time, you have to wash these. Otherwise there will be none left."

"But you and Jupiter do it for me," they say carelessly, flipping through papers. "I'm going to go play for a bit. You're all starting to look the same. I can't tell the difference between one name and the next."

"We are not all the same," I say, scrubbing angrily. "The last form I read for was for a ninety-seven-year-old woman from Osaka who died of congestive heart failure. This one before that was for a twenty-four-year-old American man who died in a mountain climbing accident."

"She's a human who is dead. That's the same." As they walk by the table, they wave a hand, and the candle there blows out. "You should take a break too."

The mug drops from my suddenly insubstantial hand into the sink with a crash.

"That was completely unnecessary," I call at their retreating back. "All I asked was for you to wash your own damn dishes for a change."

"Would you two keep it down?" Jupiter asks as she emerges from her bedroom. Her hair is mushed to one side, and there's a wrinkle on her cheek that must be from her pillow. "I still have two hours before my shift starts."

"What's going on?" Behind her, X appears, scratching sleepily at his head.

"Go back to sleep," I say.

"Can you wash some dishes before you do?" Kelly asks. "I'm out of coffee mugs."

"Do them yourself," I say. "Humans aren't your servants."

"Homo sapiens," X says with a smile, walking up the hall. He taps his temple. "You know what sapiens means? Wise." I'm not sure what that has to do with anything, but he seems pleased with himself. He struts around the kitchen, completely unconcerned he's only in his boxer briefs.

"Could you please put some clothes on?" I ask, doing my best to look anywhere but at him as he stands by the front window facing the street. His underwear is so thin I can see his ass crack through them, and when he stretches his arms over his head, he must be giving the whole neighbourhood a show, because the same woman with the shih tzu pauses right there on the sidewalk, staring with her mouth agape.

Jupiter goes to the sink and starts filling it to wash dishes in silent defeat.

I can't live like this. No, I can't die like this. Definitely can't stay dead like this.

"Let's go." Kelly re-emerges suddenly from the living room.

"Go?" Jupiter has pulled a frying pan from the stack of pots and pans that seem to permanently live in the oven, but she sets it down on the table where I'm absolutely certain it will still be this time tomorrow. "Go where?"

"Not you." Kelly jabs a finger in my direction. "You."

"What about the mug?" I call after them as they head to the side door.

"Jupiter can clean it up. Come on. Bang called."

"Bang's a person? Cool name. Did you—" X's question disappears as I pass through the door to where Kelly is waiting by the car in the driveway. Not that I want to stay to hear it. After spending more time with him, I have determined that X is sweet in that he has a personality like the inside of an Oreo. It's hard not to like him, but he's not quick to react. Even though in an unfamiliar situation he wouldn't be my first choice, I appreciate his doggedness with the research.

"What's with the driving?" I ask Kelly. "Shouldn't we slide?"

"You didn't seem to like it last time," they say, giving me their increasingly irritating arch look.

We haven't done the blender travel thing since after we saw Bang and I'm in no hurry to repeat it, but I also don't want to miss the opportunity.

"It's fine," I say. "Where are we going?"

"Bang, where we going?" Kelly asks the air, then nods when she replies. "Quebec City."

"Quebec—" I can't contain my shock. "We can't drive there."

Kelly's thumbing through their phone. "Sure we can. The maps app says it will take . . . oh."

"Exactly. Toronto to Quebec City is an eight-hour drive. The wraiths will be long gone by then."

They shake their head. "Human travel is so inefficient. How do you live like this?"

I was just asking myself the very same thing.

"Not living, remember? Part of the deal with being dead means not having to sit in traffic anymore." I hold my arms out. "Now let's go."

It's better. Or at least it's not awful. Better since we land at ground level instead of way up in the air. Still, when we set down on the boardwalk in front of Chateau Frontenac, I stumble out of Kelly's arms and have to brace on the ramparts for a second while the St. Lawrence River wheels wildly in front of me. I haven't been to Quebec City since a school trip in my last year of high school. We were supposed to be here to practice our French and learn about Canadian history, but on a free afternoon, Rebecca Zeller and I snuck away from the group and spent the afternoon drinking in a sketchy pub that didn't bother checking IDs. By the time we got back to the hotel our class was staying at, we were so drunk we could barely stand up, and the hangover on the bus ride all the way back to Toronto the following day nearly made me regret the adventure.

Nearly. Just like I nearly regret it now.

"Come on," Kelly says, oblivious or—probably more likely—uncaring to the way my head is still spinning.

"Is sliding worse the farther we travel?" I ask, stumbling after them.

They don't even look over their shoulder at me. "I've never had a problem with sliding."

Well, bully for you, then.

"Bang said the wraiths were concentrated here." They point up the hill towards the Chateau. It's not actually a castle. Never was, if my dim memories of that school trip are correct. It's a hotel, one of the ones you see on Canadian postcards and calendars sold to tourists, with round turrets and pitched copper roofs.

No one acknowledges us as we approach the entrance. The hotel reception area is all high ceilings and wood panelling. Visitors with cameras and wheeled suitcases are everywhere. No wraiths, though.

"Are you sure?" I ask, looking around. The whole place feels very normal. "I was expecting more carnage. More explosions." Unless the woman at the front desk bitching that her room doesn't have a view of the Plains of Abraham is a wraith, this is hardly ground zero.

A crash sounds in the distance, followed by a scream. Shortly after, the smoke alarm goes off.

"Guess it's that way," I say. The people coming from that direction are all glancing nervously over their shoulders, like something isn't right. Beside me, Kelly vanishes.

"Figures," I mutter to myself, running past elevators, shops, and a pop-up wedding boutique that line the ornate corridor. The shouts are getting louder now, coming from overhead. The corridor opens into a foyer bordered on each side by sweeping staircases. The sound is coming from the top, and people are descending. Everyone is well-dressed in suits and evening gowns. Behind them, the air is smoky. That can't be good.

Kelly appears at the top of the stairs, scanning the space below until their gaze lands on me.

"Are you coming?" they ask.

"Not all of us can slide from place to place," I say, dodging past the people running for the exits as I climb. "Some of us have to go the old-fashioned way."

They roll their eyes, but suddenly they appear next to me, and a second later, we're both standing at the top of the stairs.

"I was almost there," I say, slipping out of Kelly's hold.

"We're running out of time. The quarantine team will be on-site soon."

Ahead of us, the doors to the ballroom are wide open and fingers of smoke swirl slowly toward us. Beyond, the telltale laughter of wraiths echoes in the air. The ceiling stretches miles overhead. Maybe a dozen chandeliers sparkle in the air, which would be beautiful except for the way a few are swinging wildly where wraiths soar overhead. There must be ten of them, plus a half dozen more again closer to the floor, weaving between frightened wedding guests. Three tables are on fire, and two more are overturned.

"What happened?" Kelly asks, sounding almost awestruck, maybe even a little frightened.

"Pretty sure this is your area of expertise," I say.

"Not this many. Or among the living. Wraiths are solitary unless there has been a recent mass casualty. They don't approach living gatherings." They duck as a wraith swoops toward us.

At the far side of the ballroom, velvet curtains line a raised stage. They billow on an unseen wind as another dozen wraiths swoop through them, appearing seemingly out of nowhere. They howl and wheel. The people closest to them, including the bride in a confection-like wedding gown, run away, almost like they can see the spectres. What they're actually trying to escape is the way the corks are popping out of nearly a hundred bottles of champagne, set up in neat rows next to a four-tier cake. The sound is like gunshots, and it makes the guests panic.

The bride trips on her skirt, sprawling on the silvery carpet, and two men, in their haste to get away, tip over one of the heavy round dining tables. It flips up, and my cry of warning does nothing before the table lands upside down on the struggling bride. Candles from the table's centrepiece bounce across the floor before settling near an adjacent table. The tablecloth smoulders for a second before it catches fire. The flames lick upward quickly, and they're alarmingly close to the bride's veil as she tries to pull herself free of the weights of both dress and table.

"Do something," I say, shoving Kelly forward.

"Saving lives isn't my job."

I'm so shocked, for a second my hand slides all the way through them. And I mean *all the way through.* I crash against them and join the screaming in the room at the sight of my hand and fingers wiggling on the other side of Kelly's chest.

"That's unnecessary," they say, stepping forward to untangle us.

"What's unnecessary is letting her die."

Above us, a wraith screeches and Kelly watches them nervously.

"This is too much. One reaper and a ghost against all these wraiths. It's not safe." They put an arm around me, and I only have a moment to realize what they're about to do.

"No." I push one more time. "No sliding. Save the bride. Then I'll go."

Kelly's lips are pressed in a thin line. I take a step back, just out of their reach. A wraith drops low, claw-like fingers stretched toward me. At the last second, Kelly grabs hold of them, flinging them to the floor so hard the wraith screeches, then lies still.

They sigh and jab an angry finger at me. "Wait outside."

"No," I say, but they're already back to wrestling another wraith, so they don't have time to argue.

"Help!" The cry comes from behind me, eery and high.

Slowly, I turn. I expect to see a wraith. A frightened little kid-turned-monster like at the bus crash. Instead, what I see is a woman. A ghost. If the others around me could see her, she might be mistaken for a wedding guest, with her peach satin dress. The only giveaway that she is no longer among the living is the way her edges are crisp where she huddles in the corner behind one of the doors. There's no telltale oily ooze like with wraiths, though, so she must be a garden-variety ghost.

Bad idea. Kelly told me to stay safe. But she's looking right at me with watery eyes. Her hair is blonde and swept together in an updo dotted with rhinestones.

"Are you okay?" I ask.

She's cowering in a corner, but when she looks up at me, her gaze is teary but otherwise clear. No wraith has ever looked at me with so much humanity left in them.

"You can see me?" she asks.

In a second, one of two things is going to happen. I'm going to help someone, or she's going to eat me. Is the risk worth it?

I hold out a hand. "Come on. It's not safe."

Her hand in mine tingles, but it doesn't leave me with the tearing feeling like the wraith on the highway. This is so not my job. I stuff the thought aside. It sounds too much like Kelly.

Once again, whoever was supposed to take her to Afterlife dropped the ball.

"My name's Ember. What's yours?" I ask.

"Lilah. Lilah Morris." she says. Her lower lip trembles. "Where am I? Did I go back to prom? What about heaven?"

"This is Quebec City," I say.

"What?" She rips her hand from mine, shaking her head violently. "No. Heaven. I have to go back. I was on the way home from prom and . . . I'm supposed to be in heaven. I was *in* heaven. We were having ice cream. They said—"

Inside the ballroom, the screams of the wraiths are getting louder. Then they're cut off as a beam of light shoots through the open door. Lilah drops to the floor, covering her head with her arms, and there's a distinct smell of burning, though I can't tell if it's burned carpet or burned wraiths.

"It's okay," I say. "It's okay."

A rustle of white catches my attention. Aside from being dead, Lilah's in better shape than the bride who bursts through the door. Her hair has fallen out of its pins, streaming in curls behind her, and her puffy skirt is scorched. Kelly stumbles out after her. They're looking even worse for wear. Their arms are covered in scratch marks, and the cuffs of their jeans are shredded, exposing blistered skin beneath.

"Happy?" they ask me. "Let's go."

"Wait."

They sigh. "Ember."

"No, listen. This is Lilah Morris. We need to take her with us."

Kelly, who appears to have not even noticed her until I say her name, takes one look at Lilah and recoils.

"What are you doing?" they ask, eyes wide with horror.

"She's a ghost. She got lost. We have to—"

"She's a wraith. Ember, what—"

"No, she isn't. She's—" But my protest cuts off suddenly as Lilah's eyes roll back in her head. If she were alive, I'd say she was having a seizure. Her mouth opens wide as she shakes and her hand tightens so much around mine that I can feel something like pain. Like bones I don't even really have anymore grinding together. "Lilah? Lilah what's wrong?"

Her head snaps forward, gaze locked on mine. That direct, cognizant gaze is gone as her eyes swirl with tendrils of black, like ink in water, consuming her pupils. When her mouth spreads in a gruesome smile, her teeth are stained with a dark oily substance that drips over her lips.

Shit. Why does Kelly always have to be right?

She grabs my wrist again. I try to shake free, but it's like we're welded together. Lilah's crying has turned to a terrifying whine in the back of her throat that morphs into the giggle I'm learning to both hate and fear. Her claw-like fingernails dig into my flesh as the connection between us tightens. The tearing feeling replaces pain. Lilah's going to shred me to molecules, and there's nothing I can do about it.

"Please. Please let me go. I don't—" I almost say I don't want to die like this, but it's too late for that. I'm already dead. I did this to myself, and now I get to bear the consequences.

It's getting hard to breathe—only I don't breathe. Hard to

think. I can literally feel my sense of identity fading as my vision gets blurry.

"Let go!"

Strong arms wrap around me. The wraith laughs.

Everything goes dark, and all I think is I can't die like this.

chapter
seventeen

I **WAKE** up being suffocated by sixteen pounds of orange cat. Carrot Stick is spread out across my entire face. Surprising how uncomfortable that is even when you don't actually need to breathe.

Still, I gasp at the memories of a ballroom and fire and twisting fingers trying to rip my very essence to pieces.

I reach out, trying to fight Lilah off. Carrot Stick moans a protest, but he hops off my face, and I find myself staring at a plain white ceiling. The pot light over my head is burned out, but the rest glow a mundane yellow-white light over an unremarkable living room. No chandeliers. No smoking carpets.

"Are you awake?" A deep voice asks. I roll to the side. X is sitting in an armchair. We're in Jupiter and Kelly's living room.

"I thought we were in Quebec City," I say. My voice is a croak.

"Did she wake up?" Jupiter calls from the kitchen.

"She thinks she's in Quebec City," X says over his shoulder. At least he has more clothes on than last time. Pretty sure they're all Jupiter's, though. The T-shirt comes well short of his waist, exposing a hairy belly button, and the cuffs of his sweatpants barely come to the middle of his shins.

"Ember?" Jupiter comes around the corner. She's got a tray of food. Chicken noodle soup from a packet by the looks of it, as she sets the nearly overflowing bowl of yellowy green something paired with a sleeve of soda crackers down on the coffee table.

"I don't eat anymore, remember?" I say, barely speaking above a whisper.

"Oh, that's for me." X takes the bowl and a spoon, slurping in a big mouthful of noodles. "Thanks, babe."

"Are you okay?" Jupiter asks me. At least I assume she's asking me. Her gaze is still somewhere to my right, so she might be talking to the sofa, but let's assume it's me.

"How am I supposed to know?" I push upright, closing my eyes again when the world shifts too, so the whole thing is still sideways, even though I'm not lying down anymore. When I open them again, everything is situated as it should be. Two humans, one cat, and me.

"Where's Kelly?" I ask. "Lilah?"

"Kelly's out," Jupiter says. "Who's Lilah?"

"She's . . ." I have to swallow as the tattered pieces of my consciousness unravel for a moment before recongealing into something like memory. She's who? A girl who thought she was on her way to prom? A ghost? A wraith? What happened to her? I close my eyes again and focus on things I understand better. "What do you mean Kelly's out? Out where?"

"She went to Afterlife."

I leap to my feet. It's so fast I even manage to rattle the coffee table when I bump against it. "Why? Why didn't they wait for me?"

X and Jupiter glance at each other. X shrugs and eats more soup. Jupiter sits down, hands clasped between her knees. It's the posture doctors adopt when they're about to tell you bad news. But how bad can it be? I'm already dead.

"You were unconscious for the last day and a half," Jupiter says softly. "We were starting to think you weren't going to wake up."

"A day and a half?" That's impossible. Even at my most medicated, I could never manage more than twelve hours.

"What happened?" Jupiter asks. She helps herself to the second bowl on the tray. This one is also practically overflowing, but with cereal and milk. "You and Kelly popped back into the living room suddenly on Saturday night. Kelly was carrying you. She was so pissed, and X said you were practically transparent?"

"It was like you were dying," X says, sounding awed. "Again. Do you think that's possible?"

I don't bother answering.

"Can you drive me to the subway?" I push myself up on unsteady feet.

"What for?" Jupiter asks.

"I need to go to Afterlife. To the archives. I have to find out what happened to Lilah." She was so scared. And Kelly was wrong. Regardless of what happened in the last few seconds, she wasn't a wraith. Not like the others I'd seen.

"I think you should wait here," Jupiter says, sounding worried.

"Did Kelly say how long they'd be?"

She shakes her head. "Kelly waited with you. Wouldn't leave the living room. But when you were still asleep this morning, she said she'd be back later."

Jupiter's spinning wheel of pronouns makes my head hurt, though my use of "they" is no more correct than her "she" so I can't complain. More importantly, the idea of Kelly sitting at my bedside sounds preposterous. Jupiter probably means they spent the time gaming and resenting me for taking up space on their sofa. Either way, I'm awake now and need to keep moving.

"Then I need to go."

"We're not supposed to let you leave the house."

For god's sake. What are they? Jailers? "Why not?"

The two mediums give each other an uncomfortable look. Someone's keeping a secret.

"What is it?" I ask.

Jupiter bites her lip, tugging at her cuffs. It's X who leans forward and pulls back my own sleeve, exposing my wrist. Four crescents have been dug into the skin. Nail marks from Lilah. If I were alive, they wouldn't be serious enough for me to do more but put some antiseptic on them, and maybe wrap them in gauze to keep them from bleeding against the inside of my shirt.

But I'm not alive. And I don't bleed. What I do, however, is ooze, thin rings of black oily goo that seep from the cuts and smear against my forearm.

I gasp. "What's this?"

They won't meet my gaze, either of them. I rub at it, trying to clear it away, but no matter what I do, more keeps leaking out of me in slow but steady drops. Cold terror washes over me. I wondered if there would be signs, and the wounds on my wrist are pretty clear.

"Decay?" My voice shakes.

"Kelly said you had to stay here," Jupiter repeats. "She said you wouldn't . . ." Her gaze drops again. I feel sick. I know that expression. Nothing good comes from words spoken after someone makes that face.

"I'm a wraith?" I say softly. My senses turn internally, taking inventory. What hurts? What feels different?

"No. No, not . . . not yet." Jupiter blinks hard like she's trying not to cry. "Kelly said if you stay here, it wouldn't happen too fast."

I close my eyes and take a deep breath. Not because I need it, but because the exhales take the terror with it, leaving only a numb calm. It's a skill I learned in the hospital. Cancer doesn't care if you get sad or angry. It doesn't care if you weep or throw things. But the doctors and nurses do, and it makes their job a whole lot easier if you can wait until you're alone to let the big feelings out.

"Jupiter's been carving more candles," X says, looking around awkwardly. I follow his gaze and realize the living room is dotted with white pillar candles. They aren't lit, but the whole thing makes me feel like I'm on the set of a 1990s vampire movie. Each one is marked with the geometric shapes of Jupiter's runes.

"Just in case," she says, giving me what she probably hopes is a reassuring smile.

If chemo couldn't save me, what hope do a dozen candles have? But this is different. It's all different. I have to trust that they can help and that Kelly and I find answers soon.

"Do you have your phone?" I ask, lying back down.

"Sure," Jupiter said.

"Do you want us to call someone for you?" X asks. "Family? Sometimes it helps to talk to them. Jupiter and I can tell them anything you want."

I shake my head. I can't put them through this. They think I'm dead and I'm in a better, safer place now. How could I let them know I got stuck here and now I'm on my way to being something worse than dead?

"I need you to look someone up. Lilah. Lilah Morris. She looked like she was on her way to prom."

It takes less than thirty seconds for Jupiter to find her.

"Vancouver teens dead after prom night tragedy," she reads out loud, scanning the screen. "Lilah Morris, age seventeen, died Saturday morning after leaving the Borden Collegiate prom with her boyfriend. The two were killed when a drunk driver ran a red light." Jupiter holds her phone out to me. "This is from British Columbia. There's a picture. Is this who you saw?"

It is. The nice thing—if you can call it nice—about dying on prom night is there are lots of pictures showing exactly what you looked like. The blonde hair, sparkling hair stones, and peach dress are unmistakable.

"When was this written?" I ask. The details sound familiar. A pretty young white girl killed on what should have been a special night would have made the news, even in Toronto.

"Last June. End of the school year." Jupiter scrolls further, clicking on links.

"And that's why you should never drink and drive." X has finished his soup and is busy consuming the entire sleeve of crackers . . . though at least half of them are turning into crumbs that fall into the carpet. No doubt they'll stay there unless I vacuum them up.

"So she died ten months ago," I say, ignoring him. "But somehow she's still a ghost now? How is that possible?"

"Because Lilah Morris isn't dead."

Kelly has returned. They slide back into the bungalow without a sound, and their voice makes all three of us jump. Even Carrot Stick gives an annoyed meow as he saunters toward the kitchen.

"She's definitely dead," I say. "We saw her. It was in the news."

"There's even pictures of her funeral," Jupiter says, still looking at her phone.

"I know." Their brows are pinched together in a frown. They glance down at me. "You're all right?"

The question is so unexpected it takes me a few seconds to understand it's directed to me. I stammer an unintelligible answer, before finally I hold up my injured wrist and say, "Still dead."

They nod, like that's enough explanation, though their gaze lingers on me for a moment before they turn their attention back to Jupiter and X.

"There's no record of her death at Afterlife. I asked Bang to look her up when we got back, and when she couldn't find a record, I went to the archives to check. I looked through everything for the last two years. There is no record that Lilah Morris is anything but alive and well."

The room goes quiet. X and Jupiter glance at each other. I stare down at the crescent punctures on my wrist. She was so scared. Whether she was decaying in front of me or not, she was terrified. Lilah got screwed in life and screwed again in death.

"What does it mean?" Jupiter asks.

"I have no idea," Kelly says on a sigh, sinking down to the couch. They nearly sit on my feet, and I pull them back, bending my knees to make room for them. "It should have been a very straightforward collection. Accidents like that are common. Even the lowest tier reaper can manage a soul in that situation."

"So they lost the paperwork and someone forgot to go get her," I say. The very suggestion leaves a sour taste in my mouth. If a case like Lilah's is as cut-and-dried as Kelly says, and even that gets messed up, what hope do any of us have of ever crossing over safely? "How did she wind up in Quebec City? If she died in BC and she's like me, it's not like I can zip off to other parts of the country in a blink. She'd have had to walk—and why would she do that?"

"She could have stowed away on a plane," X says, nodding with enthusiasm at having had the idea, though no one else acknowledges it.

"It's the wraiths that worry me," Kelly says. "There were more than thirty of them. A swarm that big usually only comes to the scene of a large death. The bus accident. A natural disaster. Not to a very large and living wedding."

"But she wasn't a wraith," I say. "We had a whole conversation before you showed up. She told me she'd been in heaven. And I know you said it's not really called heaven, but that's what—"

"She called it heaven?" they ask, eyebrows going up in surprise.

I sigh, closing my eyes. "I don't want to fight with you, Kelly. Heaven, Afterlife, the big cloud hotel in the sky. What does it matter what she called it?"

"But she remembered it? She remembered being in heaven?" Their gaze has turned intent, like whatever I'm about to say is very important, and suddenly I feel shy. It's hard to say what I remember and what pieces I've filled in myself.

"Everything was happening really fast," I say. "But I think so, yes. She knew she'd been in heaven. She kept saying it over and over. She said they were having ice cream."

Kelly's given me the silent treatment a lot. They're not one to fill a quiet moment with chatter. But the wordless stare they give me now feels like the floor is about to swallow me whole. Without meaning to, I begin to scratch at the cuts on my wrist. They burn the more I touch them, but the pain is soothing. An outlet for the fear that starts to boil inside me.

"She shouldn't be able to remember it," Kelly says, though each word is slow, like they're considering them right down to the syllable. "They're not supposed to remember anything once they cross over."

Like when they asked me if I was all right, their statement pulls me up short as I struggle to compute.

"What do you mean?" I ask, voice threatening to choke me.

Kelly is staring down at their hands. The humanness of the action is so disconcerting. Even Jupiter and X seem to feel it, because she nudges him and whispers, "Let's go outside."

"What for?" he asks at full volume. X may have a particular set of skills, but it doesn't include knowing how to read the room. She rolls her eyes and tugs on his sleeve until he rises. They reach the front door at the same time, briefly getting stuck in the frame before they wrestle themselves free and disappear out to the porch. It would be funny, except the humour can't overpower the fluttery panic that is forming just beneath my breastbone.

"What do you mean?" I ask again. "That they're not supposed to remember?"

Kelly's lips are thin and they won't look at me. If they reach for the cat-ear headset on the coffee table I will scream. I will rip open the cuts on my arm and I won't stop until whatever poison Lilah left inside me spreads everywhere so I can tear Kelly to pieces.

"It's why I left," they say. "Minerva and I had always gutted heads."

"What?" I ask.

"Gutted heads?" Even now they sound uncertain.

"You mean butted heads?" It should be funny, but I'm not laughing.

They glare, and I'm reminded of staring into Minerva's eyes. She may be the head reaper in charge, but the depth of Kelly's eyes —slate grey today—is just as ancient. They are not human and never have been.

"Gutted heads. Fine." I spread my hands in a placating gesture. "Continue."

"Before Richard left, he told us to take care of Afterlife. Minerva took that to mean keeping it exactly the way it's always been, and I thought differently. Give the souls less supervision, move reapers around so they weren't doing the same job for eternity. Minerva refused. Then, when the human population exploded, there wasn't time for changes. We've spent four hundred years trying to keep from drowning in wraiths. We were filling Afterlife faster than souls were burning out. At the start of the twentieth century, we reached a tipping point. We were out of room, and the stress of overcrowding was creating wraiths within the districts, which only made the situation worse."

I try to follow. In my head, Afterlife's districts are a picture-perfect community like the ones you see in those heteronormative Christmas movies the streaming services all seem to make these days. As Kelly speaks, I imagine the cute shop fronts and ginger-bread houses slowly turning black with rot.

"So you walked away from it?" I don't mean to think the worst of Kelly, but their expression has turned almost guilty, and I need to know what they think they're culpable of.

"Not at first. I tried. Many of us did. We proposed sending exploration teams to the far reaches of Afterlife. It's been thou-sands of years since anyone's been out there. I thought we might be able to build new districts. I sent reapers out, but they didn't come back. Minerva insisted there wasn't time for alternatives. That we needed to find a solution with the space and resources we had. She said the best thing to do was to stop allowing souls to believe Afterlife is an extension of their human lives. If we wiped their memories at intake, we didn't have to worry about making them comfortable. We could exponentially increase the number of souls we could fit in each district and also reduce the number of reapers required to act as supervision."

My fingers are slick on my skin, and I realize I really have torn the cuts on my wrist open with my anxious scratching. Dark goo is smeared on my forearm. Carrot Stick hops up on my lap and gives it a sniff. He hisses, batting at my hand as if he's telling me to stop. I do, spreading my palm over the wound, as if I can hide what's happened from Kelly. But surely they know. They probably did from the moment we got back from Quebec City.

"And that's what she did?" I ask.

"Not long after your second World War. The population exploded with babies, and we knew what was coming. She said we had no choice. I told her I couldn't be a part of it," they say. "We're guardians. Not judge and jury. We don't get to take anything from souls, only protect them from themselves. I said that if she went ahead with her plan, I'd walk away from Afterlife and all of it. Richard is the only other reaper to ever leave. It's unheard of. Our organization is hierarchical, and everyone knows if you disobey the reapers above you, you can be downsized in a blink."

"So when I cross over," I say carefully, "you're going to erase my memories? All of them?" My family. Friends. Trips I've taken. How it feels to have the sun on my face, or the cozy sensation that is the first few seconds when I wake up in the morning before the worries and the to-do list take over. It's all gone? A tear rolls over my eyelashes, and in swiping it away, I must leave a dark smear on my cheeks, because Kelly's expression turns startled. I scrub at my face with my sleeve, ignoring the stain it leaves on the yarn.

"It's not what I wanted," they say. As if that's supposed to make me feel better.

"But you let it happen." I stand, trying to make space in my body for the rage volcano that is about to explode. "You knew and you let me believe something different. We were just talking about the districts the other day. On the way back from the bus accident. You told me they were communities. You never said they don't exist anymore."

"The reapers don't tell anyone. If we did, do you think anyone would cross over? You'd all stay here. The number of wraiths would go up exponentially. It would be a disaster." The longer they talk, the more their appearance changes. Skin tone, eye colour. Tattoos ripple over their arms and disappear. It's like I'm seeing all the faces they've ever worn as they collected unsuspecting people and walked them to the door, making promises of reunification desks and a peaceful afterlife, only to take it all away. I should be proud to have finally found the thing that cracks Kelly's perpetual shell of disinterest. The one thing that prompted them to take a stand. But it didn't matter. Standing aside is not the same as standing in the way.

"So you chose pizza and chips over helping?" I say.

"She's too powerful. There was no way . . ." They're just making excuses now. They sound weak. Powerless. They're supposed to be my ally, and they've been keeping the most important truth from me since the beginning. That this is it. There is nothing after this.

"So what now?" I ask, breathing hard. It's so odd the things my body does even though it doesn't have to anymore. "My options are to hang out here and become a wraith or, if I'm lucky, Minerva will still remember I exist in a week or a month and come get me and take me to . . . nothing?"

"You're getting off topic," Kelly says, rising so we're eye to eye. As they do, they ripple and change again so that they take the same form as when we were on the highway after they got caught in the blue beam. White skin, colourless hair, white eyes. Maybe they're trying to intimidate me, or maybe they're so caught up in this string of revelations they don't have it in them to maintain a more humanlike appearance. "We were talking about Lilah. That she remembered heaven. It shouldn't be possible, but she did."

"That doesn't matter," I say, taking a step back. "It doesn't matter what she remembers or not. She was a wraith. You said so. Maybe she was lying. Waiting for me to get close enough she could tear into me and consume what's left of me. How is that any different than what you were going to do?"

"I saved you," they say, sounding pained. Their emotional response to this whole scenario makes everything worse. If they'd remained cool, detached Kelly, I might have been able to get control of myself. But their loss of control has only accelerated mine. "I stayed with you. Watched over you so you didn't become a wraith."

"So you could do what? Let me help you get your job back, then deliver me to Minerva so she can take my memories?" I lift my arm and the sleeve falls back, exposing the black-stained skin beneath. "Or so you can wait until I'm too far gone and drop me off at HELL? Is that it? Wipe your hands of me and go back to sponging off Jupiter while she makes your meals and lets you live in her house?"

"Ember," they say. "I'm trying."

No they aren't. They've done nothing. Humoured me. Gone along with my wild schemes to save myself but probably laughing at me the whole time. Pitiful human doesn't know the truth. When you live forever, a little diversion is probably nice. A few hours at the movies aren't enough, but a few days or weeks following after a ghost with a hare-brained plan to jump the queue at Afterlife is probably fun. A nice break from the monotony of being all-powerful and responsibility-free. And if that ghost gets erased for all her trouble, who cares? There's always more where she came from.

"I have to go," I say, stumbling to the door.

"Ember, wait," Kelly says behind me.

"Hey, everything okay?" Jupiter asks as I take an unsteady step onto the porch.

"Oh wow, you're bleeding," X says. "Or not bleeding, but . . ."

I'm decaying. Dying. All over again. The cancer took my life and my dignity. Being dead is going to take everything that makes me who I am. I thought I had a choice, but I've been wrong the whole time.

chapter
eighteen

DEAR SPARKS, okay, so I finally know what haunting really is. It's not about ukeleles or revenge. It's grief.

I wander down Dundas Street. It's perfect for this kind of thing. Dundas cuts through more than half of Toronto and I'm starting on the westernmost reaches. Out here it's quiet. Residential. The closest things to businesses are houses that have been converted into daycares or lawyer's offices, but driving by you'd never know the difference. If I walk long enough, I'll pass old railyards. New condo developments. The city bus station. Strip clubs. The whole diversity Toronto has to offer.

Away from the strengthening force of Jupiter's candles, the wound on my arm throbs. Even after sitting sullenly on a park bench for a half hour, the claw marks won't close. The black fluid seeps through my sweater, so that anyone who walks by would be able to see it . . . if they could see any part of me at all. Tiny green sprigs of the earliest grass poke through the dirt beneath my feet, but they slowly turn black and shrivel again the longer I sit there. I'm sucking the life from them, just like I'll suck the last energy from unsuspecting ghosts once I become a wraith. Guilt at causing even this small amount of harm forces me to my feet and I walk a little farther.

No one from the house has followed me. Who knows what Kelly told Jupiter and X? That they can't save me. That even if they do, it's pointless, because delivering me to Afterlife is the same as taking me to HELL. There's nothing after it. It's truly the end of the line. I thought I'd get a little more time. Respite to wash away the memories of my last horrible months of life.

I'm so caught up in my swirl of misery I don't notice the man standing on the sidewalk until I bump into him, and then I'm embarrassed, not just for the collision, but because he's wearing a hard hat, reflective safety vest, and heavy steel-toed boots. He couldn't be more visible if he tried.

"Oh, I'm so sorry," I say, realizing a second too late that I shouldn't have been able to bump into him in the first place.

Also, I know him.

"Ember?" Zach asks, looking as surprised as I feel.

"You!" I stumble back. "You were at the hospital. You left me behind."

At least he has the good manners to look sheepish. "Yeah. Sorry about that. Those quarantine jerks are assholes. I came back the next day to get you, but I couldn't find you."

Does he know? Kelly said reapers lie to get ghosts to go with them to Afterlife. So all of Zach's promises of a condo and amenities were just a scam. What a shithead. I liked Zach. Maybe not the whole ditching me to the monsters and jerks part, but I liked his can-do attitude and his focus on customer service. Better than Kelly's silence and Minerva's bureaucracy. Turns out he's not any better than the rest.

Before I can launch into my lecture about that lying to the recently deceased is the height of bad behaviour, an engine roars to life on my right. We're standing in front of a construction site. The skeleton of a massive three-story house sits on a dirt lot. Someone has turned on a generator, and it rumbles noisily near the sidewalk, while workers carry two by fours up a ladder. A team of four men in hats and vests like Zach's are on the roof, nailing down sheets of plywood.

Dread coils in the pit of my stomach.

"What are you doing here?" I ask. Reapers don't just pop up for no reason. If they're here, it's because they're working. Minerva sent them.

He checks his clipboard again, oblivious to the fact I know what he's up to. "Mihai Bacau. Aged forty-nine years, two-hundred and fifty-two days. Born Bucharest, Romania. Died—" His recitation is cut short by a cry from the roof where a man stands, holding his plywood. A gust of wind has caught it, lifting it like a sail. Mihai—presumably—shouts out as he is pulled off his feet. The workers around him all rush forward, their boots thumping heavily on the barely constructed roof, but Mihai is already being dragged toward the edge. None of the workers are wearing harnesses or anything that would secure them. He finally lets go of the plywood, but it's too late. Mihai plummets over the side, dropping to the ground with a sickening thud.

"Died just now," Zach says with a sigh. "Workplace accident."

I can barely hold on to my earlier anger. I may already be dead, but watching the end of someone else's life is horrific, especially something so preventable. What if he has a family? Friends he'd made plans to see after work? I hope the media finds out about this and runs his employer through the mud.

But then Mihai runs up to Zach, shouting in a language I don't understand. Romanian, I guess. Zach answers him, and Mihai drops to his knees, face buried in his hands as he sobs. Zach kneels, continuing to offer reassurances.

"Like any of that really matters," I say. I mean to be speaking to myself, but Zach throws me a look. I smirk. "Cold comfort, right? Why don't you tell him where you're really taking him?"

Zach tilts his head. "Where do you think I'm taking him?"

"Heaven?" Mihai asks in heavily accented English. "I go to heaven?"

I open my mouth to answer, but the words get stuck. What am I supposed to tell him? That they're lying? That he'll never see his family in Romania again, alive or dead? That he's better off staying here. Only he isn't, is he? Either he becomes a wraith or gets eaten by one. I tug my sleeve down, making sure it's covering my wrist. Zach's gaze follows the motion, and I can't say if he notices the black stain seeping through or not before I tuck the whole thing behind my back.

"Go on," I say, waving at them with my other hand. "Good luck, godspeed. Whatever it is I'm supposed to say here." The words sound hollow, and I hope Mihai's English language skills aren't solid enough for him to notice. The only thing worse than going to heaven knowing you're going to be wiped clean like a kitchen counter is being afraid on the journey.

"The condo's still available if you want it," Zach says to me. "I can only take one of you at a time, but I can come back."

Sure. His "condo."

"I'm good here." Unthinking, I wave him off and my stained sleeve betrays me, flopping back to reveal my hand. Zach's eyes widen as he sees it. He doesn't say anything, but his gaze is soft. Compassionate. It doesn't really matter, does it? Compassion or not, the end would be the same.

Mihai tugs at Zach, who replies in Romanian. He gives me what is probably supposed to be a reassuring smile, but only leaves me feeling both number and angrier than I did before. Then he and Mihai slide away, disappearing with a soft rush that's drowned out by the commotion still going on at the construction site as the workers gather around Mihai's lifeless body.

How are these my choices? It's not fair. None of it is fair. I did what I was supposed to do. I fought the cancer, and the cancer won. So I chose medically assisted dying because it was faster, painless, more convenient. For everyone, not just for me. Fewer days sitting by my bedside for my family. Fewer heart emojis on my social media posts where the Sparks told me to stay strong, even when I had no strength left. So I made the tough decision, closed my eyes, and accepted my fate.

But I can't accept this. This is the rawest of raw deals.

Ember's Life Tip #1: *If you want something done, do it yourself.*

I know how to get to Afterlife. All I have to do is hop the train at Lower Bay and I'll be there by dinnertime. I'm not taking no for an answer anymore. The organization is a shit show. All I have to do is be patient and wait for my opportunity to slip through the gates unnoticed. They can't delete me if they don't know I'm there, and they barely know I'm here, so how hard can it be?

But as I turn, something like a strong wind rushes up behind me, practically blowing me off my feet. My whole body goes cold, starting at my wrist before spreading up my arm and through my chest. The sensation changes, burning with the pain of a thousand needles poking under my skin. I look around, trying to find the source—or maybe for someone who can help me. My vision has changed. Everything has gone monochrome, turned shades of blue-grey. The shaken construction team, the paramedics who are just getting out of their ambulance. They're each surrounded by a radiant border, like they're being lit up from the inside. They pulse with the energy and all I can think for a second is I want to touch it. Take it. They're so alive. Everything I'm not. I need to—

I blink. The world slides back into soft, multi-coloured reality. As the invisible electrical current leaves me, I drop to the ground, breathing hard as I brace on my hands and knees.

What the hell was that?

Except I know. Even as it fades, my mangled arm is on fire. Panic swamps me with the idea that it might be spreading, rising higher up my body.

I can't go to Afterlife like this. They'll take one look at me on the subway platform and call for quarantine to beam me up.

The tapping sound of someone running in high heels on concrete catches my attention, and I stagger to my feet as a white woman with bouncing blonde curls and a green wool trench coat hurries up the sidewalk. She's crystal clear, and I blink a few times, making sure there's no shining light around her, but that vision is gone. When she sees me, her perfectly made-up face breaks into a smile, then slips into a more familiar elfin form.

"Ember! What are you doing here?" she asks. Something like iridescent butterfly wings waver behind her coat for a moment before vanishing again.

"Cerise?" I shift uncomfortably, thinking about running. Before I can though, she pulls me into a warm hug. I hold myself stiffly. Can she feel what just happened? I can. The buzz under my skin is faint but still there. Though as she holds on to me, it recedes even further. It's like the feeling of Jupiter's candles, or when Kelly is near.

I force myself to let go. She knows too. She lies to souls every day. Those children. The very idea makes me want to throw up. They're gone. Erased.

"Still hanging out with Kelly?" she asks as she steps back.

I laugh unsteadily. "Sort of. Not really."

She sniffs the air, eyes sparkling. I shrink away. Does decay have an odour? I never noticed anything with the wraiths I've seen so far, but we've already established my olfactory senses aren't what they used to be.

"Smells like hurt feelings. Did you two have a fight?" Her laughter trills on the breeze.

I should walk away, like I did with Zach. She can't wipe my identity if she doesn't take me to Afterlife. Unless she can. What do I really know about reaper powers?

Dear Sparks, sometimes you have to ask the scary question. Whether it's asking for a date or asking for a raise. People aren't mind readers, and they don't always know what you want unless you tell them. If you put all your cards on the table and don't get the hand you want, it might hurt in the short-term, but at least then you can move on.

"Kelly told me," I say. "About Minerva. About how she decided to make more room at Afterlife."

Cerise's fairy persona is already pale, her skin nearly opalescent. But somehow, she blanches even further.

"Kelly told you . . . about . . ." Her voice is shaky.

"You can't take me," I say, shoving up my sleeve. No point in hiding it anymore, especially not since it's gotten even worse. Black tendrils run under my skin where the veins used to be. If I were alive, it's the kind of thing that would send me straight to the ER, and probably into an isolation unit. "I'm already decaying."

Her eyes go wide. "Ember."

"It's really shitty," I say. "Lying to people. We haven't done anything to deserve that. But you make us think it's going to be better when it's not."

She nods. "I know."

"Who says you get to make the decision?" I ask, voice rising. "Who put you in charge? We're not children to be corralled at the end of playtime. You don't get to say when it's over."

"You're right." Her gaze is locked on the ground.

"If you all hate your jobs so much, the solution isn't to destroy the things that make humans human." I'm gaining momentum now. I need a soapbox. A flag to wave. "You should just walk away. You try living in a failing body for eighty years if you're lucky. The only thing that makes it bearable is the hope that maybe there's something more. Something better or easier that comes after. And there was, until you took it away!"

"Ember." She grabs hold of my shoulders, shaking me. "I know, all right? I agree with everything you're saying. A lot of us do. Even Kelly."

I snort. "Kelly doesn't care. They abdicated responsibility and moved out."

"Because Minerva threatened to downsize them. She'd strip every single ounce of their power and their immortality and leave them here to age and die."

Her voice is distraught, but I don't have much sympathy left. Because downsizing is the worst thing that can happen? Their quippy jokes about food poisoning and global warming are somehow worse than the options they've left us?

Cerise's expression is grim. A grim reaper. Well, tough shit. You don't get to play the role of supernatural warden and feel bad about it.

"Minerva said either they could implement the program or she would downsize them," Cerise repeats carefully, clearly trying to control her emotions since I can't be bothered to do the same with mine. "And if she could do that to Kelly, imagine what she could do to the rest of us. They're the most powerful of us all. So they left. It was their only option."

"You didn't sound nearly so concerned the other night at the bus crash." I fold my arms over my chest, then let go again when I realize I'm leaving a new stain where my wrist has landed just beneath my breasts.

She sighs. "I was angry. About a lot of things. I shouldn't have taken it out on them. I wish they were still fighting with us at Afterlife, but I understand why they aren't. We're trying to find other options, but . . ." Her gaze drifts over me, landing on the black mark on my sweater. The corners of her mouth drop down in a frown.

"But not for me," I say. It's too late for me. Thanks a lot, Lilah. There will be no ice cream in heaven for me, even if Cerise and the others were to get things turned around today.

She winces. "I don't know. Maybe. Once decay starts, it usually happens pretty quickly, but you're holding on. How long ago did that happen?"

I flex my fingers, feeling the tug on my torn skin. "A few days ago." I don't mention my little spell from right before she arrived. It feels like I'm losing a war of attrition. The last war, even. I thought I'd already fought this battle when I signed the MAID paperwork at the hospital. Looks like there was one more fight left, where I finally accept this is really truly the end of the road. If I admit defeat soon, maybe she can take me to Afterlife. It has to be better to just go blank than decay all the way to a wraith and hurt others before I go.

Her lips quirk like she's thinking about something. She says, "I might know a way. A special place. Give me a couple days to make sure it's safe. Go back to Kelly. They'll protect you."

Tears form in my eyes. It sounds so much like Minerva's empty promises. And the idea of going back to Kelly is practically painful. Because I'm still mad. Because they still lied. But there are all those candles that Jupiter carved in the living room. Maybe if we set them up in the backyard, along with a tent, I can hang out there and not have to talk to them. Cerise said a few days, and that's probably all I have in me, regardless of whether she finds a solution or the decay takes hold fully. At least we know Kelly can call the quarantine team ASAP if it comes to that.

I nod, swallowing down the lump in my throat. "Please hurry."

"I will. By the way," she says, looking around, "you haven't seen a dead construction worker, have you? I'm late. Got stuck negotiating with a soprano who choked on a chocolate-covered strawberry at a fundraiser for the Sydney Opera House. She refused to leave until she'd done her aria and wouldn't believe me that it was too late for that."

"You mean Mihai?"

Cerise rifles through her purse, which is about the size of a credit card. Yet somehow from within, she produces a normal-sized tablet and scrolls through the screen.

"Lemme see here. Done. Done." She rolls her eyes as she passes one particular name. "Ugh, never again. I'm not dealing with dictators anymore. Syphilis does wild things to the brain. Done. Done. Oh, here it is. Yes. Mihai Bacau. Age—"

"He's already gone," I say.

She wrinkles her nose in frustration. "Dammit. I really don't have time to be chasing after more people today."

"No. Not gone like he ran away. He was picked up. Zach was waiting for him."

"Zach?" She checks her screen again, frowning. "Says here he's . . ." Cerise lets out a heavy sigh. "See, this is what I'm talking about. Even with all of Minerva's updates and efficiencies, the whole place is a mess. Now I'm double booked. It's such a waste of resources. Whatever." She stuffs the tablet back into her purse. "I had to be in Ashgabat like twenty minutes ago. Earthquake. Don't you just hate days like this?" As she speaks, she slowly transforms so her blonde hair turns black, her white skin golden brown, and her trench coat turns into a long embroidered robe that brushes the sidewalk. She hugs me one more time. "I'll be back soon."

Before I can say anything, there's a pop and she slides away.

And I'm still here. Literally decaying on the sidewalk, and my only option is to go back to Kelly's judgement and apathy.

One way or the other, death is coming. For real this time.

nineteen

THERE'S NO TENT. And a stiff breeze that picks up and blows through Toronto means Jupiter's candles won't stay lit in the backyard. So I'm stuck inside again, giving Kelly the silent treatment and pretending the black marks in my arm aren't slowly passing my elbow.

At least inside, with the candles burning, I feel better. Or at least I don't feel any worse. The decay may be spreading, but I don't have any more moments where my vision goes black and white or I have the desire to jump on Carrot Stick and eat his soul.

Do cats even have souls? If I were talking to Kelly I would ask, but they would probably call me ridiculous and sentimental and never actually answer my question anyway, so instead I spend my time sitting at the kitchen table tracing runes carved into candle wax.

"Where did you even learn to do this?" I ask Jupiter.

"The internet," she says casually. "And library books. A lot of it was trial and error. You get a lot of woo-woo practitioners who promise you a high-definition conversation with Nana but all you really get is them reading platitudes from a fortune cookie. You can't assume all their advice is good. Some of them are just online for the views."

Don't I know it? People like that give content creators a bad name, and it's nearly impossible for the average person to tell the difference.

"We should start a coven," X says, gasping at the novelty of the suggestion. "Maybe have some meet ups. I could start a Discord server."

"Aren't covens for witches?" I ask while Jupiter pats his arm. Their relationship is unusual but sweet. She knows he's odd, but she likes him anyway. I hope they live long happy lives together and don't stress too much about the reaper asshattery that awaits them at the end.

Kelly walks into the kitchen, and we all go quiet. The three of us are sitting at the table. The upside to all my hard work tidying up is now there's space to hang out. We watch silently as they pull a bag of chips from the cupboard, then walk out again. The whole scene is very high school mean girls, but I'm not doing anything to change it. When I came back to the house, I told Jupiter what Kelly and Cerise had told me. No doubt she's let X into the conversation now too. They both deserve to know.

"You shouldn't scratch that," X says, motioning toward where I've been picking at my arm without realizing. "It might get infected."

The tips of my fingernails are black. I slide my fists into my sleeves and twist them in my lap. I pretend not to notice when Jupiter lights another candle.

"Pretty sure a staph infection is the least of my worries right now," I say.

No word from Cerise so far. I'm not sure what she can actually do in so little time. Everything seems to happen at Afterlife on the scale of years and decades, not days. It's probably hopeless, but hope has to be the most human of qualities, and mine refuses to die.

Kelly reappears in the kitchen door. They linger there for a second, looking uncertainly at us.

"Are we out of coffee or something?" Jupiter asks. Carrot Stick is licking a plate on the counter and pauses long enough to add his two cents to the conversation with a hiss.

"Bang just called," they say. Their voice lacks their usual factual flatness. Instead, they look uncomfortable. Good for them. "There are wraiths downtown. A lot of them."

Their gaze is on me, and the scrutiny makes me scratch at my wrist again.

"Pretty sure we both know my wraith hunting plan was a terrible one from the beginning."

Kelly's mouth quirks up on one side. "Not completely terrible."

But their softening attitude is too little too late. I say, "Like you said . . . Life coaches think we can teach things we haven't experienced. Even if we caught one that didn't want to kill us, what am I going to do? Hold their hands and tell them this is a safe space? That they have options and they can stop being a wraith if they just have a more positive outlook on life and try yoga? Oh, wait. They're already dead. There are no options. You made sure of that."

X leaps to his feet, applauding deliriously like a right-wing voter at a political rally. Jupiter tugs on his arm until he sits back down. He looks like he might protest, but she shakes her head wordlessly and he settles, looking hurt his display of support didn't have the desired effect.

Kelly shrugs, like they expected this reception. "I'm going to go see what's possible," they say. "Afterlife is a mess. If I can identify specifically how so many wraiths are falling through the cracks, I can prove Minerva's tactics aren't working. There have to be others who would support me if I had proof."

There are, but I won't give them the satisfaction of sharing that. Not yet. Also, the plan is still flimsy, even with better support from Kelly than before. Finding out where the wraiths are coming from won't fix the staffing or overcrowding issues at Afterlife. It just proves they have more problems to solve.

But if there is any chance it can make a difference to the people who die after me, I should help. I've got nothing left to lose, but if I can stop even one more person from going through any part of this bullshit, then maybe it'll be worth it.

"I'll go with you," I say, rising from the table. Even with the candles, the effort is exhausting, like on the worst days after chemo. The decay eats me from the inside. But Kelly puts a hand on my back to steady me, and it helps a little. I take a deep breath, staring down at my hands braced on the table. The back of one has also started to turn black.

"You don't have to," Kelly says softly.

I groan, in part from the effort of straightening fully, in part because they're wrong.

"No, I do," I say. "Your bedside manner sucks. Even if you find a wraith who's still with it enough to understand you want to help, you'll do a terrible job at convincing them."

"I can go too," Jupiter says, standing as well. "If you want to talk to the wraiths, I can try to help."

The statement has Kelly leaping to the front door, blocking the way like she's about to make a break for it.

"Out of the question."

"Not sure you get a say." She grabs a hoodie from where it's been tossed on the sofa. "Ember's running out of time, and everything we've found out about how Afterlife works reminds me of the time I got a part-time job at a tattoo parlour down on Lakeshore where the owner came to work drunk every day. You've never seen so many misspellings and wobbly roses in your life. So I'm with Ember on this one; you can't be trusted."

I ignore the part about me running out of time. We don't have to state the obvious. But having her stick up for me is a relief. The two of us together can soften the spikiest of Kelly's rough edges.

"Wait," X says slowly. "Are we going ghost hunting?" He glances between us nervously.

"Wraith hunting," Kelly says, sounding annoyed at the growing movement to hijack their plan. "It's a completely different thing and very dangerous."

"Right. Right. Very serious too. Of course." He also rises, stretching his arms overhead and twisting side to side. "Count me in. If Jupiter's going, so will I."

Normally, X wouldn't be my first choice as a partner in this mission, but under normal circumstances, would I know this mission existed? And he and Jupiter are a package deal, it seems, so I loop my arms through each of theirs. We're either about to start a musical number, or we look like heroes about to take on the world.

"You're getting your goo on me," X whispers in my ear, glancing down at where my wrist presses over his forearm. Jupiter clears her throat, and he seems to realize he's spoiling the moment, lifting his chin to return Kelly's stare.

They sigh, shaking their head.

"This is a terrible idea," they say.

"Yup." I do my best to smile. Fake it 'til you make it. For all my effort providing helpful tips and actionable steps on how to craft the life you want, sometimes that's the best tip of all. "Terrible idea. Let's go."

We slide to the corner of York Street and Bremner Boulevard.

"Oh no," I say.

"Stay here," Kelly says before sliding back to the house. We have recently—as in just now—learned the all-powerful reaper isn't quite so all powerful. Sliding a ghost and two very-much-alive mediums in one go turned out to be like trying to carry all the grocery bags into the house at once. The way Jupiter shrieked made it sound like we were about to leave part of her at the bungalow, so we decided it was better to be transported one at a time.

Wish I'd gone last, though, because now I'm stuck standing alone on a street corner staring down the throng of people gathered in what the city officially calls Maple Leaf Square and affectionately calls Jurassic Park. We're in the densest part of downtown, especially on a game day. The intersection of York and Bremner is a block from two major league sports venues, the city's largest convention centre, the aquarium, and the CN Tower where Kelly and I first talked to Bang just a few days ago. On a good day, it can take twenty minutes in a car to make the crawl south from here to the Gardiner Expressway running along the waterfront. On a bad day, it can flood so badly in the rain that pedestrians are left walking through knee-deep water. Also, it's never not under construction, which only makes things worse.

Tonight, it's where people are gathered for playoffs to participate in what has to be one of the biggest tailgate parties in the country. The last block of Bremner is closed with orange barricades, while police cars line the street beyond on either side. Thousands of red-jerseyed fans have gathered on the street carrying horns and banners and cardboard signs. They're watching the Raptors play on the giant screen mounted outside the arena. It can be seen from blocks away, which is good, because even beyond the official boundaries of the square, people are backed up on the sidewalk and in the middle of the streets, cheering for their team.

A chill runs up my spine as a wraith swoops overhead. Its cackle can be heard even over the chanting crowds. I try to duck out of the way as fans walk toward me, but there's nowhere to go, so I have to close my eyes and ignore the unnerving sensation of living bodies passing through me.

Kelly and Jupiter appear on the sidewalk.

"Woah." Jupiter staggers briefly, holding on to Kelly's sleeve. I step in close because Kelly still has the effect of a rock in the stream, and fans dodge around us, giving me a chance to relax.

Unfortunately, Kelly slides away one last time. We're immediately swarmed by people. Jupiter sidesteps, and I follow. Once she bumps through my shoulder and throws an apologetic smile in my direction.

"The wraiths?" she asks.

"Up there." I point overhead. A dozen or so spectral forms float in the sky, swirling like a whirlpool.

"I can feel them." She makes a gagging sound that doesn't seem forced at all. "So gross. What are they doing?"

"Hanging out?" I suggest. "Usually, they're way more with the diving and terrifying people."

They trail in the sky, glowing like menacing comets. Toronto at night is lit up with flashing signs, cars and highway billboards that reflect off glass-covered condos and office towers. The wraiths are different. There's no reflection. More like they swallow the light around them, blocking out the urban glow above.

"Was it like this in Quebec City?" Jupiter asks.

"It had already started in Quebec," I say. "This is more like . . . they're waiting for something." Or they're waiting for everyone else to join the party. As we stand there, the whirlpool grows wider as more and more wraiths appear. My throat goes dry. Whatever is happening, it's bigger than the hotel.

A cheer erupts from the front of the crowd, rippling backward toward us. People jump and scream, and the wraiths scream with them, though they still don't approach.

"Woah, what's the score?"

X and Kelly have slid in beside us. Kelly's attention is already on the wraiths. X, of course, is focused on the big screen in the distance. Something happens—I'm not exactly a basketball fan—that makes everyone cheer again, even louder than before. The people around us start jumping up and down. X joins them, high-fiving two guys standing in front of us. I bump against Kelly's chest and they put an arm around me. It's a strangely intimate gesture. We've never talked about it, but they clearly know the contact helps steady me—all ghosts, presumably. But being close like this is a different experience. It fills me, and I relax into it without any resistance. I can almost feel the coolness of the evening air on my skin. I inhale, half convinced I can smell the crush of bodies and the distant wafting scent of hot dog carts.

The wraiths screech overhead, circling lower and lower. Even with Kelly's natural buffer, there are so many fans around us they get jostled and let go of me. I faceplant into the back of a man wearing a number 7 jersey.

"This many people isn't safe," I say, extricating myself. Getting a few hundred frightened wedding guests out of the hotel ballroom was hard enough. Thousands of hyped-up basketball fans? Impossible.

"They're coming from over there." Kelly points away from the crowd of fans, down Bremner. The gathered wraiths are so thick it's like a storm cloud, and more are floating up from the old railroad roundhouse across from the aquarium. The roundhouse is a restored semicircular building that was originally used for railyard maintenance, though these days it's equal parts museum, brewery, and event space. When I was a kid, my mom and I came down here for an open house and I pretended it was haunted. The old railcars in front seemed like the perfect place for spooky entities to lurk, waiting to jump out and scare a seven-year-old girl playing hooky from school with her mom.

Turns out I might have been right after all.

"You have to start moving people out of the way," I tell Jupiter. "When the wraiths finally break, it's going to be a nightmare in here." The arena forms the end of a dead-end street, and skyscrapers line the way out on both sides. Office towers and condos that stretch upward for sixty stories and the police barricades further restrict opportunities to exit. If the wraiths attack, people will be penned in.

"Me?" Jupiter asks. "Why me? I want to help you and Kelly."

"That is helping. Because they can't see me and Kelly won't—" I glance at them, but they're already walking toward the roundhouse. "You two have to help them."

"How do we do that?" X asks, attention still on the game.

I wave at them, following after Kelly. "I don't know. Pull the fire alarm or something."

"The fire alarm outside?" Jupiter sounds even more confused, but I don't get a chance to answer before multiple people walk through me and around me. The crowd erupts in a fresh round of cheering, louder than before. It must be some kind of signal, because an echoing scream comes from above. The crowd sounds joyous and elated. The wraiths sound hungry.

Like a swarm of ravenous hunters, they drop out of the sky to the unsuspecting people below.

chapter
twenty

"KELLY!" I call. For once, they turn around. I point at the descending mob of wailing wraiths. They watch for a moment, face unexpectedly grave with concern.

"We can't help them," they say, which is the response I expected, even though it's still infuriating.

"But the people," I say. "Jupiter."

"You told her what to do. Do you want to have a conversation with one of these things or not? Those ones are too far gone. All they'll do is try to consume you. Let's see where they're coming from."

I watch for a second longer. The effect is small at first. The cheering crowd swells again, but soon the cheers change to something else. Louder. More afraid. The people in the middle push toward the outside like they're trying to escape a threat, even if they can't see what it is.

But as much as I hate to say it, Kelly's right. Jupiter knows what's going on, and the living aren't my problem anymore. I've helped as many as I'm going to help in my lifetime. All I can do is help their afterlifetime now.

The roundhouse is dark. The antique train cars sit like silent sentries in front and wraiths fly from the massive open doorways beyond.

"This way," Kelly says, heading toward a side door. I stick close. The screaming from the square is getting louder and it seems to excite the wraiths. They rush past us with a woosh.

"Why are they leaving me alone?" I ask. Not that I should be questioning my good fortune, such as it is. One screeches past me, too close for comfort, but it doesn't even give me a backward glance. "I thought you said they hunt ghosts first."

"They may not see you as completely a ghost anymore," they say, almost apologetically.

I put a hand to my wrist. At least all this downtown supernatural adventure has taken my mind off the state of my . . . what? Soul? Existence? Leave it to Kelly to remind me at the worst possible time.

"See," I say, "this is what I mean about needing to work on your people skills."

They glance over their shoulder. "If I knew anything about what was happening right now, I'd have more than a ghost and two snappy-go-ducky psychics as backup."

I burst out laughing. Kelly scowls. It's kind of adorable. If we survive this, maybe I'll explain. "Happy-go-lucky" was ambitious for them anyway.

Still, the fact they don't know doesn't bring me much comfort. At the bus accident, the feeling of the wraiths was frenzy, like the pull of so many dead souls in one place was irresistible. At the wedding, the feeling was different. Malice. Mischief. Like boys playing pranks and enjoying watching the chaos unfold.

This, though . . . This is hungry. Predatory. The wraiths are hunting.

We step inside the roundhouse. The interior is pitch black, except for where the emergency exit signs spill red pools on the floor. Kelly and I creep forward. Finally, the space goes quiet. Empty.

"Are we too late?" I ask.

Kelly's unnaturally still, listening for something I don't think I'll ever be able to hear.

"This way," they say.

We make our way through the cavernous space. It's all wood and concrete, and the absence of our footsteps echoing on the floor is unnerving. But the silence also means we're able to hear the sound of whispered voices coming toward us from behind one of the railcars parked inside.

"Shh. Keep quiet."

"But where are we?"

"I don't know. A warehouse, maybe?"

"What happened?"

"I was just about to ask you myself," Kelly says as we come around the corner. On the ground, two women scream.

"A little tact?" I ask, which unfortunately only makes them scream more. Okay, so they're not alive. Not if they can see and hear both of us. "I think you're scaring them."

"Get away!"

Even in the dim space, they emanate some kind of light on their own, so they're visible if a little shadowed. It's different from the kind I see around X and Jupiter sometimes, or the way the living people glowed when I had that spell at the construction accident. They're two white women, both in their early twenties. No prom dresses at least, but they're also not dressed for the game. No jerseys, no team colours. In fact, they're dressed like they're about to head off on an arctic expedition. Heavy coats with fur hoods. Thick-soled boots tied halfway up their calves.

"Where are we?" the younger of the two ask me.

"Toronto. The roundhouse."

"Toronto?" the other one says. They're huddled close together and both look terrified. "How did we get to Toronto?"

"Where did you come from?" I ask.

"Did you come with the wraiths?" Kelly asks.

"Nova Scotia," the older of the two women says, looking around nervously.

"Heaven," the other says. "We were getting ice cream."

Again with the ice cream.

"Nova Scotia?" I crouch down so we're eye to eye.

"Heaven?" Kelly asks, looming over them.

"What's the last thing you remember?" we ask at the same time. The unintended stereo effect is enough to calm them both, at least a little.

"The white room," one says.

"The colours," the other says.

"Why aren't you a wraith?" Kelly's studying them both suspiciously.

"I don't think they know what wraiths are, Kelly." I roll my eyes. Kelly may think having me and Jupiter and X for backup is dicey, but they're not an ace at this sort of thing either.

"Abigail?" The younger woman tugs on the older's sleeve.

"Who are you people?" the older woman asks. She's not actually old. Or even older than me. Only older than her companion, but now that I'm closer she really can't be more than twenty.

"When did you die?" I ask her.

"Abigail."

Kelly's hand settles on my shoulder. "Get back."

"What year is it?" Abigail asks.

"Ember." The hand on my shoulder gets tighter. They're not offering comfort in the face of the wraiths. It's a warning.

"What do you—" My question cuts off sharply when the younger woman tips her head back and lets out a shriek like a hawk dive-bombing a mouse. It's like Lilah all over again. I finally listen to Kelly's warning, scrambling backward. One second, she looks scared and mostly human, the next, her heavy hood flops back to reveal streaming tar-stained hair and dripping teeth. Her eyes are completely black and her smile is hungry.

Shit.

"Meg? Meg?" Abigail's voice rises with panic. She screams when Meg grabs her shoulder, talon-like fingernails ripping through her jacket and spilling ghostly down toward the floor.

"Get her," I say, pushing at Kelly. "We need her."

I expect them to argue. Tell me we can't save anyone. But, for once, they do as I say. Abigail screams as the wraith's claws rip at her, and Kelly wades in, pulling her free, even as Abigail calls out for a Meg who isn't there anymore.

"Take her home," I say.

Their eyes go wide. "Absolutely not."

Ah, well. Our ceasefire was nice while it lasted.

"We need to talk to her. Take her home and keep her there."

The wraith lunges for me. Kelly steps in at the last second, passing Abigail off to me. It's not like wrangling scared school kids. Abigail is a fully grown adult, and even if she's dead, she thinks she's fighting for her life. She kicks and pounds at me, and all I can do is hold on while she struggles and calls Meg's name.

Kelly and the wraith are locked together. The thing that was Meg howls, full of rage. They roll across the floor until they crash into a table holding what looks like an extensive model train set. The whole set-up rattles and the wraith screeches.

An explosion rocks the floor underneath us. Even Abigail stills in my grasp. The Meg wraith slips from Kelly's hold, but instead of heading for us, she soars into the air, making a loop of the round-house before swooping out one of the open doors. The sounds outside are utter chaos. People screaming and running. Smoke wafts through the city glow.

I shove Abigail at Kelly one more time. The fight seems to have gone out of her, and she essentially falls into their arms, sobbing.

"Take her home," I say. "Light every one of Jupiter's candles."

Finally, they understand.

"I can take you both." They hold out an arm, but I step back.

"I should go after Jupiter and X. They might be hurt."

"What are you going to do if they are?"

My answer stops short in my throat. What would I do? I want to help my friends, but a quick glance through the roundhouse doors shows what has become a stampede. The thousands of fans who thought they were here for a basketball game are now running for their lives. Wraiths dive-bomb them, knocking people to the ground where both wraith and victim disappear amid running feet. The cheering has become terrified screams. Chaos. That's what Kelly said, back when this all started. Batteries on the landfill of existence. No one will be able to see or hear me. Even if I find Jupiter, if she's hurt, I can't pull her to safety or call for help.

I can't help anyone out there.

Kelly's arm around me is strong and warm and I squeeze my eyes shut as we ride the split-second roller coaster to Etobicoke. We pop back into existence in the living room. Abigail is still crying, and when Kelly lets go of her, she crumples to the floor.

"Candles," I say.

After Kelly lights the first candle on the table, I feel solid enough that I can light the one by the front door. Abigail's sobbing doesn't get any quieter. Kelly lights the ones Jupiter had put out in the living room while I was recovering from my encounter with Lilah. I raid Jupiter's room and find a half dozen more, each with precise geometric designs carved into the wax. I bring them all to the living room and light them on the coffee table. As I straighten, I jump back at the sight of my reflection in the dark TV screen.

"It's strong energy," Kelly says. "There's a reason I stayed with Jupiter."

"You mean I could have been alive this whole time? Like this?"

"You're still not alive. Only more present." They blow out two of the candles on the table, and my blurry form on the screen vanishes.

"Bring it back," I say, waving my arms over my head, trying not to smile too brightly when the motion appears on the TV once more as Kelly relights the candles.

Carrot Stick has emerged from wherever he was napping and saunters into the living room. He winds himself around my ankles, and I can almost feel the soft brush of his fur. But his casual affection turns suddenly to horror when he spots Abigail where she's still weeping on the floor. Carrot Stick puffs up until he's an angry hissing ball. He leaps into the air, landing on the back of the sofa, spitting and yowling as he tries to scale the wall before he finally gets enough traction on the upholstery to launch himself out of the room. His claws skitter on the hallway floor as he makes a hasty retreat.

Abigail manages to pull herself together to look up at us through teary eyes. If it's possible for a ghost to look sick, she's doing it. All the others I've seen so far are the picture of health. The old woman with the tube in her throat at the hospital. The kids who must have suffered terrible injuries at the bus crash. All were fine as they left their bodies behind. Even me, though I'm a little worse for wear. But Abigail looks like a Victorian consumption patient dressed for an extreme mountain trek. Even her hood hangs limply around her shoulders, like the fur used to trim it came from roadkill, not something living and healthy. Her skin has the same bluish tinge of wraiths, but her gaze is lucid and fearful.

In short, she probably looks like me. Though a whole lot more confused.

"Who are you people?" she asks. "What's going on?"

I glance at Kelly, and they jerk their head toward her. Time to put my relationship skills to use. They're just here in case things go terribly wrong. And there's every chance they will. I was playing a hunch, that Jupiter's candles would be enough to stabilize Abigail so she could tell us what happened to her and where the other wraiths came from. But I have no idea how long the effect will last. If Lilah's and Meg's transformations are anything to go by, she could be trying to rip my throat out in a matter of seconds.

Still, for now she's scared and confused, so I drop down to my knees, scooting as close to her as I dare.

"This is Kelly. They're a . . ." I don't want to freak her out more, so I skip over that part. "My name is Ember. I'm a . . ." Oops. Also tricky. "I'm a life coach."

Her brows knit in even deeper confusion. "A life coach?"

Now is not the time. I hurry onward. "What's the last thing you remember?"

She has to take a couple deep breaths before she speaks. "We were getting ice cream."

"And then you died?"

Abigail looks at me with confusion. "No, we died in Nova Scotia in 1997. We were going winter camping. Meg said she was going to get water, but she got too close to the edge of the river and fell in. I tried to save her, but I fell in too."

"Where does the ice cream fit into it?" I ask.

Abigail has slid out of her coat. Beneath, she's wearing only a tangerine-coloured T-shirt, and while she's been speaking, she picks at her arms in a nervous gesture, scratching and tugging at the skin. In some places, small welts appear where she's dug a little too deeply, but instead of shiny red blood welling up, something thicker and dark slowly oozes out. It's an all-too familiar sight. I glance up at Kelly and they look just as worried as I feel. My decay may be progressing slowly, but with Abigail, we can't be sure we have much time left.

"There's ice cream every day," she says, like she doesn't even understand why I'm asking the question.

"In heaven?" I ask and she nods.

Kelly snorts. "Don't be silly. Why would they give you ice cream when you don't even—"

I throw a hand behind me, unwilling to look away from Abigail. If they blow it right now and tell her she's not supposed to have any memories of heaven, we'll never make any progress. My palm collides with their shin and the contact is enough to distract them for a second so I can speak before Kelly alienates Abigail completely with their superiority.

"You were in heaven?" I ask.

But Abigail's eyes narrow as she studies Kelly.

"I know what you are," she says. "You're a reaper. You're from Afterlife, aren't you?"

Kelly's brows knit with confusion. "You know me?"

She sneers. The expression is a surprise after her confusion. "I know where you're from. What you represent. Where we were was perfect. Meg and I had an apartment. No one gave us a hard time for being together. It was like the life we'd dreamed about back in Antigonish, only better since we weren't broke all the time." Abigail may not be aware, but she's got a finger on her free hand halfway into a sore on her forearm, rooting around while she talks. The nails on her other fingers have grown longer, like claws.

"Since 1997?" I ask, glancing nervously at Kelly, trying to signal them silently, but all their attention is on Abigail.

"That's not possible," they say. "Minerva implemented the erasure program around 1955. But the end of the century, she—"

"We would never choose that," Abigail insists. "Zach told us—"

"Zach?" I gasp at the unexpected name. "What does Zach have to—"

The sound of breaking glass cuts me off, followed by a woman's scream. Carrot Stick wails in the hallway. The window in the front door is shattered, and the empty space is filled with a dozen swirling moaning wraiths. They claw at the jagged edges of the glass still in its frame, but some invisible barrier keeps them from entering the house.

"The runes," Kelly says, standing in the kitchen. "Jupiter's runes in the foundation will keep them out."

A slippery taloned hand reaches through the opening, dragging over the door with a sound like the worst nails on a chalkboard.

"Are you sure about that?"

They're not exactly rushing in, but they're not giving up

either. They shriek and struggle, pushing against each other and whatever power Jupiter's runes have to keep them at bay.

"Bang," Kelly says to the air. "Bang, pick up. We need help."

Another window shatters, this time in the living room. Abigail screams again. She's curled up in the far corner of the couch, her battered coat in front of her like a down shield. There's enough humanity left in her that she can see the threat, but even so, the tears that run down her cheeks are black and gooey, and even her fingernails have grown over the last few moments until they look more like claws.

A third crash comes, this time from the direction of the side door. Jupiter's going to have some serious explaining to do with her landlord when she gets back. *If* she gets back. I hope she's okay.

"Are these the wraiths from downtown?" I ask. If they aren't, Toronto is dealing with a serious infestation. Raccoons have been king for decades, but wraiths may take the crown when it comes to suburban mayhem.

"Bang!" Kelly shouts, and the way their voice rises with fear just makes me even more frightened. Finally, though, they take a deep breath, and the power I always feel from them pours clear with relief. "Holy shoot, Bang, where have you been? We need help. Send a team. Send Cerise. Whoever you've got. What? No. Wraiths. A lot of them. We're trapped."

The wailing around the house drowns out Kelly's pleas as the wraiths try everything to find a point of entry. Carrot Stick howls and squeezes himself under the couch. Abigail sobs. I crouch down at the edge of the sofa, waiting for our invisible fortifications to give way, as claws and insubstantial forms keep assaulting the barrier.

"It's okay, it's okay," I say over and over, even though no one can hear me over the wraiths. The rune barricade finally gives way, and they pour through the broken windows.

Dear Sparks, we're not getting out of this—dead or alive.

chapter
twenty-one

ABIGAIL SCREAMS and even a wailing Carrot Stick can be heard over the wild shrieking laughter. I close my eyes, thinking about the solid wall behind me, but whether it's my mounting panic or the grounding influence of the candles, I can't roadrunner my way through it into the room on the other side.

"Help!" Abigail screams as a wraith slithers toward her, gnashing its teeth. She scrambles up the back of the sofa, much like Carrot Stick did when she first arrived, but there's nowhere for her to go. I try to reach to pull her down beside me, but she's just beyond my grasp.

"Help me!"

At first I assume the plea is from Abigail, but when it comes a second time, I realize it's coming from the wraith. I've never heard one speak before. Moan, yes. Scream. Laugh. But never use words.

Abigail gasps. "Meg?"

"Abi. Help me." Her words are garbled like they're being spoken from behind too many teeth, but it's definitely words and not sounds. The wraith is close enough it should be able to attack her, but all it does is reach for her, like it's genuinely hoping for assistance.

"Ember!" Kelly calls. "Watch out!"

Beyond the shattered living room window, a blue glow consumes the darkened street. It fills the window frame and gets brighter, disintegrating the wraiths who are still trying to get inside.

I have just enough time to flatten myself on the carpet before the screaming in the house turns from ravenous ecstasy to furious rage. The beam goes on longer than it ever has before, and when it's over, the whole room is unnervingly silent. My ears ring, refusing to believe the attack is over just as quickly as it began. When I finally open my eyes, blue sparks are still shooting over the carpet. Carrot Stick is sitting on the opposite side of the room, and his whiskers curl where they've been singed, but he daintily licks a paw like nothing out of the ordinary has happened.

"Kelly? Kelly are you in there?" Cerise is in the door, eyes wide as she takes in the damage.

"I'm fine," Kelly says, standing carefully. They must have also hit the deck right before the blue doom beam shot through the whole house. Like Carrot Stick, they're looking a little crispy around the edges, and they grimace as they pick a shard of glass from their palm and drop it to the floor.

"Abigail—" I whirl around, but she's gone. The sofa is charred, and black scorch marks on the wall in the shape of flailing arms make me turn away.

"What the heck was that?" Cerise asks. She's got her silvery white hair twisted up in Marilyn Monroe–style femme fatale curls.

"It was a shoot show. That's what it was." The sounds of boots crunching more glass precedes Goran as he stomps through the front door. He looks even more intimidating than he did the night of the bus crash. His scowl is so deep his face might as well be stuck like that.

"Do you mean a shit show?" I ask, rising.

"What is all of this?" he asks, ignoring me as he points at the candles still burning on the kitchen table. With one strong breath, he blows them all out. The effect is so sudden that I drop to my knees again, shaking as all their power vanishes with their smoke. "Do you know the kind of magic you're dealing with? What were you thinking?"

For once, Kelly doesn't have a snappy comeback. They open and close their mouth a few times, then glance at me. Here we go. Throw the ghost under the supernatural bus. They're not even wrong. I was the one who told them to light all the candles.

But they remain silent. Cerise watches them, worried, while Goran scoffs.

"Do you know what's happening downtown right now?" he asks. "My team has their hands full, and you're out here lighting these things like fireworks and drawing every wraith in a ten-mile radius to you. I do not have time to split my workforce like this."

"Maybe they were trying to help?" Cerise asks hopefully, attempting to defuse the tension mounting between Kelly and Goran. "Divide and conquer?" She looks at me. "That's the expression, right?"

Great. One of them finally checks with me before saying something silly, and the last thing I need is scrutiny from three reapers.

I nod stiffly. "Yeah. That's how you say it."

"Listen, we have to talk," Kelly says, stepping between us.

But Goran isn't interested in what Kelly has to say. He pushes past them until he's standing right in front of me.

"Are you a wraith? How did you get past—"

"Listen," Kelly says, pulling at Goran's shoulder. Kelly's always taller than most of the humans around them, but Goran is just as tall, and he's currently got shoulders the width of a minivan. In his dark fatigues, he looks like a cover model for one of those vintage *Soldier of Fortune* magazines.

"What?" he asks on a growl.

"Those weren't wraiths."

Goran looks incredulous. "What do you think they were? Ponies? Bronies?"

"That's not what bronies are," I mutter, which earns me a glare from Goran and a warning glance from Kelly. I mimic zipping my lips shut.

"They were going after the living. Some of them were sentient," Kelly insists.

"Meg spoke to Abigail." I can't help myself. "She asked for help."

"So you started collecting them? Setting a beacon in case any others needed a place to sleep? Do you know how much trouble you're in right now? You deliberately undermined WQU operations creating a secondary site. The wraiths downtown were—"

"They're *not* wraiths," Kelly insists.

"Then what are they?" Cerise asks.

Goran doesn't care, though. "Whatever they are, you left Afterlife, and you're still enjoying the perks. That ends now. Bang!"

I will never get used to that. I jump like I'm the one who's been shot. But Goran's command is followed by a weary sigh as Bang appears in the living room.

"You rang?" she asks. She's dressed like a Catholic school girl in a kilt and collared shirt and clutching a tablet. She takes in her surroundings with wide eyes behind her ever-present glasses. "Yikes. What happened here?"

"Start the process for a downsizing. I'll get Minerva to sign off on it later." Goran looks meaningfully at Kelly.

Cerise gasps, putting her hands to her mouth. Bang pales, looking shocked.

"A downsizing?"

Goran sneers as he gestures to the candles on the table. "We gave Kelly enough rope to hang someone, and in the end they did it to themself."

I wince, trying to follow where Goran made the wrong turns,

but whether he got the expression right, it almost makes sense. Also, that's really not the priority right now. Cerise looks stricken. Bang looks downright terrified. I twitch, tucking my blackened hand into my sleeve, trying to think of something to say to appease Goran. He can't really do what he's suggesting, can he?

"Are you sure that's necessary?" Bang asks.

Goran waves his hands around. "We nearly lost the whole neighbourhood."

"Don't be ridiculous. The swarm barely got in the house." Kelly sounds far less concerned with this whole turn of events than literally anyone else in the room.

"Reckless use of powers, especially when it endangers ghosts and other reapers, is grounds for downsizing. This kind of meddling puts us all at risk. Do it, or I'll report you and everyone else here to Minerva for breach of protocol." Goran crowds into Bang's space, bearing down on her intimidatingly. He's a bully, through and through.

"Come on," Cerise says. "You're overreacting. It's Kelly."

Goran clearly has no interest in negotiating or listening to Cerise's plea for compassion. He just keeps looming over Bang, who hunches in protectively, glancing between him and Kelly.

"It's fine," they say finally, but the flicker of sympathy that washes over their face again is enough to turn my stomach. Whatever is happening, it's anything but fine.

"I'm really sorry," Bang says.

"What? No. What are you doing?" Cerise asks, but she can't stop Bang before the smaller reaper pokes at a few buttons on her tablet, then turns the screen toward Goran, who squiggles a finger over it like he's signing for a package. A second later, it's like the candles going out again, only worse. Every muscle in my body seems to give way all at once, while a zillion invisible bees take root under my skin. I drop to the floor gasping, and my vision goes blurry.

"Good. You." He points to one of the soldiers standing just

outside the front door. "Stay here and make sure there are no more wraiths. The rest of you, head out."

"But what about—" Cerise starts to say.

"Now," he barks, making Bang and Cerise snap to attention. Somewhere close by, Carrot Stick hisses.

There's a rushing, followed by the tinkle of shards of glass. I struggle to find the coordination to look at what's happening, and when I finally do, the living room is empty except for me and Kelly. The windows are back in their frames, with no sign the wraiths were ever here.

"Kelly." I drag myself up to my knees. They're still standing where they were, hands in their pockets. But they waver on their feet, then finally slump down to the couch. "What just happened?"

They pull their hands free, staring at their palms like they've never seen them before.

"I've been downsized." Their voice is faint. Stunned. "I've been completely disconnected from Afterlife."

On shaking limbs, I crawl to the couch. My hands go through it when I push on the cushions, but after a few deep breaths, I manage to pull myself up until I'm sitting next to them. I don't understand. Jupiter's candles are still burning brightly. Why am I like this? Was it Kelly keeping me from decaying all along?

"But you'll be okay, right? Give it a day, call Bang, and she'll undo it when Goran's less pissed off?" I can almost feel them. Or their power. The steadying wave that always announces their arrival. It's not gone entirely, but it's fading. The last remnants of ice melting in a cup on a sunny day.

They hunch forward, clasping their hands between their knees. Their usual skin tone is pale, but now they've blanched until they're bone white.

Suddenly, they lurch to their feet. "I need some air."

"Kelly? Kelly, wait." But with only the candles for help, I'm left tripping and stumbling as I try to keep up. "Wait. Hang on!"

They stride out the front door, leaving it open behind them. My legs wobble like I've just finished running a marathon. They're already to the sidewalk and I'm barely down the stairs. I can't lose them.

"Kelly? Ember?" Jupiter and X are coming up the street from the opposite direction. X is limping, but Jupiter hurries when she sees us. "Hey, are you okay?"

"Jupiter. Stop them. Something happened." I trip and fall, sprawling on the lawn. I'm not going to catch them. It has to be Jupiter. Who knows where Kelly is going or what they'll do?

"What do you mean?" X asks, but I never take my eyes off Kelly's back. They're barefoot and still in the sweats and T-shirt they wore while the rest of us stared them down at the kitchen table. This is all my fault. I'm the one who insisted on chasing wraiths. Kelly was fine here. Under the radar. I was scared and self-ish, and they've paid for it.

"Kelly? Where are you going?" Jupiter calls. "Ember? What's going on?"

She can't see me but I wave her away nonetheless. "Go after them. They've been downsized."

"What does that mean?"

"Didn't Kelly already quit?" X asks.

We're all so caught up in our various confusion and misery, no one sees the one lingering wraith lurking in the neighbour's rose bush until it zips out and descends on Kelly, claws digging into their back with a triumphant screech. They go down hard on the sidewalk.

"Kelly!" I call, but I can barely find the energy to run. I have nothing in me to fight a wraith.

A hand closes around my wrist. I whirl. I may not be up for a battle, but I'm going to try.

Only it's not a wraith who has me.

It's Cerise. The only recognizable feature is the iridescent strand of white hair that falls out of the black ball cap she has on, along with wearing head-to-toe black too.

"What are you . . ." I try to ask. The wraith screams behind me.

"Come with me," she says on a whisper.

"Come with you? Where?"

"Kelly!" Jupiter calls out. "X, help me!" They're running toward where Kelly is pinned on the ground while the wraith snaps and snarls.

"Come on." Cerise pulls harder. "While everyone's distracted. I can get you in."

Amidst the panic, part of me stills. Calms.

"Get me in? In where?"

She purses her lips in exasperation. "Where do you think? I told you to give me a day or two. I thought you understood that meant keeping out of trouble."

If my heart still beat, it would be pounding.

"Now?" I ask, glancing where she has my blackened hand in a tight grip. "I thought—"

"Yes, now. There's a place I can take you. This is your one shot, do you understand?"

Do I? Do I want this? But Kelly. I need to help Kelly.

"You'll keep your memories," Cerise says. "But only if you come with me this second."

In everything, I'd forgotten about that. About Minerva's belief in efficiency above all else. If the choice was between saving Kelly or oblivion, I might choose Kelly. Not like I have anything to lose.

But if it's a choice between Kelly and myself . . .

I look back one more time. X has joined the fray, along with the soldier Goran left behind. It's not pretty, but they wrestle the wraith away from Kelly long enough for them to scramble out of clawing distance. A shock of red pours down their temple. They don't glance in my direction, not even for a moment.

Ember's Life Tip #21: *Putting yourself first doesn't make you selfish.*

In a choice between Kelly and myself, Kelly would want me to choose me. They never wanted to be my sidekick in the first place.

"Okay," I say. "Let's go."

Dear Sparks, whatever happens next, thanks for being part of my life and afterlife. Look out for one another. The world is so much bigger and weirder than I ever expected.

chapter
twenty-two

WHAT HAPPENS NEXT IS a series of slides so fast I only have a second to see flashes of lights as we move from one point to the next. Sometimes I think I see glimpses of familiar landmarks, but they happen so quickly it might just be my mind filling in blanks.

Sliding with Kelly was a lot smoother. But Cerise's grip on me is tight, so at least I don't worry she's going to drop me as we zip from one place to the next.

We don't take the subway at Lower Bay, which makes sense. I can't see the guards with their decay scanners at intake looking real favourably on my injured arm. Finally, the endless whir of blinking lights turns into a long string of white, like we're in a glowing tunnel. A rushing sound signals the end of the trip, and I'm flung out of Cerise's arms. At least the landing is soft. My face is being cradled by the feathers of a thousand doves.

Okay, it's just a pillow.

I open one eye. I'm in bed. A cozy one. Along with the pillow, the comforter has to have been made with the down of a million baby angels. I can actually feel the slide of cool sheets against my skin too. So much of my existence lately has been a sort of numb awareness of human things that to really *feel* something is the most luxurious thing I've ever experienced.

"You okay?" Cerise asks. She looks positively ragged. Her dark clothes have been replaced with a white shift dress, and her hair is a swirly white rat's nest over her head.

"Maybe." I take inventory. Toes, feet, legs, hips. So far, so good. Chest, shoulders, arms, hands—one black, one not. Overall, everything where it should be and moving as well as can be expected. It takes a few blinks to get my eyes to focus because everything is shockingly white, but it turns out that's not a remnant of our little trans-dimensional road trip, only because the room is, in fact, whiter than fresh snow in a field on a sunny day. If I stay here long enough, I might get a tan.

"Is this heaven?" I ask, awestruck. "Did we make it?"

"Yes," Cerise says, but instead of looking pleased with herself, she's rushing around the room, pulling the long floor-to-ceiling blinds that line three of the walls.

"What are you doing?" I ask, struggling to sit up. Something is wrong.

"Don't worry," she says, but she's whispering. "No one knows you're here."

That doesn't sound promising. I certainly wasn't expecting a parade and a welcome basket, but despite the swanky accommodations, the way Cerise is scurrying around like she doesn't want to be seen is not a good sign.

"Kelly?" I ask, trying to push down the sense of unease. I did it. Afterlife. I made it and I'm still me. "Is Kelly okay?" If sliding works with Cerise the way it did with Kelly, we're only a few seconds after the scene at the house. Kelly and X could still be fighting the wraith. Cerise should go back and help them.

"I don't know," she says. "It was a mess."

And Kelly was powerless to fight back. If there was one wraith, there might be more. No way they could defend themself. My hands tighten in the sheets at the very thought.

Cerise must see the concern on my face because she puts a comforting hand on my shoulder. I expect the usual surge of power. Not like I'm used to with Kelly, but Cerise hugged me on the street at the construction site and I could feel it then. It made me feel a little better, if only for a moment. But now there's nothing more than the pressure of her palm against my skin.

"Oh shit," I say, bunching the covers around me. No one told me part of finally getting to heaven would involve losing my clothes. So long leggings and floppy sweater, I guess.

"The things you were wearing looked a little worn out," Cerise says, going to a closet and pulling out a fluffy white robe, which I hurry to put on. "This will do for now. Once we get you settled in, you can wear anything you want . . . as long as it's white."

"Settled in?" I ask. "Am I not staying here?" I pull the robe up tight around my neck and explore. Along with the bedroom, there's a bathroom that consists entirely of a giant claw foot tub. Bubbles float lazily on top, and when I dip a hand in, the water beneath is just hot enough without being painful.

"It never gets cold," Cerise says with a smile. "And you never get dirty, so you can soak whenever you want for however long you want. And no, this is just the demo suite. This area isn't officially open yet, so no one should bother you while I . . ." Her smile fades as she glances up the hallway. The tension inside me returns. Something really is wrong.

"What aren't you telling me?" I ask.

"Nothing," she says, but the answer comes too quickly. If it really were nothing, she'd have more to say, but all she can do is keep glancing around her like a wraith might pop out of a closet at any moment. Finally, she sighs. "Sorry. I didn't think I'd have to bring you here so fast. I'm not . . ." Her gaze drops to where my hand dangles from the robe's oversized sleeve. "You should be okay. If you were going to turn into a wraith, you'd have done it by now. Once the decay is so obvious, it doesn't stop. I don't know how you made it this long. But this place should . . ." She bites her lip. I miss Kelly. They were annoying, but they were almost never uncertain. "Just stay in here, okay? I need to double-check some things. Talk to . . ." She's making a hasty exit now, gauzy white dress swishing softly as she heads for the door at the end of the hall. "Just stay, okay? For a little bit longer. Don't open the door to anyone but me."

Before I can reply, she slips out the door, closing it softly behind her. I'm left alone in the hallway of the white apartment, gaping. What is this? Don't leave? She said I'd keep my memories, but does that matter if I'm not allowed to leave this room? My hand is on the doorknob, ready to escape before I realize it, and only at the last second do I pause. Slow down. I'm safe. My consciousness is still intact. I should trust Cerise, right? At least for a little while.

It's time for Ember's Life Tips for What to Do When You Find Yourself in Unfamiliar Surroundings and Don't Know Who to Trust.

#1: *Don't panic.*

Pretty sure I borrowed that from someone, but it's still sensible. If this is heaven, great. If it's somewhere else, I'll fare better if I'm not bolting down the hall in nothing but a bathrobe. And, worst of all, if this has all been some elaborate scheme to trick me into voluntarily entering HELL, then it's already too late, and panicking will get me nothing.

#2: *Confirm what you know.*

What do I know? I'm dead. My name is Ember Munro. I was in Toronto, and now I'm . . . not.

I glance at my hands. One is the same as it has been my whole adult life. A pale mole on the back of my wrist. The one fingernail that got caught in a door at a drunken party in university and never grew back properly. Funny that didn't sort itself out, even in heaven. The other hand is black and wrinkled, but when I move my fingers and flex my wrist, there's no pain. No tension. I bend my elbow and everything feels fine. Even the little tendrils that were creeping under my skin like vines don't look like they reach as far as they did the last time I checked. Though I can't be sure.

What else do I know? I'm in some kind of Afterlife apartment. Along with the bedroom and the very literal bathroom, the last room is a large space with plush carpet, a long sofa that reminds me of the one at Kelly and Jupiter's . . . without the sagging cushions and pizza stains, a white dining room table that seats twelve, and a crystal chandelier that sparkles in a million colours. Also, the same massive floor-to-ceiling windows wrap around three sides of this room, just like the bedroom, which I'm not really sure how that's possible, but I suppose I shouldn't question heavenly architecture too closely.

The curtains aren't drawn here, though. In her haste to escape or take care of business or whatever it was Cerise needs to do, she forgot to close me in here.

"Woah," I say, sounding like Jupiter.

I must be at least thirty stories up, but whereas towers like this in Toronto would give you a view of the next condo building over, here we're looking over a sprawling valley. The sky is a dazzling blue, and the fields in every direction ripple with green grass and bright yellow flowers.

Tears prick in my eyes. Maybe this is heaven after all.

"Hey, Sparks," I say as I stare out the window. The sky is blue and cloudless. Perfect. "I made it. Didn't think I'd be able to show you what it's like, but here we are."

The last words are strangled as emotion swamps me. Relief. Gratitude. Grief. Worry. I thought I'd be happier once I was here. I need a distraction.

I wonder if I can get some ice cream.

Only one way to find out. I rush for the door, and it's only when I spot my blackened hand on the white handle that I remember I'm not supposed to go anywhere. I take a step back, considering my options. There's a small peephole in the door, and when I stand on my toes and peek outside, all I see is a long white corridor. It's empty. The space around me is completely soundless. No distant sound of a radio playing or people speaking in another unit. No whir of an air conditioner. Even my feet on the floor don't make much sound. It's unnerving. I go back to the bedroom, fumbling through the curtains Cerise drew until I find a latch on the window and push it open. A waft of fresh air blows through. It smells of pine and newly cut grass. More importantly, the gentle sounds of birds chirping follow. I breathe a long exhale, blowing out unease with it. This is okay. I'm going to be okay.

I take a bath. Why not? Cerise is right. The water is the perfect temperature. I close my eyes and let the heat seep into me.

But what about Kelly, Jupiter, and X? It feels wrong to be relaxing when I don't know what happened to them. Cerise said she'd find out, but I don't like having a middleman—middle reaper—between me and the outside world.

Something to get used to. My story among the living—and the cast-out reapers—is over. For real this time. I'll never really get to find out what happened to Kelly any more than I'll find out if Lindsey and her fiancée have a happy marriage, or if my mother ever figures out how to keep the squirrels out of the birdfeeder in the backyard.

I swish the bubbles around. They shift and collide against each other but never burst.

It takes a second to realize my hands beneath the water are the same colour.

"What?" I say, splashing as I lift them out of the water. Inky black trails off my right hand, trailing into the water before vanishing like it was never there at all. The skin beneath is perfect and pink. I stare at them, turning my hands back and forth, before dunking my whole body back under the water, swirling my arms for a moment before resurfacing. This time, I lift my whole arm out of the water. Perfect. Flesh-coloured. The only sign of anything left is a single line of black that circles my wrist. It's no wider than a string and anyone looking quickly might confuse it for a bracelet or tattoo.

Am I cured? Could it be that simple? I pull myself out of the bath. There is—of course—a stack of obscenely fluffy towels waiting on a little stool. I dry off, expecting the black to return, but it never does. I'm so excited I dance naked around the bedroom, bouncing up and down on the bed for a minute before flinging myself down, making angels against the sheets.

Dear Sparks, I did it. Soon, I'm going to write down everything that happened and figure out a way to post it so you can learn from my mistakes. Step one: don't take no for an answer. This all would have been so much easier if I'd made that first reaper take me along with Hazel.

Celebration complete, I wrap myself back up in the robe. The birds are still chirping, and the breeze through the window now smells more like a distant campfire. It's perfect. Idyllic.

What else is out there?

I'm back at the door. When I look through the peephole, the coast is still clear. Can I do this? I promised Cerise I'd stay here. But she was worried someone might see my hand and freak out. The robe sleeve covers my arm all the way to the wrist, and anyone who might notice the little black line won't think anything of it, right?

I won't go far. At the first sign of trouble, I'll come back up here and lie low. But what can go wrong? It's heaven. There are no wraiths. And if I learned anything in my mostly dead time with Kelly, it's that the staff at Afterlife is so strapped, no one has the time to stop me and ask how I got in here. If I'm past intake, they'll assume I came in like everyone else.

With a deep breath, I open the door and step into the hall.

chapter
twenty-three

IT'S EXACTLY like I thought it would be. The hall is empty, but I find an elevator at the end, and when I step inside, it only has one button, so I push it, then squeak as the whole car drops with a sudden lurch. In a matter of seconds, even though I had to descend thirty floors, the doors slide open again to reveal a sprawling lobby area with sleek couches, gently trickling fountains, and a gigantic television showing bright tropical fish bobbing in turquoise water above a reef. There are people gathered around, watching like it's the most stunning thing they've ever seen. A man in a white shirt and apron stands behind a bar handing out pastel smoothies, while a woman wearing similar clothes holds a clipboard and takes down names for an afternoon croquet tournament.

I hesitate for a second, but instead of questions about who let me in, I'm greeted with friendly smiles. No one even seems to care I'm dressed in a bathrobe. Cerise wasn't kidding, though. The people around me are dressed in a wide array of clothes, from ball gowns to T-shirts, flowing garments that look straight off a fashion show catwalk in the Middle East, to one woman who appears to have constructed a whole ensemble out of pool noodles. The only thing everyone has in common is they're all wearing white.

"Excuse me," the woman with the clipboard says as she approaches.

"Yes?" I ask, hoping my smile looks relaxed.

"You look lost," she says. "Can I help you find something? The spa, maybe?"

I clutch the robe closed protectively, though doing so makes the sleeve of my robe fall back. The clipboard woman doesn't so much as glance at my wrist.

"I'm just looking around," I say. She nods and hands me a printed piece of paper.

"Here's today's schedule. Hot stone massages in the spa all day, aqua aerobics in the small pool at noon, water volleyball in the big pool at one. Goat yoga this morning at ten and this afternoon at three thirty, and of course"—her smile grows—"ice cream at sunset."

I take the sheet. It's a schedule of events, like the ones you get in your room at all-inclusive resorts. It also lists a number of spiritual and religious services, from a Buddhist meditation to a committee meeting for resident members of the Satanic Temple before their upcoming holiday, Hexenacht.

"If you need anything, just use one of the courtesy phones. Someone will be right there to help you." The woman gives me one more quick smile before walking away.

A crash rings behind me. I whirl, ready for a fight, but all I find is a man in white coveralls standing by a ladder that must have fallen over.

"For God's sake, Carl," a voice rings over the atrium. "People are existing here. They don't need your incompetence."

Heads turn, and the aforementioned people part, ducking their heads almost respectfully. A man with a thousand-watt smile and a white suit strides through the opening. He may be smiling, but the way his gaze is locked on poor Carl says those thousand watts might zap him into whatever exists beyond the rolling fields if he doesn't get the response he wants.

It's Zach.

Carl practically folds in half at the waist in his haste to apologize.

"I'm sorry, sir. I was trying to change a lightbulb. Guess I'm not as steady as I used to be."

Abigail mentioned him, and in everything, I forgot. Seeing him now makes every hair on my dead body stand on end.

Zach walks right up to Carl until they're practically nose to nose. Others have gathered around, curious at the confrontation. I duck behind two tall men. Of all the people I could meet in my first hour in heaven, I didn't expect it to be Zach, but Cerise told me to stay in my room, and if he sees me, he may not be as understanding as she's been.

He stares down the sheepish Carl for a minute longer before breaking into a friendlier smile again. Zach claps Carl on the back, hard enough for the older man to rock on his feet.

"Don't worry about it," Zach says merrily. "Mistakes happen. You shouldn't have tried to do this on your own. Everyone, who can help Carl change this lightbulb?"

I don't know what's more surprising, that even in heaven they haven't figured out how to build a better lightbulb, or the way a half dozen people all surge forward like the opportunity to help an old man is a privilege that can't be passed up.

Unfortunately, the rush means my camouflage goes with it, and in the second it takes me to look around for cover, an arm loops through mine, pulling me toward the elevator.

"What are you doing?" Cerise hisses in my ear. "I told you to stay upstairs."

I don't resist as she drags me inside. Zach is surrounded by people, smiling indulgently as they vie for his attention. The two men I was standing behind have righted the ladder, and when Carl climbs to the top, a cheer goes up around him like he's just summited Everest.

The doors slide shut. Despite the fact we're going up, I once again get the same precipitous falling sensation, before the door opens again and we're back in the long white hall.

"How . . ." Trying to understand the physics makes my brain cramp.

"I wasn't even gone that long," Cerise mutters, still towing me along. "What if someone saw you? What if Zach—"

"Look." I wrench free, holding up my hand. "It's gone. I took a bath and it washed away."

She stops short, eyes going wide. I stand still, letting her study my arm from fingertips to elbow.

"That's not . . ." she stammers. "That's amazing."

"See?" I smile. "It's all good. I'm good. You don't have to worry."

And yet she's still chewing on her bottom lip nervously. She glances around like someone might be listening even though the unit she left me in is literally the only door in this hallway.

"What's going on?" I ask as I follow her inside. I didn't expect a celebration like Carl's triumph. What's overcoming eternal decay of your soul compared to changing a lightbulb? But I'd have thought she'd be relieved. Bringing me here was a risk, I know that, and the fact her magical bathtub sent our biggest issue down the drain should at least solve part of her problem.

Her lips are thin. "Look," she says. "The decay was concerning, but . . . I don't know. Something different is going on with you. Given how far it had spread, you should be a wraith. But even if it's gone now, there's still the fact I snuck you in here. There are protocols. If anyone finds out—"

"You mean if Minerva finds out." I fold my arms over my chest. Honestly, I'm of half a mind to march up to her office and have it out. No more Little Miss Nice Ghost. I have been punted around from reaper to reaper, department to department. Afterlife has literally one job, and the reapers suck at it in a way that would make a vacuum cleaner weep.

Cerise won't meet my gaze. I miss Kelly. They would argue

back. Tell me I was being ridiculously emotional. Fragilely human. Cerise just looks apologetic. It doesn't instill me with confidence in my long-term residency here at Afterlife. At least not while I'm still cognizant.

She nods like she's made a decision. "Fine. But keep a low profile. If Zach—"

"About that," I say, jumping to a new thought. "What's he doing here? He's like a schmoozy political candidate. I thought he was on the retrieval team with you."

Her resolve wavers.

"Just stay out of trouble, okay? The way they keep track of headcounts here is very precise. It's different than in general intake. I have to go forge some paperwork." She doesn't look happy about it. I should be nicer to her. Cerise did what literally no one else could or would do. Isn't that the important thing here?

"Okay," I say, ducking my head. "I'll stay here."

She hugs me, like she did that day on the street. It helps. Hugs are powerful, regardless of whether they come from a reaper or a human being.

"It's always hard, getting here. Even back . . ." Cerise clears her throat. "Even before Minerva closed the districts, it was tough for new arrivals. You lose so much. Even when you know death is coming. It'll be okay. You'll make new friends here."

She sounds like we're talking about my first day of university. Don't let it be scary. There will be cool kids in your dorm. Little does she know I went to UofT and lived in Don Mills the whole time. I put up a good front, but branching out has never been my strong suit. I'm better at dispensing advice about experiences I haven't lived.

But I can't cling to her for the rest of eternity. I let Cerise go and she disappears out to the hall again, leaving me alone once more. I smooth my hands down the front of my robe, and something crinkles inside the plush material. The daily schedule, which I must have folded and stuffed in the pocket. I scan it again, hoping for a distraction. Goat yoga, meditation, a cooking class exploring the flavours of Tunisia. There's a memo at the bottom asking people to sign up for an upcoming pony trek to the beach. It sounds perfect. Relaxing.

I hate it.

This is what Cerise meant, right? About it being hard. Part of a new round of grief. I'm sure I've read about this, though not specifically related to heaven. You finally achieve what you wanted and realize how much you've had to give up getting there. I read the page again, trying to find any single activity that piques my interest. Instead, the thing that catches my eye is the letterhead, which I had completely glossed over the first two times. In an elegant script, it reads *The Other Life: Alternative After-Death Living Since 1992.*

I blink. Laughter rings in my ears, even though no one is around. It gets louder and louder, until suddenly I feel like I'm back in Kelly and Jupiter's kitchen on that first day.

What is that? Some discount brand service offering named for search engine purposes? Like a restaurant called Thai Food Near Me?

Is it? But that doesn't make sense. Cerise works at Afterlife. That's where she took me, right?

I turn the schedule over, like the answer might be on the back, but it's blank. I fold it up and put it back in my pocket as I pace the apartment. Something's not right. Zach. The Other Life. That's what he offered me. A perfect place to live in an unfinished building. What if it's not that my unit is the only one on this floor? What if the rest just aren't built yet?

This is silly. I'm overreacting. It's leftover adrenaline. The last of the decay leaving my system. Or maybe this anxiety is a fun side effect of being dead and I didn't feel it before because I was swamped by the protective influence of being so close to Kelly all the time. Because that's what happened, isn't it? Sure, Jupiter's candles made a difference, but whether Kelly was holding my hand or only walking up the hall, I felt connected to their power from the minute I walked into the house.

I flop down on the couch. I wish I could sleep. That's what I would tell the Sparks to do. If you've followed all the steps and the world still feels like too much, take a nap. Naps are massively underrated. Your subconscious does so much work while you sleep. And now it's not something I can do.

Frustrated, I turn on the TV. I don't even have a chance to wonder if they have cable or streaming services in heaven before I'm greeted by Zach's face on the screen. The sound is off, but he's strolling through a field of white flowers, wearing the same white suit I saw him in earlier. His smile is dazzling, and the way he keeps gently gesturing with his hands is comforting. Everything about it says this is a man you can trust.

Also, it has the vibe of an infomercial, and when I turn the sound on, the soft music sounds exactly like the royalty-free stuff I used in the early days of my channel. It's generic and soothing while Zach speaks.

"Here at The Other Life, we're all about your soul's experience. Whether you've arrived here alone or you've come with your loved ones, we will tailor your living arrangements, social calendar, and all of our amenities to your preferences. Because we believe you deserve a choice in how you spend the afterlife."

Not the afterlife. Just Afterlife. Afterlife Incorporated, officially. Kelly said that. They were so annoyed with me.

"When I founded The Other Life," Zach continues, "it was because I was tired of seeing so many souls subjected to the same one-size-fits-all solutions. You were individuals when you were alive. Why should you all be treated the same in death?"

The remote control shakes in my trembling hand. I set it down on a glass coffee table as Zach continues to promise the viewer the moon and more. Literally. If you want to take a trip to the moon, just call the Other Life ambassador courtesy line to book your trip. Want to travel back in time to see famous moments in history? Sign up for the waitlist. First departures are coming soon.

Where's the white nothing? Empty souls crammed to maximum density while reapers try to catch up on a never-ending backlog of deaths? Minerva would never allow field trips, much less waitlists for events that mean souls get to remain themselves longer than absolutely necessary.

I turn the TV off and walk to the windows on wobbling legs. Outside, paradise greets me. The yellow flowers have turned a joyful orange. A line of people dressed in white are marching toward the trees. Every so often, one of them points upwards and they all look, lifting what appears to be pairs of binoculars. Heavenly birdwatchers, maybe?

It's idyllic. Pristine. Everything you could ever hope for.

"Dear Sparks," I say. "Where the hell am I?"

chapter
twenty-four

UNSURPRISINGLY, I find no answers to my questions. Not in the apartment, anyway. I watch Zach's video on the TV a few more times. It's on a loop and takes about fifteen minutes to get through. But it doesn't tell me anything I don't already know. Why would it? The people seeing it have already made their decision to come here. It's not a sales pitch so much as reassurance that the viewer has made the right decision by coming here.

Though that assumes the people here knew they had a choice. Zach certainly never made it clear to me he wasn't taking me to Afterlife. He let me assume he was no different than Cerise or Kelly. But I have no doubt this is not the same place.

Is that a bad thing, though? Goat yoga and moon landings is so much better than Minerva's version of what comes next. Yet I can't shake the feeling that something here is too good to be true. Especially since Cerise is being so cagey. Zach knows me, and clearly he and Cerise must know each other. They both claim to be skirting the rules—Zach back at the hospital and Cerise by bringing me here at all—but neither one is telling me everything.

I jump when a chime goes off overhead. It sounds like someone ringing a doorbell, but it's followed immediately by the chirpy voice of a woman through a PA system I didn't know existed.

"Good evening, Other Life residents," she says. "It's been another beautiful day here in paradise. It's your favourite time now. Ice cream will be served in the courtyard in five minutes. Come and get it, everyone!"

The chime sounds a second time before the room goes silent again. I sit for a second.

There was ice cream every day. Was that Abigail or Lilah? Does it matter? They both said something about ice cream, though all that proves is they were here, not that anything sinister was going on. I'm seeing conspiracies and lies everywhere.

But it can't hurt to check, right?

I open the closet Cerise pulled the robe from. Can't play detective dressed like this. I probably shouldn't be surprised when the racks on either side of the walk-in closet are lined with dozens of identical robes.

Figures. I close the door again and take a deep breath. Cerise said I could wear anything I want as long as it was white. I picture my closet at home. The one from before I got sick and stopped choosing clothes based on what looked cute and started choosing them based on what would hide how quickly I was losing weight. There's the leggings and sweater Cerise took when we came here. The pencil skirt I wore in my twenties when I was trying to look professional. The skinny jeans that are out of style now but I still love. Sweatshirts from my university years and concerts that I couldn't bring myself to give away. The vintage dress I bought at a thrift shop thinking it would fit if I could just lose five pounds, only to discover I prefer Japanese cheesecake on Bay Street more than I wanted to wear the dress.

When I open the closet again, it's all there, minus the colour. That's pretty spiffy. This place really isn't that bad. Sure, the vibes are weird, but I've been through a lot in the last week, haven't I? From dying to getting caught up in the corporate shitstorm that is the afterlife in all its permutations. I can be forgiven for being a little paranoid.

The dress fits like a glove. Of course it does. It's linen and skims against my ankles. Sleeveless, but a quick glance says the black line around my wrist hasn't changed. Might as well enjoy the opportunity while I can.

When the elevator opens back up to the main floor, I tell myself to look confident. You can get in almost anywhere if you dress the part and look like you belong there. The atrium is full of people all streaming toward the front door. They talk excitedly amongst each other. There's not a single child among them, but ice cream elicits delight at any age.

"Did everyone come down for this?" I ask.

"Ice cream isn't mandatory." The woman with the clipboard has materialized next to me, making me stumble. She smiles like nothing weird has just happened. "But most people go. Who doesn't love ice cream?"

Who indeed?

A white van rolls around the corner, pulling into the front courtyard. It sings a merry tune that sounds like hot summer evenings and nostalgia. The residents of The Other Life rush outdoors and call out their orders to the smiling man in the white paper hat inside the truck. He hands out cones and sundaes. Everyone shouts cheery thank yous and gathers in little clusters, chatting without a care in the world.

When a new melody floats over the air, the relaxed chit-chat turns into an excited ripple. Even more people exit the building, waving at the oncoming vehicle. Two vans pull up to a stop right outside the main door, and two women in white uniforms run around and roll out a bright blue carpet from the first van's panel side door all the way to a small platform that another uniformed man is placing on the ground. A fanfare plays, and the door slides open, revealing Zach inside.

The crowd goes wild. He's greeted with the same enthusiasm a late-night host receives as he takes the stage, and Zach looks the part. His smile is white and his suit is even whiter. He might be a spokesman for a bleach commercial.

"Everyone!" Zach holds his arms out like he'd like to hug each person gathered before him. "How has your day been?"

The cheer is deafening. Louder than thousands of basketball fans cheering a miracle three-pointer in Jurassic Park.

Zach beams. His smile really is his brightest feature. He could suck a wraith to HELL with that thing.

"Good. Good. I'm so happy you're happy. It's been the mission of my entire afterlife to build this place for people like you. The smartest, the kindest. The people who deserved more than what the Big Death providers can offer." The way he says it, the capitalization is evident. Funny, I never got this skeezy vibe from him the other times we met. But now that he's in front of an adoring audience, he only hams it up more the longer he goes.

"I have to tell you, when I think of how we're disrupting the post-mortem industry, it makes me so proud of each and every one of you. You took a risk. You risked everything, in fact. You took what I offered on faith, and now you're at the forefront of a revolution to determine what happens to the human race for eternity."

More cheering. People stomp their feet. A few have melting ice cream dripping over their hands and down their wrists, but no one seems to care. If they're part of a revolution, I don't think Afterlife knows about it. Kelly certainly never mentioned it, and if they knew someone else opposed Minerva, they would have at least told me about him. Everything they said indicated they thought they were alone, at least on the outside of Afterlife.

So that means either Zach is lying to everyone here, or the revolution has yet to begin.

Either way, his speech is reaching a crescendo.

"I know that having choices for what happens to you after death is reward enough, but I think it's time for a little something extra. What do you think?"

The crowd moves into a frenzy. He eggs them on, waving his hands. The sound has a fever pitch like wraiths about to dive-bomb a wedding. The people around me start tearing into their ice cream. Literally. They crush the cones, peel apart the little paper cups. It's almost like their looking for something and when, with sticky fingers, they don't find anything, their attention immediately turns to their neighbours, watching excitedly.

A shout goes up from the far side of the crowd. An old man with silver hair holds his hand in the air. He's got something between his fingers, maybe a piece of paper, but he's too far away for me to see clearly.

Then a second cry rises from just behind me. An Asian woman with straight black hair and a delighted smile is also holding up a piece of paper, but she's close enough for me to identify it. A napkin, like the kind that was wrapped around the cones.

Further shouts follow, each one coming from a different part of the crowd. Each person holds up their paper, and the people around them cheer in ecstasy, like even though they haven't won whatever contest this is, they're still impossibly happy for the winners.

I'm so caught up in the collective joy I've forgotten about Zach, and when I glance back to him, he's looking right at me. His gaze is direct and his smile has dimmed slightly. He tilts his head to one side, betraying a moment of confusion. I straighten and smile, doing my best to mimic what has quickly become his trademark expression. I wave at him enthusiastically as if to say, *See? I made it after all.* His eyes narrow before the woman behind me, the one with the winning paper, whatever it is, nearly knocks me over as she rushes through the crowd and toward Zach. She flings herself at him, hugging him so tightly he winces, but he pats her on the back, and his smile returns to full wattage by the time she lets him go. Others are moving forward to join her, and the people who remain applaud them.

Finally, when the exaltation starts to wane, Zach holds his

hands up for silence. Everyone collects themselves, though many continue to whisper in hurried gasps between each other.

"Wow," Zach says, shaking his head in disbelief. "That's the most we've ever had. Are you excited? I'm excited." People clap, but he continues before they work themselves up again. "I know I've said before that we are all equal here. No one gets special treatment. But that also means we're all just as likely to get a little treat from time to time, am I right?" More clapping. Earlier, I had the thought he looked like a late-night host. Now he's gone to the daytime version. Whatever is on those papers is the equivalent of Oprah telling everyone to look under their seats because someone is about to get a new minivan.

In fact, it's so much more than that. Zach says, "Everyone, say goodbye to your friends. They have put in their time; they have enjoyed their days in The Other Life. And now, they're about to embark on the biggest journey they possibly can. It's time . . ." He pauses dramatically, watching as everyone leans forward in anticipation. "For their reincarnation!"

This time the cheer is so loud it's a wonder the glass of the tall tower behind us doesn't shatter. Some of the people around me are weeping openly. Others are clapping over their heads. A few at the back have started to trail toward the indoors again, but most remain, cheering for their fellow residents. The winners wave and are escorted toward the vans. Zach steps down from the platform. I lose track of him. I should leave. Go back up to my room. This place gives me the willies, but I can't say for sure Zach is doing anything wrong. Better to slip away and regroup. Maybe let him forget about me for a bit. He's clearly a very busy reaper. It might be time to take Cerise's advice and keep a low profile.

I turn to go and find myself facing a wall of people all moving forward to see off the not-special chosen people. What does that even mean? But the point is, I'm not going to find a way out that way. I turn again—and find myself face to face with Zach.

He's shorter than I remember. His skin is flecked with freckles.

"Hey, Ember," he says, voice smooth like honey. "I didn't think I'd see you again." His gaze drops to my hand, which is unfortunately planted on his chest in an effort to keep me from tumbling against him. I pull it away but force myself not to hide it behind my back. I have nothing to hide.

"Guess I made the cut," I say, forcing a brave smile. "Nice place you got here."

His smile grows, but his gaze is calculating.

"Thanks. I've worked really hard on it. You want a tour?"

"Oh no, that's fine." I try to back away, but I'm hemmed in by others hoping for a moment of Zach's attention.

"No, no. I insist." He puts a hand on the small of my back. I suddenly wish I were wearing something more substantial than the linen dress. The heat of Zach's palm against me is too close. I take a jerky step forward, trying to create a little more space, and he takes it as acquiescence. He guides me toward the van. I could make a run for it. Hike up my skirt and dart for the field beyond the courtyard. The flowers are snow white now. If I got far enough, I might even be able to hide among them.

But that's the opposite of not attracting notice. And there's still the very real chance I'm seeing ghosts where there aren't any. Or . . . I guess there are ghosts everywhere. But they may not be any more threatening than the vast majority of people I used to pass on the street every day. Even Zach. All that talk of revolution might have been metaphorical. It's a word that gets used in advertising everything from fast cars to breakfast cereal. It doesn't always mean marching off to glorious victory. Maybe I'm building conflict that doesn't exist in my head. Next someone will tell me I need to spend a few years in HECK scrubbing grout so I can chill out.

"Sure," I say. My smile feels frozen on my face. "Let's have a look around."

"Perfect. Come on. We'll go for a drive."

We go to the first van. Zach opens the front passenger seat door and waits for me to climb in. He goes around to the other side and gets behind the wheel. I have to fight not to fidget with the linen against my thighs as Zach gets the engine running.

"Okay, everyone. You've seen The Other Life. Are you ready for the next life?" Zach sounds like a proud dad about to take his family on an epic road trip. The people in the rows of seats behind us cheer, solidifying the image. They're convinced they're about to have the very best time. Snacks and a sing-along are imminent.

"I hope I come back as a boy," a woman whispers to her seatmate.

"I raised four boys," the other woman says. "Trust me when I say you don't want that at all."

I have questions for them. And more for Zach. But my head is spinning, my stomach is in knots, and I don't even know where to start that won't upset what are probably innocent people, so I bide my time and stare out the window, watching as we drive past the billowing field. Past that is a forest, though it looks more like a forest out of a storybook than one I've ever seen in real life. The trees are tall with wide canopies of orange and gold leaves. Back at home, the forests off the highway are mostly scrubby fir trees. Here, the trees are spaced far apart. The sunlight shines through them like it's beckoning us, asking us to take a merry adventure to meet woodland creatures for a tea party

"Where are we, anyway?" I ask.

"The Other Life!" someone calls from the back seat. "Where did you think we were?"

The others laugh. Their conversation gets louder, talking more about what they'll do when they're reincarnated.

I lean across my seat so I'm closer to Zach.

"No, but really. Where are we?"

He winks. "Just a little corner of Afterlife where no one will ever think to look. Took me a while to pick out a spot, but I think I did pretty well, don't you? And don't worry. Even if Minerva hears we're squatting on her territory, she'll never find us."

Every word ratchets my trepidation tighter in my chest.

Without meaning to, I circle the dark line on my wrist with my thumb and middle finger, rubbing at it like I can wipe the last of it away. Zach's gaze drops as he catches the motion, and he smiles.

"That was pretty lucky, wasn't it?" he asks. "You were in much rougher shape the last time I saw you."

I give him a tight grimace. "A hot bath works miracles."

He laughs like it's the funniest thing he's ever heard. Everyone else joins in, even though they can't have heard our conversation. It's like Zach is a completely different person. The bumbling new guy is gone. He's suave and charismatic. Even without changing his appearance, he's changed himself entirely. Whatever it is he's doing, whatever he wants, he's very good at presenting himself—so he gets it.

"You all want some driving music?" he asks, and our little entourage throws up another cheer. Zach punches at the van's stereo and the space fills with a pop song I don't recognize. Maybe it's not even a real song. Just like the trees aren't real, or the flowers. Everything here is as real as anything, but also a complete fantasy. Made up by Zach or some poor soul who thinks this is what people want in their afterlife.

The landscape changes again. Past the forest, things get sparse. The trees get shorter, then fade away. Literally, they get smaller and the orange and gold slowly turns to grey then white, like Zach's magical world ran out of ink. Now we're in what looks more like an empty soundstage, except for the low rectangular building at the end of the road.

"Doesn't look like much," someone says.

"The best gifts come in the plainest packages." Zach turns long enough to wink at the people in the back seat. They all giggle and sigh like that's all the reassurance they need.

I'm not so sure.

"So how does this reincarnation thing work?" I ask. Ember's Life Tip #297: *If you're not sure who you're talking to, ask the hard questions first.* People who were actually involved in the design and operation of something will give you all the nitty-gritty details of how it was built or why it only works most of the time. The ones who report to them will do their best and eventually move you up the food chain. The ones above will give a fast answer about how wonderful the whole thing is and change the subject.

Zach eyes me. His smile seems to be permanent.

"It's peasy easy. Walk through a door and boom! Back in diapers."

Unless he turns them all into lizards. Dragonflies. I'm still missing a piece to see the whole puzzle clearly. Maybe this is a trick to bring the more resistant souls within the perimeter of Afterlife and then figure out whether they go to Minerva's empty rooms or to HELL. If everyone thinks they've come back as the eldest son of a multinational CEO, who would question that they never come back?

We come to a stop in front a rolling bay door. Zach presses a button on an overhead panel, and the door slowly climbs upward. He pulls forward and the people in the back all "oooh" like they're reaching the high point of a rollercoaster.

"Last stop, everybody off!" Zach calls as he parks the van. Everyone whoops and cheers as they roll the side door back. The second van pulls up beside us. We climb out, and Zach leads us through the truck bay to a door in the back. Inside is another white room, this one lavishly decorated. White couches, white throw cushions, white tables. White cheval-style mirrors and white chandeliers hanging from the ceiling. At the far side, a woman in a short skirt and high heels is studying a clipboard, and when she sees us come in, she's all smiles.

"Welcome, welcome!" She confirms each person's name and meticulously writes it down. "And you?" she asks when she comes to me.

"Not her," Zach says, pulling me behind him. "She's just getting the deluxe tour."

The gesture reminds me of Kelly, pulling me behind them on

the Gardiner at the bus crash, when Goran started looking like he might be thinking about sucking me off to HELL with his blue beam. Reapers are so bossy and so annoying with their half-truths. Zach's all about choice and alternatives. What alternatives do I have that don't involve reapers?

The woman looks nervously between Zach and me, but she marks something down on her clipboard as she nods and steps away.

"Excuse me for a second," Zach says to me, mouth too close to my ear for comfort, but before I can reply, he walks to the others. He makes another one of his speeches about choice and opportunity and how fortunate they have all been to spend time here.

"But now," he says, pulling open a white door at the far side of the room. Everyone gasps. Instead of another room through the doorway, beyond is a shimmering, swirling nothing. It whirls and tumbles, looking like silver glitter and soap bubbles, "it's time for a new adventure. One step through here, and you're on your way to a whole new life. Who's first?"

They hesitate, which I can't blame them for. Please walk through the glowing door on a promise of something no one on Earth has ever been able to prove is true.

But, slowly, the first woman, the one who asked if she could be reborn a boy, approaches the swirling light and steps in. She disappears almost immediately. Everyone murmurs and no one makes an immediate move, like they might be waiting for a sign that something is wrong. But when it doesn't come, one by one they all go in. Some shake Zach's hand. Others hug him. Their thanks are so heartfelt. Maybe everything is as Zach says.

When everyone is gone, he whispers something to the clipboard woman, who smiles and walks back through the first door we came through. Zach and I are alone.

"Pretty cool, isn't it?" he asks. His smile is back.

It can't be that simple. "Where did they really go?"

He tsks. "Ember. I always liked you, but you're so skeptical. I sent them back. A whole new existence. It's everything I told them."

I take a few steps forward. I don't want to get too close to the door. Something inside pulses like a heartbeat. I couldn't hear it across the room, but now it's obvious. The heartbeats of the ghosts who just went through, maybe, restarting just like their mortal lives are restarting.

"I do have a question, though," Zach says. "The last time we met, you didn't make the cut anymore. You would have, of course, if you'd come the first time we met—"

"You mean the time you left me high and dry in the hospital?" The question comes out more bitter than I expect. How much simpler would this have all been if he hadn't run away? How much less I would know.

"Ember," he cajoles. "You can't blame me for that. Now that you've seen this place. Imagine what the quarantine knucklebrains would do if they found me. This isn't about assigning blame. Just like I'm not going to blame whoever helped you get here, because it certainly wasn't me."

I don't know how Cerise knows about this place or what her relationship with Zach is. Maybe they're in this together. Maybe she brought me here to spy for her. But until I know, I'm certainly not giving Zach her name.

Ember's Life Tip #1820: *When all else fails, lie your ass off.*

"I got sick of waiting," I say. "I was decaying, and no one was helping. I took the subway from Lower Bay and snuck in past intake. You know things are a disaster there. All I had to do was wait until something more interesting than a days-old ghost with a rotten hand showed up. Didn't take long. All I needed were a couple junior reapers trying to make quota and cover their asses and they couldn't tell if the alarms were going off for the souls they were trying to pass through or for me. A few quick steps through the gates and they lost track of me. Took me a while to find this place. But I'm so glad I made it." I finish off the performance with a grateful smile. Maybe I'm selling it too hard.

But all he does is smile back. He puts his hands on both my shoulders and pulls me into a hug. It feels a bit like I'm being squeezed by a malicious boa constrictor, but I close my eyes and wait for it to be over.

"I'm glad you made it too," he says, squeezing me hard. "You know why?"

I push back, giving myself a little room to take the breath I don't need. "Why's that?"

His grip on my shoulders is friendly. His smile is wide. But his voice is sinister when he says, "Because now you get to tell Kelly I said hello."

Then he shoves me, hard, sending me tumbling through the glowing door.

chapter
twenty-five

I FALL AND FALL, spiralling around a celestial whirlpool.
When I open my eyes, I immediately realize that's a terrible idea as
the world around me spins in shining pastels and jewel tones that
move too fast to be anything but colour. I squeeze my eyelids shut,
hoping simultaneously that I pass out and throw up. Anything to
make the spinning stop.

My landing is painful. One second I'm tumbling through
nothing, the next I'm colliding with something solid. My teeth
clack shut against my tongue, and only being dead saves me from
biting through it entirely.

When I open my eyes, the first thing I see is a glove. A little
purple one. Stretchy, like the kind you buy at the dollar store,
knowing full well your toddler will toss them out of the stroller at
the first opportunity. A man walks by on the sidewalk, and his
edges are blurred in the familiar way of the living.

I blink a few more times and sit up. I'm in the grass on a street
corner. The sun is down. An old woman walks by, pulling a two-
wheeled shopping cart with her groceries behind her. Over her
head, a street sign is illuminated by a car as it pulls through the
intersection.

Bloor Street.

I'm back in Toronto.

"Where are we?" a voice asks. Behind me, a dozen or so frightened people are huddled in a bus shelter.

"What's going on? Why am I still old?" someone else asks. It's the people from the van. Their white clothes are stained and torn. They're clinging to each other and watching the world around them with terrified eyes.

"Zach? Where's Zach?"

My throat hurts like I'm trying not to cry. He lied to them. Said they'd be reborn and instead we're here. Dead and betrayed and—

The woman who sat behind me stumbles away from the others. Her hands shake and she moans.

"Heather? Heather, what's wrong?" one of the other women asks, following after her.

"No," I say, trying to stand. "No, get back."

Heather screams, though the sound gargles like she's choking on something. Black spills over her lips and her fingernails lengthen to talons. The people around her cry out in fear before one by one, their cries turn to the call of predators as they become wraiths. I cower, but they have no interest in me. Heather takes off across the street, colliding with a man out for a jog. He stumbles and falls, and when he stands again, his movements are uncoordinated. An evil light flashes in his eyes as he looks toward us once before he runs on. The others chatter in unintelligible sentences before they take to the sky. They circle, then soar off, headed to other parts of the city where they can sow chaos and fear, until there's only one left.

"What is it?" she asks. "What's happening?" But before I can answer, she twists and moans. When she looks at me again, her eyes have sunk in her head, leaving black voids. She wails, lifting her head like she's scenting something on the wind. Her gait is clumsy as she stumbles down the street, disappearing into the night.

Zach. He lied to all of us, and these people paid the price. But why? There was no decay there. He didn't need to banish them like this. What was with the false promises?

A spasm rocks through me, sending me backward until I'm sprawled on the ground again. My stomach cramps with lingering nausea and I roll, vomiting into the grass, even though that shouldn't be possible. Another car drives by, casting a streak of light over me and onto the puddle of inky black goo that has just ejected itself from my insides.

Oh no.

I scramble away from it, like I can escape, but when I trip into the pool of a streetlight, my hands stay dark. Both of them, not just the right. My teeth chatter, and as I stagger to my feet, I know exactly what's happening to me.

I'm back in Toronto, and I'm in serious trouble.

Tell Kelly I said hello.

Bloor Street. Kelly's house is near the subway. Of course. Bloor runs from Etobicoke all the way to the eastern end of downtown, but if Zach wanted me to deliver his message, he wouldn't have dropped me off on Yonge Street. I would never have made it in time.

My insides feel electrified, and my thoughts swirl in a million directions, many of them dangerous or painful. All I can think about is darting into traffic or rushing the man who is coming toward me. He's got his head down and his hands stuck into his coat pockets, minding his own business as he walks home, or else to work, or maybe to meet friends. Doesn't matter. With a certainty I don't understand, I know that if I reached out and touched him, the contact would ease the gnawing feeling inside me. I could wrap my arms around him, maybe put my mouth to his or my teeth against his skin and take the glowing living energy from inside him and make it mine.

I more or less have to fling myself into an empty garbage bin at the foot of a dark driveway to avoid taking him down. He walks on, oblivious to the desperate neediness that's welling up inside me.

Shit. Shit. Shit! The knowledge that I've blown it leaves a bitter taste in my mouth. All I wanted was a quiet afterlife with no pain. I had that. I could have stuck around The Other Life to eat ice cream, go to yoga, and snuggle with a few baby goats. Instead, I let myself get suckered into falling through heaven's emergency exit, and now I'm disintegrating from the inside.

As I stumble onto Jupiter's dead-end street, a sob escapes from my chest. The little bungalow has a light on in the front window, like it's calling me home. The street is full of the buzz of living energy from the families in each of the other homes. But the candle in the window beckons me, pulling me along.

Still, ignoring the call of so many oblivious lives is painful. I stagger up the short concrete steps in front of Jupiter's house. I pitch forward, thinking about the door and what it will feel like to fall through it, but the cartoon physics fail me and I collide with it instead, like I'm as solid as I ever was in life.

"Please," I beg, banging on the front window. "Please! Jupiter? Hello? Anyone? Is anyone home?"

The door swings open, and I tumble into strong arms that catch me before I can crash to the floor.

Kelly. Thank god and whatever other entities are watching over me. I open myself up, welcoming the rush of their power that always helps me feel slightly more human. It's there, but far away, like the sound of voices in another room. It does nothing to ease the need inside me. A frustrated whimper escapes from my throat.

I expect their flat disdain as I glance up. Here's Ember. First she couldn't get to heaven on her own, then she did, only to immediately fall back to earth to haunt the living as a wraith. Punishment for her stubborn hubris.

Instead, all I see is concern. Kelly's brows are pinched together, their nostrils flared as they study me.

"Where have you been?" They sound bewildered. Angry.

Nearly human in their emotion. "Jupiter and I have been looking for you for weeks."

"Help," I say, swallowing down a wave of nausea. I grab for their forearm and my fingernails bite into their skin. "I need— help, please."

I growl. No, wait. That's not me. I look down, and Carrot Stick is winding around my ankles, making the deep throaty sound of a cat establishing dominance. His fur is all puffed up, and when his green eyes meet mine, the threat is clear. He will fuck me up if he has to.

"Kelly?" Jupiter's voice comes from down the hall. "Kelly? What's going on?"

"Stay there," Kelly says. They wrap their arms around me tighter.

"What is it?" She pops her head out of her bedroom door. Her eyes go wide. "Ember?"

"Woah." X appears behind her, mouth open. "You don't look good."

"Don't get close," Kelly says. "Something's . . . She's . . ."

But their warning is too late. Now that I can see them, I can feel them too. Tease their essence out from all the other living, breathing humans around us and the siren call of the candles. They're so close. So vital. I can practically taste it and now I get a choice of who I consume first.

It shouldn't be possible for me to break free of Kelly's hold, but I do. With a howl I didn't know I could make, I rush up the hall. The surprise on Jupiter's face turns to fear and she retreats, tripping over X as they try to close the door. They won't be fast enough. I know it even before I get there. They're only human, and I am . . . something else.

At the last second, as Jupiter lifts her hands up in a defensive posture that won't save her, something catches my ankle and slams me to the ground. A heavy weight presses on top of me as I snarl. X has fallen backward onto the bed, pulling Jupiter with him.

"Stop. Ember, stop!" A hand tangles in my hair. Kelly's voice is so close to my ear. I twist and struggle, trying to break free, but without the element of surprise, I can't escape. They know what I am now. They won't make the same mistake twice.

"Help." The word is faint. Frightened.

Oh. It came from me.

I clear my throat and try again. "Kelly. Help. I need—"

"Jupiter. More candles."

She hesitates, eyeing me cautiously. Can't blame her, really. As she scurries past me, I snap at her ankles. Just one bite. A nibble. But Kelly's still holding me down, and they won't be thrown off, so all I can do is whine at the sound of Jupiter's feet running up the hall.

"Where have you been?" they ask.

Weeks. They said they'd been looking for weeks. But I was at The Other Life for less than a day.

"You vanished," X says, rising from the bed. He at least has the sense to keep a safe distance between us. "One second you were there, then poof."

A warm calm settles over me as the questions swirl like a spinning vortex in my head.

"Here," Jupiter says softly. She sets something on the floor. When I open my eyes, a lit candle flickers by my head. A few of them, in fact. I didn't even hear her put them down. They still call to me, but with each amplifying the next, it's more like an anchor weighing me to reality rather than an invitation to destroy.

"I'm okay," I say. My voice is rough, like I've been shouting. Or growling, I guess. Human vocal cords, even undead ones, were not created to make those kinds of sounds.

Kelly doesn't move. There's a flick of a lighter, and Jupiter sets down more candles, just out of sight. Each one leaves me feeling less desperate, though the hunger and need never vanish completely.

"All right?" Kelly asks. They're breathing hard. I can feel the rise and fall of their stomach against my back. I nod, though I'm shaking beneath them. I'm not going to attack anyone, but I don't exactly feel stable.

"We can't leave this many lit too long. There could be more like Em—like her." Jupiter's words are tense. Wait until she hears about the wraiths that came from Zach's with me.

Slowly, Kelly rises off me. I lie still a moment longer, focusing on the steadying influence of Jupiter's runes in the glowing candles, and the distant intangible sensation that is still Kelly.

When I open my eyes again, Carrot Stick is back, staring me down. I truly do swear the look on his face is a warning not to mess with the residents of this house. But when I reach to give him a reassuring pat, he hisses and swats at me before turning and sauntering up the hall, leaving me to watch his wrinkly butthole and fluffy tail.

When I get up to my knees and turn, Kelly is watching me with familiar unbothered detachment. The sight of it is almost a comfort. But when my gaze settles on Jupiter, just behind them, she flinches.

"Sorry about that," I say. I shouldn't have come here. I knew what was happening. There's no excuse. I've put them all in danger now.

"You're a wraith?" Jupiter sounds stricken.

"I—" I shake my head. "Maybe? I don't know." I should be gone by now. My arms are blackened all the way to the shoulders like I've been tattooed. There shouldn't be any of me left, just the monster that's living inside my skin.

"Where did you go?" Kelly asks.

I try to stand and accidentally kick over a candle. Jupiter's on it in a second, righting it, though she still won't quite look at me. She scurries until she's standing close to X, who takes a protective step forward.

"I don't suppose there's any way we could take this to the living room?" I ask. "Having burning candles on the floor in the middle of traffic is a fire hazard, and—"The candles aren't only on the floor. There are another four or five on the kitchen counter. More on the little dining table. The flickering light that reflects through the entry says there are more in there too. It's like the set of a gothic opera. Also, you can't light that many candles quickly. "How long was I out of it?"

"A few minutes," Jupiter says. The way she brushes a stray hair out of her face with a shaking hand says it was longer than that. My gaze travels to Kelly and . . . oh.

I can't help the way I blink as I suddenly realize it's Kelly, but they don't look the same. The coloured hair and architectural cheekbones are gone. They don't exactly look human, but it's the closest they've ever been. Like seeing a pop star without their makeup. Their hair is a dark brown and hangs limply on each side of their head. Their eyebrows are the same colour and thicker than I remember. Even the long nose they looked down at me so disapprovingly from seems smaller, less angled.

"What happened?" I ask.

Jupiter's nervous attention swings from me to Kelly. They press their lips into something displeased. Whatever's happened, they still prefer to be in control, and somehow that's not the case anymore.

We go to the living room. Even Carrot Stick reappears and strolls after us, though he gives me a wide berth, settling on the windowsill and carelessly licking one paw. Kelly sits next to me. X takes the armchair. Jupiter lingers in the doorway, like she might make a break for it, which is good self-preservation on her part. I wouldn't blame her if she never spoke to me again.

"Start at the beginning," Kelly says. "You were outside. There was a wraith. Then . . ."

I tell them. It's surprising how little there is to say. The fears and revelations came so fast. But when I present them, it sums up to a few short sentences. Zach has built his own Afterlife. He's holding court and making monsters.

"Then he pushed me through the door, and I wound up back here." I can't make myself look at the rest of them. Their judgement would be too much to bear.

"As a wraith?" Jupiter asks. As I've been speaking, she's crept closer until she's sitting on the arm of X's chair. She still picks at her clothes and the upholstery nervously, but she doesn't look like a deer about to leap into the woods at the first crack of a twig.

"I don't know." I hold my hands up. "I shouldn't be able to form a sentence by now, much less be able to control myself. None of the others lasted more than a few minutes. I don't know why I haven't."

"You'll be safe here," Kelly says flatly. "With the candles, you should—"

"You help too," I say.

They cock their head to one side.

"That's not possible. I've been downsized."

"Your power. I don't know." I drop my gaze to my knees, suddenly feeling shy. "Now that I'm calm again, I don't think I need so many candles. Not with you so close. Something about your magic reaper mojo has always made me feel more . . . alive? Steady? I could feel it with Cerise too, but it's always been strongest with you."

"My magic reaper mo—" Kelly sounds bewildered, but Jupiter jumps in.

"Kelly doesn't have any powers."

The living room gets quiet. The only sounds are the hum of the furnace pushing warm air I can't feel through the ductwork, and the wet determined sound of Carrot Stick gnawing on a particularly difficult knot of fur near his crotch.

"You really can't get your powers back?" I ask softly.

Kelly's eyes crinkle in the corners, but their voice is still dispassionate when they say, "I don't work there anymore."

We stare at each other for a moment. Something wordless passes between us. Neither one of us is where we expected to be.

But that doesn't mean the situation is hopeless. I can still feel their power, even if they can't access it. And maybe my chance at a peaceful afterlife is gone, but that doesn't mean our story is over. I can still help Kelly.

"The wraiths," I say. "There are so many because Zach is sending them back from The Other Life. We have to tell Minerva. Maybe she'll—"

"We're not going back there," they say with the blunt finality that always sets my teeth on edge.

"How would we even do it?" Jupiter asks. "Kelly can't . . ." She mimics folding someone into a big hug then makes wooshing sounds. "The thing anymore."

"We can take the subway," I say. "Lower Bay. We can—"

"We're not going to Afterlife," Kelly says, holding firm. "They've made it very clear they don't want us involved."

Rage simmers inside me. Maybe it's my decayed soul. Maybe it's the knowledge that even though we finally have answers, Kelly's gone back to not getting involved.

"Since when do you listen to what they say?" I ask. "When you weren't supposed to use your powers in the first place? When you got Bang to tip you off before the quarantine team was deployed?"

"It's different now," they say. "If we go, Minerva will send you to HELL. You know that, right? Look at you."

I stiffen, soft feelings toward Kelly evaporating.

"I'm not here to be shamed. Nothing that's happened to me is my fault."

They huff impatiently. "I didn't say it was."

I spring up to my feet. "Minerva is still wiping memories. The people at The Other Life think they're safe, but they aren't because Zach is bribing them with ice cream and promises of new lives, only to dump them for some kind of prank. What does he even get out of this? How is any of this fair?"

Something inside me cracks. Something I've been holding together for a very long time. Longer than I've been dead. "I did everything right. I went to the doctor's appointments. I posted the videos about staying strong. I didn't get upset when friends stopped visiting because it was too hard to see me dying. I picked a medically assisted death because it was tidy and painless." I'm yelling as I pace. Carrot Stick yowls in what I hope is solidarity. "I did everything right, and it turns out it was all for this bullshit? It's not fair. It's not okay. And if you won't do something about it, then I'll—" I whirl with every intention of marching right out the front door. Let the decay take me. If Jupiter thought I was an awesome girlboss when we first met, wait until she meets me as a pissed-off wraith.

But before I can complete my perfect exit, fuelled entirely by righteous indignation and no plan whatsoever, a hand catches my wrist, wrapping around the place where Abigail first attacked me. I try to shake it off, but the grip is too strong, and before I can fight back more, Kelly drags me back to the sofa.

"I can't protect you," they say through gritted teeth. "It's all stacked against us, and I have no way to keep you from getting hurt . . . more than you've already been hurt."

"It doesn't matter." I shake my head, not wanting their sympathy. Not now when it's too late. "I'm not worried about me. I'm already dead. I've seen behind the curtain. But if I can change something. Help anyone who dies from here forward . . ."

"Maybe we should go," X says softly to Jupiter. She shushes him, watching us with worried eyes.

"They're not your problem," Kelly says, tone almost plaintive. "Why do you have to make everything your problem? If you would only look out for yourself, none of this would have happened."

I scoff. "I'm just another annoying ghost who won't do what they're supposed to. Why don't you call Goran and tell him to beam me up? What do you even care?"

"Because I missed you, all right?" they say. Their voice is so loud it makes Carrot Stick flatten himself against the windowsill, ears back as he hisses. Jupiter gasps in the silence that follows, and

X's eyes have gone bright, ping-ponging between us with excitement. He opens his mouth to say something, but Jupiter takes his hand, pulling him up from the chair.

"Let's go," she whispers.

He whines. "But Kelly just said—"

She doesn't let him finish. Only puts all her weight into it as she tugs him from the room and up the hall with hurried footsteps. I glance at Carrot Stick, and even he seems to realize he's intruding. He gives me one slow blink before hopping down and following after X and Jupiter.

"You missed me?" I ask when Kelly and I are alone. It's hardly a declaration of undying devotion, but for Kelly they might as well have gotten my name tattooed over their heart.

One of the things they lost in their downsizing is the ability to hide their emotions as expertly as they used to. The tips of their ears go bright pink and they won't meet my gaze. But they don't let go of me either. The connection helps. Maybe downsizing doesn't destroy their powers so much as it disconnected them. Like unplugging something from the electrical outlet. The current is still there.

They wrinkle their nose and clear their throat uncomfortably. "Remember when I said I'd never met a human who talked to me like you do?"

"Yes," I say. It had felt like goodbye as we'd ridden the elevator to Minerva's office. How wrong we'd both been.

They finally do look at me. Their eyes are a perfectly normal brown, and it leaves me feeling warm, even against the wraith chill that teases me inside.

"It's been one surprise after another," they say. "You confront wraiths and even reapers. Very few humans I've met are like that. Having someone advocate for the dead like you do has made me question how things are done at Afterlife. Even before Minerva made her changes. We've always viewed you as an obligation. A burden. But maybe there's something more. A partnership, even."

And we're both blushing. Because that really was a compliment, and after all the indifferent and thoughtless things Kelly has said to me, it feels extra special. Not that I'm going to get all moony-eyed over them. But I'll keep holding their hand.

"Why did he lie to them?" I ask. "What is Zach getting out of it?"

Kelly groans. "You're not going to let this go, are you?"

"It feels wrong," I say. "You weren't there. They adore him. He's made himself a saviour. He's like the exact opposite of you." I take a risk and give them an arch of my eyebrow.

They, of course, don't pick up on the joke. "He's lied about more than reincarnation. There are no reapers named Zach."

"But he said to say hello. You really don't know him?"

They shake their head.

"So it's an alias," I say. A thought occurs to me and, still in a lighter mood, I ask, "Maybe it's part of his longer full name? You never did tell me what Kelly was short for."

They scowl. "That's not important right now, Ember."

I laugh, storing the question for another day. They'll tell me eventually.

"Even if he's not using his real name, he's still a reaper, and he's preying on people for his own gratification and—"

"He's not a reaper," an unexpected voice says from the front door. The shock is enough to make my new wraith instincts surge to the forefront. I lunge for the intruder, and only Kelly's reflexes and strong arms around my waist keep me from tearing Cerise's throat out as she reels back.

"That's not good," she says, looking afraid as she watches me struggle.

"What are you doing here?" Kelly asks. Whether they've spent the weeks of my absence working out or they're naturally strong even without powers, I'm grateful either way right now. I take a few deep breaths, waiting for the hunger to subside.

"You were supposed to stay out of sight," Cerise says. "I told you not to piss on Zach."

"It's piss off," I say, spitting black goo on the floor. "And you didn't tell me he was tricking people into believing he could reincarnate them in new lives, only to create more wraiths."

I expect her to argue. To say there's no choice, because that seems to be the universal reaper answer for everything, but instead she freezes, eyes going wide.

"He's doing what?" She slumps into the chair X and Jupiter so recently vacated. Speaking of them, they may have slipped off to give Kelly and me some privacy, but they must have had their ears pressed to Jupiter's bedroom door, because they pop out into the hallway almost immediately.

"Who's here?" Jupiter asks, then her eyes get big when she sees Cerise in the living room. "Hey, you were here that night. When Ember disappeared."

Cerise waves weakly. "How's it going?"

"Hi." X crosses the room, hand outstretched. "I'm Alexander Lester Roddick the fourth. Pleasure to meet you."

I give Jupiter a questioning look at the litany of names, raising my eyebrows, and all she can do is shrug. Apparently, she's never heard X's full name either.

Cerise grins as she shakes X's offered hand. "Cerise Cherry Cereza. Nice to meet you."

Jupiter gives a lopsided smile. "Don't those all mean Cherry?"

Cerise beams at her. Now I really want to know what Kelly is short for. But we're getting sidetracked here. I quickly fill Cerise in on my last few moments in The Other Life. She looks like the floor has dropped out from under her and keeps collapsing no matter how far she falls.

"So you really didn't know about this?" I ask.

She's been crying little crystal tears for the last few minutes, which she wipes away.

"No. Zach, he . . . he wanted a place where ghosts could be

safe. Where they could keep their memories and live together peacefully. It's still new. We've been working out some kinks, so it's not fully open yet, but he never said anything about . . ."

"Who is Zach?" Kelly asks.

Cerise's words dry up immediately, though her tears fall harder. Whoever he is, she obviously cares about him.

"He's a lost soul," she says on a long exhale.

X snorts. "Not that lost. Sounds like you know exactly where he is."

"That's impossible. Lost souls are a myth." Kelly sounds stunned. I squeeze their hand, trying to head off an inevitable argument, but they don't respond.

Cerise shakes her head, sniffling. "They're real. We were just too proud to admit it."

"Wait, is 'lost soul' an official thing?" I ask. The way they're talking about it sounds like it might be more than yet another ghost they lost track of. "You can't be introducing new job descriptions now. I was just starting to make sense of it all."

"No. Lost souls aren't a thing," Kelly says emphatically.

"Yes they are," Cerise says immediately. "Zach has been in and out of Afterlife countless times. He knows all the back entrances."

Once again, they're doing that thing that reapers do where they talk in shorthand that I don't understand. It's dialogue born of long years working shoulder to shoulder. It makes my head hurt.

"When this is all over, I really am going to draw that Afterlife organizational chart," I mutter to myself.

"You won't find lost souls in the Afterlife organization," Kelly says. "They're mistakes. Defective. And they don't exist."

"I'm not sure they can be both," I say, squaring for a fight. They're going to decide they didn't miss me so much after all. "Either they're imaginary, or they're yet another screw-up. Which is it?"

Cerise and Kelly give each other a long look before Kelly stands.

"Let's go," they say.

"Go where?" I ask.

"To see this Zach person."

Cerise looks troubled. "You can't. He hates you."

"And I don't even know him." They slide into their leather jacket, the same one they wore the day we met. They may not be an all-powerful reaper anymore, but Kelly still gives off the aura of someone you don't want to mess with. "He's hurting people and interfering with Afterlife business. And he's upsetting Ember." They throw me an unreadable glance. "I think it's time for a conversation. Either that, or we're taking the subway to Afterlife and telling Minerva that you helped a lost soul escape and that you've been kidnapping souls instead of doing your sworn duty to bring them to Afterlife."

Ember's Life Tip #987: *Blackmail is wrong. But sometimes it's the only option.*

I don't believe for a second Kelly would actually follow through. Only a few moments earlier they were refusing to confront Minerva, and even if we have more information now, they still don't have any powers to stand their ground with against her. But Cerise wasn't there for that part of the conversation. She droops. Even her shimmering hair has turned dull like it's ashamed to be there. But finally, she nods.

"Okay," she says. "Let's go to The Other Life."

chapter
twenty-six

ONE OF MY most popular videos was called "On a Tuesday Morning." The exercise is relatively simple. I ask the viewer to envision their perfect Tuesday morning five or ten years from now. It helps them think of their goals in a holistic way. Instead of something specific like "get a raise" or "publish a book" it makes them look at the overall impact those dreams will have on their lives. Where do they live? Who else is there? What are they going to do with their day? After that, it's easier to pin down what they truly value and who and what can help them achieve their goals. We can talk through the steps that will get them from where they are now to where they want to be on a Tuesday morning sometime in the future.

But I can't imagine what steps I've taken and goals I set that end with me squeezed between X and Jupiter in the back of Kelly's car while they bicker with Cerise in the front.

"We've been down this alley three times," Kelly mutters, clearly annoyed.

"I haven't come this way in years," Cerise says. "And it wasn't dark then. Everything looks different."

"Berating her isn't helping," I growl, shifting uncomfortably. Both Jupiter and X are slowly seeping inside me, melting through my shoulders, and each time it happens they wince or clear their throat and make new room. No one wants my decay, stable or otherwise. The presence of two reapers in the front seat helps me stay myself, but the threat still simmers beneath my skin, waiting for a chance to slip free.

"Are you sure it was this way?" Kelly asks, squinting through the windshield.

"Pretty sure. That graffiti bear looks familiar," Cerise says, but she doesn't sound certain at all.

"We've already passed that bear twice," Jupiter mutters next to me.

I close my eyes and focus on breathing. My nervousness has nothing to do with decay and everything to do with simple yet explosive human frustration. Seriously. Reapers travel the world collecting souls, but Kelly and Cerise can't even navigate their way around the alleys of the Parkdale neighbourhood in Toronto.

In their defence, it's an old part of town, and the laneways that run between the century-old houses are barely wider than our car. They make space for small single-car garages that range from nearly as old as the original houses to new ones that have been fixed up and even turned into rental suites. Unfortunately, the laneways look very similar from one to the next, especially in the wee hours of the morning, and we've been up and down at least a dozen.

"So does anyone want to explain what a lost soul is?" I ask, hoping to de-escalate the tension. It does the exact opposite. Kelly and Cerise go deadly quiet.

"Uh-oh," X breathes. "They don't like that question."

Doesn't really matter. We can't help if we don't have all the information, and reapers have been frustratingly stingy with sharing details, even when it would benefit them. How many times have I wished Afterlife had a self-serve option? No need to wait for a reaper. Just a flyer on your deathbed telling you to make your way to Lower Bay, or whatever the closest place to hitch a ride to Afterlife might be in other places. We don't need handholding as long as the instructions are clear. The retrieval and quarantine teams would only need to pick up the stragglers.

Like Kelly's full name, I file that question away for a future conversation.

Finally, Cerise says, "Ghosts aren't supposed to be able to cross the boundary. Once they're past the Afterlife intake team, they can't return. But every so often, a ghost slips back out again."

"No they don't," Kelly says emphatically. "Now can we get back to finding this garage?"

"They do," Cerise says. I grimace. I was trying to avoid an argument, not start a new one. "You can ask Zach when we see him. Or just ask Ember."

I go cold with shock. I wasn't expecting to hear my name in this conversation. Even X and Jupiter try to put a little more space between us. Jupiter crosses her legs. X grabs the handle over the door and pulls himself as snug against it as he can.

"Me?" I ask.

She glances over her seat at me. "The Other Life is technically inside the confines of Afterlife, so—"

"What?" Kelly's shout echoes so loud in the car I have to clap my hands over my ears. Cerise shrinks back. We're probably lucky they have no powers anymore, because the look on their face as they glance at me in the rearview then at Cerise said they would zap us both to HELL now if they could.

Cerise winces. "I was hoping we could talk about that after we got there. It was—" She gasps. "There. There. Stop the car."

"What do you mean it's in Afterlife?" they ask again. Their expression is murderous.

"Zach figured Minerva would never find it if he put it right under her nose. Now stop the car!" She bangs the roof, then vanishes, reappearing a second later in front of us on the road, arms outspread like she'll stop the vehicle with her bare hands if it comes to it. Kelly slams on the brakes, cursing.

"Ah," Jupiter says next to me. "A little warning. Some of us have human bones that break." She tugs on her seat belt, but it's locked in place from the momentum of our sudden halt. Kelly doesn't reply as they turn the car off and get out. Jupiter and X do the same, and I follow.

We're at the end of the laneway, next to something that could barely be called a garage. It's hardly even a shed. More like a dozen or so pieces of scrap metal held together by chicken wire, desiccated grapevines, and plywood so rotted it makes wraiths look like members of the royal family.

"This is a portal to a supernatural realm?" X asks, looking around.

"Zach wanted something inconspicuous," Cerise says.

"Or else he was hoping anyone who got nosy would be crushed when the whole thing collapses and he'd have an easy pickup," I say. Nothing facing us was built to code. Doesn't mean someone in Toronto wouldn't rent it for a thousand dollars a month just to have a roof over their head, even if it's a leaky one. But as far as portals to the underworld go, this is as sketchy as it gets. "How did he know where to find ghosts in the first place? The first time I met him, he played it up like he was some intern still learning the ropes. But he definitely didn't want anyone who was really from Afterlife to see him."

"I sent him death notices," Cerise says. "He said he wanted to help. After Minerva started wiping memories. After Kelly—" Her glance toward them is nervous. Even if she's the more powerful reaper now, she knows Kelly shouldn't be messed with. I feel a little bad for her though. Kelly walked away, and Zach proposed a solution. It's not her fault her good faith was taken advantage of.

Kelly doesn't respond to her confession, though. They shove open the door, making the whole structure wobble, and we're greeted with a snarling hiss before the fattest racoon I've ever seen waddles out, growling its displeasure at being disturbed.

"Ugh. I don't remember it smelling so bad last time." Cerise gags and puts a hand over her mouth and nose.

The garage's interior is a disaster. Maybe this is how it's still staying upright. Crap is piled from floor to ceiling. And I truly mean crap. Scrap wood. Tools that are more rust than tool. Four cracked porcelain toilets stacked precariously one on top of each other in a corner. Heaps of baskets like the kind you get when you buy bushels of produce at the farmer's market. Old paint cans, a box with a riot of Christmas decorations exploding from it, and one of those bouncy horses that were all the rage before I was born and undoubtedly fell out of favour after too many little kids got pinched in the exposed metal springs. Worse than the springs, the horse's head has been smashed in, leaving it looking mangled and haunted.

"Nice place you've got here," I say.

"It was in better shape when we started." She grimaces when she pulls a door away from where it's been leaning against the wall, causing an avalanche of screws, nails, and other hardware that were previously balanced on the ancient shelving unit the door had also apparently been holding up. "Well, slightly better shape."

Kelly coughs as a cloud of dust wafts up from the disturbed contents of the garage.

"Where are we going? Is it really some unexplored part of Afterlife?"

Cerise laughs as she moves another door. Fortunately, this one seems less crucial to the building's structural integrity.

"Unexplored? More like unattended. When was the last time anyone did any real patrols? They're all so confident in the infallibility of reapers and Afterlife. This is why things have gone to spit." She frowns and glances over her shoulder at me. "Spit?"

"Shit," I say. On my list, along with an org chart and glossary, I should also publish a list of common English idioms and how to use them properly. "Though spit's not bad."

"Shit." She smiles. "This is why Afterlife has gone to shit. The vision is so narrow. They think they know all there is to know and never look for alternatives. They squeeze in soul after soul and never take the time to ask if what we're doing is the best way. The kindest."

Her mission statement is passionate, but she's missing the part where Zach brings people in, then punts them out on a whim and a lie. Maybe the original vision was a better alternative, but something went sideways when she wasn't looking. Seems to be a common problem with reapers.

"Ah." Cerise pulls on yet another door. "I knew it was back here." The knob wobbles in her grip, and she has to put her shoulder against the panel, but finally it swings open, revealing a shining void beyond. It's the same as the one I went through that landed me back in Toronto, and I recoil, hissing like Carrot Stick's long lost wraith cousin. Something beyond the door pulses. Whether it's friend or foe is unclear. Is this what being a lost soul means? Every trip from here to wherever changes you a little bit?

"What about the others?" I ask suddenly, the tendrils of an idea beginning to consolidate.

"Which others?" Cerise asks.

"The ones Zach sent through here, from The Other Life back to Toronto. Are they lost souls too?" I still don't know exactly what it means to be a lost soul, but if the definition is a human ghost who has left Afterlife, then don't they all fit the criteria?

The garage gets quiet. Even Jupiter and X pause where they've been poking around on other shelves to look toward me and the reapers.

Cerise shakes her head like she's dismissing a thought she hasn't even given voice to. "Lost souls are very rare. It's never more than one at a time. Escaping from Afterlife is nearly impossible once you've crossed over."

"Unless someone forced a group of them out," Kelly says. "How many did you say there were?"

"A dozen?" I say. "Enough to fill a couple passenger vans." I didn't bother counting. I was too busy trying to guess what Zach was up to, and now I'm starting to think I was never going to put the pieces together. Not on my own.

"And the ones at Jurassic Park?" X asks, and I go cold.

"They were wraiths," I say.

Kelly presses their mouth into a grim line. "What if they weren't?"

"But you said—" I hesitate. Wasn't that one of the last things Kelly said before Goran had them downsized? That the wraiths weren't wraiths. But Goran was so busy being an asshat he didn't take the time to listen.

We're listening now.

Kelly says, "They looked like wraiths, but the swarms were abnormally large, and they went after the living, not the dead. You spoke with them, and they were coherent."

They were, but they were decaying rapidly. Zach is out there pretending to be a reaper, and I survived my trip back from The Other Life only a little more broken down than I was before. If they were lost souls, why didn't they make it?

"Zach's powerful," Cerise says. "He's been dead a long time. He says with enough practice, lost souls can be even more powerful than reapers. Maybe he figured out something that keeps him from decaying when he's here."

"And me?" I ask, though I'm not sure I want to hear the answer. Humans always want to find out they're special, but not necessarily "transcending the bonds of life and death" special. That sounds like a lot of responsibility. Possibly a lot of learning. No one wants extra homework once they're dead.

Kelly comes to stand beside me. They put a hand on my back. The gesture makes me think of Zach walking me toward the glowing door, but Kelly's touch is only about comfort. I lean into it, then flush when I catch Cerise watching us with a bemused quirk of her lips.

"You might have some help," she says.

"Can we get back to the others?" Kelly asks impatiently,

though they don't break the contact between us. "Are they lost souls, or are they wraiths?"

The five of us look between each other. It's pretty clear no one knows for sure.

"If the ones at my house were lost souls and not wraiths," Jupiter says slowly, "and the reapers came and took them away . . ."

"Woah," X says. "Lost souls escape Afterlife, then go straight to HELL. What a sucky ending."

But Kelly stiffens behind me, and Cerise's eyes go wide.

"What happens when lost souls go to HELL?" I ask.

"Nothing good. HELL is designed very specifically for wraiths. If they put lost souls in the cells—" Suddenly, Kelly lets go of me, and I stumble at the loss of contact. But they don't look back as they rush toward the garage door, Cerise close behind them. Jupiter, X, and I share a quick look, then run after them. Wherever the reapers are going, we're not getting left behind.

Kelly barely waits until we're all in the back seat before they put the car in gear and reverses. Turning around in the narrow laneway would involve something like a fifteen-point turn. Instead, they back up at a speed that would make a stunt driver proud.

"What's going on?" I ask. "What about Zach?"

"We have much bigger problems," Kelly says, swinging the wheel so the car veers wildly around the ninety-degree turn that takes us out to the street.

"Bigger than a lost soul making other lost souls and releasing them onto the streets of Toronto?" I ask. "Because the people at Jurassic Park would say that's a pretty big deal."

"It was a mess," Jupiter says. "You weren't there, Ember, after. The city is launching a whole investigation. There were hundreds of injuries. Thirteen people got trampled to death. You're saying this Zach guy made it all happen?"

"And then Goran . . ." Kelly says, then swears again, like even the mention of the quarantine leader's name is foul. "Then Goran and his minions gathered them all up and swept them off to HELL."

"Where . . ." Jupiter lets the word hang.

I watch Kelly from the rearview mirror. They look toward Cerise, who is sitting silently in the front seat.

"Just wait until we get there," Kelly says softly. Their brown eyes flash to me in the mirror.

Time to go to HELL.

chapter
twenty-seven

TURNS out the way to HELL follows the same path many commuters follow in Toronto every day: you take the subway.

When we reach Lower Bay station, the platform is empty.

"Where is everyone?" I ask.

"Oh, this isn't good," Cerise says, looking around.

"You mean we could have come down here any time and rode over to Afterlife and asked for a tour?" X asks, sounding delighted at the idea. Nothing really seems to faze him. I'm starting to see the appeal, even if men still aren't my thing romantically. The weirder it all gets, the more it helps to have a member of our little group who takes it all in stride. Not everyone needs to be a problem solver or a leader. Foot soldiers, especially unflappable ones, are important too.

The train pulls in and we get on board. There is no one else. No ghosts, no reapers. Yet it leaves the station promptly, so someone's working the controls. I sit next to Kelly, pressing my knee against theirs. Cerise sits on their other side. Jupiter and X spend the whole trip watching the flashing lights whiz by outside, and when we emerge from the tunnel, Jupiter gasps.

"Oh, it's so beautiful."

It looks so ugly to me. Inhumane. Whatever is going on, an

organization this size should be able to identify trouble and address it. Instead, the gleaming tower sparkles like it doesn't have a care in the world, and the only cavalry on its way is the five of us. Two reapers, including one with no access to their powers, two mediums who are still acting like this is all a fun adventure, and me, a ghost who might be some kind of mythical lost soul, but who also might go to pieces if Kelly lets go of my hand for too long.

As far as rescue parties go, we're not inspiring confidence.

The platform at Afterlife is just as deserted. So are the twisting corrals where the souls were lined up the last time we were here.

"Are we too late?" Cerise asks. No one replies.

Kelly leads us to the tower. There isn't a single office light on in any of the stories rising above us. But the front doors are still open and Bang is still sitting at the front desk as we walk in.

"Kelly? Cerise? What's going on?" She hurries forward to meet us, pushing her glasses up on her nose as she goes.

"Where's Minerva?" Kelly asks. They don't stop for small talk. "Goran?"

"They're not here. No one's here."

My stomach drops. Maybe we really are too late. Zach's smart. Sneaky. Whatever his plan is, he had to know that once Kelly started piecing things together, he was running out of time to execute.

"Where did they go?" Cerise asks.

Bang sighs, looking tired. "Minerva pulled everyone out of the field. She said we needed to go to some kind of town half and sort out some operational issues as a team."

"Town hall?" I ask.

Bang frowns as she mouths the words before her expression clears. "Ohhh. Yeah. That would make more sense, wouldn't it? Minerva said it was time to air some grievances and figure out why we can't get our numbers up. I thought she meant we weren't even hitting half the towns we were supposed to, but your version sounds better."

"Bang!" Kelly says, making us all jump. "What do you mean she pulled everyone out of the field?"

Bang rolls her eyes. "She said something about needing a reset. Wiping the slate clean. Everyone gets on board or they can get out. You know Minerva. Big talk, but nothing ever changes."

"What about the quarantine team? HELL?" They twitch in agitation, looking around the vacant lobby. I try to take their hand, hoping the calming energy they offer me goes both ways, but Kelly shrugs me off and paces instead.

"Ziggy left a skeleton crew. Goran argued the WQU were essential personnel who couldn't leave their posts, but Minerva wasn't having it."

"Too late, too little. Let's go." They stride to the elevators, but instead of entering the first bank like we did when we went to Minerva's office, they go to the second. A single call button is marked with a large red H.

"We're going directly to HELL? Shouldn't we wait?" Cerise asks, sounding worried.

"Dude! We're going to hell!" X crows like it's the best news he's heard all day. Jupiter looks uncomfortable; if Kelly doesn't want my immediate support, I wish I could offer it to her instead, but even here in Afterlife I still can't touch her.

"Call Minerva," Kelly says to Bang as the doors open. "Call Goran and Ziggy. Whoever you can reach. Tell them we have lost souls in HELL."

"Lost souls?" Bang asks, but the doors are already closing with the rest of us inside. The elevator drops with a jolt, like the one at The Other Life. Jupiter, X, and Cerise scream. Kelly stumbles into me, and I grab hold of them.

"It's a bit of a ride down," they say, glancing down to study me. "And I don't know what we're in for. Cerise and I—"

"I want to help." I squeeze their arm. I have to. It's too late for me. My only option now is HELL. But if I can help today, that can only help the ghosts that come after me. Maybe that's the purpose of my afterlife.

The drop stops with a second jerk.

"Stay behind me," Kelly says, and I nod. Helping and diving headlong into an unknown situation are two very different things.

One by one, we step into HELL.

It's nicer than I expected, though I don't know why I keep being surprised when Afterlife refuses to meet my expectations. The hallway glows blue, and the light ripples like we're underwater. A simple desk with a computer monitor sits at the end. A reaper in a blue and silver jumpsuit is sitting behind it. He's slumped against one arm, staring at the screen like he's about thirty seconds from falling asleep. Slow day in HELL, I guess. But they sit up straight when they see us.

"Who are you? What are you doing here?"

"I'm Kelly, head of retrieval team," they say.

The reaper at the desk frowns. "The retrieval team?"

"SRU," Cerise says impatiently. "What are you, new?"

"No." The reaper laughs. "You know there haven't been new reapers in—"

"Let us through," Kelly says, motioning to a heavy gate behind the desk.

The other reaper gapes. They're young. Maybe nineteen. Not that it means anything. Thanks to the famous Richard's disappearing act, they have to be at least fourteen hundred years old. But the sneer they give Kelly is a hundred percent the look of a summer intern who has been given too much authority while the rest of the office goes out for a staff appreciation day at the golf course.

"You're not authorized to go back there," they say.

"Can't you just slide us through?" Jupiter asks. "Kelly did before."

Cerise shakes her head. "HELL is seriously warded. Reapers can't slide here. You can only go in or out through the gates."

"We have reason to believe you're containing lost souls," Kelly says, obviously trying to keep their voice steady. "I'm surprised you haven't had a meltdown yet."

The reaper smirks. "Lost souls? Next you're going to tell me the bogeyman is real too." They pronounce bogey with a hard O, like it rhymes with "fogey." I don't have time to explain why that's wrong.

"I'm a lost soul," I say, stepping forward. "Now let us in before —" I don't actually know what I'm going to threaten them with, but it doesn't matter. Before I can finish, an explosion rocks the floor beneath us. Jupiter cries out, and Cerise stumbles back. The reaper at the desk ducks. A deafening bellow comes from beyond the gate, and the lights glow brighter for a second before the whole room plunges into darkness.

"What was that?" X asks. For once he sounds worried.

"Let us in now," Kelly barks as the space floods with dim lighting from a backup system. The reaper doesn't argue again. They put their hand to a panel by the wall, and the gate slides back soundlessly. Or it might make a horrible shrieking sound of unoiled hinges. There's no way to know because it's all drowned out by the crashes and roaring coming from deeper inside HELL.

Running toward the screaming is a terrible idea, but it's what we do. Heavy doors line the hallway. They're the kind that, in the living world, are designed to be fireproof, possibly even waterproof. Here, they must be wraith-proof, because through the small window near the top, all I can make out is the dark swirl of a wraith floating around like a leaf in the wind. After a half dozen doors, a long corridor splits off on either side. The lighting is poor, but even so, more doors like these extend in both directions as far as I can see.

"How far do they go?" Jupiter asks, just ahead of me.

"It's HELL," Kelly says. "How far do you think?"

A sound like dozens of flapping wings sounds on the air, and we only have a minute for Cerise to shout, "Get down!" before a swarm of wraiths flies toward us. We all drop to the floor. Kelly's got a hand over my head. Jupiter and X cry out. But the wraiths have no interest in us. They swoop past, screeching as they make a beeline for the gate. At the last second, they crash against an invisible barrier, like bugs against a windshield. They make a sickening thudding sound, one after the next, as they collide with it and hit the ground, where they twitch but don't move.

"How did they get out?" Cerise asks. "The containment has held for thousands of years."

"It works for wraiths," Kelly says, pushing up to their feet before helping me do the same. "We have no idea if the cells will hold lost souls." They glance at me, gaze searching. "We don't know enough about lost souls to be certain of anything."

One thing I'm certain of, though, is the screaming and the banging is still coming from further inside. The immobilized wraiths on the floor aren't the only beings who have been let free. It's a nearly rhythmic sound, like someone slamming a door over and over. With each slam, the screaming gets louder, and slowly it's punctuated by footsteps, and the unmistakable people marching in lockstep.

"Someone's coming," I say. I really wish I still had a heartbeat right now. Not having it means it's not pounding in my chest warning me of danger. It leaves a strange feeling of calm when I should be very, *very* afraid.

"Down the hall," Kelly says, pulling me with them. The others follow. When we're far enough down that we won't be visible unless someone comes searching for us, I strain, listening for even the slightest hint of what's going on.

"Hello? Hello? Is someone there?" a voice behind us calls, then bangs on a door. I whirl, looking around, but it's nearly impossible to tell which one it was coming from. The voice is familiar, though.

"Stay down," Kelly says, but I stand up, peering through the window of the closest door. A wraith lunges at me, all teeth and rage. It slams against the window, making the door shake in its frame, but it holds tight.

"Ember," Jupiter says, sounding scared.

"One second." I work down the hall. Each one has a wraith in it.

"Hello? Hello?" the voice comes again, this time directly behind me.

I turn, and Lilah is staring right at me through her little window. She looks terrified, even though she's exactly the same as she was the last time I saw her. Hair still pinned up. Face still young.

"Lilah?" I ask.

"Yes. Yes, please. Let me out," she says. "I don't know where I am. No one will talk to me." Tears stream down her cheeks. They're black and inky, but she's undeniably still herself.

There's another whooshing sound, and a fresh swarm of wraiths passes the opening at the end of the hall. There might be twice as many, and when they hit the barrier, the whole floor under my feet shakes.

"What are they doing?" Jupiter asks.

"They're trying to get out," Kelly says.

Lilah resumes her banging on the door, louder and harder than before.

"You can't keep me here! I'm not dead. I'm supposed to be alive. A new person! Let me out!" She flings herself against the door over and over. It's the sound I heard earlier. The rhythmic banging. It goes on and on as I struggle with the door. The handle doesn't budge. There's a keypad to the side, but when I push a few buttons, nothing happens.

"Help me," I plead. "Kelly? Cerise? Help me get her out of here."

Kelly grabs hold of me, arms around my shoulders, pulling me across the hall.

"You can't do that," they say. "It's not safe."

"She didn't know." I struggle against them. "He lied to her, and now she's a prisoner."

But as the protest leaves my lips, the door of Lilah's cell crashes open. She stands in the doorway for a moment. She looks glorious as the stones shine in her hair and her peach dress shimmers in the light. She might be an avenging angel, particularly when her mouth opens to let out an ear-piercing shriek. Once again, we drop to the floor and I wrap my arms around my head.

"I don't think we should be here," Jupiter says. She and X are huddled across from us with Cerise. They look frightened. We shouldn't have brought them with us. If anyone has anything to lose here, it's them.

Lilah's head swings in their direction. The sparkling prom queen is gone. Black oil pulls her hair loose of its pins, streaming over her shoulders and staining her dress. Her blackened eyes narrow as she smiles. I have a split second to be afraid before she moves faster than any wraith I've seen. Jupiter is pulled off her feet, arching as Lilah collides with her. For a second, it's like Jupiter has twice as many arms and legs as she should. X pulls desperately at one hand, but she cries out, writhing painfully, before she crumples.

"Jupiter!" I struggle in Kelly's hold, but they won't let me go. X kneels next to her still form. Lilah has vanished. Or has she? Jupiter snaps her head up, smiling a gruesome smile. Her teeth and lips have turned black, and her eyes flash with a terrifying blue glow. And I don't mean that metaphorically. There are no sparkling sapphires as she looks up in delight. Only pulsing consciousness as the monster that has taken residence inside Jupiter makes its presence known.

"Babe?" X asks, sounding scared. Jupiter's inhuman gaze swings to him, and she licks her lips.

"Hello, dear."

Wraiths attack the dead. But lost souls attack the living. It's like Jurassic Park all over again, except the only living people here are—

X is knocked off his feet as another dark spectre slams into him. Jupiter grins as she watches. He twitches, flailing on the ground for a moment, before he rises, moving in fluid motions that are nothing like his usual bouncy manner.

"What's going on?" Cerise asks.

Lost souls need a home. And they've chosen my friends.

I glance up at Kelly. Even they look scared. All those eons alive, and we're finally face to face with something they've never seen before.

"We have to help them," I say. X and Jupiter—or the things inside them—look at each other laughing in twin choruses of a high-pitched giggle that will never not frighten me, then turn. They don't acknowledge us in any way. Instead, they go to opposite sides of the hall. X puts his hands on either side of the closest cell door, and without much effort at all, he rips it from its hinges. The wraith inside bursts forth with a howl, joined shortly by a second one as Jupiter does the same thing. They don't even wait to see where the wraiths go. Simply move up the hall and do the same thing again, one door at a time.

A new crash comes from the entrance, followed by a flash of light so bright I have to turn away. Panic threatens to finish up what the decay started when Kelly lets go of me and crawls up the hall until they can look around the corner.

"The barrier is failing," they say when they return. "They're trying to get up to Afterlife."

Somehow, I don't think that one intern reaper at the desk will be enough to hold them back. The escapees soar over my head, with only one destination in mind. HELL shudders and shakes as each one tries their luck at freedom.

"Ember!" Jupiter trips, moving awkwardly toward me. For a moment, her darkened eyes clear and her face contorts in terror. Then Lilah rises up behind her, expression sinister. She wraps her arms around Jupiter, and melds into her, disappearing once again.

Jupiter trembles, before her features go slack and she returns to pulling open doors.

We have to help them. We have to stop the wraiths. We need so much support and no one is coming. Who knows if Bang called Minerva, or if she'd even believe Kelly's hasty message enough to wrap up her retreat or town hall or whatever it is she felt was more important than keeping Afterlife safe? They might even be off somewhere like the reaper equivalent of Bali that would take them a day or a week to make the return trip.

A wraith swoops low, knocking me to the floor.

"Ember!" Kelly's at my side in a moment, pulling me out of the way. The hall is clogged with wraiths, and our means of exit is closed. Now would be a really good time for sliding to work. Or any part of Kelly's powers. We never talked about what they could and couldn't do. Maybe they had some secret wraith-blasting skill that would come in really handy right now.

My hand on their wrist turns hot. I pull it back on a hiss and they look at me in confusion.

"What just happened?" they ask.

"I—" With the contact broken, my hand feels fine. But when I touch them again, the heat returns. I take a breath, focusing on controlling the pain, exploring it, finding the source.

"Ember?" Kelly asks. They sound uncertain, but I don't answer. I can't let doubt find its way in.

When I open my eyes, everything is in the flat monochrome like the day at the construction accident. Black and white, grainy at the edges. I was so scared then, but I can't be now. I look around. The wraiths are empty shapes swarming heedlessly past us. Cerise is bright white, standing at the corner where the two hallways meet. Kelly is grey, except for their centre, which shines even brighter than Cerise, and a single white line that runs from that core, up their arm toward me.

I look down the hall toward where Jupiter and X continue their jailbreak. It's easy to see how. They're bright living auras, like

I saw that afternoon on the porch, but with the growing darkness inside where the lost souls are taking hold.

Well, they can't have them.

"Hold on," I say, looking back to Kelly. Now it's like I can see them in double; their black and white version, and the everyday form who looks from my face to our joined hands. "This might hurt."

Honestly, I don't even know what it will do.

I've been able to feel their power from the very beginning, even when they can't, and now I grab hold and set it loose, letting it run through me. The wraiths howl, but I don't let go. I picture the blue beam. The light so bright I have to shield my eyes every time the quarantine team deploys it. The way it shoots forward so fast the world goes from dark to light in an instant. I picture the wraiths howling, protesting their captivity. Then I imagine it stretching further down the hall. I picture it changing until it forms a long claw. A skeletal hand that reaches forward, grabbing first at Jupiter, then the thing that has possessed her. The screams get louder, mingling the sounds of wraiths, humans, and lost souls. I close my eyes and picture the tearing sensation as I drag the soul from Jupiter, flinging it into the beam along with the wraiths. Then I do the same for X, taking hold and tearing. The souls protest their eviction. Either Jupiter or X cries out in pain. But I've put in all this effort. I can't lose them now.

"Ember." Kelly sounds breathless. I squeeze my eyes tight, concentrating on the line of power and what I need it to do. The wraiths scream louder. I wait until it stops. I can't let go until there's silence, but the howls and shrieks echo endlessly in my ears. "Ember, open your eyes."

When I do, the hallway is clear. Every single wraith has disappeared. Jupiter and X lie in a heap in the middle of the floor, but as I look, she sits up, shaking him desperately while he groans. There's no sign of Lilah. My hand is on Kelly's chest, and their heart beats wildly beneath my palm. Funny. I didn't expect them to have a heartbeat.

"What happened?" I ask, blinking. My vision is blurry, like I'm just waking from sleep. Everything is in three-dimensional colour again, and when I flex my fingers carefully against Kelly's shirt, their power feels far away.

"They're gone," Cerise says, sounding awestruck. "You vaporized them."

"That. Was. Awesome!" This is X, looking pale and shaken, but still endlessly excited to be on this quest. Nothing bothers him, not even being taken over by a lost soul. "You're like a superhero."

"Ember?" Jupiter's eyes are wide. She's just as pale as X, but more surprisingly her gaze is fixed directly on me.

"Can you see me?" I ask. What the hell did I just do? She nods, but I don't have time to think about it further before my legs give way.

"Ember!" Kelly's got me, holding me close as all my strength leaves me.

"How did I do that?" I ask.

"I'd like to know too," a new voice says. Zach has come around the corner, at the head of a group of people all dressed in white. If The Other Life gave off weirdly happy, culty vibes, it's ten times worse now against the dark backdrop of HELL.

"Zach," Cerise says, voice faint. She shrinks back behind the rest of us, but that doesn't keep Zach from tracking her with a snake-like gaze.

"Hey, sweetheart," he says, grinning his salesman's smile. "We'll talk in a minute, but for now, I have questions for Ember." His gaze turns back to me, and his smile turns wicked. "That was a neat trick. Wanna show me how you did it?"

twenty-eight

WE'RE GATHERED in the corridor. The odds aren't exactly fair. There are five of us. Zach has easily fifty people with him, probably more. Possibly a lot more. The hallway only has room for us to stand about four across, and I can't see how far back Zach's group goes.

"What are you doing here?" I ask.

His smile is slippery. Smug.

"We're taking back what we're owed."

"You're taking over HELL?" X asks, sounding confused. I expect him to once again proclaim it's cool, but instead he just looks perplexed.

"Are you all right?" Kelly asks me again, soft enough so the others can't hear. They take my hand, and to be honest, I'm not sure. Little lights float in my vision like I've been staring at a flame for too long. I still feel weak, and the black on my arms has begun to move, like something alive is crawling beneath my skin, or maybe I'm turning into a human lava lamp.

Zach tsks. "Kelly. So considerate. But not always, right? It's been a while. How have you been?"

Kelly jerks their head back and scowls, obviously annoyed to be interrupted by someone as insignificant as Zach. "I don't know you."

"That's what you think." His tone hardens. It's the same look he gave me before pushing me through the door. "Can't be bothered to remember the people you crossed over, can you?"

I close my eyes as certainty settles in my stomach like a lead weight. Of all the times for Kelly's superiority complex to get us into trouble, now is the worst possible moment.

"Kelly took you to Afterlife?" I ask.

Zach's lip curls. "Hurricane Creek mine. 1970. One minute I was laying primer cord, the next Kelly was standing over me and telling me to follow or get left behind."

Sounds about right. I sigh wearily. Kelly, of course, decides now is the perfect opportunity to argue their case.

"Over thirty of you died in a single explosion, and I was the only reaper on-site. It didn't leave much time for pleasantries."

My turn to take their hand and squeeze. Hard. Shut up, shut up. We don't know why Zach is here or what he wants. There's no need to antagonize him.

Fortunately, Cerise drags us back to more pressing issues.

"Zach, what are you doing? We made The Other Life to be an alternative. Ember said you're lying to people? Turning them into lost souls?" Her voice cracks on the last question.

He sneers. "It was never going to be enough. Don't you get it? It's too small to hold everyone . . . Or everyone who will want to come. We need more." He glances around at the darkened hallway. It's silent now. I don't even see any wraiths in the cells where the doors are still closed. "This place lacks the right atmosphere. We'll renovate eventually. For now, though . . ."

"You think you're taking over Afterlife?" I ask. Talk about goal setting. It's audacious on any scale.

"Someone has to," he says. "You're going to leave it to the reapers?

"You think you can take on Minerva?" Kelly asks.

Zach shrugs. "Maybe not when I died, but I've had time. To plan. Learn." He lifts a hand, staring at it. "Her little wraith problem has kept her distracted. I had to sacrifice a few residents to make sure she was looking the other way, but the team down here didn't even bother to lock the back door. I've been coming back and forth through HELL for years. In fact, I've picked up quite a few new tricks. Things Ember is only just starting to dream of. Want to see?" He lifts a hand and snaps his fingers.

For a second, nothing happens. I'm about to roll my eyes at Zach's theatrics when a rattling gasp comes from behind me. It's Cerise, hands at her throat like she's choking.

"Stop!" Jupiter says. She and X are clinging to each other's sleeves. My gaze swings back to Zach, and he's watching Cerise with a sick twist in his lips.

"She shouldn't have betrayed me. We were so close to reaching the top of the mountain," he says.

She drops to her knees. Her hair colour ripples, swirling like a pastel rainbow. But she's not dying. She's fading. Shrinking. Like a balloon losing air until suddenly, there's nothing left. She vanishes, disappearing between one breath and the next. The last thing I see is her terrified gaze as she silently begs Zach for release. Then she's gone.

"What did you do?" I ask, whirling on Zach. The people behind him shift nervously, but he holds up a hand, stilling them.

"I gave her what she deserved. What they all deserve. It's all lies, Ember. You know it. It starts from the minute they tell us we're off to a better place, then shuttle us into a white room and strip us of anything that makes us ourselves. Everything is a lie."

It's not an answer to my question. Did he kill her? Send her back to The Other Life? Lock her up in one of the endless cells in the endless hallways that make up HELL?

"What about *your* lies?" I ask. "Reincarnation? You turned them into monsters."

There's more restless murmuring among the residents of The Other Life, but also a few flashes of sharp teeth and blackened eyes.

Zach's teeth also flash as his smile widens. "I made them powerful. In the living world, lost souls aren't much more stable than wraiths. They need a human host to survive more than a few hours. But inside Afterlife, we have capabilities reapers don't even know about."

Which means it's time for Kelly, never one to be distracted by the predicament at hand, to say, "1970. That's just over fifty years ago."

They're still holding on to me. Slowly, I'm feeling more like myself again. If I concentrate, I can feel Kelly's power, but the idea of accessing it again leaves me with a sick feeling. I don't understand what happened, other than I knew in that moment I had to save Jupiter and X while protecting the rest of us. If I tried again, I'd just as likely melt myself down into a puddle as fry Zach and anyone else who wants to hurt us.

But his focus shifts to Kelly, and his features darken in wicked pleasure. How could I have not seen Zach isn't a reaper? Every time I saw him, he looked the same. Not even a different haircut.

"1970," he says. "What does that date mean to you?"

Kelly flinches, but they say, "Nothing specific, other than that was after Minerva decided—"

"To start depriving the souls of their memories and identities." Zach's voice is sharp like a knife. "But not mine. You were in such a hurry. You walked me to the gate and left me there. No one else was around, so I entered Afterlife by myself. I spent ten years inside alone. Do you know what that was like?" His eyes are furious. "Nothing but white walls and emptiness. No one to talk to. No one to ask for help. I wandered around for years and never met another person."

Kelly's indignant expression turns to shock. "You were aware?"

"You bet I was. You were so busy being an all-powerful reaper, you never thought to make sure I was processed properly, did you?" Zach's words are punctuated by livid spittle, his temper rising. "Everyone else had been wiped. Everyone who came in after me was scrubbed clean like a new penny. It was torture, and no one even knew."

The room goes quiet. My mind races in a kind of secondary horror. Even though I wasn't there with Zach, the very idea of so much isolation makes me want to cling to every shred of sentience I still have. Even Kelly blinks a few times, finally realizing the full implication of what Zach is saying.

"So you chose to become a lost soul to exact some kind of revenge on us?" Kelly asks.

"That's all you think there is, don't you?" Zach snaps. "Ghosts, reapers, and wraiths. The occasional lost soul. Trust me when I tell you there's so much more." His eyes flicker, going completely black for a second. Pupils, irises. All of it. Then he blinks again, and he's back to basic Zach. Did I ever think he was approachable? Now everything about him radiates tech bro douchebag. He's about to tell us about the rounds of financing he went through to fund his passion project, even while someone else is laying all the employees off in the next room. Then he'll burn the whole thing down around us.

"Everyone stay where you are!" a new voice bellows. Goran, coming up behind us. We're now effectively trapped between Zach and the troops of Afterlife. Goran's once again in full tactical gear. I wonder if he ever wears anything else. He doesn't strike me as a T-shirt and sneakers on the weekends kind of reaper.

Minerva pushes her way to the front though, and she's gone from goth diva to first lady, dressed from head to toe in a plum pantsuit. Even her hair has been cut into a black helmet-like bob. But the fury in her eyes is unmistakably Minerva.

"What is going on here?" she says, glaring at all of us. I take a step back, pressing against Kelly. "We were having a corporate retreat, and you're downstairs—"

"Actually solving problems." Zach spreads his arms. "Look at all these empty cells. Another day or two and we will have resolved your overcrowding issue."

She glances around, but she doesn't look like she appreciates the help. Her gaze narrows, and she pinches her lips.

"Check it out," she says, motioning to Goran, who in turn flicks a finger at two of the soldiers who flank him. They pass by us without a glance, checking the open cells one at a time, officiously announcing that each is just as empty as Zach said they were.

"I don't know who you think you are," she says slowly. The smell of something burning begins to permeate the air, and small flames lick at her fingertips. Kelly's arm around my middle draws me backward ever so slightly. "But you have no authorization to—"

A shriek fills the air. A man standing behind Zach throws his head back, mouth agape. When he looks down again, his eyes have sunk in and turned hungry, while black goo drips from the corner of his mouth. One by one, the other people behind Zach do the same, their shrieks growing like a terrible chorus.

Zach only smiles. "I may have forgot to mention that we came in through the back door, but we took a little detour on our way here. A farewell tour to the world we left behind before we make the world we want to live in forever." The he lifts a hand, two fingers held upward like he's about to bless everyone, before he flicks them, mimicking Goran's motion from a second ago. The lost souls—and they're all lost souls—swarm forward, whirling around Zach. For a second, it almost looks like they're running away, but it becomes clear they are running in every direction. Toward us, away. Down the side halls. As they run, they wrench open the cell doors and wraiths pour out, filling the space with their screaming. They make a beeline for the reapers. And we are right in the way.

"Grab them." I shove Kelly toward Jupiter and X. They do, and we all stumble toward the cell that once housed Lilah. It's the only one close by that still has a door, and I struggle to pull it closed, but the crash as the first wraith collides with it is enough to slam it shut. I fly backward, sprawling on the floor.

"Ember!" Jupiter yells.

"I'm all right." It's not even the worst fall I've taken tonight.

Outside in the hall, a brawl has started, if the sounds are anything to go by. The shrieks of the wraiths are answered by the cries of reapers and lost souls. More than once, a heavy body bangs against our door, making us all jump, but no one opens the door.

"Guys, I think it's locked," X says, pulling on the handle.

"Why would you want to go out there?" Kelly asks.

"What, like we're supposed to stay here?" Jupiter fires back.

"Wait it out? How long will that take?" I ask. If Zach's goal is to release all the wraiths from HELL, that could take a long time. And I don't mean a couple hours. With billions of people dead, even if only a small percentage are sent to HELL, we're still talking about waiting for millions and millions of wraiths to find their way out. That's a traffic jam I don't want to be a part of.

And regardless, whoever comes out on top when the dust settles, we're unlikely to be popular with the winners in either camp. There's also a small chance Zach's ultimate goal is mutually assured destruction, in which case we're going to literally be trapped in HELL with no way to call for help.

X is peering through the small window. "Guys, it really doesn't look good out there. They keep trying to set up something that looks like tent poles, and the other guys keep tearing them down. One little old lady just snapped one of them like a toothpick."

I close my eyes. The last thing I need is X's play by play. I need to think.

"The lost souls will want to keep the quarantine team from collecting them," Kelly says.

"Can they even use that thing down here?" I ask. "They're already in HELL. Where will the beam send them?"

"There's a holding area while new wraiths get processed. It's more secure. Minerva needs space to plan next steps."

Great. So she's going to lock them all up while she leads focus groups. More time for Zach to plan too. It'll be chaos down here, which will mean chaos back in Toronto and everywhere else while more and more souls aren't being retrieved and turning to wraiths.

Another crash comes against the door. Something that might have been human once appears in the window, roaring as it exposes long fangs. The hinges creak. The glass of the window has a long crack through the middle. I can only see what's happening directly in front of us, but from this vantage point, the whole thing is a bloodbath.

"Is this really all because I wasn't nice to him at the mine disaster?" Kelly asks.

I bang my head a few times against the door because it's better than yelling at Kelly, until another wraith slams against it on the other side, making the whole thing rattle.

"It's because you treat us like a chore." I sigh. "You said so yourself. Reapers view us as a burden, and eventually we figured that out."

The door shudders again. The glass bursts from the frame. A clawed hand slides through the opening, feeling around like it's looking for a way to unlock the door from the inside.

We have to get out of here. We can't wait for the fight to be over or someone to rescue us. There's no one left. Cerise is . . . somewhere not here. I refuse to believe she's dead. Bang no doubt has her hands full. It's just the four of us. A powerless reaper, two frightened mediums, and me. A life coach ghost who has somehow become a lost soul . . . whatever that means.

Inside Afterlife, we have capabilities reapers don't even know about.

Does that include vaporizing wraiths by imagining I can control Goran's light machine and exorcising lost souls? It certainly seems to. Would it also include being able to slide my friends away?

"Give me your hand," I say, holding mine out. Kelly does, but they give me a questioning look too. "I'm getting us out of here."

They pull free immediately. "What? No."

"You have a better idea?" I ask, arching a brow. They scowl, but finally shake their head. "Then give me your hand."

"What's going on?" Jupiter and X look between us. One is wearing a worried frown. The other grins like they're waiting for a magic trick.

"We're leaving," I say.

"This is a terrible idea. I cannot overstate the risk," Kelly says, but they place their hand in mine. My chest swells with pride at their trust. Power zings beneath their skin, begging me to tap into it.

I give them a reassuring smile, even though I feel very much less than sure. "I did it once before. I can do it again."

"Are you going to zap us out of here?" X asks.

"Cerise said sliding can't be done in HELL." Jupiter swallows nervously, so I smile even wider. We all have to believe this will be successful.

"She said reapers can't slide here. Doesn't mean a lost soul can't. What choice do we have?"

"You don't have to do this," Kelly says.

A new wraith shoves their hand through the shattered window. Their claws leave gouges in the metal as shards of glass fall through the opening.

"Pretty sure I do." I study them because I'm very likely about to take us through a cosmic cheese grater, and neither of us will ever be seen again.

Their smile is almost fond when they say, "I'll go first. If it works, come back for X and Jupiter." They glance at the two of them, huddled by the door. "If she doesn't return, wait until it's quiet, then wait some more. Find a way to get out and call Bang. She'll help."

Poor Bang. The stopgap for so many unsolvable problems. She's going to have so much paperwork to fill out when this is over.

"This might hurt . . . again," I say, holding Kelly's hand firmly. Unexpectedly, they pull me in for a tight hug.

"You're the most astonishing ghost I've ever met, Ember Munro," they say.

I hug them just as hard. Kelly. They're infuriating, annoying, self-absorbed. But I think we're friends too, and if I don't make it, I hope they miss me, just a little.

"I'm not just a ghost," I say, ignoring the way my face is crushed against their chest. "I'm the best goddamn afterlife coach you ever met."

I close my eyes and open myself to the power Kelly can't touch. I imagine it filling us, wrapping around us, like I imagined the blue light taking the wraiths in the hall. I picture it lifting us off the ground like we're in a bubble. We're safe. On our way home. When I open my eyes, we'll be back in Etobicoke. Yes, that's all I need. Trust that I am strong and powerful and that I can keep the people—and reapers—I care about safe.

Ember's Life Tip #1993: *You make your own—*

The bubble bursts as worries intrude. Sliding must be a precise thing. What if I mix up the living room in Etobicoke with my old condo? Will half of us go one place and half the other? What if we wind up in Tanzania or Peru? What if I can't figure out how to go back for Jupiter and X? Did I just trap them forever in HELL?

Pain explodes in my chest as I lose hold of Kelly's power, and of Kelly too. The force of the disconnection sends me spiralling off into nothingness with only the distant sound of wraiths screaming for company. Then, just as suddenly, I'm enveloped in something cool and supportive, like a bed made of clouds. It's even more comfortable than the divine feather bed in Zach's demo suite.

Someone grunts next to me, and when I open my eyes, Kelly is there, lying face down on what really does look like a cloud. I push myself up to sitting only to find we're in yet another white room, though this one feels vast and empty and lacks Zach's penchant for overdecorating.

"Are you all right?" Kelly asks.

"I think so." My arms are still black, with the inky whatever still moving beneath my skin, but every so often, streaks of blue shoot through it. It's like a meteor shower inside me, and when I poke at the blue lines, they burst into a thousand fragments. "What about you?"

They nod. Their hair is disheveled, and their expression is stunned, but other than that they seem fine

Around us, other clouds—with their own guests—have wafted over until they form a little circle. Minerva. Bang. They both look utterly confused to be here, which makes me feel a little better.

I gasp as Zach sits up on the cloud immediately to my right. Unlike me and Kelly, he looks so much worse for wear. His clothes are shredded and his lip is bleeding. A lump is forming in the middle of his forehead, and when he lifts his hands, at least one finger is broken and bent at a painful angle.

"Where are we?" he asks.

"Somewhere safe."

Jupiter walks between the clouds. Her worn combat boots make no noise as she moves. She's holding Carrot Stick. How on earth did the cat get here? Wherever *here* is. When she sets him on the ground, he arches and stretches, wraps himself around her ankles once, before he finally hops up on a little cloud that has floated in like it has arrived specifically for the occasion. It rises until he's bobbing in the centre of our little formation, then revolves slowly, so he can take in all of us like the ruler all cats believe they are.

When he faces me, I gasp. Carrot Stick is smiling at me. His whiskers twitch, and the little puffballs between his nose and mouth turn upward, revealing a straight row of square very-much-not-catlike teeth.

Then, in a voice that is way more California surfer dude than feline meow, he says, "I think that's quite enough excitement for one eternity, don't you?"

WHICH IS WEIRDER: Discovering that death isn't harps and angels, but actually egos and administrative errors? Or meeting a talking cat with human teeth?

No. Wait. It gets weirder.

Carrot Stick winks, sitting back on his haunches. Then he gets big. Really big. He's like an inflatable snowman coming to life, shaking off yesterday's snow to rule over the yard once more. The orange hair falls away as he straightens.

What in the *Alice in Wonderland* nonsense is going on?

He's a person. Carrot Stick. Where once sat a cat, now is a person. Or . . . maybe a reaper? A god? The Carrot Stick–person has the same unearthly aura of power Kelly used to have, only multiplied by a factor of a thousand.

Minerva gasps. "Richard?"

He glances down at her from his cloud perch with the same detached indifference reapers look at humans. Even in this personish shape, there are still traces of the cat visible. His skin is a ruddy copper, his hair is striped in shades of orange and cream, and his eyes are sandy yellow. At least his transformation has included clothes, even if it's batik-printed shorts, battered dollar store flip-flops, and a T-shirt that says *Vamos Abuelo!* in bright bubble-shaped lettering.

"Hello, Minerva." His voice is a rumble like a purr. "Sounds like you've been busy."

Minerva crosses her arms over her chest. "It's been four centuries, Dick. Things change."

His eyes go big. "Four centuries? No way. Really?" He stretches his arms over his head, and muscles from his forearms to his shoulders ripple. "Man. Time flies when you're busy being a cat."

"For four hundred years?" Even Zach sounds impressed.

"You have no authorization to speak here," Minerva says, still looking decidedly pissed, but when Richard's cloud wafts toward her, she scrambles back as far as her own cloud will permit, which admittedly isn't very far.

While they're squaring off, Jupiter scurries toward me, crawling onto the cloud I'm already sharing with Kelly. It gets cozy very quickly.

"Ember?" she asks.

"Yeah?"

"I think my cat might be . . . God?"

Minerva calls Richard a bloated jackass, and he tips his head back to laugh. It echoes through the nothingness around us, and even his hair seems to grow with his amusement, creating golden waves that cascade down his back. He's like a walking shampoo commercial.

"How did you get out of HELL?" I ask.

"I don't know what happened. One second, we were in that cell, and the next—Wait." Her gaze turns fearful as she takes in the people gathered around us. "Where's X?"

Richard's sandy gaze turns to us. "I dropped him off at home. He's sweet, but he doesn't need to be part of this conversation. Seriously, honey, you could do a lot better. My last human guardian would be a perfect partner . . ." He pauses, running a finger through his beard like he's considering something. "Except she died in 1881. Would that be a problem for you?"

All poor Jupiter can do is stare. We won't even begin to guess whether it's because her cat is a deity, is basically doing a Jeff Bridges impression, or thinks her taste in men sucks.

"He's not a god," Minerva says. Her politician persona has also changed. She's closer to the punky teenager I first met, and she looks furious. "He's—"

"The father of Afterlife," Bang says, eyes enormous behind her glasses.

"Hi, Bang," Richard says with a curling smile. "Nice to see you again." His attention makes her flush, and she drags her fingers through her cloud, pulling up little tufts of fluffy vapour.

"He's not the father of Afterlife either." Minerva pounds her fists at her sides, but it doesn't have the desired effect, given they just plunge through the cloud, causing her to flop onto her back.

"I prefer the term chairman," Richard says.

"Please," she scoffs, struggling back up to sitting. "Retired chairman at best. We've been doing fine without you."

He folds himself onto his cloud, crossing his legs so he can pick at one of his toenails. "Not from what I've heard. That's why I brought you all here. It's time to have a little kit-kat."

"Chit-chat," I say, then pinch my lips together. Maybe correcting a god—or a chairman—is a bad idea.

But Richard's eyes crinkle in delight. His attention is like the sun coming after a rainy day. I actually feel teary, as though I've been looking for someone like him my whole life.

"Chit-chat," he says again. "I like you, Ember. I hope you stick around. Yes, let's have a chit-chat."

"Are we in heaven?" Jupiter asks. "Like, *really* heaven?"

Richard winks. "You humans are the best. Your hope is even more eternal than I am. I regret to inform you there truly is no heaven, only constructed spaces like Afterlife, and those are still flawed."

Zach scoffs. "I told you."

"Come on," Richard says, ignoring him. He motions to us, and the clouds all drift forward until they bump against each other. "Gather round. Let's talk it out. Sounds like there's some steak here."

"Not as much steak as I have with you," Minerva says, glaring. But she hasn't gone full dragon mode on him, so he must hold some clout. "Where the hell have you been? Do you know what it's been like?"

Jupiter giggles. "Steak. I think they mean beef. They have beef with each other." I have to bite my lip to keep from laughing with her.

Richard shrugs, careless. "I've been learning. Do you know how much humanity has changed in the last four hundred years? Colonialism, the Industrial Revolution? The technology." He throws his hands up in the air and laughs delightedly. "I paid for a coffee with a smartwatch the other day. Didn't need a wallet or anything. Isn't that incredible?"

"Wait. A coffee?" Jupiter asks. "How did you get out of the house? You're an indoor cat. And where did you get a smartwatch?"

"You know he's not really a cat, right?" Bang asks her, sounding genuinely concerned for Jupiter's mental acuity. "He's a—"

"Don't think we're going to celebrate your return," Minerva says, and I practically thank her for dragging us back to the more important topic. If we can accept Kelly owns a castle, and somehow I'm able to use the power they can't, we can accept that Richard the cat god can escape Jupiter's bungalow without much trouble. "You abandoned us when we needed you. Do you know how hard it's been?"

"Oh, I'm getting an idea." He glances at Zach. "Do you have feedback you wish to share with the customer experience team?"

His whole countenance sparkles when his gaze meets mine again. "You? I think you have a lot to say."

Do I? I struggle to organize my thoughts, remembering back to the last few days in the hospital when everything had felt so certain and clear. My time among the living was coming to an end. I wasn't sad or scared. I had finally taken control of my fate. Except then it turned out no one has any control, not even the reapers who claim to.

"I think there's some flaws at Afterlife. More than they're willing to admit," I say slowly. "But organizational change is some of the hardest to successfully accomplish, especially in a big, well-established entity."

Richard snaps his fingers. "Exactly. Minerva, you old spoon in the road, has it never occurred to you that if you have too many mice in the trap, it's time to build a better *and* bigger trap?"

I open my mouth to correct him, then close it again. As far as mixed reaper idioms go, those weren't bad. Also, the spoon in the road thing could be fork in the road or stick in the mud, but it's probably not worth wasting too much mental energy trying to figure it out.

Minerva doesn't look nearly as appeased. She's sitting so upright it looks painful, and her fingers are clenched around each other in her lap.

"The job's not the same as it was when you left," she says, speaking tightly. "Do you know how many more of them there are? We've been over capacity for almost a hundred years. We're overdue for an increased workforce by centuries."

"But you had the capability to make new reapers all along." He glances between Zach and Minerva. "Both of you. Why did you never talk to each other instead of playing your little pranks and storming off to your rooms like angry siblings?"

Minerva looks like smoke will start pouring from her ears at any moment. Zach looks thoughtful. Kelly slides a hand into mine, and I take it. Something tells me they're about to have their world rocked. A little comfort never hurt anyone, even a reaper who may not know how to ask for it.

Richard notices our joined hands and smiles. He always seems to be smiling, even though he basically just headed off a supernatural war. Funny he doesn't think much of X. They'd probably get along well.

"You two have been the most fun of all. Ember, you're so on the ball. Escaping HELL like that. Though you need to work on your accuracy. If I hadn't grabbed you both, you'd have found yourself trapped inside a glacier in Alberta. It's melting pretty quickly these days, but you'd have still needed a few decades to get out. But I'm sure you would have made it eventually. You and Kelly make quite the team. Humans amaze me over and over. It's why I spent so long with you. Things at home were getting kind of stuffy, you know?"

"Stuffy?" Minerva's exasperation is only growing. She finally leaps from her seat like a jack-in-the-box on a spring. "We were barely surviving, and you were doing what? Sunbathing and begging for treats!"

"Ah." Richard wags a finger. "Cats never beg."

"Is this actually solving anything?" I whisper to Kelly.

"Give it a minute," they murmur. "He's building to something. Richard always likes a show."

"What do you mean we could have made more reapers?" Minerva asks. Actually, it's more like she's pleading, and I do feel the tiniest bit sorry for her. She's been an ass to everyone, but she truly did believe she was making the best of a very bad situation.

Richard spreads his hands. "You had all the pieces. Lost souls and the erasure of human memories. That's all it takes."

Our little cloud space gets quiet. Minerva and Zach continue to glare at each other. I try to put the pieces together, but once again I don't have enough information. I never have enough information when it comes to Afterlife. Fortunately, in this case for once, I'm not alone.

Bang says, "Reapers are lost souls?"

Jupiter says, "Reapers were human?"

Richard laughs at their confusion. "Well, of course! Where did you think they came from? That they just spontaneously came into existence every thousand years?"

More silence. Minerva looks like she's just about to break a stick in half using only the force of her ass cheeks. Zach has his face in his hands and appears to be laughing as his shoulders shake. Bang is pinching her arms, while Jupiter stares up in shock at Kelly. Kelly, who always looked human, but not quite. Kelly, who sits next to me frozen. They don't even blink.

"You were a person?" Jupiter asks softly. They don't respond. My hand is still in theirs, and I squeeze. The answering reflexive squeeze is so tight even my ghostly senses can feel the pain.

"What do you mean 'memory erasure'?" Bang asks. A tear slips over her cheek. "We were . . . we . . ."

"Naturally," Richard says, looking extra feline as he blinks slowly. "To do the work for as long as we do, you can't have any sentimentality. No attachments to the human world. What would you do if you discovered your granddaughter had become a wraith? And where do you think we'd put new souls if we couldn't make room by taking the strongest and brightest who refuse to burn out and give them a new purpose?"

Okay, now Minerva looks like she's on the verge of a stroke. One eye is distinctly larger than the other, and her lower lip trembles as she undoubtedly tries to suppress a scream.

"And you never thought to write any of this down?" she asks. Each syllable is punctuated with a healthy dose of spittle. "Or tell anyone else?"

Richard shrugs nonchalantly, which only seems to enrage Minerva even more. Kelly still hasn't said anything, but when I scoot a little closer to them, anticipating an epic blow-up in the very near future, they put a protective arm around my shoulder, which I'm grateful for. I find Jupiter's hand with my free one, then do some mental rooting around until I find Kelly's power. If I have to, I will swoop us out of here. Better to end up in a glacier than get obliterated by a reaper pissed off she didn't get a formal Standard Operating Procedure before Richard started his sabbatical.

"You were always a smart girl, Minerva," Richard says, giving her a knowing eye. "I assumed you'd figure it out. Maybe I overestimated you."

Zach lets out a long, low *Oooh*. "Someone's in trouble."

"What do you know?" Minerva snaps at him. Something like electricity is arcing between her fingertips. Her cloud turns an ominous grey, and thunder rumbles through the air.

"Yes! Yes." Richard claps excitedly. "See! Conversation. This is what I've been waiting for. Instead, you just set up competing camps and pretended like nothing was broken. And you." He points at Jupiter, who flinches, trying to hide behind me, only there's not enough room. "You're in charge now."

My jaw drops open. Talk about a plot twist.

"Me?" Jupiter looks just as shocked. In fact, she looks like she's about to fling herself off our cloud or a cliff or whatever there is at the edge of Richard's personal chill-out room. I pull her toward me, trying to offer some comfort.

"You." Richard smiles broadly. "Those candles are so impressive. Shame they burn out so fast, but we can work on that. And you're good with wraiths. I've seen it myself."

I snort. She should put that on her resume. Detail-oriented. Effective communicator. Good with wraiths.

Jupiter just shakes her head. "I can't. I'm not even dead."

Richard purses his lips in disappointment, clearly having forgotten that little detail. Finally, he shrugs. "Okay. Kelly, then."

"What?" Minerva squawks.

Beside me, Kelly stiffens even further. Maybe in shock. Excitement, I hope. I take a deep breath. This is it. Our deal. Get Kelly's job back, get me a peaceful afterlife. Surely after everything, I can negotiate with Richard for a quiet little island away from the conflict.

"You can't," Minerva is still saying. "Kelly quit. They've never had any interest in management at Afterlife. And now you want to reward them?"

"I'll do it if no one else wants the job," Zach says.

"Oh, I have plans for you," Richard says, "but it's not putting you in charge. Kelly, though . . . you've got the experience. The desire for innovation. I have no doubt that under your watch, things would change pretty quickly at Afterlife."

It's perfect. They'll get everything they've ever wanted. It's all working out even better than I imagined.

"No."

The cloud circle goes quiet again. For once, even Richard looks taken aback.

"No?" He bounces like a toddler on the verge of a tantrum, before an idea occurs to him, and he stills. "You got downsized, didn't you?"

"He was interfering with—" Minerva starts, but Richard snaps his fingers, cutting off her protest. It also has the effect of filling the whole space with a rush. A tsunami that crashes over us all, making us gasp and shiver. The wave pours down, before it redirects straight at Kelly. When it hits them, I'm knocked backward, basically into Jupiter's lap. Kelly throws their head back, mouth open. It's like the moment lost souls lose control, but I'm not afraid. This isn't about Kelly losing something. It's about regaining what they never should have lost.

But I still have Kelly's hand, and the flood pushes toward me. It's so strong. Overwhelming. I should let go, but I can't make myself do it. Instead, I close my eyes and accept my fate, waiting for the incoming tide to drown me, but it only reaches my toes before the wave breaks and softens, swirling around my ankles before draining away.

"Sorry about that," they say softly. "I'm out of practice."

I open my eyes. Kelly is sitting next to me. Blue and purple hair. Eyes pale blue and a little far apart. A single black chain sprouts in their earlobe, dangling down into a tiny metal skull. Their thin lips turn up in a smile.

"Hi," I say softly, feeling almost shy to look them directly in the eye. Kelly, the second most powerful reaper, stares down at me fondly.

"Hi," they say.

"See?" Richard says. His smile has turned gleeful. "There's something in this for everyone. Help me out." He holds out his hands, and a new *Vamos Abuelo!* T-shirt unfurls itself out of nowhere. It's exactly the same as the one he wears. "We can even have team shirts. Casual Fridays. You know you want to."

"Actually, I don't." Kelly sounds more like themself than I've heard in a while. Self-assured. Aloof. Whatever game Richard is playing, Kelly has no interest in participating. But their next words are unexpected. "I think there's more for me to do in Toronto. I'd be terrible in an office. But down there . . . that's the kind of change you need."

Richard's smile turns appreciative, and his eyes twinkle some more. If this ends with him staying among the living, I should suggest he apply to be a mall Santa this Christmas. He'd be legendary. For now, though, he watches Kelly for a moment longer, looking them up and down, before nodding and whirling his gaze to me. "You. Do you want it?"

"Me?" I ask, putting a hand to my chest.

"Why not?" He shrugs. "You're bossy. Unafraid. Maybe it's time to put the humans in charge. You like to do things like cleaning, and it sounds like Afterlife HR needs more of that. And you're dead, which makes you more qualified than Jupiter, even if I like her better because she feeds me." He flicks a hand at his ear like a cat scratching an itch, then seems to realize what he's doing and tucks it back in his lap.

I glance around at everyone. Jupiter's staring at me like I've already gained superpowers. Bang is nodding eagerly, which I can't blame her for. Minerva looks like she'd rather eat glass forever than work with me—or worse, *for* me. Zach's gaze is assessing. No doubt he's already envisioning how he will manipulate me to get more than his share of authority.

In short, it would be hell. The politics, the attitude. It's always tempting to see things like this as an opportunity. Even a promotion. Instead of being one of the billions of souls burning out after a few centuries, I'd run the place.

But that's not what I want my death to be. If I've learned anything so far, it's that change won't come from the inside. It's too big. Too cumbersome.

"No thank you," I say. "I'm more of a consultant than an executive. I think I'm better suited to death coaching."

"Death coaching?" Richard sounds intrigued.

"Those who can't do, teach, right?" I glance at Kelly, and they wink at me. Wink! The warm thing inside me settles. It's like every time I'm close to them, but this time feels bigger. Final. I'm making the right choice. "I haven't been very successful at dying, but I think I can help others not repeat my mistakes." I'll write my handbook. The glossary. Also, you can be damn sure I will advocate for new ghosts long and hard whenever a reaper says they're too busy to do their job.

We all get quiet again. Richard watches us for a minute before licking the back of his hand and running it over his forehead and behind his ear. He repeats the gesture a few times before he laughs softly to himself. He hangs his head and sighs.

"Okay, fine. Bang. The job is yours."

"Yes!" She practically flies in the air, punching her fists upward. "Yes. Yes, oh thank you. Yes! I've been waiting. No one ever—"

"Her?" Minerva practically screeches. "She's not qualified. She's an assistant. She's—"

"I'm twenty-six hundred years old, Minerva," Bang says. "How many more centuries do I have to put in before I make the cut?"

Yes. Definitely the right choice. I do not need to be doing an eternal nine-to-five with these folks.

"We should go," Kelly says, like they can read my mind. "This is going to get ugly."

Minerva's face is mottled. Not red with fury. Blue. With scales. She's shouting and Bang is dancing and Richard is watching the whole thing like it's the most entertainment he's had in a while.

Yup. Time to go. The business of dying is about to get very messy indeed.

"You're taking me too, right?" Jupiter says as Kelly and I climb to our feet.

"Your name is on the lease," Kelly says. "Can't leave you here."

"You can own a castle, but you can't sign a lease?" I ask.

Kelly's smile is sharp. They hold out their arms, and we both join them.

"Hey, Kelly?" I can barely contain my smile.

"Yes?" They glance down their long nose at me, and their expression turns exasperated, like they already know what's coming.

"What's Kelly really short for?"

They shake their head, but I catch the ghost of a smile as it wafts over their lips.

"Ready?" they ask.

I risk one last glance at the others. Bang is still celebrating on her cloud, but Minerva climbs up, yanking at her ankle and dragging her down. Bang screams, and Minerva grabs hold of her hair, pulling hard. It's all very reality TV cat fight. Zach's cloud is drifting away on an invisible current while he shouts about reparations and modernization. Meanwhile, Richard has paddled his cloud toward a waving palm tree. A frond dips toward him, and he bats at it like a cat with a string. Centuries of feline habits die hard.

"Ready." I press my cheek to Kelly's chest. Jupiter puts hers on my shoulder. This is right. This is the answer. And I guess we can keep X too, as long as Jupiter likes him. Like Richard said, he's sweet in his own way.

Living is hard. Dying is easy. Being dead is going to be the toughest thing I've ever done.

"We're going to need a new cat," Jupiter says.

"We don't have enough bedrooms at home," I say. Home. Back to the little house in Etobicoke that is going to be mine now as much as it's theirs.

"Neither of you sleep," Jupiter says. "You can share."

I glance up to where Kelly is watching me.

"You better not eat any of my thinking pizza," they say.

"Wouldn't dream of it," I say, then squeeze my eyes tight, waiting for the sickening blender feeling to take hold. Someday, I hope I get used to it.

Dear Sparks, it's time for Ember's Afterlife Tip #1: *Never stop learning.*

My name is Ember Munro, and I have a lot to learn about being dead.

about the author

Alli lives in Toronto with her very patient husband and a growing pack of rescue pets. She tries to split her time between writing, community theatre stage management, and traveling anywhere that has good wine. Tragically, this leaves no time to clean the house.

lgbtq+ fantasy by alli temple

Afterlife Incorporated

Only Mostly Dead

Hate to Haunt You (coming soon)

The Pirate & Her Princess

Uncharted

Unbroken

Unleashed

lgbtq+ romances by allison temple

Out & About

Work-Love Balance

Honeymoon Sweet

The Seacroft Series

Top Shelf

Cold Pressed

Hot Potato

Shared Series

My Not-So-Super Blind Date (part of Subparheroes)

Under Her Roof (part of Accidentally Undercover)

Puppuccino (part of Bold Brew)

Standalone

Destination Bedding

The Neighbourly Thing

Up North

Boyfriend With Benefits

The Pick Up

www.ingramcontent.com/pod-product-compliance
Lightning Source LLC
Chambersburg PA
CBHW060432310726
48977CB00001B/149